THE RESEARCH MAGNIFICENT

THE RESEARCH
MAGNIFICENT

BY

H. G. WELLS

CONTENTS

THE PRELUDE

THE STORY

THE PRELUDE

THE RESEARCH
MAGNIFICENT

THE PRELUDE

ON FEAR AND ARISTOCRACY

§ 1

THE story of William Porphyry Benham is the
story of a man who was led into adventure by an
idea. It was an idea that took possession of his
imagination quite early in life, it grew with him
and changed with him, it interwove at last completely with his being. His story is its story. It
was traceably germinating in the schoolboy; it
was manifestly present in his mind at the very
last moment of his adventurous life. He belonged
to that fortunate minority who are independent of
daily necessities, so that he was free to go about
the world under its direction. It led him far. It
led him into situations that bordered upon the
fantastic, it made him ridiculous, it came near to
making him sublime. And this idea of his was of
such a nature that in several aspects he could docu-
ment it. Its logic forced him to introspection and
to the making of a record.

3

An idea that can play so large a part in a life must necessarily have something of the complication and protean quality of life itself. It is not to be stated justly in any formula, it is not to be rendered by an epigram. As well one might show a man's skeleton for his portrait. Yet, essentially, Benham's idea was simple. He had an incurable, an almost innate persuasion that he had to live life nobly and thoroughly. His commoner expression for that thorough living is "the aristocratic life." But by "aristocratic" he meant something very different from the quality of a Russian prince, let us say, or an English peer. He meant an intensity, a clearness. . . . Nobility for him was to get something out of his individual existence, a flame, a jewel, a splendour — it is a thing easier to understand than to say.

One might hesitate to call this idea "innate," and yet it comes soon into a life when it comes at all. In Benham's case we might trace it back to the Day Nursery at Seagate, we might detect it stirring already at the petticoat stage, in various private struttings and valiant dreamings with a helmet of pasteboard and a white-metal sword. We have most of us been at least as far as that with Benham. And we have died like Horatius, slaying our thousands for our country, or we have perished at the stake or faced the levelled muskets of the firing party — "No, do not bandage my eyes" — because we would not betray the secret path that meant destruction to our city. But with

Benham the vein was stronger, and it increased instead of fading out as he grew to manhood. It was less obscured by those earthy acquiescences, those discretions, that saving sense of proportion, which have made most of us so satisfactorily what we are. "Porphyry," his mother had discovered before he was seventeen, "is an excellent boy, a brilliant boy, but, I begin to see, just a little unbalanced."

The interest of him, the absurdity of him, the story of him, is that.

Most of us are — balanced; in spite of occasional reveries we do come to terms with the limitations of life, with those desires and dreams and discretions that, to say the least of it, qualify our nobility, we take refuge in our sense of humour and congratulate ourselves on a certain amiable freedom from priggishness or presumption, but for Benham that easy declension to a humorous acceptance of life as it is did not occur. He found his limitations soon enough; he was perpetually rediscovering them, but out of these interments of the spirit he rose again — remarkably. When we others have decided that, to be plain about it, we are not going to lead the noble life at all, that the thing is too ambitious and expensive even to attempt, we have done so because there were other conceptions of existence that were good enough for us, we decided that instead of that glorious impossible being of ourselves, we would figure in our own eyes as jolly fellows, or sly dogs, or sane, sound, capable men or brilliant successes, and so forth — practicable things. For Benham, exceptionally, there were not these practicable things. He blundered, he fell short of himself, he had—as you will be told—some astonishing rebuffs, but they never turned him aside for long. He went by nature for this preposterous idea of nobility as a linnet hatched in a cage will try to fly.

And when he discovered — and in this he was assisted not a little by his friend at his elbow — when he discovered that Nobility was not the simple thing he had at first supposed it to be, he set himself in a mood only slightly disconcerted to the discovery of Nobility. When it dawned upon him, as it did, that one cannot be noble, so to speak, *in vacuo*, he set himself to discover a Noble Society. He began with simple beliefs and fine attitudes and ended in a conscious research. If he could not get through by a stride, then it followed that he must get through by a climb. He spent the greater part of his life studying and experimenting in the noble possibilities of man. He never lost his absurd faith in that conceivable splendour. At first it was always just round the corner or just through the wood ; to the last it seemed still but a little way beyond the distant mountains.

For this reason this story has been called *The Research Magnificent*. It was a real research, it was documented. In the rooms in Westhaven Street that at last were as much as one could call his home, he had accumulated material for — one hesitates to call it a book — let us say it was an analysis of, a guide to the noble life. There after his tragic death came his old friend White, the journalist and novelist, under a promise, and found these papers; he found them to the extent of a crammed bureau, half a score of patent files quite distended and a writing-table drawer-full, and he was greatly exercised to find them. They were, White declares, they are still after much experienced handling, an indigestible aggregation. On this point White is very assured. When Benham thought he was gathering together a book he was dreaming, White says. There is no book in it. . . .

Perhaps too, one might hazard, Benham was dreaming when he thought the noble life a human possibility. Perhaps man, like the ape and the hyæna and the tapeworm and many other of God's necessary but less attractive creatures, is not for such exalted ends. That doubt never seems to have got a lodgment in Benham's skull; though at times one might suppose it the basis of White's thought. You will find in all Benham's story, if only it can be properly told, now subdued, now loud and amazed and distressed, but always traceable, this startled, protesting question, *"But why the devil aren't we?"* As though necessarily we ought to be. He never faltered in his persuasion that behind the dingy face of this world, the earthy stubbornness, the baseness and dulness of himself and all of us, lurked the living jewels of heaven, the light of glory, things unspeakable. At first it seemed to him that one had only just to hammer and will, and at the end, after a life of willing and hammering, he was still convinced there was something, something in the nature of an Open Sesame, perhaps a little more intricate than one had supposed at first, a little more difficult to secure, but still in that nature, which would suddenly roll open for mankind the magic cave of the universe, that precious cave at the heart of all things, in which one must believe.

And then life — life would be the wonder it so perplexingly just isn't. . . .

§ 2

Benham did not go about the world telling people of this consuming research. He was not the prophet or preacher of his idea. It was too living and intricate and uncertain a part of him to speak freely about. It was his secret self; to expose it casually would have shamed him. He drew all sorts of reserves about him, he wore his manifest imperfections turned up about him like an overcoat in bitter wind. He was content to be inexplicable. His thoughts led him to the conviction that this magnificent research could not be, any more than any other research can be, a solitary enterprise, but he delayed expression; in a mighty writing and stowing away of these papers he found a relief from the unpleasant urgency to confess and explain himself prematurely. So that White, though he knew Benham with the intimacy of an old schoolfellow who had renewed his friendship, and had shared his last days and been a witness of his death, read the sheets of manuscript often with surprise and with a sense of added elucidation.

And, being also a trained maker of books, White as he read was more and more distressed that an accumulation so interesting should be so entirely unshaped for publication. "But this will never make a book," said White with a note of personal grievance. His hasty promise in their last moments together had bound him, it seemed, to a task he now found impossible. He would have to work upon it tremendously; and even then he did not see how it could be done.

This collection of papers was not a story, not an essay, not a confession, not a diary. It was — nothing definable. It went into no conceivable covers. It was just, White decided, a proliferation. A vast proliferation. It wanted even a title. There were signs that Benham had intended to call it *The Aristocratic Life*, and that he had tried at some other time the title of *An Essay on Aristocracy*. Moreover, it would seem that towards the end he had been disposed to drop the word "aristocratic" altogether, and adopt some such phrase as *The Larger Life*. Once it was *Life Set Free*. He had fallen away more and more from nearly everything that one associates with aristocracy — at the end only its ideals of fearlessness and generosity remained.

Of all these titles *The Aristocratic Life* seemed at first most like a clue to White. Benham's erratic movements, his sudden impulses, his angers, his unaccountable patiences, his journeys to strange places, and his lapses into what had seemed to be pure adventurousness, could all be put into system

with that. Before White had turned over three
pages of the great fascicle of manuscript that was
called Book Two, he had found the word "Bushido"
written with a particularly flourishing capital letter
and twice repeated. "That was inevitable," said
White with the comforting regret one feels at a
friend's banalities. "And it dates . . . Yes —
this was early. . . ."

"Modern aristocracy, the new aristocracy," he
read presently, "has still to be discovered and understood. This is the necessary next step for mankind.
As far as possible I will discover and understand it,
and as far as I know it I will be it. This is the essential disposition of my mind. God knows I have
appetites and sloths and habits and blindnesses,
but so far as it is in my power to release myself I
will escape to this. . . ."

§ 3

White sat far into the night and for several nights
turning over papers and rummaging in untidy
drawers. Memories came back to him of his dead
friend and pieced themselves together with other
memories and joined on to scraps in this writing.
Bold yet convincing guesses began to leap across
the gaps. A story shaped itself. . . .

The story began with the schoolfellow he had
known at Minchinghampton School.

Benham had come up from his father's preparatory school at Seagate. He had been a boy reserved
rather than florid in his acts and manners, a boy with

a pale face, incorrigible hair and brown eyes that went dark and deep with excitement. Several times White had seen him excited, and when he was excited Benham was capable of tensely daring things. On one occasion he had insisted upon walking across a field in which was an aggressive bull. It had been put there to prevent the boys taking a short cut to the swimming place. It had bellowed tremendously and finally charged him. He had dodged it and got away; at the time it had seemed an immense feat to White and the others who were safely up the field. He had walked to the fence, risking a second charge by his deliberation. Then he had sat on the fence and declared his intention of always crossing the field so long as the bull remained there. He had said this with white intensity, he had stopped abruptly in mid-sentence, and then suddenly he had dropped to the ground, clutched the fence, struggled with heaving shoulders, and been sick.

The combination of apparently stout heart and manifestly weak stomach had exercised the Minchinghampton intelligence profoundly.

On one or two other occasions Benham had shown courage of the same rather screwed-up sort. He showed it not only in physical but in mental things. A boy named Prothero set a fashion of religious discussion in the school, and Benham, after some self-examination, professed an atheistical republicanism rather in the manner of Shelley. This brought him into open conflict with Roddles, the History Master.

Roddles had discovered these theological controversies in some mysterious way, and he took upon
himself to talk at Benham and Prothero. He
treated them to the common misapplication of that
fool who "hath said in his heart there is no God."
He did not perceive there was any difference between
the fool who says a thing in his heart and one who
says it in the dormitory. He revived that delectable anecdote of the Eton boy who professed dis-
belief and was at once "soundly flogged" by his head
master. "Years afterwards that boy came back
to thank ——"

"Gurr," said Prothero softly. "*Stew* — ard!"

"Your turn next, Benham," whispered an orthodox controversialist.

"Good Lord! I'd like to see him," said Benham
with a forced loudness that could scarcely be ignored.

The subsequent controversy led to an interview
with the head. From it Benham emerged more
whitely strung up than ever. "He said he would
certainly swish me if I deserved it, and I said I
would certainly kill him if he did."

"And then?"

"He told me to go away and think it over. Said
he would preach about it next Sunday. . . . Well,
a swishing isn't a likely thing anyhow. But I
would. . . . There isn't a master here I'd stand
a thrashing from — not one. . . . And because I
choose to say what I think! . . . I'd run amuck."

For a week or so the school was exhilarated by a
vain and ill-concealed hope that the head might

try it just to see if Benham would. It was tanta-
lizingly within the bounds of possibility. . . .

These incidents came back to White's mind as he
turned over the newspapers in the upper drawer of
the bureau. The drawer was labelled "Fear — the
First Limitation," and the material in it was evidently designed for the opening volume of the great
unfinished book. Indeed, a portion of it was already
arranged and written up.

As White read through this manuscript he was
reminded of a score of schoolboy discussions Benham
and he and Prothero had had together. Here was
the same old toughness of mind, a kind of intellectual hardihood, that had sometimes shocked his
schoolfellows. Benham had been one of those boys
who do not originate ideas very freely, but who go
out to them with a fierce sincerity. He believed and
disbelieved with emphasis. Prothero had first set
him doubting, but it was Benham's own temperament took him on to denial. His youthful atheism
had been a matter for secret consternation in White.
White did not believe very much in God even then,
but this positive disbelieving frightened him. It was
going too far. There had been a terrible moment in
the dormitory, during a thunderstorm, a thunderstorm
so vehement that it had awakened them all, when
Latham, the humourist and a quietly devout boy, had
suddenly challenged Benham to deny his Maker.

"*Now* say you don't believe in God?"

Benham sat up in bed and repeated his negative
faith, while little Hopkins, the Bishop's son, being

less certain about the accuracy of Providence than His aim, edged as far as he could away from Benham's cubicle and rolled his head in his bed-clothes.

"And anyhow," said Benham, when it was clear that he was not to be struck dead forthwith, "you show a poor idea of your God to think he'd kill a schoolboy for honest doubt. Even old Roddles —"

"I can't listen to you," cried Latham the humourist, "I can't listen to you. It's — *horrible.*"

"Well, who began it?" asked Benham.

A flash of lightning lit the dormitory and showed him to White white-faced and ablaze with excitement, sitting up with the bed-clothes about him. "Oh *wow!*" wailed the muffled voice of little Hopkins as the thunder burst like a giant pistol overhead, and he buried his head still deeper in the bed-clothes and gave way to unappeasable grief.

Latham's voice came out of the darkness. "This *Atheism* that you and Billy Prothero have brought into the school —"

He started violently at another vivid flash, and every one remained silent, waiting for the thunder. . . .

But White remembered no more of the controversy because he had made a frightful discovery that filled and blocked his mind. Every time the lightning flashed, there was a red light in Benham's eyes. . . .

It was only three days after when Prothero discovered exactly the same phenomenon in the School

House boothole and talked of cats and cattle, that
White's confidence in their friend was partially
restored. . . .

§ 4

"Fear, the First Limitation" — his title indicated
the spirit of Benham's opening book very clearly.
His struggle with fear was the very beginning of his
soul's history. It continued to the end. He had
hardly decided to lead the noble life before he came
bump against the fact that he was a physical coward.
He felt fear acutely. "Fear," he wrote, "is the foremost and most persistent of the shepherding powers
that keep us in the safe fold, that drive us back to
the beaten track and comfort and — futility. The
beginning of all aristocracy is the subjugation of
fear."

At first the struggle was so great that he hated
fear without any qualification ; he wanted to abol-
ish it altogether.

"When I was a boy," he writes, "I thought I
would conquer fear for good and all, and never more
be troubled by it. But it is not to be done in that
way. One might as well dream of having dinner for
the rest of one's life. Each time and always I have
found that it has to be conquered afresh. To this
day I fear, little things as well as big things. I have
to grapple with some little dread every day — urge
myself. . . . Just as I have to wash and shave
myself every day. . . . I believe it is so with every
one, but it is difficult to be sure ; few men who go
into dangers care very much to talk about fear. . . ."

Later Benham found some excuses for fear, came even to dealings with fear. He never, however, admits that this universal instinct is any better than a kindly but unintelligent nurse from whose fostering restraints it is man's duty to escape. Discretion, he declared, must remain; a sense of proportion, an "adequacy of enterprise," but the discretion of an aristocrat is in his head, a tactical detail, it has nothing to do with this visceral sinking, this ebb in the nerves. "From top to bottom, the whole spectrum of fear is bad, from panic fear at one extremity down to that mere disinclination for enterprise, that reluctance and indolence which is its lowest phase. These are things of the beast, these are for creatures that have a settled environment, a life history, that spin in a cage of instincts. But man is a beast of that kind no longer, he has left his habitat, he goes out to limitless living. . . ."

This idea of man going out into new things, leaving securities, habits, customs, leaving his normal life altogether behind him, underlay all Benham's aristocratic conceptions. And it was natural that he should consider fear as entirely inconvenient, treat it indeed with ingratitude, and dwell upon the immense liberations that lie beyond for those who will force themselves through its remonstrances. . . .

Benham confessed his liability to fear quite freely in these notes. His fear of animals was ineradicable. He had had an overwhelming dread of bears until he was twelve or thirteen, the child's irrational dread of impossible bears, bears lurking under the

bed and in the evening shadows. He confesses that
even up to manhood he could not cross a field
containing cattle without keeping a wary eye upon
them — his bull adventure rather increased than
diminished that disposition — he hated a strange
dog at his heels and would manœuvre himself as
soon as possible out of reach of the teeth or heels of
a horse. But the peculiar dread of his childhood
was tigers. Some gaping nursemaid confronted
him suddenly with a tiger in a cage in the menagerie
annexe of a circus. "My small mind was overwhelmed."

"I had never thought," White read, "that a tiger
was much larger than a St. Bernard dog. . . .
This great creature! . . . I could not believe any
hunter would attack such a monster except by stealth
and with weapons of enormous power. . . .

"He jerked himself to and fro across his cramped,
rickety cage and looked over my head with yellow
eyes — at some phantom far away. Every now and
then he snarled. The contempt of his detestable
indifference sank deeper and deeper into my soul.
I knew that were the cage to vanish I should stand
there motionless, his helpless prey. I knew that
were he at large in the same building with me I
should be too terror-stricken to escape him. At
the foot of a ladder leading clear to escape I should
have awaited him paralyzed. At last I gripped my
nurse's hand. 'Take me away,' I whispered.

"In my dreams that night he stalked me. I made
my frozen flight from him, I slammed a door on him,

c

and he thrust his paw through a panel as though it
had been paper and clawed for me. The paw got
longer and longer. . . .

"I screamed so loudly that my father came up
from his study.

"I remember that he took me in his arms.

"'It's only a big sort of pussy, Poff,' he said.
'*Felis tigris.* *Felis*, you know, means cat.'

"But I knew better. I was in no mood then for
my father's insatiable pedagoguery.

"'And my little son mustn't be a coward.' . . .

"After that I understood I must keep silence
and bear my tigers alone.

"For years the thought of that tiger's immensity
haunted my mind. In my dreams I cowered before it a thousand times; in the dusk it rarely failed
me. On the landing on my way to bed there was
a patch of darkness beyond a chest that became a
lurking horror for me, and sometimes the door of
my father's bedroom would stand open and there was
a long buff and crimson-striped shape, by day indeed
an ottoman, but by night—. Could an ottoman
crouch and stir in the flicker of a passing candle?
Could an ottoman come after you noiselessly, and so
close that you could not even turn round upon it?
No!"

§ 5

When Benham was already seventeen and, as he
supposed, hardened against his fear of beasts, his
friend Prothero gave him an account of the killing
of an old labouring man by a stallion which had

escaped out of its stable. The beast had careered across a field, leapt a hedge and come upon its victim suddenly. He had run a few paces and stopped, trying to defend his head with the horse rearing over him. It beat him down with two swift blows of its fore hoofs, one, two, lifted him up in its long yellow teeth and worried him as a terrier does a rat — the poor old wretch was still able to make a bleating sound at that — dropped him, trampled and kicked him as he tried to crawl away, and went on trampling and battering him until he was no more than a bloody inhuman bundle of clothes and mire. For more than half an hour this continued, and then its animal rage was exhausted and it desisted, and went and grazed at a little distance from this misshapen, hoof-marked, torn, and muddy remnant of a man. No one it seems but a horror-stricken child knew what was happening. . . .

This picture of human indignity tortured Benham's imagination much more than it tortured the teller of the tale. It filled him with shame and horror. For three or four years every detail of that circumstantial narrative seemed unforgettable. A little lapse from perfect health and the obsession returned. He could not endure the neighing of horses: when he saw horses galloping in a field with him his heart stood still. And all his life thereafter he hated horses.

§ 6

A different sort of fear that also greatly afflicted Benham was due to a certain clumsiness and insecurity he felt in giddy and unstable places. There he was more definitely balanced between the hopelessly rash and the pitifully discreet.

He had written an account of a private struggle between himself and a certain path of planks and rock edges called the Bisse of Leysin. This happened in his adolescence. He had had a bad attack of influenza and his doctor had sent him to a little hotel — the only hotel it was in those days — at Montana in Valais. There, later, when he had picked up his strength, his father was to join him and take him mountaineering, that second-rate mountaineering which is so dear to dons and schoolmasters. When the time came he was ready for that, but he had had his experiences. He had gone through a phase of real cowardice. He was afraid, he confessed, before even he reached Montana; he was afraid of the steepness of the mountains. He had to drive ten or twelve miles up and up the mountain-side, a road of innumerable hairpin bends and precipitous banks, the horse was gaunt and ugly with a disposition to shy, and he confesses he clutched the side of the vehicle and speculated how he should jump if presently the whole turnout went tumbling over. . . .

"And afterwards I dreamt dreams of precipices. I made strides over precipices, I fell and fell with a floating swiftness towards remote valleys, I was assailed by eagles upon a perilous ledge that crumbled away and left me clinging by my nails to nothing."

The Bisse of Leysin is one of those artificial water-courses which bring water from some distant source to pastures that have an insufficient or uncertain supply. It is a little better known than most because of a certain exceptional boldness in its construction; for a distance of a few score yards it runs supported by iron staples across the front of a sheer precipice, and for perhaps half a mile it hangs like an eyebrow over nearly or quite vertical walls of pine-set rock. Beside it, on the outer side of it, runs a path, which becomes an offhand gangway of planking at the overhanging places. At one corner, which gives the favourite picture postcard from Montana, the rocks project so sharply above the water that the passenger on the gangway must crouch down upon the bending plank as he walks. There is no hand-hold at all.

A path from Montana takes one over a pine-clad spur and down a precipitous zig-zag upon the middle of the Bisse, and thither Benham came, fascinated by the very fact that here was something of which the mere report frightened him. He had to walk across the cold clear rush of the Bisse upon a pine log, and then he found himself upon one of the gentler interludes of the Bisse track. It was a scrambling path nearly two feet wide, and below it were slopes, but not so steep as to terrify. At a vast distance below he saw through tree-stems and blue haze a twisted strand of bright whiteness, the river that joins the Rhone at Sion. It looped about and passed out of sight remotely beneath his feet.

He turned to the right, and came to a corner that
overhung a precipice. He craned his head round
this corner and saw the evil place of the picture-post-
cards.

He remained for a long time trying to screw
himself up to walk along the jagged six-inch edge of
rock between cliff and torrent into which the path
has shrunken, to the sagging plank under the overhanging rock beyond.

He could not bring himself to do that.

"It happened that close to the corner a large lump
of rock and earth was breaking away, a cleft was
opening, so that presently, it seemed possible at any
moment, the mass would fall headlong into the
blue deeps below. This impending avalanche was
not in my path along the Bisse, it was no sort of
danger to me, but in some way its insecurity gave a
final touch to my cowardice. I could not get myself round that corner."

He turned away. He went and examined the
planks in the other direction, and these he found less
forbidding. He crossed one precipitous place, with
a fall of twoscore feet or less beneath him, and found
worse ahead. There also he managed. A third
place was still more disagreeable. The plank was
worn and thin, and sagged under him. He went
along it supporting himself against the rock above
the Bisse with an extended hand. Halfway the
rock fell back, so that there was nothing whatever
to hold. He stopped, hesitating whether he should
go back — but on this plank there was no going

back because no turning round seemed practicable. While he was still hesitating there came a helpful intervention.   Behind him he saw a peasant appearing and disappearing behind trees and projecting rock masses, and coming across the previous plank at a vigorous trot. . . .

Under the stimulus of a spectator Benham got to the end of this third place without much trouble.   Then very politely he stood aside for the expert to go ahead so that he could follow at his own pace.

There were, however, more difficulties yet to come, and a disagreeable humiliation.   That confounded peasant developed a parental solicitude. After each crossing he waited, and presently began to offer advice and encouragement.   At last came a place where everything was overhanging, where the Bisse was leaking, and the plank wet and slippery. The water ran out of the leak near the brim of the wooden channel and fell in a long shivering thread of silver.   *There was no sound of its fall.*   It just fell— into a void.   Benham wished he had not noted that. He groaned, but faced the plank; he knew this would be the slowest affair of all.

The peasant surveyed him from the further side.

"Don't be afraid!" cried the peasant in his clumsy Valaisian French, and returned, returning along the plank that seemed quite sufficiently loaded without him, extending a charitable hand.

"Damn!" whispered Benham, but he took the hand.

Afterwards, rather ignobly, he tried to explain in his public-school French. "Pas de peur," he said. "Pas de peur. Mais la tête, n'a pas l'habitude."

The peasant, failing to understand, assured him again that there was no danger.

("Damn!")

Benham was led over all the other planks, he was led as if he was an old lady crossing a glacier. He was led into absolute safety, and shamefacedly he rewarded his guide. Then he went a little way and sat down, swore softly, and watched the honest man go striding and plunging down towards Lens until he was out of sight.

"Now," said Benham to himself, "if I do not go back along the planks my secret honour is gone for ever."

He told himself that he had not a good head, that he was not well, that the sun was setting and the light no longer good, that he had a very good chance indeed of getting killed. Then it came to him suddenly as a clear and simple truth, as something luminously plain, that it is better to get killed than go away defeated by such fears and unsteadiness as his. The change came into his mind as if a white light were suddenly turned on — where there had been nothing but shadows and darkness. He rose to his feet and went swiftly and intently the whole way back, going with a kind of temperate recklessness, and, because he was no longer careful, easily. He went on beyond his starting place toward the corner, and did that supreme bit, to and fro, that

bit where the lump was falling away, and he had
to crouch, as gaily as the rest. Then he recrossed the
Bisse upon the pine log, clambered up through the
pines to the crest, and returned through the meadows
to his own hotel.

After that he should have slept the sleep of con-
tentment, but instead he had quite dreadful nightmares, of hanging in frozen fear above incredible
declivities, of ill-aimed leaps across chasms to slippery
footholds, of planks that swayed and broke suddenly
in the middle and headed him down and down. . . .

The next day in the sunshine he walked the Bisse
again with those dreams like trailing mists in his
mind, and by comparison the path of the Bisse was
nothing, it was like walking along a kerbstone, it
was an exercise for young ladies. . . .

§ 7

In his younger days Benham had regarded Fear
as a shameful secret and as a thing to be got rid of
altogether. It seemed to him that to feel fear was
to fall short of aristocracy, and in spite of the deep
dreads and disgusts that haunted his mind, he set
about the business of its subjugation as if it were a
spiritual amputation. But as he emerged from the
egotism of adolescence he came to realize that this
was too comprehensive an operation; every one
feels fear, and your true aristocrat is not one who
has eliminated, but one who controls or ignores it.
Brave men are men who do things when they are
afraid to do them, just as Nelson, even when he

was seasick, and he was frequently seasick, was still master of the sea.   Benham developed two leading ideas about fear; one that it is worse at the first onset, and far worse than any real experience, and the other that fear is essentially a social instinct.   He set himself upon these lines to study — what can we call it? — the taming of fear, the nature, care, and management of fear. . . .

"Fear is very like pain in this, that it is a deterrent thing.   It is superficial.   Just as a man's skin is infinitely more sensitive than anything inside. . . . Once you have forced yourself or have been forced through the outward fear into vivid action or experience, you feel very little.   The worst moment is before things happen.   Rowe, the African sportsman, told me that he had seen cowardice often enough in the presence of lions, but he had never seen any one actually charged by a lion who did not behave well.   I have heard the same thing of many sorts of dangers.

"I began to suspect this first in the case of falling or jumping down.   Giddiness may be an almost intolerable torture, and falling nothing of the sort. I once saw the face of an old man who had flung himself out of a high window in Rome, and who had been killed instantly on the pavement; it was not simply a serene face, it was glad, exalted.   I suspect that when we have broken the shell of fear, falling may be delightful.   Jumping down is, after all, only a steeper tobogganing, and tobogganing a milder jumping down.   Always I used to funk at the top of the Cresta run. I suffered sometimes almost intolerably; I found it almost impossible to get away. The first ten yards was like being slashed open with a sharp sword. But afterwards there was nothing but joyful thrills. All instinct, too, fought against me when I tried high diving. I managed it, and began to like it. I had to give it up because of my ears, but not until I had established the habit of stepping through that moment of disinclination.

"I was Challoner's passenger when he was killed at Sheerness. That was a queer unexpected experience, you may have supposed it an agony of terror, but indeed there was no fear in it at all. At any rate, I do not remember a moment of fear; it has gone clean out of my memory if ever it was there. We were swimming high and fast, three thousand feet or so, in a clear, sweet air over the town of Sheerness. The river, with a string of battleships, was far away to the west of us, and the endless grey-blue flats of the Thames to the north. The sun was low behind a bank of cloud. I was watching a motor-car, which seemed to be crawling slowly enough, though, no doubt, it was making a respectable pace, between two hedges down below. It is extraordinary how slowly everything seems to be going when one sees it from such an height.

"Then the left wing of the monoplane came up like a door that slams, some wires whistled past my head, and one whipped off my helmet, and then, with the seat slipping away from me, down we went. I snatched unavailingly for the helmet, and then gripped the sides. It was like dropping in a boat suddenly into the trough of a wave — and going on dropping. We were both strapped, and I got my feet against the side and clung to the locked second wheel.

"The sensation was as though something like an intermittent electric current was pouring through me. It's a ridiculous image to use, I can't justify it, but it was as if I was having cold blue light squirted through every pore of my being. There was an astonishment, a feeling of confirmation. 'Of course these things do happen sometimes,' I told myself. I don't remember that Challoner looked round or said anything at all. I am not sure that I looked at him. . . .

"There seemed to be a long interval of intensely excited curiosity, and I remember thinking, 'Lord, but we shall come a smash in a minute!' Far ahead I saw the grey sheds of Eastchurch and people strolling about apparently unaware of our disaster. There was a sudden silence as Challoner stopped the engine. . . .

"But the point I want to insist upon is that I did not feel afraid. I was simply enormously, terribly *interested*. . . .

"There came a tremendous jolt and a lunge, and we were both tipped forward, so that we were hanging forehead down by our straps, and it looked as if the sheds were in the sky, then I saw nothing but sky, then came another vast swerve, and we were falling sideways, sideways. . . .

"I was altogether out of breath and *physically* astonished, and I remember noting quite intelligently as we hit the ground how the green grass had an effect of *pouring out* in every direction from below us. . . .

"Then I remember a jerk and a feeling that I was flying up again. I was astonished by a tremendous popping—fabric, wires, everything seemed going pop, pop, pop, like a machine-gun, and then came a flash of intense pain as my arm crumpled up. It was quite impersonal pain. As impersonal as seeing intense colour. *Splinters!* I remember the word came into my head instantly. I remember that very definitely.

"I thought, I suppose, my arm was in splinters. Or perhaps of the scraps and ends of rods and wires flying about us. It is curious that while I remember the word I cannot recall the idea. . . .

"When I became conscious again the chief thing present in my mind was that all those fellows round were young soldiers who wouldn't at all understand bad behaviour. My arm was — orchestral, but still far from being real suffering *in* me. Also I wanted to know what Challoner had got. They wouldn't understand my questions, and then I twisted round and saw from the negligent way his feet came out from under the engine that he must be dead. And dark red stains with bright red froth—

"Of course!

"There again the chief feeling was a sense of oddity. I wasn't sorry for him any more than I was for myself.

"It seemed to me that it was all right with us both, remarkable, vivid, but all right. . . ."

§ 8

"But though there is little or no fear in an aeroplane, even when it is smashing up, there is fear about aeroplanes. There is something that says very urgently, 'Don't,' to the man who looks up into the sky. It is very interesting to note how at a place like Eastchurch or Brooklands the necessary discretion trails the old visceral feeling with it, and how men will hang about, ready to go up, resolved to go up, but delaying. Men of indisputable courage will get into a state between dread and laziness, and waste whole hours of flying weather on any excuse or no excuse. Once they are up that inhibition vanishes. The man who was delaying and delaying half an hour ago will now be cutting the most venturesome capers in the air. Few men are in a hurry to get down again. I mean that quite apart from the hesitation of landing, they like being up there."

Then, abruptly, Benham comes back to his theory.

"Fear, you see, is the inevitable janitor, but it is not the ruler of experience. That is what I am driving at in all this. The bark of danger is worse than its bite. Inside the portals there may be events and destruction, but terror stays defeated at the door. It may be that when that old man was killed by a horse the child who watched suffered more than he did. . . .

"I am sure that was so. . . ."

§ 9

As White read Benham's notes and saw how his
argument drove on, he was reminded again and
again of those schoolboy days and Benham's hardihood, and his own instinctive unreasonable reluctance to follow those gallant intellectual leads.
If fear is an ancient instinctive boundary that the
modern life, the aristocratic life, is bound to ignore
and transcend, may this not also be the case with
pain? We do a little adventure into the "life beyond fear"; may we not also think of adventuring
into the life beyond pain? Is pain any saner a
warning than fear?   May not pain just as much as
fear keep us from possible and splendid things?
But why ask a question that is already answered in
principle in every dentist's chair? Benham's idea,
however, went much further than that, he was
clearly suggesting that in pain itself, pain endured
beyond a certain pitch, there might come pleasure
again, an intensity of sensation that might have the
colour of delight. He betrayed a real anxiety to
demonstrate this possibility, he had the earnestness
of a man who is sensible of dissentient elements
within. He hated the thought of pain even more
than he hated fear. His arguments did not in the
least convince White, who stopped to poke the fire
and assure himself of his own comfort in the midst
of his reading.

Young people and unseasoned people, Benham
argued, are apt to imagine that if fear is increased

and carried to an extreme pitch it becomes unbear-
able, one will faint or die; given a weak heart, a
weak artery or any such structural defect and that
may well happen, but it is just as possible that as
the stimulation increases one passes through a brief
ecstasy of terror to a new sane world, exalted but as
sane as normal existence. There is the calmness
of despair. Benham had made some notes to en-
force this view, of the observed calm behaviour of
men already hopelessly lost, men on sinking ships,
men going to execution, men already maimed and
awaiting the final stroke, but for the most part
these were merely references to books and period-
icals. In exactly the same way, he argued, we exaggerate the range of pain as if it were limitless. We
think if we are unthinking that it passes into agony
and so beyond endurance to destruction. It probably does nothing of the kind. Benham compared
pain to the death range of the electric current. At a
certain voltage it thrills, at a greater it torments
and convulses, at a still greater it kills. But at
enormous voltages, as Tesla was the first to demonstrate, it does no injury. And following on this
came memoranda on the recorded behaviour of
martyrs, on the self-torture of Hindoo ascetics, of the
defiance of Red Indian prisoners.

"These things," Benham had written, "are
much more horrible when one considers them from
the point of view of an easy-chair" ; — White
gave an assenting nod — "*are they really horrible at
all?* Is it possible that these charred and slashed

and splintered persons, those Indians hanging from
hooks, those walkers in the fiery furnace, have had
glimpses through great windows that were worth
the price they paid for them? Haven't we allowed
those checks and barriers that are so important a
restraint upon childish enterprise, to creep up into
and distress and distort adult life? . . .

"The modern world thinks too much as though
painlessness and freedom from danger were ultimate
ends. It is fear-haunted, it is troubled by the
thoughts of pain and death, which it has never met
except as well-guarded children meet these things,
in exaggerated and untestable forms, in the menagerie or in nightmares. And so it thinks the discovery of anæsthetics the crowning triumph of
civilization, and cosiness and innocent amusement,
those ideals of the nursery, the whole purpose of
mankind. . . ."

"Mm," said White, and pressed his lips together
and knotted his brows and shook his head.

§ 10

But the bulk of Benham's discussion of fear was
not concerned with this perverse and overstrained
suggestion of pleasure reached through torture, this
exaggeration of the man resolved not to shrink at
anything; it was an examination of the present
range and use of fear that led gradually to something
like a theory of control and discipline. The second
of his two dominating ideas was that fear is an
instinct arising only in isolation, that in a crowd

D

there may be a collective panic, but that there is
no real individual fear. Fear, Benham held, drives
the man back to the crowd, the dog to its master,
the wolf to the pack, and when it is felt that the
danger is pooled, then fear leaves us. He was quite
prepared to meet the objection that animals of a
solitary habit do nevertheless exhibit fear. Some
of this apparent fear, he argued, was merely discretion, and what is not discretion is the survival of an
infantile characteristic. The fear felt by a tiger
cub is certainly a social emotion, that drives it
back to the other cubs, to its mother and the dark
hiding of the lair. The fear of a fully grown tiger
sends it into the reeds and the shadows, to a refuge,
that must be "still reminiscent of the maternal lair."
But fear has very little hold upon the adult solitary
animal, it changes with extreme readiness to resentment and rage.

"Like most inexperienced people," ran his notes,
"I was astonished at the reported feats of men in
war; I believed they were exaggerated, and that
there was a kind of unpremeditated conspiracy of
silence about their real behaviour. But when on
my way to visit India for the third time I turned off
to see what I could of the fighting before Adrianople,
I discovered at once that a thousand casually selected
conscripts will, every one of them, do things together
that not one of them could by any means be induced
to do alone. I saw men not merely obey orders that
gave them the nearly certain prospect of death, but
I saw them exceeding orders; I saw men leap out of

cover for the mere sake of defiance, and fall shot
through and smashed by a score of bullets. I saw a
number of Bulgarians in the hands of the surgeon,
several quite frightfully wounded, refuse chloroform
merely to impress the English onlooker, some of their
injuries I could scarcely endure to see, and I watched
a line of infantry men go on up a hill and keep on
quite manifestly cheerful with men dropping out
and wriggling, and men dropping out and lying
still until every other man was down. . . . Not
one man would have gone up that hill alone, without onlookers. . . ."

Rowe, the lion hunter, told Benham that only on
one occasion in his life had he given way to ungovern-
able fear, and that was when he was alone. Many
times he had been in fearful situations in the face of
charging lions and elephants, and once he had been
bowled over and carried some distance by a lion,
but on none of these occasions had fear demoralized
him. There was no question of his general pluck.
But on one occasion he was lost in rocky waterless
country in Somaliland. He strayed out in the
early morning while his camels were being loaded,
followed some antelope too far, and lost his bearings.
He looked up expecting to see the sun on his right
hand and found it on his left. He became bewildered.
He wandered some time and then fired three signal
shots and got no reply. Then losing his head he
began shouting. He had only four or five more
cartridges and no water-bottle. His men were
accustomed to his going on alone, and might not

begin to remark upon his absence until sundown. . . .
It chanced, however, that one of the shikari noted
the water-bottle he had left behind and organized
a hunt for him.

Long before they found him he had passed to an
extremity of terror. The world had become hideous
and threatening, the sun was a pitiless glare, each
rocky ridge he clambered became more dreadful
than the last, each new valley into which he looked
more hateful and desolate, the cramped thorn bushes
threatened him gauntly, the rocks had a sinister
lustre, and in every blue shadow about him the
night and death lurked and waited. There was no
hurry for them, presently they would spread out
again and join and submerge him, presently in the
confederated darkness he could be stalked and
seized and slain. Yes, this he admitted was real
fear. He had cracked his voice, yelling as a child
yells. And then he had become afraid of his own
voice. . . .

"Now this excess of fear in isolation, this comfort
in a crowd, in support and in a refuge, even when
support or refuge is quite illusory, is just exactly
what one would expect of fear if one believed it to
be an instinct which has become a misfit. In the
case of the soldier fear is so much a misfit that instead
of saving him for the most part it destroys him.
Raw soldiers under fire bunch together and armies
fight in masses, men are mowed down in swathes,
because only so is the courage of the common men
sustained, only so can they be brave, albeit spread

out and handling their weapons as men of unqualified daring would handle them they would be infinitely safer and more effective. . . .

"And all of us, it may be, are restrained by this misfit fear from a thousand bold successful gestures of mind and body, we are held back from the attainment of mighty securities in pitiful temporary shelters that are perhaps in the end no better than traps. . . ."

From such considerations Benham went on to speculate how far the crowd can be replaced in a man's imagination, how far some substitute for that social backing can be made to serve the same purpose in neutralizing fear. He wrote with the calm of a man who weighs the probabilities of a riddle, and with the zeal of a man lost to every material consideration. His writing, it seemed to White, had something of the enthusiastic whiteness of his face, the enthusiastic brightness of his eyes. We can no more banish fear from our being at present than we can carve out the fleshy pillars of the heart or the pineal gland in the brain. It is deep in our inheritance. As deep as hunger. And just as we have to satisfy hunger in order that it should leave us free, so we have to satisfy the unconquerable importunity of fear. We have to reassure our faltering instincts. There must be something to take the place of lair and familiars, something not ourselves but general, that we must carry with us into the lonely places. For it is true that man has now not only to learn to fight in open order instead of in a phalanx, but he has to think and plan and act in open order, to live in open order. . . .

Then with one of his abrupt transitions Benham had written, "This brings me to God."

"The devil it does!" said White, roused to a keener attention.

"By no feat of intention can we achieve courage in loneliness so long as we feel indeed alone. An isolated man, an egoist, an Epicurean man, will always fail himself in the solitary place. There must be something more with us to sustain us against this vast universe than the spark of life that began yesterday and must be extinguished to-morrow. There can be no courage beyond social courage, the sustaining confidence of the herd, until there is in us the sense of God. But God is a word that covers a multitude of meanings. When I was a boy I was a passionate atheist, I defied God, and so far as God is the mere sanction of social traditions and pressures, a mere dressing up of the crowd's will in canonicals, I do still deny him and repudiate him. That God I heard of first from my nursemaid, and in very truth he is the proper God of all the nursemaids of mankind. But there is another God than that God of obedience, God the immortal adventurer in me, God who calls men from home and country, God scourged and crowned with thorns, who rose in a nail-pierced body out of death and came not to bring peace but a sword."

With something bordering upon intellectual consternation, White, who was a decent self-respecting

sceptic, read these last clamberings of Benham's
spirit. They were written in pencil; they were
unfinished when he died.

(Surely the man was not a Christian!)

"You may be heedless of death and suffering
because you think you cannot suffer and die, or
you may be heedless of death and pain because you
have identified your life with the honour of mankind
and the insatiable adventurousness of man's imagination, so that the possible death is negligible and the
possible achievement altogether outweighs it." . . .

White shook his head over these pencilled fragments.

He was a member of the Rationalist Press Association, and he had always taken it for granted that
Benham was an orthodox unbeliever. But this was
hopelessly unsound, heresy, perilous stuff; almost, it
seemed to him, a posthumous betrayal. . . .

§ 11

One night when he was in India the spirit of adventure came upon Benham. He had gone with Kepple,
of the forestry department, into the jungle country
in the hills above the Tápti. He had been very
anxious to see something of that aspect of Indian
life, and he had snatched at the chance Kepple had
given him. But they had scarcely started before
the expedition was brought to an end by an accident,
Kepple was thrown by a pony and his ankle broken.
He and Benham bandaged it as well as they could,
and a litter was sent for, and meanwhile they had

to wait in the camp that was to have been the centre
of their jungle raids. The second day of this waiting
was worse for Kepple than the first, and he suffered
much from the pressure of this amateurish bandag-
ing. In the evening Benham got cool water from
the well and rearranged things better; the two men
dined and smoked under their thatched roof beneath
the big banyan, and then Kepple, tired out by his
day of pain, was carried to his tent. Presently he
fell asleep and Benham was left to himself.

Now that the heat was over he found himself
quite indisposed to sleep. He felt full of life and
anxious for happenings.

He went back and sat down upon the iron bedstead
beneath the banyan, that Kepple had lain upon
through the day, and he watched the soft immensity
of the Indian night swallow up the last lingering
colours of the world. It left the outlines, it obliterated nothing, but it stripped off the superficial
reality of things. The moon was full and high
overhead, and the light had not so much gone as
changed from definition and the blazing glitter and
reflections of solidity to a translucent and unsubstantial clearness. The jungle that bordered the
little encampment north, south, and west seemed
to have crept a little nearer, enriched itself with
blackness, taken to itself voices.

(Surely it had been silent during the day.)

A warm, faintly-scented breeze just stirred the
dead grass and the leaves. In the day the air had
been still.

Immediately after the sunset there had been a
great crying of peacocks in the distance, but that
was over now; the crickets, however, were still
noisy, and a persistent sound had become predomi-
nant, an industrious unmistakable sound, a sound
that took his mind back to England, in midsummer.
It was like a watchman's rattle — a nightjar!

So there were nightjars here in India, too! One
might have expected something less familiar. And
then came another cry from far away over the heat-
stripped tree-tops, a less familiar cry. It was
repeated. Was that perhaps some craving leopard,
a tiger cat, a panther? —

"*Hunt, Hunt*"; that might be a deer.

Then suddenly an angry chattering came from
the dark trees quite close at hand. A monkey? . . .

These great, scarce visible, sweeping movements
through the air were bats. . . .

Of course, the day jungle is the jungle asleep.
This was its waking hour. Now the deer were
arising from their forms, the bears creeping out of
their dens amidst the rocks and blundering down
the gullies, the tigers and panthers and jungle cats
stalking noiselessly from their lairs in the grass.
Countless creatures that had hidden from the heat
and pitiless exposure of the day stood now awake and
alertly intent upon their purposes, grazed or sought
water, flitting delicately through the moonlight
and shadows. The jungle was awakening. Again
Benham heard that sound like the belling of a
stag. . . .

This was the real life of the jungle, this night life, into which man did not go. Here he was on the verge of a world that for all the stuffed trophies of the sportsman and the specimens of the naturalist is still almost as unknown as if it was upon another planet. What intruders men are, what foreigners in the life of this ancient system!

He looked over his shoulder, and there were the two little tents, one that sheltered Kepple and one that awaited him, and beyond, in an irregular line, glowed the ruddy smoky fires of the men. One or two turbaned figures still flitted about, and there was a voice — low, monotonous — it must have been telling a tale. Further, sighing and stirring ever and again, were tethered beasts, and then a great pale space of moonlight and the clumsy out-lines of the village well. The clustering village itself slept in darkness beyond the mango trees, and still remoter the black encircling jungle closed in. One might have fancied this was the encampment of newly-come invaders, were it not for the larger villages that are overgrown with thickets and alto-gether swallowed up again in the wilderness, and for the deserted temples that are found rent asunder by the roots of trees and the ancient embankments that hold water only for the drinking of the sambur deer. . . .

Benham turned his face to the dim jungle again. . . .

He had come far out of his way to visit this strange world of the ancient life, that now recedes and dwin-dles before our new civilization, that seems fated

to shrivel up and pass altogether before the dry
advance of physical science and material organization. He was full of unsatisfied curiosities about
its fierce hungers and passions, its fears and cruelties,
its instincts and its well-nigh incommunicable
and yet most precious understandings. He had
long ceased to believe that the wild beast is wholly
evil, and safety and plenty the ultimate good for
men. . . .

Perhaps he would never get nearer to this mysterious jungle life than he was now.

It was intolerably tantalizing that it should be so
close at hand and so inaccessible. . . .

As Benham sat brooding over his disappointment
the moon, swimming on through the still circle of the
hours, passed slowly over him. The lights and
shadows about him changed by imperceptible grada-
tions and a long pale alley where the native cart
track drove into the forest, opened slowly out of
the darkness, slowly broadened, slowly lengthened.
It opened out to him with a quality of invitation. . . .

There was the jungle before him. Was it after all
so inaccessible?

"Come!" the road said to him.

Benham rose and walked out a few paces into the
moonlight and stood motionless.

Was he afraid?

Even now some hungry watchful monster might
lurk in yonder shadows, watching with infinite
still patience. Kepple had told him how they would

sit still for hours — staring unblinkingly as cats
stare at a fire — and then crouch to advance.
Beneath the shrill overtone of the nightjars, what
noiseless grey shapes, what deep breathings and
cracklings and creepings might there not be? . . .

Was he afraid?

That question determined him to go.

He hesitated whether he should take a gun. A
stick? A gun, he knew, was a dangerous thing to
an inexperienced man. No! He would go now,
even as he was with empty hands. At least he
would go as far as the end of that band of moonlight.
If for no other reason than because he was afraid.
Now!

For a moment it seemed to him as though his feet
were too heavy to lift and then, hands in pockets,
khaki-clad, an almost invisible figure, he strolled
towards the cart-track.

Come to that, he halted for a moment to regard
the distant fires of the men. No one would miss
him. They would think he was in his tent. He
faced the stirring quiet ahead. The cart-track
was a rutted path of soft, warm sand, on which he
went almost noiselessly. A bird squabbled for an
instant in a thicket. A great white owl floated like
a flake of moonlight across the track and vanished
without a sound among the trees.

Along the moonlit path went Benham, and when
he passed near trees his footsteps became noisy
with the rustle and crash of dead leaves. The
jungle was full of moonlight; twigs, branches,

creepers, grass-clumps came out acutely vivid.
The trees and bushes stood in pools of darkness,
and beyond were pale stretches of misty moonshine
and big rocks shining with an unearthly lustre.
Things seemed to be clear and yet uncertain. It
was as if they dissolved or retired a little and then
returned to solidity.

A sudden chattering broke out overhead, and black
across the great stars soared a flying squirrel and
caught a twig, and ran for shelter. A second
hesitated in a tree-top and pursued. They chased
each other and vanished abruptly. He forgot his
sense of insecurity in the interest of these active
little silhouettes. And he noted how much bigger
and more wonderful the stars can look when one
sees them through interlacing branches.

Ahead was darkness, but not so dark when he
came to it that the track was invisible. He was at
the limit of his intention, but now he saw that that
had been a childish project. He would go on, he
would walk right into the jungle. His first disinclination was conquered, and the soft intoxication of the
subtropical moonshine was in his blood. . . . But
he wished he could walk as a spirit walks, without
this noise of leaves. . . .

Yes, this was very wonderful and beautiful, and
there must always be jungles for men to walk in.
Always there must be jungles. . . .

Some small beast snarled and bolted from under
his feet. He stopped sharply. He had come into
a darkness under great boughs, and now he stood

still as the little creature scuttled away.   Beyond
the track emerged into a dazzling whiteness. . . .

In the stillness he could hear the deer belling again
in the distance, and then came a fuss of monkeys
in a group of trees near at hand.   He remained
still until this had died away into mutterings.

Then on the verge of movement he was startled by
a ripe mango that slipped from its stalk and fell
out of the tree and struck his hand.   It took a little
time to understand that, and then he laughed, and
his muscles relaxed, and he went on again.

A thorn caught at him and he disentangled himself.

He crossed the open space, and the moon was like a
great shield of light spread out above him.   All the
world seemed swimming in its radiance.   The
stars were like lamps in a mist of silvery blue.

The track led him on across white open spaces
of shrivelled grass and sand, amidst trees where
shadows made black patternings upon the silver, and
then it plunged into obscurities.   For a time it
lifted, and then on one hand the bush fell away,
and he saw across a vast moonlit valley wide undula-
tions of open cultivation, belts of jungle, copses, and
a great lake as black as ebony.   For a time the path
ran thus open, and then the jungle closed in again
and there were more thickets, more levels of grass,
and in one place far overhead among the branches
he heard and stood for a time perplexed at a vast
deep humming of bees. . . .

Presently a black monster with a hunched back
went across his path heedless of him and making a

great noise in the leaves. He stood quite still until it had gone. He could not tell whether it was a boar or hyæna; most probably, he thought, a boar because of the heaviness of its rush.

The path dropped downhill for a time, crossed a ravine, ascended. He passed a great leafless tree on which there were white flowers. On the ground also, in the darkness under the tree, there were these flowers; they were dropping noiselessly, and since they were visible in the shadows, it seemed to him that they must be phosphorescent. And they emitted a sweetish scent that lay heavily athwart the path. Presently he passed another such tree. Then he became aware of a tumult ahead of him, a smashing of leaves, a snorting and slobbering, grunting and sucking, a whole series of bestial sounds. He halted for a little while, and then drew nearer, picking his steps to avoid too great a noise. Here were more of those white-blossomed trees, and beneath, in the darkness, something very black and big was going to and fro, eating greedily. Then he found that there were two and then more of these black things, three or four of them.

Curiosity made Benham draw nearer, very softly.

Presently one showed in a patch of moonlight, startlingly big, a huge, black hairy monster with a long white nose on a grotesque face, and he was stuffing armfuls of white blossom into his mouth with his curved fore claws. He took not the slightest notice of the still man, who stood perhaps twenty yards away from him. He was too blind and careless. He snorted and smacked his slobbering lips, and plunged into the shadows again. Benham heard him root among the leaves and grunt appreciatively. The air was heavy with the reek of the crushed flowers.

For some time Benham remained listening to and peering at these preoccupied gluttons. At last he shrugged his shoulders, and left them and went on his way. For a long time he could hear them, then just as he was on the verge of forgetting them altogether, some dispute arose among them, and there began a vast uproar, squeals, protests, comments, one voice ridiculously replete and authoritative, ridiculously suggestive of a drunken judge with his mouth full, and a shrill voice of grievance high above the others. . . .

The uproar of the bears died away at last, almost abruptly, and left the jungle to the incessant nightjars. . . .

For what end was this life of the jungle?

All Benham's senses were alert to the sounds and appearances about him, and at the same time his mind was busy with the perplexities of that riddle. Was the jungle just an aimless pool of life that man must drain and clear away? Or is it to have a use in the greater life of our race that now begins? Will man value the jungle as he values the precipice, for the sake of his manhood? Will he preserve it?

Man must keep hard, man must also keep fierce. Will the jungle keep him fierce?

For life, thought Benham, there must be insecurity. . . .

He had missed the track. . . .

He was now in a second ravine. He was going downward, walking on silvery sand amidst great boulders, and now there was a new sound in the air —. It was the croaking of frogs. Ahead was a solitary gleam. He was approaching a jungle pool. . . . .

Suddenly the stillness was alive, in a panic uproar. *"Honk!"* cried a great voice, and *"Honk!"* There was a clatter of hoofs, a wild rush — a rush as it seemed towards him. Was he being charged? He backed against a rock. A great pale shape leaped by him, an antlered shape. It was a herd of big deer bolting suddenly out of the stillness. He heard the swish and smash of their retreat grow distant, disperse. He remained standing with his back to the rock.

Slowly the strophe and antistrophe of frogs and goat-suckers resumed possession of his consciousness. But now some primitive instinct perhaps or some subconscious intimation of danger made him meticulously noiseless.

He went on down a winding sound-deadening path of sand towards the drinking-place. He came to a wide white place that was almost level, and beyond it under clustering pale-stemmed trees shone the mirror surface of some ancient tank, and, sharp and black, a dog-like beast sat on its tail in the midst of this space, started convulsively and went slinking

E

into the undergrowth. Benham paused for a moment and then walked out softly into the light, and, behold! as if it were to meet him, came a monster, a vast dark shape drawing itself lengthily out of the blackness, and stopped with a start as if it had been instantly changed to stone.

It had stopped with one paw advanced. Its striped mask was light and dark grey in the moonlight, grey but faintly tinged with ruddiness; its mouth was a little open, its fangs and a pendant of viscous saliva shone vivid. Its great round-pupilled eyes regarded him stedfastly. At last the nightmare of Benham's childhood had come true, and he was face to face with a tiger, uncaged, uncontrolled.

For some moments neither moved, neither the beast nor the man. They stood face to face, each perhaps with an equal astonishment, motionless and soundless, in that mad Indian moonlight that makes all things like a dream.

Benham stood quite motionless, and body and mind had halted together. That confrontation had an interminableness that had nothing to do with the actual passage of time. Then some trickle of his previous thoughts stirred in the frozen quiet of his mind.

He spoke hoarsely. "I am Man," he said, and lifted a hand as he spoke. "The Thought of the world."

His heart leapt within him as the tiger moved. But the great beast went sideways, gardant, only that its head was low, three noiseless instantaneous strides it made, and stood again watching him.

"Man," he said, in a voice that had no sound, and took a step forward.

"Wough!"   With two bounds the monster had become a great grey streak that crackled and rustled in the shadows of the trees.   And then it had vanished, become invisible and inaudible with a kind of instantaneousness.

For some seconds or some minutes Benham stood rigid, fearlessly expectant, and then far away up the ravine he heard the deer repeat their cry of alarm, and understood with a new wisdom that the tiger had passed among them and was gone. . . .

He walked on towards the deserted tank and now he was talking aloud.

"I understand the jungle.   I understand. . . .   If a few men die here, what matter?   There are worse deaths than being killed. . . .

"What is this fool's trap of security?

"Every time in my life that I have fled from security I have fled from death. . . .

"Let men stew in their cities if they will.   It is in the lonely places, in jungles and mountains, in snows and fires, in the still observatories and the silent laboratories, in those secret and dangerous places where life probes into life, it is there that the masters of the world, the lords of the beast, the rebel sons of Fate come to their own. . . .

"You sleeping away there in the cities!   Do you know what it means for you that I am here to-night?

"Do you know what it means to you?

"I am just one — just the precursor.

"Presently, if you will not budge, those hot cities must be burnt about you. You must come out of them. . . ."

He wandered now uttering his thoughts as they came to him, and he saw no more living creatures because they fled and hid before the sound of his voice. He wandered until the moon, larger now and yellow tinged, was low between the black bars of the tree stems. And then it sank very suddenly behind a hilly spur and the light failed swiftly.

He stumbled and went with difficulty. He could go no further among these rocks and ravines, and he sat down at the foot of a tree to wait for day.

He sat very still indeed.

A great stillness came over the world, a velvet silence that wrapped about him, as the velvet shadows wrapped about him. The corncrakes had ceased, all the sounds and stir of animal life had died away, the breeze had fallen. A drowsing comfort took possession of him. He grew more placid and more placid still. He was enormously content to find that fear had fled before him and was gone. He drifted into that state of mind when one thinks without ideas, when one's mind is like a starless sky, serene and empty.

§ 12

Some hours later Benham found that the trees and rocks were growing visible again, and he saw a

very bright star that he knew must be Lucifer
rising amidst the black branches. He was sitting upon a rock at the foot of a slender-stemmed
leafless tree. He had been asleep, and it was
daybreak. Everything was coldly clear and colourless.

He must have slept soundly.

He heard a cock crow, and another answer —
jungle fowl these must be, because there could
be no village within earshot — and then far away
and bringing back memories of terraced houses
and ripe walled gardens, was the scream of peacocks. And some invisible bird was making a
hollow beating sound among the trees near at hand.
Tunk. . . . *Tunk*, and out of the dry grass came a
twittering.

There was a green light in the east that grew
stronger, and the stars after their magnitudes were
dissolving in the blue; only a few remained faintly
visible. The sound of birds increased. Through
the trees he saw towering up a great mauve thing
like the back of a monster, — but that was nonsense,
it was the crest of a steep hillside covered with woods
of teak.

He stood up and stretched himself, and wondered
whether he had dreamed of a tiger.

He tried to remember and retrace the course of his
over-night wanderings.

A flight of emerald parakeets tore screaming
through the trees, and then far away uphill he heard
the creaking of a cart.

He followed the hint of a footmark, and went back up the glen slowly and thoughtfully.

Presently he came to a familiar place, a group of trees, a sheet of water, and the ruins of an old embankment. It was the ancient tank of his over-night encounter. The pool of his dream?

With doubt still in his mind, he walked round its margin to the sandy level beyond, and cast about and sought intently, and at last found, and then found clearly, imposed upon the tracks of several sorts of deer and the footprints of many biggish birds, first the great spoor of the tiger and then his own. Here the beast had halted, and here it had leapt aside. Here his own footmarks stopped. Here his heels had come together.

It had been no dream.

There was a white mist upon the water of the old tank like the bloom upon a plum, and the trees about it seemed smaller and the sand-space wider and rougher than they had seemed in the moonshine. Then the ground had looked like a floor of frosted silver.

And thence he went on upward through the fresh morning, until just as the east grew red with sun-rise, he reached the cart-track from which he had strayed overnight. It was, he found, a longer way back to the camp than he remembered it to be. Perhaps he had struck the path further along. It curved about and went up and down and crossed three ravines. At last he came to that trampled place of littered white blossom under great trees where he had seen the bears.

The sunlight went before him in a sheaf of golden spears, and his shadow, that was at first limitless, crept towards his feet. The dew had gone from the dead grass and the sand was hot to his dry boots before he came back into the open space about the great banyan and the tents. And Kepple, refreshed by a night's rest and coffee, was wondering loudly where the devil he had gone.

THE STORY

CHAPTER THE FIRST

THE BOY GROWS UP

§ 1

BENHAM was the son of a schoolmaster. His father was assistant first at Cheltenham, and subsequently at Minchinghampton, and then he became head and later on sole proprietor of Martindale House, a high-class preparatory school at Seagate. He was extremely successful for some years, as success goes in the scholastic profession, and then disaster overtook him in the shape of a divorce. His wife, William Porphyry's mother, made the acquaintance of a rich young man named Nolan, who was recuperating at Seagate from the sequelæ of snake-bite, malaria, and a gun accident in Brazil. She ran away with him, and she was divorced. She was, however, unable to marry him because he died at Wiesbaden only three days after the Reverend Harold Benham obtained his decree absolute. Instead, therefore, being a woman of great spirit, enterprise and sweetness, she married Godfrey Marayne, afterwards Sir Godfrey Marayne, the great London surgeon.

Nolan was a dark, rather melancholy and sentimental young man, and he left about a third of his

59

very large fortune entirely to Mrs. Benham and the rest to her in trust for her son, whom he deemed himself to have injured. With this and a husband already distinguished, she returned presently to London, and was on the whole fairly well received there.

It was upon the reverend gentleman at Seagate that the brunt of this divorce fell. There is perhaps a certain injustice in the fact that a schoolmaster who has lost his wife should also lose the more valuable proportion of his pupils, but the tone of thought in England is against any association of a schoolmaster with matrimonial irregularity. And also Mr. Benham remarried. It would certainly have been better for him if he could have produced a sister. His school declined and his efforts to resuscitate it only hastened its decay. Conceiving that he could now only appeal to the broader-minded, more progressive type of parent, he became an educational reformer, and wrote upon modernizing the curriculum with increasing frequency to the *Times*. He expended a considerable fraction of his dwindling capital upon a science laboratory and a fives court; he added a London Bachelor of Science with a Teaching Diploma to the school staff, and a library of about a thousand volumes, including the Hundred Best Books as selected by the late Lord Avebury, to the school equipment. None of these things did anything but enhance the suspicion of laxity his wife's escapade had created in the limited opulent and discreet class to which his establishment appealed.

One boy who, under the influence of the Hundred
Best Books, had quoted the *Zend-Avesta* to an iras-
cible but influential grandfather, was withdrawn
without notice or compensation in the middle of the
term. It intensifies the tragedy of the Reverend
Harold Benham's failure that in no essential respect
did his school depart from the pattern of all other
properly-conducted preparatory schools.

In appearance he was near the average of scholastic English gentlemen. He displayed a manifest
handsomeness somewhat weakened by disregard and
disuse, a large moustache and a narrow high forehead. His rather tired brown eyes were magnified
by glasses. He was an active man in unimportant
things, with a love for the phrase "ship-shape,"
and he played cricket better than any one else on
the staff. He walked in wide strides, and would
sometimes use the tail of his gown on the blackboard.
Like so many clergymen and schoolmasters, he had
early distrusted his natural impulse in conversation,
and had adopted the defensive precaution of a rather
formal and sonorous speech, which habit had made
a part of him. His general effect was of one who is
earnestly keeping up things that might otherwise
give way, keeping them up by act and voice, keeping
up an atmosphere of vigour and success in a school
that was only too manifestly attenuated, keeping
up a pretentious economy of administration in a
school that must not be too manifestly impoverished,
keeping up a claim to be in the scientific van and
rather a flutterer of dovecots — with its method of

manual training for example — keeping up *esprit de corps* and the manliness of himself and every one about him, keeping up his affection for his faithful second wife and his complete forgetfulness of and indifference to that spirit of distracting impulse and insubordination away there in London, who had once been his delight and insurmountable difficulty. "After my visits to her," wrote Benham, "he would show by a hundred little expressions and poses and acts how intensely he wasn't noting that anything of the sort had occurred."

But one thing that from the outset the father seemed to have failed to keep up thoroughly was his intention to mould and dominate his son.

The advent of his boy had been a tremendous event in the reverend gentleman's life. It is not improbable that his disposition to monopolize the pride of this event contributed to the ultimate disruption of his family. It left so few initiatives within the home to his wife. He had been an early victim to that wave of philoprogenitive and educational enthusiasm which distinguished the closing decade of the nineteenth century. He was full of plans in those days for the education of his boy, and the thought of the youngster played a large part in the series of complicated emotional crises with which he celebrated the departure of his wife, crises in which a number of old school and college friends very generously assisted — spending weekends at Seagate for this purpose, and mingling tobacco, impassioned handclasps and suchlike consola-

tion with much patient sympathetic listening to his
carefully balanced analysis of his feelings. He declared that his son was now his one living purpose in
life, and he sketched out a scheme of moral and intellectual training that he subsequently embodied in
five very stimulating and intimate articles for the
School World, but never put into more than partial
operation.

"I have read my father's articles upon this sub-
ject," wrote Benham, "and I am still perplexed to
measure just what I owe to him. Did he ever
attempt this moral training he contemplated so
freely? I don't think he did. I know now, I knew
then, that he had something in his mind. . . .
There were one or two special walks we had together,
he invited me to accompany him with a certain
portentousness, and we would go out pregnantly
making superficial remarks about the school cricket
and return, discussing botany, with nothing said.

"His heart failed him.

"Once or twice, too, he seemed to be reaching out
at me from the school pulpit.

"I think that my father did manage to convey
to me his belief that there were these fine things,
honour, high aims, nobilities. If I did not get this
belief from him then I do not know how I got it.
But it was as if he hinted at a treasure that had got
very dusty in an attic, a treasure which he hadn't
himself been able to spend. . . ."

The father who had intended to mould his son
ended by watching him grow, not always with sym-

pathy or understanding. He was an overworked man assailed by many futile anxieties. One sees him striding about the establishment with his gown streaming out behind him urging on the groundsman or the gardener, or dignified, expounding the particular advantages of Seagate to enquiring parents, one sees him unnaturally cheerful and facetious at the midday dinner table, one imagines him keeping up high aspirations in a rather too hastily scribbled sermon in the school pulpit, or keeping up an enthusiasm for beautiful language in a badly-prepared lesson on Virgil, or expressing unreal indignation and unjustifiably exalted sentiments to evil doers, and one realizes his disadvantage against the quiet youngster whose retentive memory was storing up all these impressions for an ultimate judgment, and one understands, too, a certain relief that mingled with his undeniable emotion when at last the time came for young Benham, "the one living purpose" of his life, to be off to Minchinghampton and the next step in the mysterious ascent of the English educational system.

Three times at least, and with an increased interval, the father wrote fine fatherly letters that would have stood the test of publication. Then his communications became comparatively hurried and matter-of-fact. His boy's return home for the holidays was always rather a stirring time for his private feelings, but he became more and more inexpressive. He would sometimes lay a hand on those growing shoulders and then withdraw it. They felt braced-up shoulders, stiffly inflexible or — they would wince. And when one has let the habit of indefinite feelings grow upon one, what is there left to say? If one did say anything one might be asked questions. . . .

One or two of the long vacations they spent abroad together. The last of these occasions followed Benham's convalescence at Montana and his struggle with the Bisse ; the two went to Zermatt and did several peaks and crossed the Theodule, and it was clear that their joint expeditions were a strain upon both of them. The father thought the son reckless, unskilful, and impatient ; the son found the father's insistence upon guides, ropes, precautions, the recognized way, the highest point and back again before you get a chill, and talk about it sagely but very, very modestly over pipes, tiresome. He wanted to wander in deserts of ice and see over the mountains, and discover what it is to be benighted on a precipice. And gradually he was becoming familiar with his father's repertory of Greek quotations. There was no breach between them, but each knew that holiday was the last they would ever spend together. . . .

The court had given the custody of young William Porphyry into his father's hands, but by a generous concession it was arranged that his mother should have him to see her for an hour or so five times a year. The Nolan legacy, however, coming upon the top of this, introduced a peculiar complication that provided much work for tactful intermediaries, and gave great and increasing scope for painful delicacies on the part of Mr. Benham as the boy grew up.

"I see," said the father over his study pipe and with his glasses fixed on remote distances above the head of the current sympathizer, "I see more and more clearly that the tale of my sacrifices is not yet at an end. . . . In many respects he is like her. . . . Quick. Too quick. . . . He must choose. But I know his choice. Yes, yes, — I'm not blind. She's worked upon him. . . . I have done what I could to bring out the manhood in him. Perhaps it will bear the strain. . . . It will be a wrench, old man — God knows."

He did his very best to make it a wrench.

§ 2

Benham's mother, whom he saw quarterly and also on the first of May, because it was her birthday, touched and coloured his imagination far more than his father did. She was now Lady Marayne, and a prominent, successful, and happy little lady. Her dereliction had been forgiven quite soon, and whatever whisper of it remained was very completely forgotten during the brief period of moral kindliness which followed the accession of King Edward the Seventh. It no doubt contributed to her social reinstatement that her former husband was entirely devoid of social importance, while, on the other hand, Sir Godfrey Marayne's temporary monopoly of the cæcal operation which became so fashionable in the last decade of Queen Victoria's reign as to be practically epidemic, created a strong feeling in her favour.

She was blue-eyed and very delicately complexioned, quick-moving, witty, given to little storms of clean enthusiasm; she loved handsome things, brave things, successful things, and the respect and affection of all the world. She did quite what she liked upon impulse, and nobody ever thought ill of her.

Her family were the Mantons of Blent, quite good west-country people. She had broken away from them before she was twenty to marry Benham, whom she had idealized at a tennis party. He had talked of his work and she had seen it in a flash, the noblest work in the world, him at his daily divine toil and herself a Madonna surrounded by a troupe of Blessed Boys — all of good family, some of quite the best. For a time she had kept it up even more than he had, and then Nolan had distracted her with a realization of the heroism that goes to the ends of the earth. She became sick with desire for the forests of Brazil, and the Pacific, and — a peak in Darien. Immediately the school was frowsty beyond endurance, and for the first time she let herself perceive how dreadfully a gentleman and a scholar can smell of pipes and tobacco. Only one course lay open to a woman of spirit. . . .

For a year she did indeed live like a woman of spirit, and it was at Nolan's bedside that Marayne was first moved to admiration. She was plucky. All men love a plucky woman.

Sir Godfrey Marayne smelt a good deal of anti-septic soap, but he talked in a way that amused her, and he trusted as well as adored her. She did what she liked with his money, her own money, and her son's trust money, and she did very well. From the earliest Benham's visits were to a gracious presence amidst wealthy surroundings. The transit from the moral blamelessness of Seagate had an entirely misleading effect of ascent.

Their earlier encounters became rather misty in his memory; they occurred at various hotels in Seagate. Afterwards he would go, first taken by a governess, and later going alone, to Charing Cross, where he would be met, in earlier times by a maid and afterwards by a deferential manservant who called him "Sir," and conveyed, sometimes in a hansom cab and later in a smart brougham, by Trafalgar Square, Lower Regent Street, Piccadilly, and streets of increasing wealth and sublimity to Sir Godfrey's house in Desborough Street. Very naturally he fell into thinking of these discreet and well-governed West End streets as a part of his mother's atmosphere.

The house had a dignified portico, and always before he had got down to the pavement the door opened agreeably and a second respectful manservant stood ready. Then came the large hall, with its noiseless carpets and great Chinese jars, its lacquered cabinets and the wide staircase, and floating down the wide staircase, impatient to greet him, light and shining as a flower petal, sweet and welcoming, radiating a joyfulness as cool and clear as a dewy morning, came his mother. "*Well*, little man, my son," she would cry in her happy singing voice, "*Well?*"

So he thought she must always be, but indeed these meetings meant very much to her, she dressed for them and staged them, she perceived the bright advantages of her rarity and she was quite determined to have her son when the time came to possess him. She kissed him but not oppressively, she caressed him cleverly; it was only on these rare occasions that he was ever kissed or caressed, and she talked to his shy boyishness until it felt a more spirited variety of manhood. "What have you been doing?" she asked, "since I saw you last."

She never said he had grown, but she told him he looked tall; and though the tea was a marvellous display it was never an obtrusive tea, it wasn't poked at a fellow; a various plenty flowed well within reach of one's arm, like an agreeable accompaniment to their conversation.

"What have you done? All sorts of brave things? Do you swim now? I can swim. Oh! I can swim half a mile. Some day we will swim races together. Why not? And you ride? . . .

"The horse bolted — and you stuck on? Did you squeak? I stick on, but I *have* to squeak. But you — of course, No! you mustn't. I'm just a little woman. And I ride big horses. . . ."

And for the end she had invented a characteristic little ceremony.

She would stand up in front of him and put her hands on his shoulders and look into his face.

"Clean eyes?" she would say. " — still?"

Then she would take his ears in her little firm hands and kiss very methodically his eyes and his forehead and his cheeks and at last his lips. Her own eyes would suddenly brim bright with tears.

"*Go*," she would say.

That was the end.

It seemed to Benham as though he was being let down out of a sunlit fairyland to this grey world again.

§ 3

The contrast between Lady Marayne's pretty amenities and the good woman at Seagate who urged herself almost hourly to forget that William Porphyry was not her own son, was entirely unfair. The second Mrs. Benham's conscientious spirit and a certain handsome ability about her fitted her far more than her predecessor for the onerous duties of a schoolmaster's wife, but whatever natural buoyancy she possessed was outweighed by an irrepressible conviction derived from an episcopal grandparent that the remarriage of divorced persons is sinful, and by a secret but well-founded doubt whether her husband loved her with a truly romantic passion. She might perhaps have borne either of these troubles singly, but the two crushed her spirit.

Her temperament was not one that goes out to meet happiness. She had reluctant affections and suspected rather than welcomed the facility of other people's. Her susceptibility to disagreeable impressions was however very ample, and life was fenced about with protections for her "feelings." It filled young Benham with inexpressible indignations that his sweet own mother, so gay, so brightly cheerful that even her tears were stars, was never to be mentioned in his stepmother's presence, and it was not until he had fully come to years of reflection that he began to realize with what honesty, kindness and patience this naturally not very happy lady had nursed, protected, mended for and generally mothered him.

§ 4

As Benham grew to look manly and bear himself with pride, his mother's affection for him blossomed into a passion. She made him come down to London from Cambridge as often as she could ; she went about with him ; she made him squire her to theatres and take her out to dinners and sup with her at the Carlton, and in the summer she had him with her at Chexington Manor, the Hertfordshire house Sir Godfrey had given her. And always when they parted she looked into his eyes to see if they were still clean — whatever she meant by that — and she kissed his forehead and cheeks and eyes and lips. She began to make schemes for his career, she contrived introductions she judged would be useful to him later.

Everybody found the relationship charming. Some of the more conscientious people, it is true, pretended to think that the Reverend Harold Ben-

ham was a first husband and long since dead, but
that was all. As a matter of fact, in his increasingly
futile way he wasn't, either at Seagate or in the
Educational Supplement of the *Times*. But even
the most conscientious of us are not obliged to go to
Seagate or read the Educational Supplement of the
Times.

Lady Marayne's plans for her son's future varied
very pleasantly. She was an industrious reader of
biographies, and more particularly of the large fair
biographies of the recently contemporary ; they mentioned people she knew, they recalled scenes, each
sowed its imaginative crop upon her mind, a crop
that flourished and flowered until a newer growth
came to oust it. She saw her son a diplomat, a
prancing pro-consul, an empire builder, a trusted
friend of the august, the bold leader of new movements, the saviour of ancient institutions, the young-
est, brightest, modernest of prime ministers — or a
tremendously popular poet. As a rule she saw him
unmarried — with a wonderful little mother at his
elbow. Sometimes in romantic flashes he was
adored by German princesses or eloped with Russian
grand-duchesses! But such fancies were *hors d'œuvre*.
The modern biography deals with the career.
Every project was bright, every project had *go* —
tremendous go. And they all demanded a hero,
débonnaire and balanced. And Benham, as she began to perceive, wasn't balanced. Something of
his father had crept into him, a touch of moral stiff-
ness. She knew the flavour of that so well. It was

a stumbling, an elaboration, a spoil-sport and weakness. She tried not to admit to herself that even in the faintest degree it was there. But it was there.

"Tell me all that you are doing *now*," she said to him one afternoon when she had got him to herself during his first visit to Chexington Manor. "How do you like Cambridge? Are you making friends? Have you joined that thing — the Union, is it? — and delivered your maiden speech? If you're for politics, Poff, that's your game. Have you begun it?"

She lay among splashes of sunshine on the red cushions in the punt, a little curled-up figure of white, with her sweet pale animated face warmed by the reflection of her red sunshade, and her eyes like little friendly heavens. And he, lean, and unconsciously graceful, sat at her feet and admired her beyond measure, and rejoiced that now at last they were going to be ever so much together, and doubted if it would be possible ever to love any other woman so much as he did her.

He tried to tell her of Cambridge and his friends and the undergraduate life he was leading, but he found it difficult. All sorts of things that seemed right and good at Trinity seemed out of drawing in the peculiar atmosphere she created about her. All sorts of clumsiness and youthfulness in himself and his associates he felt she wouldn't accept, couldn't accept, that it would be wrong of her to accept. Before they could come before her they must wear a bravery. He couldn't, for instance, tell her how

Billy Prothero, renouncing vanity and all social
pretension, had worn a straw hat into November
and the last stages of decay, and how it had been
burnt by a special commission ceremonially in the
great court.   He couldn't convey to her the long
sessions of beer and tobacco and high thinking that
went on in Prothero's rooms into the small hours.
A certain Gothic greyness and flatness and muddi-
ness through which the Cambridge spirit struggles
to its destiny, he concealed from her.   What remained to tell was — attenuated.   He could not
romance.   So she tried to fill in his jejune outlines.
She tried to inspire a son who seemed most unac-
countably up to nothing.

"You must make good friends," she said.   "Isn't
young Lord Breeze at your college?   His mother
the other day told me he was.   And Sir Freddy Quen-
ton's boy.   And there are both the young Baptons
at Cambridge."

He knew one of the Baptons.

"Poff," she said suddenly, "has it ever occurred
to you what you are going to do afterwards.   Do
you know you are going to be quite well off?"

Benham looked up with a faint embarrassment.
"My father said something.   He was rather vague.
It wasn't his affair — that kind of thing."

"You will be quite well off," she repeated, without
any complicating particulars.   "You will be so well
off that it will be possible for you to do anything
almost that you like in the world.   Nothing will tie
you.   Nothing. . . ."

"But — *how* well off?"

"You will have several thousands a year."

"Thousands?"

"Yes. Why not?"

"But — Mother, this is rather astounding. . . . Does this mean there are estates somewhere, responsibilities?"

"It is just money. Investments."

"You know, I've imagined—. I've thought always I should have to *do* something."

"You *must* do something, Poff. But it needn't be for a living. The world is yours without that. And so you see you've got to make plans. You've got to know the sort of people who'll have things in their hands. You've got to keep out of — holes and corners. You've got to think of Parliament and abroad. There's the army, there's diplomacy. There's the Empire. You can be a Cecil Rhodes if you like. You can be a Winston. . . ."

§ 5

Perhaps it was only the innate eagerness of Lady Marayne which made her feel disappointed in her son's outlook upon life. He did not choose among his glittering possibilities, he did not say what he was going to be, proconsul, ambassador, statesman, for days. And he talked *vaguely* of wanting to do something fine, but all in a fog. A boy of nearly nineteen ought to have at least the beginnings of *savoir faire*.

Was he in the right set? Was he indeed in the right college? Trinity, by his account, seemed a huge featureless place — and might he not conceivably be *lost* in it? In those big crowds one had to insist upon oneself. Poff never insisted upon himself — except quite at the wrong moment. And there was this Billy Prothero. *Billy!* Like a goat or something. People called William don't get their Christian name insisted upon unless they are vulnerable somewhere. Any form of William stamps a weakness, Willie, Willy, Will, Billy, Bill; it's a fearful handle for one's friends. At any rate Poff had escaped that. But this Prothero!

"But who *is* this Billy Prothero?" she asked one evening in the walled garden.

"He was at Minchinghampton."

"But who *is* he? Who is his father? Where does he come from?"

Benham sought in his mind for a space. "I don't know," he said at last. Billy had always been rather reticent about his people. She demanded descriptions. She demanded an account of Billy's furniture, Billy's clothes, Billy's form of exercise. It dawned upon Benham that for some inexplicable reason she was hostile to Billy. It was like the unmasking of an ambuscade. He had talked a lot about Prothero's ideas and the discussions of social reform and social service that went on in his rooms, for Billy read at unknown times, and was open at all hours to any argumentative caller. To Lady Marayne all ideas were obnoxious, a form of fogging; all ideas, she held, were queer ideas. "And does he call himself a Socialist?" she asked. "I *thought* he would."

"Poff," she cried suddenly, "you're not a *Socialist?*"

"Such a vague term."

"But these friends of yours — they seem to be *all* Socialists. Red ties and everything complete."

"They have ideas," he evaded. He tried to express it better. "They give one something to take hold of."

She sat up stiffly on the garden-seat. She lifted her finger at him, very seriously. "I hope," she said with all her heart, "that you will have nothing to do with such ideas. Nothing. *Socialism!*"

"They make a case."

"Pooh! Any one can make a case."

"But —"

"There's no sense in them. What is the good of talking about upsetting everything? Just disorder. How can one do anything then? You mustn't. You mustn't. No. It's nonsense, little Poff. It's absurd. And you may spoil so much. . . . I *hate* the way you talk of it. . . . As if it wasn't all — absolutely — *rubbish*. . . ."

She was earnest almost to the intonation of tears.

Why couldn't her son go straight for his ends, clear tangible ends, as she had always done? This thinking about everything! She had never thought about anything in all her life for more than half an hour — and it had always turned out remarkably well.

Benham felt baffled. There was a pause. How on earth could he go on telling her his ideas if this was how they were to be taken?

"I wish sometimes," his mother said abruptly, with an unusually sharp note in her voice, "that you wouldn't look quite so like your father."

"But I'm *not* like my father!" said Benham puzzled.

"No," she insisted, and with an air of appealing to his soberer reason, "so why should you go *looking* like him? That *concerned* expression. . . ."

She jumped to her feet. "Poff," she said, "I want to go and see the evening primroses pop. You and I are talking nonsense. *They* don't have ideas anyhow. They just pop — as God meant them to do. What stupid things we human beings are!"

Her philosophical moments were perhaps the most baffling of all.

§ 6

Billy Prothero became the symbol in the mind of Lady Marayne for all that disappointed her in Benham. He had to become the symbol, because she could not think of complicated or abstract things, she had to make things personal, and he was the only personality available. She fretted over his existence for some days therefore (once she awakened and thought about him in the night), and then suddenly she determined to grasp her nettle. She decided to seize and obliterate this Prothero. He must come to Chexington and be thoroughly and conclusively led on, examined, ransacked, shown up, and disposed of for ever. At once. She was not quite clear how she meant to do this, but she was quite resolved that it had to be done. Anything is better than inaction.

There was a little difficulty about dates and engagements, but he came, and through the season of expectation Benham, who was now for the first time in contact with the feminine nature, was delighted at the apparent change to cordiality. So that he talked of Billy to his mother much more than he had ever done before.

Billy had been his particular friend at Minchinghampton, at least during the closing two years of his school life. Billy had fallen into friendship with Benham, as some of us fall in love, quite suddenly, when he saw Benham get down from the fence and be sick after his encounter with the bull. Already Billy was excited by admiration, but it was the incongruity of the sickness conquered him. He went back to the school with his hands more than usually in his pockets, and no eyes for anything but this remarkable strung-up fellow-creature. He felt he had never observed Benham before, and he was astonished that he had not done so.

Billy Prothero was a sturdy sort of boy, generously wanting in good looks. His hair was rough, and his complexion muddy, and he walked about with his hands in his pockets, long flexible lips protruded in a whistle, and a rather shapeless nose well up to show he didn't care. Providence had sought to console him by giving him a keen eye for the absurdity of

other people.   He had a suggestive tongue, and he
professed and practised cowardice to the scandal
of all his acquaintances.   He was said never to wash
behind his ears, but this report wronged him.   There
had been a time when he did not do so, but his mother
had won him to a promise, and now that operation
was often the sum of his simple hasty toilet.   His
desire to associate himself with Benham was so
strong that it triumphed over a defensive reserve.
It enabled him to detect accessible moments, do
inobtrusive friendly services, and above all amuse his
quarry.   He not only amused Benham, he stimulated
him.   They came to do quite a number of things
together.   In the language of schoolboy stories
they became "inseparables."

Prothero's first desire, so soon as they were on a
footing that enabled him to formulate desires, was to
know exactly what Benham thought he was up to in
crossing a field with a bull in it instead of going
round, and by the time he began to understand that,
he had conceived an affection for him that was to
last a lifetime.

"I wasn't going to be bullied by a beast," said
Benham.

"Suppose it had been an elephant?" Prothero
cried. . . .   "A mad elephant? . . . A pack of
wolves?"

Benham was too honest not to see that he was
entangled.   "Well, suppose in *your* case it had been
a wild cat? . . . A fierce mastiff? . . . A mastiff? . . . A terrier? . . . A lap dog?"

"Yes, but my case is that there are limits."

Benham was impatient at the idea of limits. With a faintly malicious pleasure Prothero lugged him back to that idea.

"We both admit there are limits," Prothero concluded. "But between the absolutely impossible and the altogether possible there's the region of risk. You think a man ought to take that risk —" He reflected. "I think — no — I think *not*."

"If he feels afraid," cried Benham, seeing his one point. "If he feels afraid. Then he ought to take it. . . ."

After a digestive interval, Prothero asked, "*Why?* Why should he?"

The discussion of that momentous question, that Why? which Benham perhaps might never have dared ask himself, and which Prothero perhaps might never have attempted to answer if it had not been for the clash of their minds, was the chief topic of their conversation for many months. From Why be brave? it spread readily enough to Why be honest? Why be clean? — all the great whys of life. . . . Because one believes. . . . But why believe it? Left to himself Benham would have felt the mere asking of this question was a thing ignoble, not to be tolerated. It was, as it were, treason to nobility. But Prothero put it one afternoon in a way that permitted no high dismissal of their doubts. "You can't build your honour on fudge, Benham. Like committing sacrilege — in order to buy a cloth for the altar."

G

By that Benham was slipped from the recognized code and launched upon speculations which became the magnificent research.

It was not only in complexion and stature and ways of thinking that Billy and Benham contrasted. Benham inclined a little to eloquence, he liked very clean hands, he had a dread of ridiculous outlines. Prothero lapsed readily into ostentatious slovenliness, when his hands were dirty he pitied them sooner than scrubbed them, he would have worn an overcoat with one tail torn off rather than have gone cold. Moreover, Prothero had an earthy liking for animals, he could stroke and tickle strange cats until they wanted to leave father and mother and all earthly possessions and follow after him, and he mortgaged a term's pocket money and bought and kept a small terrier in the school house against all law and tradition, under the baseless pretence that it was a stray animal of unknown origin. Benham, on the other hand, was shy with small animals and faintly hostile to big ones. Beasts he thought were just beasts. And Prothero had a gift for caricature, while Benham's aptitude was for music.

It was Prothero's eyes and pencil that first directed Benham to the poor indolences and evasions and insincerities of the masters. It was Prothero's wicked pictures that made him see the shrivelled absurdity of the vulgar theology. But it was Benham who stood between Prothero and that rather coarsely conceived epicureanism that seemed his logical destiny. When quite early in their Cam-

bridge days Prothero's revolt against foppery reached
a nadir of personal neglect, and two philanthropists
from the rooms below him, goaded beyond the
normal tolerance of Trinity, and assisted by two
sportsmen from Trinity Hall, burnt his misshapen
straw hat (after partly filling it with gunpowder and
iron filings) and sought to duck him in the fountain
in the court, it was Benham, in a state between distress and madness, and armed with a horn-handled
cane of exceptional size, who intervened, turned the
business into a blend of wrangle and scuffle, introduced the degrading topic of duelling into a simple
wholesome rag of four against one, carried him off
under the cloud of horror created by this impro-
priety and so saved him, still only slightly wetted,
not only from this indignity but from the experiment in rationalism that had provoked it.

Because Benham made it perfectly clear what he
had thought and felt about this hat.

Such was the illuminating young man whom Lady
Marayne decided to invite to Chexington, into the
neighbourhood of herself, Sir Godfrey, and her circle
of friends.

§ 7

He was quite anxious to satisfy the requirements
of Benham's people and to do his friend credit. He
was still in the phase of being a penitent pig, and he
inquired carefully into the needs and duties of a
summer guest in a country house. He knew it was
quite a considerable country house, and that Sir
Godfrey wasn't Benham's father, but like most

people, he was persuaded that Lady Marayne had
divorced the parental Benham. He arrived dressed
very neatly in a brown suit that had only one fault,
it had not the remotest suggestion of having been
made for him. It fitted his body fairly well, it did
annex his body with only a few slight incompatibil-
ities, but it repudiated his hands and face. He had
a conspicuously old Gladstone bag and a conspicuously new despatch case, and he had forgotten black
ties and dress socks and a hair brush. He arrived
in the late afternoon, was met by Benham, in tennis
flannels, looking smartened up and a little unfamiliar, and taken off in a spirited dog-cart driven
by a typical groom. He met his host and hostess
at dinner.

Sir Godfrey was a rationalist and a residuum.
Very much of him, too much perhaps, had gone into
the acquirement and perfect performance of the
cæcal operation ; the man one met in the social
world was what was left over. It had the effect of
being quiet, but in its unobtrusive way knobby.
He had a knobby brow, with an air about it of having recently been intent, and his conversation was
curiously spotted with little knobby arrested anec-
dotes. If any one of any distinction was named,
he would reflect and say, "Of course, — ah, yes, I
know him, I know him. Yes, I did him a little service — in '96."

And something in his manner would suggest a
satisfaction, or a dissatisfaction with confidential
mysteries.

He welcomed Billy Prothero in a colourless manner, and made conversation about Cambridge. He had known one or two of the higher dons. One he had done at Cambridge quite recently. "The inns are better than they are at Oxford, which is not saying very much, but the place struck me as being changed. The men seemed younger. . . ."

The burden of the conversation fell upon Lady Marayne. She looked extraordinarily like a flower to Billy, a little diamond buckle on a black velvet band glittered between the two masses of butter-coloured hair that flowed back from her forehead, her head was poised on the prettiest neck conceivable, and her shapely little shoulders and her shapely little arms came decidedly but pleasantly out of a softness and sparkle of white and silver and old rose. She talked what sounded like innocent commonplaces a little spiced by whim, though indeed each remark had an exploratory quality, and her soft blue eyes rested ever and again upon Billy's white tie. It seemed she did so by the merest inadvertency, but it made the young man wish he had after all borrowed a black one from Benham. But the manservant who had put his things out had put it out, and he hadn't been quite sure. Also she noted all the little things he did with fork and spoon and glass. She gave him an unusual sense of being brightly, accurately and completely visible.

Chexington, it seemed to Billy, was done with a large and costly and easy completeness. The table with its silver and flowers was much more beauti-

fully done than any table he had sat at before, and
in the dimness beyond the brightness there were
two men to wait on the four of them. The old grey
butler was really wonderfully good. . . .

"You shoot, Mr. Prothero?"

"You hunt, Mr. Prothero?"

"You know Scotland well, Mr. Prothero?"

These questions disturbed Prothero. He did not
shoot, he did not hunt, he did not go to Scotland for
the grouse, he did not belong, and Lady Marayne
ought to have seen that he did not belong to the class
that does these things.

"You ride much, Mr. Prothero?"

Billy conceived a suspicion that these innocent
inquiries were designed to emphasize a contrast in
his social quality. But he could not be sure. One
never could be sure with Lady Marayne. It might
be just that she did not understand the sort of man
he was. And in that case ought he to maintain the
smooth social surface unbroken by pretending as
far as possible to be this kind of person, or ought he
to make a sudden gap in it by telling his realities.
He evaded the shooting question anyhow. He left
it open for Lady Marayne and the venerable butler
and Sir Godfrey and every one to suppose he just
happened to be the sort of gentleman of leisure who
doesn't shoot. He disavowed hunting, he made it
appear he travelled when he travelled in directions
other than Scotland. But the fourth question
brought him to bay. He regarded his questioner
with his small rufous eye.

"I have never been across a horse in my life, Lady Marayne."

"Tut, tut," said Sir Godfrey. "Why! — it's the best of exercise. Every man ought to ride. Good for the health. Keeps him fit. Prevents lodgments. Most trouble due to lodgments."

"I've never had a chance of riding. And I think I'm afraid of horses."

"That's only an excuse," said Lady Marayne. "Everybody's afraid of horses and nobody's really afraid of horses."

"But I'm not used to horses. You see — I live on my mother. And she can't afford to keep a stable."

His hostess did not see his expression of discomfort. Her pretty eyes were intent upon the peas with which she was being served.

"Does your mother live in the country?" she asked, and took her peas with fastidious exactness.

Prothero coloured brightly. "She lives in London."

"All the year?"

"All the year."

"But isn't it dreadfully hot in town in the summer?"

Prothero had an uncomfortable sense of being very red in the face. This kept him red. "We're suburban people," he said.

"But I thought — isn't there the seaside?"

"My mother has a business," said Prothero, redder than ever.

"O-oh!" said Lady Marayne. "What fun that must be for her?"

"It's a real business, and she has to live by it. Sometimes it's a worry."

"But a business of her own!" She surveyed the confusion of his visage with a sweet intelligence. "Is it an amusing sort of business, Mr. Prothero?"

Prothero looked mulish. "My mother is a dressmaker," he said. "In Brixton. She doesn't do particularly badly — or well. I live on my scholarship. I have lived on scholarships since I was thirteen. And you see, Lady Marayne, Brixton is a poor hunting country."

Lady Marayne felt she had unmasked Prothero almost indecently. Whatever happened there must be no pause. There must be no sign of a hitch.

"But it's good at tennis," she said. "You *do* play tennis, Mr. Prothero?"

"I — I gesticulate," said Prothero.

Lady Marayne, still in flight from that pause, went off at a tangent.

"Poff, my dear," she said, "I've had a diving-board put at the deep end of the pond."

The remark hung unanswered for a moment. The transition had been too quick for Benham's state of mind.

"Do you swim, Mr. Prothero?" the lady asked, though a moment before she had determined that she would never ask him a question again. But this time it was a lucky question.

"Prothero mopped up the lot of us at Minchinghampton with his diving and swimming," Benham explained, and the tension was relaxed.

Lady Marayne spoke of her own swimming, and became daring and amusing at her difficulties with local feeling when first she swam in 'the pond. The high road ran along the far side of the pond — "And it didn't wear a hedge or anything," said Lady Marayne. "That was what they didn't quite like. Swimming in an undraped pond. . . ."

Prothero had been examined enough. Now he must be entertained. She told stories about the village people in her brightest manner. The third story she regretted as soon as she was fairly launched upon it; it was how she had interviewed the village dressmaker, when Sir Godfrey insisted upon her supporting local industries. It was very amusing but technical. The devil had put it into her head. She had to go through with it. She infused an extreme innocence into her eyes and fixed them on Prothero, although she felt a certain deepening pinkness in her cheeks was betraying her, and she did not look at Benham until her unhappy, but otherwise quite amusing anecdote, was dead and gone and safely buried under another. . . .

But people ought not to go about having dressmakers for mothers. . . .

And coming into other people's houses and influencing their sons. . . .

§ 8

That night when everything was over Billy sat at the writing-table of his sumptuous bedroom—the bed was gilt wood, the curtains of the three great windows were tremendous, and there was a cheval glass that showed the full length of him and seemed to look over his head for more, — and meditated upon this visit of his. It was more than he had been prepared for. It was going to be a great strain. The sleek young manservant in an alpaca jacket, who said "Sir" whenever you looked at him, and who had seized upon and unpacked Billy's most private Gladstone bag without even asking if he might do so, and put away and displayed Billy's things in a way that struck Billy as faintly ironical, was unexpected. And it was unexpected that the brown suit, with its pockets stuffed with Billy's personal and confidential sundries, had vanished. And apparently a bath in a bathroom far down the corridor was prescribed for him in the morning; he hadn't thought of a dressing-gown. And after one had dressed, what did one do? Did one go down and wander about the house looking for the breakfast-room or wait for a gong? Would Sir Godfrey read Family Prayers? And afterwards did one go out or hang about to be entertained? He knew now quite clearly that those wicked blue eyes would mark his every slip. She did not like him. She did not like him, he supposed, because he was common stuff. He didn't play up to her world and her. He was a discord in this rich, cleverly elaborate household. You could see it in the servants' attitudes. And he was committed to a week of this.

Billy puffed out his cheeks to blow a sigh, and then decided to be angry and say "Damn!"

This way of living which made him uncomfortable was clearly an irrational and objectionable way of living. It was, in a cumbersome way, luxurious. But the waste of life of it, the servants, the observances, all concentrated on the mere detail of existence? There came a rap at the door. Benham appeared, wearing an expensive-looking dressing-jacket which Lady Marayne had bought for him. He asked if he might talk for a bit and smoke. He sat down in a capacious chintz-covered easy chair beside Prothero, lit a cigarette, and came to the point after only a trivial hesitation.

"Prothero," he said, "you know what my father is."

"I thought he ran a preparatory school."

There was the profoundest resentment in Prothero's voice.

"And, all the same, I'm going to be a rich man."

"I don't understand," said Prothero, without any shadow of congratulation.

Benham told Prothero as much as his mother had conveyed to him of the resources of his wealth. Her version had been adapted to his tender years and the delicacies of her position. The departed Nolan had become an eccentric godfather. Benham's manner was apologetic, and he made it clear that only recently had these facts come to him. He had never suspected that he had had this eccentric godfather. It altered the outlook tremendously. It was one of the reasons that made Benham glad to have Prothero there, one wanted a man of one's own age, who understood things a little, to try over one's new ideas. Prothero listened with an unamiable expression.

"What would you do, Prothero, if you found yourself saddled with some thousands a year?"

"Godfathers don't grow in Brixton," said Prothero concisely.

"Well, what am I to do, Prothero?"

"Does all *this* belong to you?"

"No, this is my mother's."

"Godfather too?"

"I've not thought. . . . I suppose so. Or her own."

Prothero meditated.

"*This* life," he said at last, "this large expensiveness — . . ."

He left his criticism unfinished.

"I agree. It suits my mother somehow. I can't understand her living in any other way. But — for me. . . ."

"What can one do with several thousands a year?"

Prothero's interest in this question presently swamped his petty personal resentments. "I suppose," he said, "one might have rather a lark with money like that. One would be free to go anywhere. To set all sorts of things going. . . . It's clear you can't sell all you have and give it to the poor. That is pauperization nowadays. You might run a tremendously revolutionary paper. A real upsetting paper. How many thousands is it?"

"I don't know. *Some.*"

Prothero's interest was growing as he faced the possibilities.

"I've dreamt of a paper," he said, "a paper that should tell the brute truth about things."

"I don't know that I'm particularly built to be a journalist," Benham objected.

"You're not," said Billy. . . . "You might go into Parliament as a perfectly independent member. . . . Only you wouldn't get in. . . ."

"I'm not a speaker," said Benham.

"Of course," said Billy, "if you don't decide on a game, you'll just go on like this. You'll fall into a groove, you'll — you'll hunt. You'll go to Scotland for the grouse."

For the moment Prothero had no further suggestions.

Benham waited for a second or so before he broached his own idea.

"Why, first of all, at any rate, Billy, shouldn't one use one's money to make the best of oneself? To learn things that men without money and leisure find it difficult to learn? By an accident, however unjust it is, one is in the position of a leader and a privileged person. Why not do one's best to give value as that?"

"Benham, that's the thin end of aristocracy!"

"Why not?"

"I hate aristocracy. For you it means doing what you like. While you are energetic you will kick about and then you will come back to this."

"That's one's own look-out," said Benham, after reflection.

"No, it's bound to happen."

Benham retreated a little from the immediate question.

"Well, we can't suddenly at a blow change the world. If it isn't to be plutocracy to-day it has to be aristocracy."

Prothero frowned over this, and then he made a sweeping proposition.

"*You cannot have aristocracy,*" he said, "*because, you see — all men are ridiculous.* Democracy has to fight its way out from under plutocracy. There is nothing else to be done."

"But a man in my position —?"

"It's a ridiculous position. You may try to escape being ridiculous. You won't succeed."

It seemed to Benham for a moment as though Prothero had got to the bottom of the question, and then he perceived that he had only got to the bottom of himself. Benham was pacing the floor.

He turned at the open window, held out a long forefinger, and uttered his countervailing faith.

"Even if he is ridiculous, Prothero, a man may still be an aristocrat. A man may anyhow be as much of an aristocrat as he can be."

Prothero reflected. "No," he said, "it sounds all right, but it's wrong. I hate all these advantages and differences and distinctions. A man's a man. What you say sounds well, but it's the beginning of pretension, of pride —"

He stopped short.

"Better pride than dishonour," said Benham, "better the pretentious life than the sordid life. What else is there?"

"A life isn't necessarily sordid because it isn't pretentious," said Prothero, his voice betraying a defensive disposition.

"But a life with a large income *must* be sordid unless it makes some sort of attempt to be fine. . . ."

§ 9

By transitions that were as natural as they were complicated and untraceable Prothero found his visit to Chexington developing into a tangle of discussions that all ultimately resolved themselves into an antagonism of the democratic and the aristocratic idea. And his part was, he found, to be the exponent of the democratic idea. The next day he came down early, his talk with Benham still running through his head, and after a turn or so in the garden he was attracted to the front door by a sound of voices, and found Lady Marayne had been up still earlier and was dismounting from a large effective black horse. This extorted an unwilling admiration from him. She greeted him very pleasantly and made a kind of introduction of her steed. There had been trouble at a gate, he was a young horse and fidgeted at gates; the dispute was still bright in her. Benham she declared was still in bed. "Wait till I have a mount for him." She reappeared fitfully in the breakfast-room, and then he was left to Benham until just before lunch. They read and afterwards, as the summer day grew hot, they swam in the nude pond. She joined them in the water, splashing about in a costume of some elaboration and being very careful not to wet her hair. Then she came and sat with them on the seat under the big cedar and talked with them in a wrap that was pretty rather than prudish and entirely unmotherly. And she began a fresh attack upon him by asking him if he wasn't a Socialist and whether he didn't want to pull down Chexington and grow potatoes all over the park.

This struck Prothero as an inadequate statement of the Socialist project and he made an unsuccessful attempt to get it amended.

The engagement thus opened was renewed with great energy at lunch. Sir Godfrey had returned to London and the inmost aspect of his fellow-creatures, but the party of three was supplemented by a vague young lady from the village and an alert agent from the neighbouring Tentington estate who had intentions about a cottage. Lady Marayne insisted upon regarding Socialism as a proposal to reinaugurate the first French Revolution, as an inversion of society so that it would be bottom upward, as an attack upon rule, order, direction. "And what good are all these proposals? If you had the poor dear king beheaded, you'd only get a Napoleon. If you divided all the property up between everybody, you'd have rich and poor again in a year."

Billy perceived no way of explaining away this
version of his Socialism that would not involve un-
civil contradictions — and nobody ever contradicted
Lady Marayne.

"But, Lady Marayne, don't you think there is
a lot of disorder and injustice in the world?" he
protested.

"There would be ever so much more if your
Socialists had their way."

"But still, don't you think — . . ."

It is unnecessary even to recapitulate these universal controversies of our time. The lunch-table
and the dinner-table and the general talk of the house
drifted more and more definitely at its own level in
the same direction as the private talk of Prothero
and Benham, towards the antagonism of the privileged few and the many, of the trained and tradi-
tioned against the natural and undisciplined, of aristocracy against democracy. At the week-end Sir
Godfrey returned to bring fresh elements. He said
that democracy was unscientific. "To deny aristocracy is to deny the existence of the fittest. It
is on the existence of the fittest that progress de-
pends."

"But do our social conditions exalt the fittest?"
asked Prothero.

"That is another question," said Benham.

"Exactly," said Sir Godfrey. "That is another
question. But speaking with some special knowledge, I should say that on the whole the people
who are on the top of things *ought* to be on the top

of things.   I agree with Aristotle that there is such
a thing as a natural inferior."

"So far as I can understand Mr. Prothero," said
Lady Marayne, "he thinks that all the inferiors are
the superiors and all the superiors inferior.   It's quite
simple. . . ."

It made Prothero none the less indignant with
this, that there was indeed a grain of truth in it.
He hated superiors, he felt for inferiors.

§ 10

At last came the hour of tipping.   An embarrassed and miserable Prothero went slinking about
the house distributing unexpected gold.

It was stupid, it was damnable; he had had to
borrow the money from his mother. . . .

Lady Marayne felt he had escaped her.   The controversy that should have split these two young
men apart had given them a new interest in each
other.   When afterwards she sounded her son, very
delicately, to see if indeed he was aware of the clumsiness, the social ignorance and uneasiness, the
complete unsuitability of his friend, she could get
no more from him than that exasperating phrase,
"He has ideas!"

What are ideas?   England may yet be ruined by
ideas.

He ought never to have gone to Trinity, that monster packet of everything.   He ought to have gone
to some little *good* college, good all through.   She
ought to have asked some one who *knew*.

§ 11

One glowing afternoon in October, as these two young men came over Magdalen Bridge after a long disputatious and rather tiring walk to Drayton — they had been talking of Eugenics and the "family" — Benham was almost knocked down by an American trotter driven by Lord Breeze. "Whup there!" said Lord Breeze in a voice deliberately brutal, and Benham, roused from that abstraction which is partly fatigue, had to jump aside and stumbled against the parapet as the gaunt pacer went pounding by.

Lord Breeze grinned the sort of grin a man remembers. And passed.

"Damnation!" said Benham with a face that had become suddenly very white.

Then presently. "Any fool can do that who cares to go to the trouble."

"That," said Prothero, taking up their unquenchable issue, "that is the feeling of democracy."

"I walk because I choose to," said Benham.

The thing rankled.

"This equestrianism," he began, "is a matter of time and money — time even more than money. I want to read. I want to deal with ideas. . . .

"Any fool can drive. . . ."

"Exactly," said Prothero.

"As for riding, it means no more than the elaborate study and cultivation of your horse. You have to know him. All horses are individuals. A made horse perhaps goes its round like an omnibus, but for the rest. . . ."

Prothero made a noise of sympathetic assent.

"In a country where equestrianism is assertion I suppose one must be equestrian. . . ."

That night some malignant spirit kept Benham awake, and great American trotters with vast wide-striding feet and long yellow teeth, uncontrollable, hard-mouthed American trotters, pounded over his angry soul.

"Prothero," he said in hall next day, "we are going to drive to-morrow."

Next day, so soon as they had lunched, he led the way towards Maltby's, in Crosshampton Lane. Something in his bearing put a question into Prothero's mind. "Benham," he asked, "have you ever driven before?"

"*Never*," said Benham.

"Well?"

"I'm going to now."

Something between pleasure and alarm came into Prothero's eyes. He quickened his pace so as to get alongside his friend and scrutinize his pale determination. "Why are you doing this?" he asked.

"I want to do it."

"Benham, is it — *equestrian?*"

Benham made no audible reply. They proceeded resolutely in silence.

An air of expectation prevailed in Maltby's yard. In the shafts of a high, bleak-looking vehicle with

vast side wheels, a throne-like vehicle that impressed
Billy Prothero as being a gig, a very large angular
black horse was being harnessed.

"This is mine," said Benham compactly.

"This is yours, sir," said an ostler.

"He looks — *quiet*."

"You'll find him fresh enough, sir."

Benham made a complicated ascent to the driver's
seat and was handed the reins. "Come on," he said,
and Prothero followed to a less exalted seat at Benham's side. They seemed to be at a very great
height indeed. The horse was then led out into
Crosshampton Lane, faced towards Trinity Street
and discharged. "Check," said Benham, and
touched the steed with his whip. They started
quite well, and the ostlers went back into the
yard, visibly unanxious. It struck Prothero that
perhaps driving was less difficult than he had supposed.

They went along Crosshampton Lane, that high-
walled gulley, with dignity, with only a slight suggestion of the inaccuracy that was presently to become
apparent, until they met a little old bearded don on
a bicycle. Then some misunderstanding arose between Benham and the horse, and the little bearded
don was driven into the narrow pavement and had
to get off hastily. He made no comment, but his
face became like a gargoyle. "Sorry," said Benham,
and gave his mind to the corner. There was some
difficulty about whether they were to turn to the
right or the left, but at last Benham, it seemed,

carried his point, and they went along the narrow street, past the grey splendours of King's, and rather in the middle of the way.

Prothero considered the beast in front of him, and how proud and disrespectful a horse in a dog-cart can seem to those behind it! Moreover, un-accustomed as he was to horses, he was struck by the strong resemblance a bird's-eye view of a horse bears to a fiddle, a fiddle with devil's ears.

"Of course," said Prothero, "this isn't a trotter."

"I couldn't get a trotter," said Benham.

"I thought I would try this sort of thing before I tried a trotter," he added.

And then suddenly came disaster.

There was a butcher's cart on the right, and Ben-ham, mistrusting the intelligence of his steed, in-sisted upon an excessive amplitude of clearance. He did not reckon with the hand-barrow on his left, piled up with dirty plates from the lunch of Trinity Hall. It had been left there; its custodian was away upon some mysterious errand. Heaven knows why Trinity Hall exhibited the treasures of its crockery thus stained and defiled in the Cambridge streets. But it did — for Benham's and Prothero's undoing. Prothero saw the great wheel over which he was poised entangle itself with the little wheel of the barrow. "God!" he whispered, and craned, fascinated. The little wheel was manifestly in-trigued beyond all self-control by the great wheel; it clung to it, it went before it, heedless of the barrow, of which it was an inseparable part. The

barrow came about with an appearance of unwilling-
ness, it locked against the great wheel; it reared
itself towards Prothero and began, smash, smash,
smash, to shed its higher plates. It was clear that
Benham was grappling with a crisis upon a basis of
inadequate experience. A number of people shouted
haphazard things. Then, too late, the barrow had
persuaded the little wheel to give up its fancy
for the great wheel, and there was an enormous
crash.

"Whoa!" cried Benham. "Whoa!" but also,
unfortunately, he sawed hard at the horse's mouth.

The animal, being in some perplexity, danced a
little in the narrow street, and then it had come about
and it was backing, backing, on the narrow pavement
and towards the plate-glass window of a book and
newspaper shop. Benham tugged at its mouth
much harder than ever. Prothero saw the window
bending under the pressure of the wheel. A sense
of the profound seriousness of life and of the folly
of this expedition came upon him. With extreme
nimbleness he got down just as the window burst.
It went with an explosion like a pistol shot, and then
a clatter of falling glass. People sprang, it seemed,
from nowhere, and jostled about Prothero, so that
he became a peripheral figure in the discussion.
He perceived that a man in a green apron was holding the horse, and that various people were engaged
in simultaneous conversation with Benham, who
with a pale serenity of face and an awful calm of
manner, dealt with each of them in turn.

"I'm sorry," he was saying. "Somebody ought to have been in charge of the barrow. Here are my cards. I am ready to pay for any damage. . . .

"The barrow ought not to have been there. . . .

"Yes, I am going on. Of course I'm going on. Thank you."

He beckoned to the man who had held the horse and handed him half-a-crown. He glanced at Prothero as one might glance at a stranger. "Check!" he said. The horse went on gravely. Benham lifted out his whip. He appeared to have clean forgotten Prothero. Perhaps presently he would miss him. He went on past Trinity, past the ruddy brick of St. John's. The curve of the street hid him from Prothero's eyes.

Prothero started in pursuit. He glimpsed the dog-cart turning into Bridge Street. He had an impression that Benham used the whip at the corner, and that the dog-cart went forward out of sight with a startled jerk. Prothero quickened his pace.

But when he got to the fork between the Huntingdon Road and the Cottenham Road, both roads were clear.

He spent some time in hesitation. Then he went along the Huntingdon Road until he came upon a road-mender, and learnt that Benham had passed that way. "Going pretty fast 'e was," said the road-mender, "and whipping 'is 'orse. Else you might 'a thought 'e was a boltin' with 'im." Prothero decided that if Benham came back at all he would return by way of Cottenham, and it was on the Cottenham Road that at last he encountered his friend again.

Benham was coming along at that good pace which all experienced horses when they are fairly turned back towards Cambridge display. And there was something odd about Benham, as though he had a large circular halo with a thick rim. This, it seemed, had replaced his hat. He was certainly hatless. The warm light of the sinking sun shone upon the horse and upon Benham's erect figure and upon his face, and gleams of fire kept flashing from his head to this rim, like the gleam of drawn swords seen from afar. As he drew nearer this halo detached itself from him and became a wheel sticking up behind him. A large, clumsy-looking bicycle was attached to the dog-cart behind. The expression of Benham's golden face was still a stony expression; he regarded his friend with hard eyes.

"You all right, Benham?" cried Prothero, advancing into the road.

His eye examined the horse. It looked all right, if anything it was a trifle subdued; there was a little foam about its mouth, but not very much.

"Whoa!" said Benham, and the horse stopped. "Are you coming up, Prothero?"

Prothero clambered up beside him. "I was anxious," he said.

"There was no need to be."

"You've broken your whip."

"Yes. It broke. . . . *Get* up!"

They proceeded on their way to Cambridge.

"Something has happened to the wheel," said Prothero, trying to be at his ease.

"Merely a splinter or so. And a spoke perhaps."

"And what is this behind?"

Benham made a half-turn of the head. "It's a motor-bicycle."

Prothero took in details.

"Some of it is missing."

"No, the front wheel is under the seat."

"Oh!"

"Did you find it?" Prothero asked, after an interval.

"No."

"You mean?"

"He ran into a motor-car — as I was passing. I was perhaps a little to blame. He asked me to bring his machine to Cambridge. He went on in the car. . . . It is all perfectly simple."

Prothero glanced at the splinters in the wheel with a renewed interest.

"Did your wheel get into it?" he asked.

Benham affected not to hear. He was evidently in no mood for story-telling.

"Why did you get down, Prothero?" he asked abruptly, with the note of suppressed anger thickening his voice.

Prothero became vividly red. "I don't know," he said, after an interval.

"I *do*," said Benham, and they went on in a rich and active silence to Cambridge, and the bicycle repair shop in Bridge Street, and Trinity College.

At the gate of Trinity Benham stopped, and conveyed rather by acts than words that Prothero was to descend. He got down meekly enough, although he felt that the return to Maltby's yard might have many points of interest. But the spirit had gone out of him.

§ 12

For three days the two friends avoided each other, and then Prothero went to Benham's room. Benham was smoking cigarettes — Lady Marayne, in the first warmth of his filial devotion, had prohibited his pipe — and reading Webb's *Industrial Democracy*. "Hello!" he said coldly, scarcely looking up, and continued to read that absorbing work.

"I keep on thinking how I jumped down from that damned dog-cart," said Prothero, without any preface.

"It didn't matter in the least," said Benham distantly.

"Oh! *Rot*," said Prothero. "I behaved like a coward."

Benham shut his book.

"Benham," said Prothero. "You are right about aristocracy, and I am wrong. I've been thinking about it night and day."

Benham betrayed no emotion. But his tone changed. "Billy," he said, "there are cigarettes and whiskey in the corner. Don't make a fuss about a trifle."

"No whiskey," said Billy, and lit a cigarette. "And it isn't a trifle."

He came to Benham's hearthrug. "That business," he said, "has changed all my views. No — don't say something polite! I see that if one hasn't the habit of pride one is bound to get off a dog-cart when it seems likely to smash. You have the habit of pride, and I haven't. So far as the habit of pride goes, I come over to the theory of aristocracy."

Benham said nothing, but he put down Sidney and Beatrice Webb, and reached out for and got and lit a cigarette.

"I give up 'Go as you please.' I give up the natural man. I admit training. I perceive I am lax and flabby, unguarded, I funk too much, I eat too much, and I drink too much. And, yet, what I have always liked in you, Benham, is just this—that you don't."

"I do," said Benham.

"Do what?"

"Funk."

"Benham, I believe that naturally you funk as much as I do. You're more a thing of nerves than I am, far more. But you keep yourself up to the mark, and I have let myself get flabby. You're so right. You're so utterly right. These last nights I've confessed it — aloud. I had an inkling of it — after that rag. But now it's as clear as daylight. I don't know if you mean to go on with me, after what's happened, but anyhow I want you to know, whether you end our friendship or not —"

"Billy, don't be an old ass," said Benham.

Both young men paused for a moment. They made no demonstrations. But the strain was at an end between them.

"I've thought it all out," Billy went on with a sudden buoyancy. "We two are both of the same kind of men. Only you see, Benham, you have a natural pride and I haven't. You have pride. But we are both intellectuals. We both belong to what the Russians call the Intelligentsia. We have ideas, we have imagination, that is our strength. And that is our weakness. That makes us moral light-weights. We are flimsy and uncertain people. All intellectuals are flimsy and uncertain people. It's not only that they are critical and fastidious; they are weak-handed. They look about them; their attention wanders. Unless they have got a habit of controlling themselves and forcing themselves and holding themselves together."

"The habit of pride."

"Yes. And then — then we are lords of the world."

"All this, Billy," said Benham, "I steadfastly believe."

"I've seen it all now," said Prothero. "Lord! how clearly I see it! The intellectual is either a prince or he is a Greek slave in a Roman household. He's got to hold his chin up or else he becomes — even as these dons we see about us — a thing that talks appointments, a toady, a port-wine bibber, a mass of detail, a conscious maker of neat sayings, a growing belly under a dwindling brain. Their gladness is drink or gratified vanity or gratified malice, their sorrow is indigestion or — old maid's melancholy. They are the lords of the world who will not take the sceptre. . . . And what I want to say to you, Benham, more than anything else is, *you* go on — *you* make yourself equestrian. You drive your horse against Breeze's, and go through the fire and swim in the ice-cold water and climb the precipice and drink little and sleep hard. And — I wish I could do so too."

"But why not?"

"Because I can't. Now I admit I've got shame in my heart and pride in my head, and I'm strung up. I might do something — this afternoon. But it won't last. *You* — you have pride in your bones. My pride will vanish at a laugh. My honour will go at a laugh. I'm just exalted by a crisis. That's all. I'm an animal of intelligence. Soul and pride are weak in me. My mouth waters, my cheek brightens, at the sight of good things. And I've got a lickerish tail, Benham. You don't know. You don't begin to imagine. I'm secretive. But I quiver with hot and stirring desires. And I'm indolent — dirty indolent. Benham, there are days when I splash my bath about without getting into it. There are days when I turn back from a walk because there's a cow in the field. . . . But, I spare you the viler details. . . . And it's that makes me hate fine people and try so earnestly to persuade myself that any man is as good as any man, if not a trifle better. Because I know it isn't so. . . ."

"Billy," said Benham, "you've the boldest mind that ever I met."

Prothero's face lit with satisfaction. Then his countenance fell again. "I know I'm better there," he said, "and yet, see how I let in a whole system of lies to cover my secret humiliations. There, at least, I will cling to pride. I will at least *think* free and clean and high. But you can climb higher than I can. You've got the grit to try and *live* high. There you are, Benham."

Benham stuck one leg over the arm of his chair.

"Billy," he said, "come and be — equestrian and stop this nonsense."

"No."

"Damn it — you *dive!*"

"You'd go in before me if a woman was drowning."

"Nonsense. I'm going to ride. Come and ride too. You've a cleverer way with animals than I have. Why! that horse I was driving the other day would have gone better alone. I didn't drive it. I just fussed it. I interfered. If I ride for ever, I shall never have decent hands, I shall always hang on my horse's mouth at a gallop, I shall never be sure at a jump. But at any rate I shall get hard. Come and get hard too."

"You can," said Billy, "you can. But not I! Heavens, the *trouble* of it! The riding-school! The getting up early! No! — for me the Trumpington Road on foot in the afternoon. Four miles an hour and panting. And my fellowship and the combination-room port. And, besides, Benham, there's the expense. I can't afford the equestrian order."

"It's not so great."

"Not so great! I don't mean the essential expense. But — the incidentals. I don't know whether any one can realize how a poor man is hampered by the dread of minor catastrophes. It isn't so much that he is afraid of breaking his neck, Benham, as that he is afraid of breaking something he will have to pay for. For instance —. Benham! how much did your little expedition the other day —?"

He stopped short and regarded his friend with round eyes and raised eyebrows.

A reluctant grin overspread Benham's face. He was beginning to see the humour of the affair.

"The claim for the motor-bicycle isn't sent in yet. The repair of the mudguards of the car is in dispute. Trinity Hall's crockery, the plate-glass window, the whip-lash and wheel and so forth, the hire of the horse and trap, sundry gratuities. . . . I doubt if the total will come very much under fifty pounds. And I seem to have lost a hat somewhere."

Billy regarded his toes and cleared his throat.

"Depending as I do on a widowed mother in Brixton for all the expenditure that isn't covered by my pot-hunting —"

"Of course," said Benham, "it wasn't a fair sample afternoon."

"Still —"

"There's footer," said Benham, "we might both play footer."

"Or boxing."

"And, anyhow, you must come with me when I drive again. I'm going to start a trotter."

"If I miss another drive may I be — lost for ever," said Billy, with the utmost sincerity. "Never more will I get down, Benham, wherever you may take me. Short of muffing my fellowship I'm with you always. . . . Will it be an American trotter?"

"It will be the rawest, gauntest, ungainliest brute that ever scared the motor-bicycles on the North-ampton Road. It will have the legs and stride of an ostrich. It will throw its feet out like dealing cards. It will lift its head and look the sun in the eye like a vulture. It will have teeth like the English spinster in a French comic paper. . . . And we will fly. . . ."

"I shall enjoy it very much," said Prothero in a small voice after an interval for reflection. "I wonder where we shall fly. It will do us both a lot of good. And I shall insure my life for a small amount in my mother's interest. . . . Benham, I think I will, after all, take a whiskey. . . . Life is short. . . ."

He did so and Benham strolled to the window and stood looking out upon the great court.

"We might do something this afternoon," said Benham.

"Splendid idea," reflected Billy over his whiskey. "Living hard and thinking hard. A sort of Intelligentsia that is *blooded*. . . . I shall, of course come as far as I can with you."

I

§ 13

In one of the bureau drawers that White in this
capacity of literary executor was examining, there
were two documents that carried back right to these
early days. They were both products of this long
wide undergraduate argumentation that had played
so large a part in the making of Benham. One
recorded the phase of maximum opposition, and one
was the outcome of the concluding approach of the
antagonists. They were debating club essays. One
had been read to a club in Pembroke, a club called
the *Enquirers*, of which White also had been a member,
and as he turned it over he found the circumstances
of its reading coming back to his memory. He had
been present, and Carnac's share in the discussion
with his shrill voice and stumpy gestures would alone
have sufficed to have made it a memorable occasion.
The later one had been read to the daughter club of
the *Enquirers*, the *Social Enquirers*, in the year after
White had gone down, and it was new to him.

Both these papers were folded flat and neatly
docketed; they were rather yellow and a little dog-
eared, and with the outer sheet pencilled over with
puzzling or illegible scribblings, Benham's memoranda for his reply. White took the earlier essay in
his hand. At the head of the first page was written
in large letters, "Go slowly, speak to the man at
the back." It brought up memories of his own
experiences, of rows of gaslit faces, and of a friendly
helpful voice that said, "Speak up?"

Of course this was what happened to every intelligent contemporary, this encounter with ideas, this restatement and ventilation of the old truths and the old heresies. Only in this way does a man make a view his own, only so does he incorporate it. These are our real turning points. The significant, the essential moments in the life of any one worth consideration are surely these moments when for the first time he faces towards certain broad ideas and certain broad facts. Life nowadays consists of adventures among generalizations. In class-rooms after the lecture, in studies in the small hours, among books or during solitary walks, the drama of the modern career begins. Suddenly a man sees his line, his intention. Yet though we are all of us writing long novels — White's world was the literary world, and that is how it looked to him — which profess to set out the lives of men, this part of the journey, this crucial passage among the Sphinxes, is still done — when it is done at all — slightly, evasively. Why?

White fell back on his professionalism. "It does not make a book. It makes a novel into a treatise, it turns it into a dissertation."

But even as White said this to himself he knew it was wrong, and it slid out of his thoughts again. Was not this objection to the play of ideas merely the expression of that conservative instinct which fights for every old convention? The traditional novel is a love story and takes ideas for granted, it professes a hero but presents a heroine. And to

begin with at least, novels were written for the
reading of heroines. Miss Lydia Languish sets no
great store upon the contents of a man's head.
That is just the stuffing of the doll. Eyes and heart
are her game. And so there is never any more
sphinx in the story than a lady may impersonate.
And as inevitably the heroine meets a man. In his
own first success, White reflected, the hero, before
he had gone a dozen pages, met a very pleasant young
woman very pleasantly in a sunlit thicket; the
second opened at once with a bicycle accident that
brought two young people together so that they
were never afterwards disentangled; the third,
failing to produce its heroine in thirty pages, had to
be rearranged. The next —

White returned from an unprofitable digression to
the matter before him.

§ 14

The first of Benham's early essays was written in
an almost boyish hand, it was youthfully amateurish
in its nervous disposition to definitions and distinctions, and in the elaborate linking of part to part.
It was called *True Democracy*. Manifestly it was
written before the incident of the Trinity Hall
plates, and most of it had been done after Prothero's
visit to Chexington. White could feel that now
inaudible interlocutor. And there were even traces
of Sir Godfrey Marayne's assertion that democracy
was contrary to biology. From the outset it was
clear that whatever else it meant, True Democracy,

following the analogy of True Politeness, True
Courage, True Honesty and True Marriage, did not
mean democracy at all.   Benham was, in fact, taking
Prothero's word, and trying to impose upon it his
own solidifying and crystallizing opinion of life.

They were not as yet very large or well-formed
crystals.   The proposition he struggled to develop
was this, that True Democracy did not mean an equal
share in the government, it meant an equal opportunity to share in the government.   Men were by
nature and in the most various ways unequal.
True Democracy aimed only at the removal of
artificial inequalities. . . .

It was on the truth of this statement, that men
were by nature unequal, that the debate had turned.
Prothero was passionately against the idea at that
time.   It was, he felt, separating himself from
Benham more and more.   He spoke with a personal
bitterness.   And he found his chief ally in a rigorous
and voluble Frenchman named Carnac, an aggressive Roman Catholic, who opened his speech by
saying that the first aristocrat was the devil, and
shocked Prothero by claiming him as probably the
only other sound Christian in the room.   Several
biologists were present, and one tall, fair youth with
a wearisome forefinger tried to pin Carnac with
questions.

"But you must admit some men are taller than
others?"

"Then the others are broader."

"Some are smaller altogether."

"Nimbler — it's notorious."

"Some of the smaller are less nimble than the others."

"Then they have better nightmares. How can you tell?"

The biologist was temporarily incapacitated, and the talk went on over his prostrate attempts to rally and protest.

A second biologist seemed to Benham to come nearer the gist of the dispute when he said that they were not discussing the importance of men, but their relative inequalities. Nobody was denying the equal importance of everybody. But there was a virtue of this man and a virtue of that. Nobody could dispute the equal importance of every wheel in a machine, of every atom in the universe. Prothero and Carnac were angry because they thought the denial of absolute equality was a denial of equal importance. That was not so. Every man mattered in his place. But politically, or economically, or intellectually that might be a lowly place. . . .

At this point Carnac interrupted with a whooping and great violence, and a volley of obscure French colloquialisms.

He was understood to convey that the speaker was a Jew, and did not in the least mean what he was saying. . . .

§ 15

The second paper was an altogether maturer and more characteristic production. It was no longer necessary to answer Prothero. Prothero had been

incorporated. And Benham had fairly got away
with his great idea. It was evident to White that
this paper had been worked over on several occasions
since its first composition and that Benham had
intended to make it a part of his book. There were
corrections in pencil and corrections in a different
shade of ink, and there was an unfinished new per-
oration, that was clearly the latest addition of all.
Yet its substance had been there always. It gave
the youth just grown to manhood, but anyhow fully
grown. It presented the far-dreaming intellectualist
shaped.

Benham had called it *Aristocracy*. But he was far
away by now from political aristocracy.

This time he had not begun with definitions and
generalizations, but with a curiously subjective
appeal. He had not pretended to be theorizing at
large any longer, he was manifestly thinking of his
own life and as manifestly he was thinking of life
as a matter of difficulty and unexpected thwartings.

"We see life," he wrote, "not only life in the
world outside us, but life in our own selves, as an
immense choice of possibilities; indeed, for us in
particular who have come up here, who are not under
any urgent necessity to take this line or that, life is
apparently pure choice. It is quite easy to think
we are all going to choose the pattern of life we like
best and work it out in our own way. . . . And,
meanwhile, there is no great hurry. . . .

"I want to begin by saying that choice isn't so
easy and so necessary as it seems. We think we are

going to choose presently, and in the end we may
never choose at all. Choice needs perhaps more
energy than we think.   The great multitude of older
people we can observe in the world outside there,
haven't chosen either in the matter of the world
outside, where they shall go, what they shall do,
what part they shall play, or in the matter of the
world within, what they will be and what they are
determined they will never be.   They are still in
much the same state of suspended choice as we seem
to be in, but in the meanwhile *things happen to them*.
And things are happening to us, things will happen
to us, while we still suppose ourselves in the wings
waiting to be consulted about the casting of the
piece. . . .

"Nevertheless this immense appearance of choice
which we get in the undergraduate community here,
is not altogether illusion ; it is more reality than
illusion even if it has not the stable and complete
reality it appears to have.   And it is more a reality
for us than it was for our fathers, and much more a
reality now than it was a few centuries ago.   The
world is more confused and multitudinous than ever
it was, the practicable world far wider, and ourselves
far less under the pressure of inflexible moulding
forces and inevitable necessities than any preceding
generations.   I want to put very clearly how I see
the new world, the present world, the world of novel
choice to which our youth and inexperience faces,
and I want to define to you a certain selection of
choices which I am going to call aristocratic, and to

which it is our manifest duty and destiny as the elect and favoured sons of our race to direct ourselves.

"It isn't any choice of Hercules I mean, any mere alternative whether we will be, how shall I put it? — the bridegrooms of pleasure or the bridegrooms of duty. It is infinitely vaster and more subtly moral than that. There are a thousand good lives possible, of which we may have one, lives which are soundly good, or a thousand bad lives, if you like, lives which are thoroughly bad — that's the old and perpetual choice, that has always been — but what is more evident to me and more remarkable and disconcerting is that there are nowadays ten thousand muddled lives lacking even so much moral definition, even so much consistency as is necessary for us to call them either good or bad, there are planless indeterminate lives, more and more of them, opening out as the possible lives before us, a perfect wilderness between salvation and damnation, a wilderness so vast and crowded that at last it seems as though the way to either hell or heaven would be lost in its interminable futility. Such planless indeterminate lives, plebeian lives, mere lives, fill the world, and the spectacle of whole nations, our whole civilization, seems to me to re-echo this planlessness, this indeterminate confusion of purpose. Plain issues are harder and harder to find, it is as if they had disappeared. Simple living is the countryman come to town. We are deafened and jostled and perplexed. There are so many things afoot that we get nothing. . . .

"That is what is in my mind when I tell you that
we have to gather ourselves together much more
than we think. We have to clench ourselves upon
a chosen end. We have to gather ourselves together
out of the swill of this brimming world.

"Or — we are lost. . . ."

("Swill of this brimming world," said White.
"Some of this sounds uncommonly like Prothero."
He mused for a moment and then resumed his
reading.)

"That is what I was getting at when, three years
ago, I made an attack upon Democracy to the
mother society of this society, an attack that I
expressed ill and failed to drive home. That is
what I have come down now to do my best to make
plainer. This age of confusion is Democracy; it is
all that Democracy can ever give us. Democracy,
if it means anything, means the rule of the planless
man, the rule of the unkempt mind. It means as a
necessary consequence this vast boiling up of collectively meaningless things.

"What is the quality of the common man, I mean
of the man that is common to all of us, the man who
is the Standard for such men as Carnac, the man
who seems to be the ideal of the Catholic Democrat?
He is the creature of a few fundamental impulses.
He begins in blind imitation of the life about him.
He lusts and takes a wife, he hungers and tills a field
or toils in some other way to earn a living, a mere
aimless living, he fears and so he does not wander,
he is jealous and stays by his wife and his job, is

fiercely yet often stupidly and injuriously defensive
of his children and his possessions, and so until he
wearies. Then he dies and needs a cemetery. He
needs a cemetery because he is so afraid of dissolu-
tion that even when he has ceased to be, he still
wants a place and a grave to hold him together and
prevent his returning to the All that made him.
Our chief impression of long ages of mankind comes
from its cemeteries. And this is the life of man, as
the common man conceives and lives it. Beyond
that he does not go, he never comprehends himself
collectively at all, the state happens about him ; his
passion for security, his gregarious self-defensiveness,
makes him accumulate upon himself until he congests
in cities that have no sense of citizenship and states
that have no structure ; the clumsy, inconsecutive
lying and chatter of his newspapers, his hoardings
and music-halls gives the measure of his congested
intelligences, the confusion of ugly, half empty
churches and chapels and meeting-halls gauge the
intensity of his congested souls, the tricks and slow
blundering dishonesties of Diet and Congress and
Parliament are his statecraft and his wisdom. . . .

"I do not care if this instant I am stricken dead
for pride. I say here now to you and to High Heaven
that *this life is not good enough for me*. I know there
is a better life than this muddle about us, a better
life possible now. I know it. A better individual
life and a better public life. If I had no other
assurances, if I were blind to the glorious intimations
of art, to the perpetually widening promise of science,

to the mysterious beckonings of beauty in form and colour and the inaccessible mockery of the stars, I should still know this from the insurgent spirit within me. . . .

"Now this better life is what I mean when I talk of Aristocracy. This idea of a life breaking away from the common life to something better, is the consuming idea in my mind.

"Constantly, recurrently, struggling out of the life of the farm and the shop, the inn and the market, the street and the crowd, is something that is not of the common life. Its way of thinking is Science, its dreaming is Art, its will is the purpose of mankind. It is not the common thing. But also it is not an unnatural thing. It is not as common as a rat, but it is no less natural than a panther.

"For it is as natural to be an explorer as it is to be a potato grower, it is rarer but it is as natural; it is as natural to seek explanations and arrange facts as it is to make love, or adorn a hut, or show kindness to a child. It is a folly I will not even dispute about, that man's only natural implement is the spade. Imagination, pride, exalted desire are just as much Man, as are hunger and thirst and sexual curiosities and the panic dread of unknown things. . .

"Now you see better what I mean about choice. Now you see what I am driving at. We have to choose each one for himself and also each one for the race, whether we will accept the muddle of the common life, whether we ourselves will be muddled, weakly nothings, children of luck, steering our artful courses for mean success and tawdry honours, or whether we will be aristocrats, for that is what it amounts to, each one in the measure of his personal quality an aristocrat, refusing to be restrained by fear, refusing to be restrained by pain, resolved to know and understand up to the hilt of his understanding, resolved to sacrifice all the common stuff of his life to the perfection of his peculiar gift, a purged man, a trained, selected, artificial man, not simply free, but lordly free, filled and sustained by pride. Whether you or I make that choice and whether you or I succeed in realizing ourselves, though a great matter to ourselves, is, I admit, a small matter to the world. But the great matter is this, that *the choice is being made*, that it will continue to be made, and that all around us, so that it can never be arrested and darkened again, is the dawn of human possibility. . . ."

(White could also see his dead friend's face with its enthusiastic paleness, its disordered hair and the glowing darknesses in the eyes. On such occasions Benham always had an expression of *escape*. Temporary escape. And thus would his hand have clutched the reading-desk; thus would his long fingers have rustled these dry papers.)

"Man has reached a point when a new life opens before him. . . .

"The old habitual life of man is breaking up all about us, and for the new life our minds, our imaginations, our habits and customs are all unprepared. . . .

"It is only now, after some years of study and living, that I begin to realize what this tremendous beginning we call Science means to mankind. Every condition that once justified the rules and imperatives, the manners and customs, the sentiments, the morality, the laws and limitations which make up the common life, has been or is being destroyed. . . . Two or three hundred years more and all that life will be as much a thing past and done with as the life that was lived in the age of unpolished stone. . . .

"Man is leaving his ancestral shelters and going out upon the greatest adventure that ever was in space or time, he is doing it now, he is doing it in us as I stand here and read to you."

CHAPTER THE SECOND

THE YOUNG MAN ABOUT TOWN

§ 1

THE oldest novel in the world at any rate, White reflected, was a story with a hero and no love interest worth talking about. It was the story of Tobias and how he came out from the shelters of his youth into this magic and intricate world. Its heroine was incidental, part of the spoil, a seven times relict. . . .

White had not read the book of Tobit for many years, and what he was really thinking of was not that ancient story at all, but Botticelli's picture, that picture of the sunlit morning of life. When you say "Tobias" that is what most intelligent people will recall. Perhaps you will remember how gaily and confidently the young man strides along with the armoured angel by his side. Absurdly enough, Benham and his dream of high aristocracy reminded White of that. . . .

"We have all been Tobias in our time," said White.

If White had been writing this chapter he would have in all probability called it *The Tobias Stage*, forgetful that there was no Tobit behind Benham and an entirely different Sara in front of him.

§ 2

From Cambridge Benham came to London. For
the first time he was to live in London. Never
before had he been in London for more than a few
days at a time. But now, guided by his mother's
advice, he was to have a flat in Finacue Street, just
round the corner from Desborough Street, a flat
very completely and delightfully furnished under
her supervision. It had an admirable study, in
which she had arranged not only his books, but a
number of others in beautiful old leather bindings
that it had amused her extremely to buy; it had a
splendid bureau and business-like letter-filing cabinets, a neat little drawing-room and a dining-room,
well-placed abundant electric lights, and a man
called Merkle whom she had selected very carefully
and who she felt would not only see to Benham's
comfort but keep him, if necessary, up to the
mark.

This man Merkle seemed quite unaware that
humanity "here and now" — even as he was engaged in meticulously putting out Benham's clothes
— was "leaving its ancestral shelters and going out
upon the greatest adventure that ever was in space
or time." If he had been told as much by Benham
he would probably have said, "Indeed, sir," and
proceeded accurately with his duties. And if Benham's voice had seemed to call for any additional
remark, he would probably have added, "It's 'igh
time, sir, something of the sort was done. Will you

have the white wesket as before, sir, or a fresh one
this evening? . . . Unless it's a very special occasion, sir. . . . Exactly, sir. *Thank* you, sir."

And when her son was properly installed in his
apartments Lady Marayne came round one morning with a large experienced-looking portfolio and
rendered an account of her stewardship of his estate
that was already some months overdue. It was all
very confused and confusing, and there were inexplicable incidents, a heavy overdraft at the bank for
example, but this was Sir Godfrey's fault, she explained. "He never would help me with any of this
business," she said. "I've had to add sometimes
for *hours*. But, of course, you are a man, and when
you've looked through it all, I know you'll understand."

He did look through it enough to see that it was
undesirable that he should understand too explicitly,
and, anyhow, he was manifestly very well off indeed, and the circumstances of the case, even as he
understood them, would have made any business-
like book-keeping ungracious. The bankers sub-
mitted the corroborating account of securities, and
he found himself possessed of his unconditional
six thousand a year, with, as she put it, "the world
at his feet." On the whole it seemed more wonderful to him now than when he had first heard of it.
He kissed her and thanked her, and left the portfolio
open for Merkle's entirely honest and respectful
but very exact inspection, and walked back with her
to Desborough Street, and all the while he was

K

craving to ask the one tremendous question he
knew he would never ask, which was just how
exactly this beneficent Nolan came in. . . .

Once or twice in the small hours, and on a number
of other occasions, this unspeakable riddle assumed
a portentous predominance in his mind. He was
forced back upon his inner consciousness for its
consideration. He could discuss it with nobody
else, because that would have been discussing his
mother.

Probably most young men who find themselves
with riches at large in the world have some such
perplexity as this mixed in with the gift. Such
men as the Cecils perhaps not, because they are in
the order of things, the rich young Jews perhaps
not, because acquisition is their principle, but for
most other intelligent inheritors there must be this
twinge of conscientious doubt. "Why particularly
am *I* picked out for so tremendous an advantage?"
If the riddle is not Nolan, then it is rent, or it is the
social mischief of the business, or the particular
speculative *coup* that established their fortune.

"*Pecunia non olet*," Benham wrote, "and it is just
as well. Or the west-ends of the world would reek
with deodorizers. Restitution is inconceivable; how
and to whom? And in the meanwhile here we are
lifted up by our advantage to a fantastic appearance
of opportunity. Whether the world looks to us or
not to do tremendous things, it ought to look to us.
And above all we ought to look to ourselves.
Richesse oblige."

§ 3

It is not to be supposed that Benham came to
town only with a general theory of aristocracy.   He
had made plans for a career.   Indeed, he had plans
for several careers.   None of them when brought
into contrast with the great spectacle of London
retained all the attractiveness that had saturated
them at their inception.

They were all more or less political careers.   Whatever a democratic man may be, Prothero and he had
decided that an aristocratic man is a public man.   He
is made and protected in what he is by laws and the
state and his honour goes out to the state.   The
aristocrat has no right to be a voluptuary or a mere
artist or a respectable nonentity, or any such purely
personal things.   Responsibility for the aim and
ordering of the world is demanded from him as
imperatively as courage.

Benham's deliberate assumption of the equestrian
rôle brought him into contact with a new set of
acquaintances, conscious of political destinies.   They
were amiable, hard young men, almost affectedly
unaffected ; they breakfasted before dawn to get in a
day's hunting, and they saw to it that Benham's
manifest determination not to discredit himself
did not lead to his breaking his neck.   Their bodies
were beautifully tempered, and their minds were as
flabby as Prothero's body.   Among them were
such men as Lord Breeze and Peter Westerton, and
that current set of Corinthians who supposed them-

selves to be resuscitating the Young England movement and Tory Democracy.   Poor movements which
indeed have never so much lived as suffered chronic
resuscitation.   These were days when Tariff Reform
was only an inglorious possibility for the Tory Party,
and Young England had yet to demonstrate its mental
quality in an anti-socialist campaign.   Seen from the
perspectives of Cambridge and Chexington, the Tory
party was still a credible basis for the adventure of a
young man with an aristocratic theory in his mind.

These were the days when the strain and extremity
of a dangerous colonial war were fresh in people's
minds, when the quality of the public consciousness
was braced up by its recent response to unanticipated
demands.   The conflict of stupidities that had
caused the war was overlaid and forgotten by a
hundred thousand devotions, by countless heroic
deaths and sufferings, by a pacification largely conceived and broadly handled.   The nation had displayed a belated regard for its honour and a sustained passion for great unities.   It was still possible
for Benham to regard the empire as a splendid
opportunity, and London as the conceivable heart of
the world.   He   could   think   of Parliament as a
career, and of a mingling of aristocratic socialism
based on universal service with a civilizing imperialism as a purpose. . . .

But his thoughts had gone wider and deeper than
that. . . .

Already when Benham came to London he had
begun to dream of possibilities that went beyond the

accidental states and empires of to-day.   Prothero's
mind, replete with historical detail, could find nothing
but absurdity in the alliances and dynasties and
loyalties of our time.   "Patched up things, Benham,
temporary, pretentious.   All very well for the undignified man, the democratic man, to take shelter
under, all very well for the humourist to grin and
bear, all very well for the crowd and the quack, but
not for the aristocrat—No!—his mind cuts like steel
and burns like fire.   Lousy sheds they are, plastered
hoardings . . . and such a damned nuisance too !
For any one who wants to do honourable things !
With their wars and their diplomacies, their tariffs
and their encroachments;   all their humbugging
struggles, their bloody and monstrous struggles,
that finally work out to no end at all. . . .   If you
are going for the handsome thing in life then the
world has to be a united world, Benham, as a matter
of course.   That was settled when the railways and
the telegraph came. Telephones, wireless teleg-
raphy, aeroplanes insist on it.   We've got to
mediatise all this stuff, all these little crowns and
boundaries and creeds, and so on, that stand in the
way.   Just as Italy had to be united in spite of all
the rotten little dukes and princes and republics, just
as Germany had to be united in spite of its scores of
kingdoms and duchies and liberties, so now the world.
Things as they are may be fun for lawyers and politicians and court people and — douaniers; they may
suit the loan-mongers and the armaments share-
holders, they may even be more comfortable for

the middle-aged, but what, except as an inconvenience, does that matter to you or me?

Prothero always pleased Benham when he swept
away empires. There was always a point when the
rhetoric broke into gesture.

"We've got to sweep them away, Benham," he
said, with a wide gesture of his arm. "We've got
to sweep them all away."

Prothero helped himself to some more whiskey,
and spoke hastily, because he was afraid some one
else might begin. He was never safe from interruption in his own room. The other young men
present sucked at their pipes and regarded him
doubtfully. They were never quite certain whether
Prothero was a prophet or a fool. They could not understand a mixed type, and he was so manifestly both.

"The only sane political work for an intelligent
man is to get the world-state ready. For that we
have to prepare an aristocracy —"

"Your world-state will be aristocratic?" some one
interpolated.

"Of course it will be aristocratic. How can
uninformed men think all round the globe? Democracy dies five miles from the parish pump. It will
be an aristocratic republic of all the capable men in
the world. . . ."

"Of course," he added, pipe in mouth, as he
poured out his whiskey, "it's a big undertaking.
It's an affair of centuries. . . ."

And then, as a further afterthought: "All the
more reason for getting to work at it. . . ."

In his moods of inspiration Prothero would discourse through the tobacco smoke until that great
world-state seemed imminent — and Part Two in
the Tripos a thing relatively remote. He would
talk until the dimly-lit room about him became
impalpable, and the young men squatting about it
in elaborately careless attitudes caught glimpses of
cities that are still to be, bridges in wild places,
deserts tamed and oceans conquered, mankind no
longer wasted by bickerings, going forward to the
conquest of the stars. . . .

An aristocratic world-state ; this political dream
had already taken hold of Benham's imagination
when he came to town.   But it was a dream, something that had never existed, something that indeed
may never materialize, and such dreams, though
they are vivid enough in a study at night, fade and
vanish at the rustle of a daily newspaper or the
sound of a passing band.   To come back again. . . .
So it was with Benham. Sometimes he was set
clearly towards this world-state that Prothero had
talked into possibility. Sometimes he was simply
abreast of the patriotic and socially constructive
British Imperialism of Breeze and Westerton.   And
there were moods when the two things were confused
in his mind, and the glamour of world dominion
rested wonderfully on the slack and straggling British
Empire of Edward the Seventh — and Mr. Rudyard
Kipling and Mr. Chamberlain.   He did go on for a
time honestly entertaining both these projects in his
mind, each at its different level, the greater impal-

pable one and the lesser concrete one within it.   In
some unimaginable way he could suppose that the
one by some miracle of ennoblement — and neglecting the Frenchman, the Russian, the German, the
American, the Indian, the Chinaman, and, indeed,
the greater part of mankind from the problem —
might become the other. . . .

All of which is recorded here, without excess of
comment, as it happened, and as, in a mood of
astonished reminiscences, he came finally to perceive
it, and set it down for White's meditative perusal.

§ 4

But to the enthusiasm of the young, dreams have
something of the substance of reality and realities,
something of the magic of dreams.   The London to
which Benham came from Cambridge and the dis-
quisitions of Prothero was not the London of a
mature and disillusioned vision.   It was London
seen magnified and distorted through the young
man's crystalline intentions.   It had for him a
quality of multitudinous, unquenchable activity.
Himself filled with an immense appetite for life, he
was unable to conceive of London as fatigued.   He
could not suspect these statesmen he now began to
meet and watch, of jaded wills and petty spites, he
imagined that all the important and influential persons
in this large world of affairs were as frank in their
private lives and as unembarrassed in their financial relationships as his untainted self.   And he had
still to reckon with stupidity.   He believed in the

statecraft of leader-writers and the sincerity of
political programmes. And so regarded, what an
avenue to Empire was Whitehall! How momentous
was the sunrise in St. James's Park, and how significant the clustering knot of listeners and speakers beneath the tall column that lifts our Nelson to the
windy sky!

For a time Benham was in love with the idea of
London. He got maps of London and books about
London. He made plans to explore its various regions. He tried to grasp it all, from the conscious
picturesqueness of its garden suburbs to the factories
of Croydon, from the clerk-villadoms of Ealing to
the inky streams of Bow. In those days there were
passenger steamboats that would take one from the
meadows of Hampton Court past the whole spectacle
of London out to the shipping at Greenwich and the
towed liners, the incessant tugs, the heaving portals
of the sea. . . . His time was far too occupied for
him to carry out a tithe of these expeditions he had
planned, but he had many walks that bristled with
impressions. Northward and southward, eastward
and westward a dreaming young man could wander
into a wilderness of population, polite or sombre, poor,
rich, or middle-class, but all ceaselessly active, all
urgently pressing, as it seemed, to their part in the
drama of the coming years. He loved the late afternoon, when every artery is injected and gorged with
the multitudinous home-going of the daily workers,
he loved the time of lighting up, and the clustering
excitements of the late hours. And he went out

southward and eastward into gaunt regions of reeking toil. As yet he knew nothing of the realities of industrialism. He saw only the beauty of the great chimneys that rose against the sullen smoke-barred sunsets, and he felt only the romance of the lurid shuddering flares that burst out from squat stacks of brickwork and lit the emptiness of strange and slovenly streets. . . .

And this London was only the foreground of the great scene upon which he, as a prosperous, well-befriended young Englishman, was free to play whatever part he could. This narrow turbid tidal river by which he walked ran out under the bridges eastward beneath the grey-blue clouds towards Germany, towards Russia, and towards Asia, which still seemed in those days so largely the Englishman's Asia. And when you turned about at Blackfriars Bridge this sense of the round world was so upon you that you faced not merely Westminster, but the icy Atlantic and America, which one could yet fancy was a land of Englishmen — Englishmen a little estranged. At any rate they assimilated, they kept the tongue. The shipping in the lower reaches below the Tower there carried the flags of every country under the sky. . . . As he went along the riverside he met a group of dusky students, Chinese or Japanese. Cambridge had abounded in Indians, and beneath that tall clock tower at Westminster it seemed as though the world might centre. The background of the Englishman's world reached indeed to either pole, it went about the earth, his background it was

—for all that he was capable of doing. All this had awaited him. . . .

Is it any wonder if a young man with an excitable imagination came at times to the pitch of audible threats? If the extreme indulgence of his opportunity and his sense of ability and vigour lifted his vanity at moments to the kingly pitch? If he ejaculated and made a gesture or so as he went along the Embankment?

§ 5

In the disquisition upon choice that opened Benham's paper on *Aristocracy*, he showed himself momentarily wiser than his day-dreams. For in these day-dreams he did seem to himself to be choosing among unlimited possibilities. Yet while he dreamt other influences were directing his movements. There were for instance his mother, Lady Marayne, who saw a very different London from what he did, and his mother Dame Nature, who cannot see London at all. She was busy in his blood as she is busy in the blood of most healthy young men; common experience must fill the gaps for us; and patiently and thoroughly she was preparing for the entrance of that heroine, whom not the most self-centred of heroes can altogether avoid. . . .

And then there was the power of every day. Benham imagined himself at large on his liberating steed of property while indeed he was mounted on the made horse of Civilization; while he was speculating whither he should go, he was already starting out upon the round.   One hesitates upon the magnificent plan and devotion of one's lifetime and meanwhile there is usage, there are engagements.   Every morning came Merkle, the embodiment of the established routine, the herald of all that the world expected and required Benham to be and do.   Usually he awakened Benham with the opening of his door and the soft tinkle of the curtain rings as he let in the morning light.   He moved softly about the room, gathering up and removing the crumpled hulls of yesterday; that done he reappeared at the bedside with a cup of admirable tea and one thin slice of bread-and-butter, reported on the day's weather, stood deferential for instructions.   "You will be going out for lunch, sir.   Very good, sir. White slips of course, sir.   You will go down into the country in the afternoon?   Will that be the serge suit, sir, or the brown?"

These matters settled, the new aristocrat could yawn and stretch like any aristocrat under the old dispensation, and then as the sound of running water from the bathroom ceased, stick his toes out of bed.

The day was tremendously indicated.   World-states and aristocracies of steel and fire, things that were as real as coal-scuttles in Billy's rooms away there at Cambridge, were now remoter than Sirius.

He was expected to shave, expected to bath, expected to go in to the bright warmth and white linen and silver and china of his breakfast-table.

And there he found letters and invitations, loaded with expectation.   And beyond the coffee-pot, neatly folded, lay the *Times*, and the *Daily News* and the *Telegraph* all with an air of requiring his attention. There had been more fighting in Thibet and Mr. Ritchie had made a Free Trade speech at Croydon. The Japanese had torpedoed another Russian iron-clad and a British cruiser was ashore in the East Indies.   A man had been found murdered in an empty house in Hoxton and the King had had a conversation with General Booth.   Tadpole was in for North Winchelsea, beating Toper by nine votes, and there had been a new cut in t·1e Atlantic passenger rates.   He was expected to be interested and excited by these things.

Presently the telephone bell would ring and he would hear the clear little voice of his mother full of imperative expectations.   He would be round for lunch?   Yes, he would be round to lunch.   And the afternoon, had he arranged to do anything with his afternoon?   No! — put off Chexington until to-morrow.   There was this new pianist, it was really an *experience*, and one might not get tickets again. And then tea at Panton's.   It was rather fun at Panton's. . . .   Oh!—Weston Massinghay was coming to lunch.   He was a useful man to know. So *clever*. . . .   So long, my dear little Son, till I see you. . . .

So life puts out its Merkle threads, as the poacher puts his hair noose about the pheasant's neck, and while we theorize takes hold of us. . . .

It came presently home to Benham that he had
been down from Cambridge for ten months, and
that he was still not a step forward with the realization of the new aristocracy. His political career
waited. He had done a quantity of things, but
their net effect was incoherence. He had not been
merely passive, but his efforts to break away into
creative realities had added to rather than diminished
his accumulating sense of futility.

The natural development of his position under the
influence of Lady Marayne had enormously enlarged
the circle of his acquaintances. He had taken part
in all sorts of social occasions, and sat and listened to
a representative selection of political and literary and
social personages, he had been several times to the
opera and to a great number and variety of plays, he
had been attentively inconspicuous in several really
good week-end parties. He had spent a golden
October in North Italy with his mother, and
escaped from the glowing lassitude of Venice for
some days of climbing in the Eastern Alps. In
January, in an outbreak of enquiry, he had gone
with Lionel Maxim to St. Petersburg and had eaten
zakuska, brightened his eyes with vodka, talked
with a number of charming people of the war that
was then imminent, listened to gipsy singers until
dawn, careered in sledges about the most silent and
stately of capitals, and returned with Lionel, dis-
coursing upon autocracy and assassination, Japan,
the Russian destiny, and the government of Peter
the Great. That excursion was the most after his

heart of all the dispersed employments of his first year. Through the rest of the winter he kept himself very fit, and still further qualified that nervous dislike for the horse that he had acquired from Prothero by hunting once a week in Essex. He was incurably a bad horseman; he rode without sympathy, he was unready and convulsive at hedges and ditches, and he judged distances badly. His white face and rigid seat and a certain joylessness of bearing in the saddle earned him the singular nickname, which never reached his ears, of the "Galvanized Corpse." He got through, however, at the cost of four quite trifling spills and without damaging either of the horses he rode. And his physical self-respect increased.

On his writing-desk appeared a few sheets of manuscript that increased only very slowly. He was trying to express his Cambridge view of aristocracy in terms of Finacue Street, West.

The artistic and intellectual movements of London had made their various demands upon his time and energies. Art came to him with a noble assumption of his interest and an intention that presently became unpleasantly obvious to sell him pictures that he did not want to buy and explain away pictures that he did. He bought one or two modern achievements, and began to doubt if art and aristocracy had any necessary connection. At first he had accepted the assumption that they had. After all, he reflected, one lives rather for life and things than for pictures of life and things or pictures arising out

of life and things. This Art had an air of saying
something, but when one came to grips with it
what had it to say? Unless it was Yah! The
drama, and more particularly the intellectual drama,
challenged his attention. In the hands of Shaw,
Bar er, Masefield, Galsworthy, and Hankin, it, too,
had an air of saying something, but he found it
extremely difficult to join on to his own demands
upon life anything whatever that the intellectual
drama had the air of having said. He would sit
forward in the front row of the dress-circle with his
cheek on his hand and his brow slightly knit. His
intentness amused observant people. The drama
that did not profess to be intellectual he went to
with Lady Marayne, and usually on first nights.
Lady Marayne loved a big first night at St. James's
Theatre or His Majesty's. Afterwards, perhaps,
Sir Godfrey would join them at a supper party, and
all sorts of clever and amusing people would be there
saying keen intimate things about each other. He
met Yeats, who told amusing stories about George
Moore, and afterwards he met George Moore, who
told amusing stories about Yeats, and it was all, he
felt, great fun for the people who were in it. But
he was not in it, and he had no very keen desire to be
in it. It wasn't his stuff. He had, though they were
nowadays rather at the back of his mind, quite
other intentions. In the meanwhile all these things
took up his time and distracted his attention.

There was, as yet, no practicable aviation to
beguile a young man of spirit, but there were times

when Benham found himself wondering whether there might not be something rather creditable in the possession and control of a motor-car of exceptional power. Only one might smash people up. Should an aristocrat be deterred by the fear of smashing people up? If it is a selfish fear of smashing people up, if it is nerves rather than pity? At any rate it did not come to the car.

§ 6

Among other things that delayed Benham very greatly in the development of his aristocratic experiments was the advice that was coming to him from every quarter. It came in extraordinary variety and volume, but always it had one unvarying feature. It ignored and tacitly contradicted his private intentions.

We are all of us disposed to be propagandists of our way of living, and the spectacle of a wealthy young man quite at large is enough to excite the most temperate of us without distinction of age or sex. "If I were you," came to be a familiar phrase in his ear. This was particularly the case with political people; and they did it not only from the natural infirmity of humanity, but because, when they seemed reluctant or satisfied with him as he was, Lady Marayne egged them on.

There was a general assumption that he was to go into Parliament, and most of his counsellors assumed further that on the whole his natural sympathies would take him into the Conservative

L

party. But it was pointed out to him that just at
present the Liberal party was the party of a young
man's opportunity ; sooner or later the swing of the
pendulum which would weed the Conservatives and
proliferate Liberals was bound to come, there was
always more demand and opportunity for candidates
on the Liberal side, the Tariff Reformers were
straining their ministerial majority to the splitting
point, and most of the old Liberal leaders had
died off during the years of exile. The party was no
longer dominated ; it would tolerate ideas. A young
man who took a distinctive line — provided it was
not from the party point of view a vexatious or
impossible line — might go very rapidly far and
high. On the other hand, it was urged upon him
that the Tariff Reform adventure called also for
youth and energy. But there, perhaps, there was
less scope for the distinctive line — and already
they had Garvin. Quite a number of Benham's
friends pointed out to him the value of working
out some special aspect of our national political
interests. A very useful speciality was the Balkans.
Mr. Pope, the well-known publicist, whose very
sound and considerable reputation was based on
the East Purblow Labour Experiment, met Benham
at lunch and proposed to go with him in a spirit
of instructive association to the Balkans, rub
up their Greek together, and settle the problem of
Albania. He wanted, he said, a foreign speciality
to balance his East Purblow interest. But Lady
Beach Mandarin warned Benham against the Bal-

kans; the Balkans were getting to be too handy for
Easter and summer holidays, and now that there
were several good hotels in Servia and Montenegro
and Sofia, they were being overdone. Everybody
went to the Balkans and came back with a pet na-
tionality. She loathed pet nationalities. She believed most people loathed them nowadays. It was
stale : it was *Gladstonian*. She was all for specializa-
tion in social reform. She thought Benham ought
to join the Fabian Society and consult the Webbs.
Quite a number of able young men had been placed
with the assistance of the Webbs. They were,
she said, "a perfect fount. . . ." Two other people,
independently of each other, pointed out to Benham
the helpfulness of a few articles in the half-crown
monthlies. . . .

"What are the assumptions underlying all this?"
Benham asked himself in a phase of lucidity.

And after reflection. "Good God! The assumptions! What do they think will satisfy me? . . ."

Everybody, however, did not point to Parliament.
Several people seemed to think Travel, with a
large T, was indicated. One distant cousin of Sir
Godfrey's, the kind of man of the world who has
long moustaches, was for big game shooting. "Get
right out of all this while you are young," he said.
"There's nothing to compare with stopping a charg-
ing lion at twenty yards. I've done it, my boy.
You can come back for all this pow-wow afterwards."
He gave the diplomatic service as a second choice.
"There you are," he said, "first-rate social position,

nothing to do, theatres, operas, pretty women, colour, life. The best of good times. Barring Washington, that is. But Washington, they say, isn't as bad as it used to be—since Teddy has Europeanized 'em. . . ."

Even the Reverend Harold Benham took a subdued but thoughtful share in his son's admonition. He came up to the flat — due precautions were taken to prevent a painful encounter — he lunched at his son's new club, and he was visibly oppressed by the contrast between the young man's youthful fortunes and his own. As visibly he bore up bravely. "There are few men, Poff, who would not envy you your opportunities," he said. "You have the Feast of Life spread out at your feet. . . . I hope you have had yourself put up for the Athenæum. They say it takes years. When I was a young man — and ambitious — I thought that some day I might belong to the Athenæum. . . . One has to learn. . . ."

§ 7

And with an effect of detachment, just as though it didn't belong to the rest of him at all, there was beginning a sort of backstairs and underside to Benham's life. There is no need to discuss how inevitable that may or may not be in the case of a young man of spirit and large means, nor to embark upon the discussion of the temptations and opportunities of large cities. Several ladies, of various positions and qualities, had reflected upon his manifest need of education. There was in particular Mrs. Skelmersdale, a very pretty little widow with hazel eyes, black hair, a mobile mouth, and a pathetic history, who talked of old music to him and took him to a Dolmetsch concert in Clifford's Inn, and expanded that common interest to a general participation in his indefinite outlook. She advised him about his probable politics — everybody did that — but when he broke through his usual reserve and suggested views of his own, she was extraordinarily sympathetic. She was so sympathetic and in such a caressing way that she created a temporary belief in her understanding, and it was quite imperceptibly that he was drawn into the discussion of modern ethical problems. She herself was a rather stimulating instance of modern ethical problems. She told him something of her own story, and then their common topics narrowed down very abruptly. He found he could help her in several ways. There is, unhappily, a disposition on the part of many people, who ought to know better, to regard a rôle played by Joseph during his earlier days in Egypt as a ridiculous one. This point of view became very inopportunely dominant in Benham's mind when he was lunching *tête à tête* with Mrs. Skelmersdale at her flat. . . .

The ensuing intimacy was of an entirely concealed and respectable nature, but a certain increased preoccupation in his manner set Lady Marayne thinking. He had as a matter of fact been taken by surprise.

Still he perceived that it is no excuse for a man that he has been taken by surprise. Surprises in one's own conduct ought not to happen. When they do happen then an aristocrat ought to stick to what he had done. He was now in a subtle and complicated relationship to Mrs. Skelmersdale, a relationship in which her pride had become suddenly a matter of tremendous importance. Once he had launched himself upon this affair, it was clear to him that he owed it to her never to humiliate her. And to go back upon himself now would be a tremendous humiliation for her. You see, he had helped her a little financially. And she looked to him, she wanted him. . . .

She wasn't, he knew, altogether respectable. Indeed, poor dear, her ethical problems, already a little worn, made her seem at times anything but respectable. He had met her first one evening at Jimmy Gluckstein's when he was forming his opinion of Art. Her manifest want of interest in pictures had attracted him. And that had led to music. And to the mention of a Clementi piano, that short, gentle, sad, old, little sort of piano people will insist upon calling a spinet, in her flat.

And so to this. . . .

It was very wonderful and delicious, this first indulgence of sense.

It was shabby and underhand.

The great god Pan is a glorious god. (And so was Swinburne.) And what can compare with the warmth of blood and the sheen of sunlit limbs?

But Priapus. . . .

She was the most subtle, delightful and tender of created beings.

She had amazing streaks of vulgarity.

And some astonishing friends.

Once she had seemed to lead the talk deliberately to money matters.

She loved him and desired him. There was no doubt of it.

There was a curious effect about her as though when she went round the corner she would become somebody else. And a curious recurrent feeling that round the corner there was somebody else.

He had an extraordinary feeling that his mother knew about this business. This feeling came from nothing in her words or acts, but from some indefinable change in her eyes and bearing towards him. But how could she know?

It was unlikely that she and Mrs. Skelmersdale would ever meet, and it seemed to him that it would be a particularly offensive incident for them to meet.

There were times now when life took on a grey and boring quality such as it had never had before he met Mrs. Skelmersdale, and the only remedy was to go to her. She could restore his nervous tranquillity, his feeling of solidity and reality, his pride in himself. For a time, that is.

Nevertheless his mind was as a whole pervaded by the feeling that he ought not to have been taken by surprise.

And he had the clearest conviction in his mind that if now he could be put back again to the day before that lunch. . . .

No! he should not have gone there to lunch.

He had gone there to see her Clementi piano.

Had he or had he not thought beforehand of any other possibility?

On a point so vital his memory was curiously unsure.

§ 8

The worry and disorganization of Benham's life and thoughts increased as the spring advanced. His need in some way to pull things together became overpowering. He began to think of Billy Prothero, more and more did it seem desirable to have a big talk with Billy and place everything that had got disturbed. Benham thought of going to Cambridge for a week of exhaustive evenings. Small engagements delayed that expedition. . . .

Then came a day in April when all the world seemed wrong to Benham. He was irritable; his will was unstable; whatever presented itself to be done presented itself as undesirable; he could settle to nothing. He had been keeping away from Mrs. Skelmersdale and in the morning there came a little note from her designed to correct this abstention. She understood the art of the attractive note. But he would not decide to go to her. He left the note unanswered.

Then came his mother at the telephone and it became instantly certain to Benham that he could not play the dutiful son that evening. He answered her that he could not come to dinner. He had engaged himself. "Where?"

"With some men."

There was a pause and then his mother's voice came, flattened by disappointment. "Very well then, little Poff.   Perhaps I shall see you to-morrow."

He replaced the receiver and fretted back into his study, where the notes on aristocracy lay upon his desk, the notes he had been pretending to work over all the morning.

"Damned liar!" he said, and then, "Dirty liar!"

He decided to lunch at the club, and in the afternoon he was moved to telephone an appointment with his siren.   And having done that he was bound to keep it.

About one o'clock in the morning he found himself walking back to Finacue Street.   He was no longer a fretful conflict of nerves, but if anything he was less happy than he had been before.   It seemed to him that London was a desolate and inglorious growth.

London ten years ago was much less nocturnal than it is now.   And not so brightly lit.   Down the long streets came no traffic but an occasional hansom.   Here and there a cat halted or bolted in the road.   Near Piccadilly a policeman hovered artfully in a doorway, and then came a few belated prostitutes waylaying the passers-by, and a few youths and men, wearily lust driven.

As he turned up New Bond Street he saw a figure that struck him as familiar.   Surely! — it was Billy Prothero!   Or at any rate it was astonishingly like Billy Prothero.   He glanced again and the likeness

was more doubtful. The man had his back to
Benham, he was halting and looking back at a
woman.

By some queer flash of intuition it came to Benham
that even if this was not Prothero, still Prothero did
these things. It might very well be Prothero even,
though, as he now saw, it wasn't. Everybody did
these things. . . .

It came into Benham's head for the first time that
life could be tiresome.

This Bond Street was a tiresome place; with its
shops all shut and muffled, its shops where in the
crowded daytime one bought costly furniture, costly
clothes, costly scent, sweets, bibelots, pictures,
jewellery, presents of all sorts, clothes for Mrs.
Skelmersdale, sweets for Mrs. Skelmersdale, presents
for Mrs. Skelmersdale, all the elaborate fittings and
equipage of — *that!*

"Good night, dear," a woman drifted by him.

"I've *said* good night," he cried, "I've *said* good
night," and so went on to his flat. The unquenchable demand, the wearisome insatiability of sex!
When everything else has gone, then it shows itself
bare in the bleak small hours. And at first it had
seemed so light a matter! He went to bed, feeling
dog-tired, he went to bed at an hour and with a
finished completeness that Merkle would have
regarded as entirely becoming in a young gentleman
of his position.

And a little past three o'clock in the morning he
awoke to a mood of indescribable desolation. He

awoke with a start to an agony of remorse and self-reproach.

§ 9

For a time he lay quite still staring at the darkness, then he groaned and turned over. Then, suddenly, like one who fancies he hears a strange noise, he sat up in bed and listened.

"Oh, God!" he said at last.

And then: "Oh! The *dirtiness* of life! The dirty muddle of life!

"What are we doing with life? What are we all doing with life?

"It isn't only this poor Milly business. This only brings it to a head. Of course she wants money. . . ."

His thoughts came on again.

"But the ugliness!

"Why did I begin it?"

He put his hands upon his knees and pressed his eyes against the backs of his hands and so remained very still, a blankness beneath his own question.

After a long interval his mind moved again.

And now it was as if he looked upon his whole existence, he seemed to see in a large, clear, cold comprehensiveness, all the wasted days, the fruitless activities, the futilities, the perpetual postponements that had followed his coming to London. He saw it all as a joyless indulgence, as a confusion of playthings and undisciplined desires, as a succession of days that began amiably and weakly, that became steadily more crowded with ignoble and trivial occupations, that had sunken now to indignity and uncleanness. He was overwhelmed by that persuasion, which only freshly soiled youth can feel in its extreme intensity, that life was slipping away from him, that the sands were running out, that in a little while his existence would be irretrievably lost.

By some trick of the imagination he saw life as an interminable Bond Street, lit up by night lamps, desolate, full of rubbish, full of the very best rubbish, trappings, temptations, and down it all he drove, as the damned drive, wearily, inexplicably.

What are we up to with life! What are we making of life!

But hadn't he intended to make something tremendous of life? Hadn't he come to London trailing a glory? . . .

He began to remember it as a project. It was the project of a great World-State sustained by an aristocracy of noble men. He was to have been one of those men, too fine and far-reaching for the dull manœuvres of such politics as rule the world to-day. The project seemed still large, still whitely noble, but now it was unlit and dead, and in the foreground he sat in the flat of Mrs. Skelmersdale, feeling dissipated and fumbling with his white tie. And she was looking tired. "God!" he said. "How did I get there?"

And then suddenly he reached out his arms in the darkness and prayed aloud to the silences.

"Oh, God! Give me back my visions! Give me back my visions!"

He could have imagined he heard a voice calling upon him to come out into life, to escape from the body of this death. But it was his own voice that called to him. . . .

§ 10

The need for action became so urgent in him, that he got right out of his bed and sat on the edge of it. Something had to be done at once. He did not know what it was but he felt that there could be no more sleep, no more rest, no dressing nor eating nor going forth before he came to decisions. Christian before his pilgrimage began was not more certain of this need of flight from the life of routine and vanities.

What was to be done?

In the first place he must get away and think about it all, think himself clear of all these — these immediacies, these associations and relations and holds and habits. He must get back to his vision, get back to the God in his vision. And to do that he must go alone.

He was clear he must go alone. It was useless to go to Prothero, one weak man going to a weaker. Prothero he was convinced could help him not at all, and the strange thing is that this conviction had come to him and had established itself incontestably because of that figure at the street corner, which had for just one moment resembled Prothero. By some fantastic intuition Benham knew that Prothero would not only participate but excuse. And he knew that he himself could endure no excuses. He must cut clear of any possibility of qualification. This thing had to be stopped. He must get away, he must get free, he must get clean. In the extravagance of his reaction Benham felt that he could endure nothing but solitary places and to sleep under the open sky.

He wanted to get right away from London and everybody and lie in the quiet darkness and stare up at the stars.

His plans grew so definite that presently he was in his dressing-gown and turning out the maps in the lower drawer of his study bureau. He would go down into Surrey with a knapsack, wander along the North Downs until the Guildford gap was reached, strike across the Weald country to the South Downs and then beat eastward. The very thought of it brought a coolness to his mind. He knew that over those southern hills one could be as lonely as in the wilderness and as free to talk to God. And there he would settle something. He would make a plan for his life and end this torment.

When Merkle came in to him in the morning he was fast asleep.

The familiar curtain rings awakened Benham. He turned his head over, stared for a moment and then remembered.

"Merkle," he said, "I am going for a walking tour. I am going off this morning. Haven't I a rücksack?"

"You 'ave a sort of canvas bag, sir, with pockets

to it," said Merkle. "Will you be needing the *very*
'eavy boots with 'obnails — Swiss, I fancy, sir —
or your ordinary shooting boots?"

"And when may I expect you back, sir?" asked
Merkle as the moment for departure drew near.

"God knows," said Benham, "I don't."

"Then will there be any address for forwarding
letters, sir?"

Benham hadn't thought of that. For a moment
he regarded Merkle's scrupulous respect with a
transient perplexity.

"I'll let you know, Merkle," he said. "I'll let
you know."

For some days at least, notes, telephone messages,
engagements, all this fuss and clamour about
nothing, should clamour for him in vain. . . .

§ 11

"But how closely," cried White, in a mood of
cultivated enthusiasm; "how closely must all the
poor little stories that we tell to-day follow in the
footsteps of the Great Exemplars! A little while
ago and the springtime freshness of Tobias irradiated
the page. Now see! it is Christian —."

Indeed it looked extremely like Christian as Benham went up across the springy turf from Epsom
Downs station towards the crest of the hill. Was he
not also fleeing in the morning sunlight from the
City of Destruction? Was he not also seeking that
better city whose name is Peace? And there was a
bundle on his back. It was the bundle, I think, that

seized most firmly upon the too literary imagination of White.

But the analogy of the bundle was a superficial one. Benham had not the slightest desire to lose it from his shoulders. It would have inconvenienced him very greatly if he had done so. It did not contain his sins. Our sins nowadays are not so easily separated. It contained a light, warm cape-coat he had bought in Switzerland and which he intended to wrap about him when he slept under the stars, and in addition Merkle had packed it with his silk pyjamas, an extra pair of stockings, tooth-brush, brush and comb, a safety razor. . . . And there were several sheets of the Ordnance map.

§ 12

The urgency of getting away from something dominated Benham to the exclusion of any thought of what he might be getting to. That muddle of his London life had to be left behind. First, escape. . . .

Over the downs great numbers of larks were singing. It was warm April that year and early. All the cloud stuff in the sky was gathered into great towering slow-sailing masses, and the rest was blue of the intensest. The air was so clean that Benham felt it clean in the substance of his body. The chestnuts down the hill to the right were flowering, the beeches were luminously green, and the oaks in the valley foaming gold. And sometimes it was one lark filled his ears, and sometimes he seemed to be

hearing all the larks for miles about him.   Presently
over the crest he would be out of sight of the grand
stand and the men exercising horses, and that brace
of red-jacketed golfers. . . .

What was he to do?

For a time he could think of nothing to do except
to keep up and out of the valley.   His whole being
seemed to have come to his surfaces to look out at
the budding of the year and hear the noise of the
birds.   And then he got into a long road from which
he had to escape, and trespassing southward through
plantations he reached the steep edge of the hills
and sat down over above a great chalk pit somewhere near Dorking and surveyed all the tumbled
wooded spaces of the Weald. . . .   It is after all
not so great a country this Sussex, nor so hilly,
from deepest valley to highest crest is not six hundred
feet, yet what a greatness of effect it can achieve!
There is something in those downland views which,
like sea views, lifts a mind out to the skies.   All
England it seemed was there to Benham's vision,
and the purpose of the English, and his own purpose
in the world.   For a long time he surveyed the large
delicacy of the detail before him, the crests, the tree-
protected houses, the fields and farmsteads, the
distant gleams of water.   And then he became
interested in the men who were working in the chalk
pit down below.

They at any rate were not troubled with the
problem of what to do with their lives.

M

§ 13

Benham found his mind was now running clear, and
so abundantly that he could scarcely, he felt, keep
pace with it. As he thought his flow of ideas was
tinged with a fear that he might forget what he was
thinking. In an instant, for the first time in his
mental existence, he could have imagined he had
discovered Labour and seen it plain. A little while
ago and he had seemed a lonely man among the
hills, but indeed he was not lonely, these men had
been with him all the time, and he was free to wander, to sit here, to think and choose simply because
those men down there were not free. *He was spending their leisure.* . . . Not once but many times
with Prothero had he used the phrase *Richesse
oblige*. Now he remembered it. He began to
remember a mass of ideas that had been overlaid
and stifling within him. This was what Merkle
and the club servants and the entertainments and
engagements and his mother and the artistic touts
and the theatrical touts and the hunting and the
elaboration of games and — Mrs. Skelmersdale
and all that had clustered thickly round him in
London had been hiding from him. Those men
below there had not been trusted to choose their
work; they had been given it. And he had been
trusted. . . .

And now to grapple with it! Now to get it clear!
What work was he going to do? That settled,
he would deal with his distractions readily enough.

Until that was settled he was lax and exposed to every passing breeze of invitation.

"What work am I going to do? What work am I going to do?" He repeated it.

It is the only question for the aristocrat. What amusement? That for a footman on holiday. That for a silly child, for any creature that is kept or led or driven. That perhaps for a tired invalid, for a toiler worked to a rag. But able-bodied amusement! The arms of Mrs. Skelmersdale were no worse than the solemn aimlessness of hunting, and an evening of dalliance not an atom more reprehensible than an evening of chatter. It was the waste of him that made the sin. His life in London had been of a piece together. It was well that his intrigue had set a light on it, put a point to it, given him this saving crisis of the nerves. That, indeed, is the chief superiority of idle love-making over other more prevalent forms of idleness and self-indulgence; it does at least bear its proper label. It is reprehensible. It brings your careless honour to the challenge of concealment and shabby evasions and lies. . . .

But in this pellucid air things took their proper proportions again.

And now what was he to do?

"Politics," he said aloud to the turf and the sky.

Is there any other work for an aristocratic man?
. . . Science? One could admit science in that larger sense that sweeps in History, or Philosophy. Beyond that whatever work there is is work for which men are paid. Art? Art is nothing aristo-

cratic except when it is a means of scientific or philosophical expression.   Art that does not argue nor
demonstrate nor discover is merely the craftsman's
impudence.

He pulled up at this and reflected for a time with
some distinguished instances in his mind.   They
were so distinguished, so dignified, they took their
various arts with so admirable a gravity that the
soul of this young man recoiled from the verdicts to
which his reasoning drove him.   "It's not for me
to judge them," he decided, "except in relation to
myself.   For them there may be tremendous signifi-
cances in Art.   But if these do not appear to me,
then so far as I am concerned they do not exist for
me.   They are not in my world.   So far as they
attempt to invade me and control my attitudes or
my outlook, or to judge me in any way, there is no
question of their impudence.   Impudence is the
word for it.   My world is real.   I want to be really
aristocratic, really brave, really paying for the privilege of not being a driven worker.   The things the
artist makes are like the things my private dream-
artist makes, relaxing, distracting.   What can Art at
its greatest be, pure Art that is, but a more splendid,
more permanent, transmissible reverie!   The very
essence of what I am after is *not* to be an artist. . . ."

After a large and serious movement through his
mind he came back to Science, Philosophy or Politics
as the sole three justifications for the usurpation of
leisure.

So far as devotion to science went, he knew he had

no specific aptitude for any departmentalized sub-
ject, and equally he felt no natural call to philosophy.
He was left with politics. . . .

"Or else, why shouldn't I go down there and pick
up a shovel and set to work? To make leisure for
my betters. . . ."

And now it was that he could take up the real
trouble that more than anything else had been keeping him ineffective and the prey of every chance
demand and temptation during the last ten months.
He had not been able to get himself into politics,
and the reason why he had not been able to do so
was that he could not induce himself to fit in.   Statecraft was a remote and faded thing in the political
life of the time; politics was a choice of two sides
in a game, and either side he found equally unattractive. Since he had come down from Cambridge
the Tariff Reform people had gone far to capture the
Conservative party. There was little chance of a
candidature for him without an adhesion to that.
And he could find nothing he could imagine himself
working for in the declarations of the Tariff Reform
people. He distrusted them, he disliked them.
They took all the light and pride out of imperialism,
they reduced it to a shabby conspiracy of the
British and their colonies against foreign industrialism. They were violent for armaments and hostile
to education. They could give him no assurance
of any scheme of growth and unification, and no
guarantees against the manifest dangers of economic
disturbance and political corruption a tariff involves.

Imperialism without noble imaginations, it seemed
to him, was simply nationalism with megalomania.
It was swaggering, it was greed, it was German; its
enthusiasm was forced, its nobility a vulgar lie.   No.
And when he turned to the opposite party he found
little that was more attractive.   They were prepared, it seemed, if they came into office, to pull the
legislature of the British Isles to pieces in obedience
to the Irish demand for Home Rule, and they were
totally unprepared with any scheme for doing this
that had even a chance of success.   In the twenty
years that had elapsed since Gladstone's hasty and
disastrous essay in political surgery they had studied
nothing, learnt nothing, produced no ideas whatever in the matter.   They had not had the time.
They had just negotiated, like the mere politicians
they were, for the Nationalist vote.   They seemed
to hope that by a marvel God would pacify Ulster.
Lord Dunraven, Plunkett, were voices crying in the
wilderness.   The sides in the party game would as
soon have heeded a poet. . . .   But unless Benham
was prepared to subscribe either to Home Rule or
Tariff Reform there was no way whatever open to
him into public life.   He had had some decisive
conversations.   He had no illusions left upon that
score. . . .

Here was the real barrier that had kept him in-
active for ten months.   Here was the problem he
had to solve.   This was how he had been left out of
active things, a prey to distractions, excitements,
idle temptations — and Mrs. Skelmersdale.

Running away to shoot big game or explore wildernesses was no remedy.   That was just running away. Aristocrats do not run away.   What of his debt to those men down there in the quarry?   What of his debt to the unseen men in the mines away in the north?   What of his debt to the stokers on the liners, and to the clerks in the city?   He reiterated the cardinal article of his creed : The aristocrat is a privileged man in order that he may be a public and political man.

But how is one to be a political man when one is not in politics?

Benham frowned at the Weald.   His ideas were running thin.

He might hammer at politics from the outside. And then again how?   He would make a list of all the things that he might do.   For example he might write.   He rested one hand on his knee and lifted one finger and regarded it.   *Could* he write?   There were one or two men who ran papers and seemed to have a sort of independent influence.   Strachey, for example, with his *Spectator;* Maxse, with his *National Review*.   But they were grown up, they had formed their ideas.   He had to learn first.

He lifted a second finger.   How to learn?   For it was learning that he had to do.

When one comes down from Oxford or Cambridge one falls into the mistake of thinking that learning is over and action must begin.   But until one perceives clearly just where one stands action is impossible.

How is one with no experience of affairs to get an

experience of affairs when the door of affairs is closed
to one by one's own convictions?   Outside of affairs
how can one escape being flimsy?   How can one
escape becoming merely an intellectual like those
wordy Fabians, those writers, poseurs, and sham
publicists whose wrangles he had attended?   And,
moreover, there is danger in the leisure of your
intellectual.   One cannot be always reading and
thinking and discussing and inquiring. . . . *Would
it not be better after all to make a concession, swallow
Home Rule or Tariff Reform, and so at least get his
hands on things?*

And then in a little while the party conflict would
swallow him up?

Still it would engage him, it would hold him.
If, perhaps, he did not let it swallow him up.   If
he worked with an eye open for opportunities of
self-assertion. . . .

The party game had not altogether swallowed
"Mr. Arthur." . . .

But every one is not a Balfour. . . .

He reflected profoundly.   On his left knee his left
hand rested with two fingers held up.   By some rapid
mental alchemy these fingers had now become Home
Rule and Tariff Reform.   His right hand which had
hitherto taken no part in the controversy, had raised
its index finger by imperceptible degrees.   It had
been raised almost subconsciously.   And by still
obscurer processes this finger had become Mrs.
Skelmersdale.   He recognized her sudden reappear-
ance above the threshold of consciousness with mild

surprise. He had almost forgotten her share in these problems. He had supposed her dismissed to an entirely subordinate position. . . .

Then he perceived that the workmen in the chalk pit far below had knocked off and were engaged upon their midday meal. He understood why his mind was no longer moving forward with any alacrity.

Food?

The question where he should eat arose abruptly and dismissed all other problems from his mind. He unfolded a map.

Here must be the chalk pit, here was Dorking. That village was Brockham Green. Should he go down to Dorking or this way over Box Hill to the little inn at Burford Bridge. He would try the latter.

§ 14

The April sunset found our young man talking to himself for greater emphasis, and wandering along a turfy cart-track through a wilderness mysteriously planted with great bushes of rhododendra on the Downs above Shere. He had eaten a belated lunch at Burford Bridge, he had got some tea at a little inn near a church with a splendid yew tree, and for the rest of the time he had wandered and thought. He had travelled perhaps a dozen or fifteen miles, and a good way from his first meditations above the Dorking chalk pit.

He had recovered long ago from that remarkable

conception of an active if dishonest political career as a means of escaping Mrs. Skelmersdale and all that Mrs. Skelmersdale symbolized. That would be just louting from one bad thing to another. He had to settle Mrs. Skelmersdale clean and right, and he had to do as exquisitely right in politics as he could devise. If the public life of the country had got itself into a stupid antagonism of two undesirable things, the only course for a sane man of honour was to stand out from the parties and try and get them back to sound issues again. There must be endless people of a mind with himself in this matter. And even if there were not, if he was the only man in the world, he still had to follow his lights and do the right. And his business was to find out the right. . . .

He came back from these imaginative excursions into contemporary politics with one idea confirmed in his mind, an idea that had been indeed already in his mind during his Cambridge days. This was the idea of working out for himself, thoroughly and completely, a political scheme, a theory of his work and duty in the world, a plan of the world's future that should give a rule for his life. The Research Magnificent was emerging. It was an alarmingly vast proposal, but he could see no alternative but submission, a plebeian's submission to the currents of life about him.

Little pictures began to flit before his imagination of the way in which he might build up this tremendous inquiry. He would begin by hunting up people,

everybody who seemed to have ideas and promise
ideas he would get at.   He would travel far — and
exhaustively.   He would, so soon as the ideas seemed
to indicate it, hunt out facts.   He would learn how
the world was governed.   He would learn how it did
its thinking.   He would live sparingly.   ("Not *too*
sparingly," something interpolated.)   He would
work ten or twelve hours a day.   Such a course of
investigation must pass almost of its own accord
into action and realization.   He need not trouble
now how it would bring him into politics.   Inevitably somewhere it would bring him into politics.
And he would travel.   Almost at once he would
travel.   It is the manifest duty of every young
aristocrat to travel.   Here he was, ruling India.
At any rate, passively, through the mere fact of
being English, he was ruling India.   And he knew
nothing of India.   He knew nothing indeed of Asia.
So soon as he returned to London his preparations
for this travel must begin, he must plot out the men
to whom he would go, and so contrive that also he
would go round the world.   Perhaps he would get
Lionel Maxim to go with him.   Or if Maxim could
not come, then possibly Prothero.   Some one surely
could be found, some one thinking and talking of
statecraft and the larger idea of life.   All the world
is not swallowed up in every day. . . .

§ 15

His mind shifted very suddenly from these large
proposals to an entirely different theme.   These

mental landslips are not unusual when men are thinking hard and wandering. He found himself holding
a trial upon himself for Presumptuousness, for setting
himself up against the wisdom of the ages, and the
decisions of all the established men in the world, for
being in short a Presumptuous Sort of Ass. He was
judge and jury and prosecutor, but rather inexplicably the defence was conducted in an irregular and
undignified way by some inferior stratum of his
being.

At first the defence contented itself with arguments
that did at least aim to rebut the indictment. The
decisions of all the established men in the world were
notoriously in conflict. However great was the
gross wisdom of the ages the net wisdom was remarkably small. Was it after all so very immodest
to believe that the Liberals were right in what they
said about Tariff Reform, and the Tories right in their
criticism of Home Rule?

And then suddenly the defence threw aside its
mask and insisted that Benham had to take this
presumptuous line because there was no other
tolerable line possible for him.

"Better die with the Excelsior chap up the mountains," the defence interjected.

Than what?

Consider the quality Benham had already betrayed. He was manifestly incapable of a decent
modest mediocre existence. Already he had ceased
to be — if one may use so fine a word for genteel
abstinence — virtuous. He didn't ride well, he

hadn't good hands, and he hadn't good hands for
life.   He must go hard and harsh, high or low.   He
was a man who needed *bite* in his life.   He was exceptionally capable of boredom.   He had been bored
by London.   Social occasions irritated him, several
times he had come near to gross incivilities, art annoyed him, sport was an effort, wholesome perhaps,
but unattractive, music he loved, but it excited him.
The defendant broke the sunset calm by uttering
amazing and improper phrases.

"I can't smug about in a state of falsified righteousness like these Crampton chaps.

"I shall roll in women.   I shall rollick in women.
If, that is, I stay in London with nothing more to do
than I have had this year past.

"I've been sliding fast to it. . . .

"No!   I'm damned if I do! . . ."

§ 16

For some time he had been bothered by a sense
of something, something else, awaiting his attention.
Now it came swimming up into his consciousness.
He had forgotten.   He was, of course, going to sleep
out under the stars.

He had settled that overnight, that was why he had
this cloak in his rücksack, but he had settled none of
the details.   Now he must find some place where he
could lie down.   Here, perhaps, in this strange forgotten wilderness of rhododendra.

He turned off from the track and wandered among
the bushes.   One might lie down anywhere here.

But not yet; it was as yet barely twilight. He consulted his watch. *Half-past seven.*

Nearly dinner-time. . . .

No doubt Christian during the earlier stages of his pilgrimage noticed the recurrence of the old familiar hours of his life of emptiness and vanity. Or rather of vanity — simply. Why drag in the thought of emptiness just at this point? . . .

It was very early to go to bed.

He might perhaps sit and think for a time. Here for example was a mossy bank, a seat, and presently a bed. So far there were only three stars visible but more would come. He dropped into a reclining attitude. *Damp!*

When one thinks of sleeping out under the stars one is apt to forget the dew.

He spread his Swiss cloak out on the soft thick carpeting of herbs and moss, and arranged his knapsack as a pillow. Here he would lie and recapitulate the thoughts of the day. (That squealing might be a young fox.) At the club at present men would be sitting about holding themselves back from dinner. Excellent the clear soup always was at the club! Then perhaps a Chateaubriand. That — what was that? Soft and large and quite near and noiseless. An owl!

The damp feeling was coming through his cloak. And this April night air had a knife edge. Early ice coming down the Atlantic perhaps. It was wonderful to be here on the top of the round world and feel the icebergs away there. Or did this wind

come from Russia? He wasn't quite clear just how
he was oriented, he had turned about so much.
Which was east? Anyhow it was an extremely cold
wind.

What had he been thinking? Suppose after all
that ending with Mrs. Skelmersdale was simply a
beginning. So far he had never looked sex in the
face. . . .

He sat up and sneezed violently.

It would be ridiculous to start out seeking the clue
to one's life and be driven home by rheumatic fever.
One should not therefore incur the risk of rheumatic
fever.

Something squealed in the bushes.

It was impossible to collect one's thoughts in this
place. He stood up. The night was going to be
bitterly cold, savagely, cruelly cold. . . .

No. There was no thinking to be done here, no
thinking at all. He would go on along the track
and presently he would strike a road and so come to
an inn. One can solve no problems when one is
engaged in a struggle with the elements. The thing
to do now was to find that track again. . . .

It took Benham two hours of stumbling and
walking, with a little fence climbing and some barbed
wire thrown in, before he got down into Shere to the
shelter of a friendly little inn. And then he negotiated a satisfying meal, with beef-steak as its central fact, and stipulated for a fire in his bedroom.

The landlord was a pleasant-faced man; he attended to Benham himself and displayed a fine sense

of comfort. He could produce wine, a half-bottle
of Australian hock, Big Tree brand No. 8, a virile
wine, he thought of sardines to precede the meal, he
provided a substantial Welsh rarebit by way of a
savoury, he did not mind in the least that it was
nearly ten o'clock. He ended by suggesting coffee.
"And a liqueur?"

Benham had some Benedictine!

One could not slight such sympathetic helpfulness.
The Benedictine was genuine. And then came the
coffee.

The cup of coffee was generously conceived and
honestly made.

A night of clear melancholy ensued. . . .

§ 17

Hitherto Benham had not faced in any detail the
problem of how to break with Mrs. Skelmersdale.
Now he faced it pessimistically. She would, he
knew, be difficult to break with. (He ought never
to have gone there to lunch.) There would be something ridiculous in breaking off. In all sorts of ways
she might resist. And face to face with her he might
find himself a man divided against himself. That
opened preposterous possibilities. On the other hand
it was out of the question to do the business by
letter. A letter hits too hard; it lies too heavy on
the wound it has made. And in money matters
he could be generous. He must be generous. At
least financial worries need not complicate her distresses of desertion. But to suggest such gener-

osities on paper, in cold ink, would be outrageous.
And, in brief — he ought not to have gone there
to lunch. After that he began composing letters
at a great rate. Delicate — explanatory. Was it
on the whole best to be explanatory? . . .

It was going to be a tremendous job, this breaking
with her. And it had begun so easily. . . .

There was, he remembered with amazing vivid-
ness, a little hollow he had found under her ear, and
how when he kissed her there it always made her
forget her worries and ethical problems for a time
and turn to him. . . .

"No," he said grimly, "it must end," and rolled
over and stared at the black. . . .

Like an insidious pedlar, that old rascal whom
young literary gentlemen call the Great God Pan,
began to spread his wares in the young man's
memory. . . .

After long and feverish wanderings of the mind,
and some talking to himself and walking about the
room, he did at last get a little away from Mrs.
Skelmersdale.

He perceived that when he came to tell his mother
about this journey around the world there would be
great difficulties. She would object very strongly,
and if that did not do then she would become extremely abusive, compare him to his father, cry
bitterly, and banish him suddenly and heartbrokenly
from her presence for ever. She had done that
twice already — once about going to the opera
instead of listening to a lecture on Indian ethnology

N

and once about a week-end in Kent. . . . He hated hurting his mother, and he was beginning to know now how easily she was hurt. It is an abominable thing to hurt one's mother — whether one has a justification or whether one hasn't.

Recoiling from this, he was at once resumed by Mrs. Skelmersdale. Who had in fact an effect of really never having been out of the room. But now he became penitent about her. His penitence expanded until it was on a nightmare scale. At last it blotted out the heavens. He felt like one of those unfortunate victims of religious mania who are convinced they have committed the Sin against the Holy Ghost. (Why had he gone there to lunch? That was the key to it. *Why* had he gone there to lunch?) . . . He began to have remorse for everything, for everything he had ever done, for everything he had ever not done, for everything in the world. In a moment of lucidity he even had remorse for drinking that stout honest cup of black coffee. . . .

And so on and so on and so on. . . .

When daylight came it found Benham still wide awake. Things crept mournfully out of the darkness into a reproachful clearness. The sound of birds that had been so delightful on the yesterday was now no longer agreeable. The thrushes, he thought, repeated themselves a great deal.

He fell asleep as it seemed only a few minutes before the landlord, accompanied by a great smell of frying bacon, came to call him.

§ 18

The second day opened rather dully for Benham.
There was not an idea left in his head about anything in the world. It was — *solid*. He walked
through Bramley and Godalming and Witley and
so came out upon the purple waste of Hindhead.
He strayed away from the road and found a sunny
place of turf amidst the heather and lay down and
slept for an hour or so. He arose refreshed. He
got some food at the Huts Inn on the Hindhead
crest and went on across sunlit heathery wildernesses
variegated by patches of spruce and fir and silver
birch. And then suddenly his mental inanition was
at an end and his thoughts were wide and brave
again. He was astonished that for a moment he
could have forgotten that he was vowed to the
splendid life.

"Continence by preoccupation;" he tried the
phrase. . . .

"A man must not give in to fear; neither must
he give in to sex. It's the same thing really. The
misleading of instinct."

This set the key of his thought throughout the
afternoon — until Amanda happened to him.

CHAPTER THE THIRD

AMANDA

§ 1

AMANDA happened to Benham very suddenly.

From Haslemere he had gone on to further heaths and gorse beyond Liphook, and thence he had wandered into a pretty district beset with Hartings. He had found himself upon a sandy ridge looking very beautifully into a sudden steep valley that he learnt was Harting Coombe; he had been through a West Harting and a South Harting and read finger-posts pointing to others of the clan; and in the evening, at the foot of a steep hill where two roads met, he sat down to consider whether he should go back and spend the night in one of the two kindly-looking inns of the latter place or push on over the South Downs towards the unknown luck of Singleton or Chichester. As he sat down two big retrievers, black and brown, came headlong down the road. The black carried a stick, the brown disputed and pursued. As they came abreast of him the foremost a little relaxed his hold, the pursuer grabbed at it, and in an instant the rivalry had flared to rage and a first-class dog-fight was in progress.

Benham detested dog-fights. He stood up, pale

180

and distressed. "Lie down!" he cried. "Shut up, you brutes!" and was at a loss for further action.

Then it was Amanda leapt into his world, a light, tall figure of a girl, fluttering a short petticoat. Hatless she was, brown, flushed, and her dark hair tossing loose, and in a moment she had the snarling furious dogs apart, each gripped firmly by its collar. Then with a wriggle black was loose and had closed again. Inspired by the best traditions of chivalry Benham came to her assistance. He was not expert with dogs. He grasped the black dog under its ear. He was bitten in the wrist, rather in excitement than malice, and with a certain excess of zeal he was strangling the brute before you could count ten.

Amanda seized the fallen stick and whacked the dog she held, reasonably but effectively until its yelps satisfied her. "There!" she said pitching her victim from her, and stood erect again. She surveyed the proceedings of her helper for the first time.

"You needn't," she said, "choke Sultan any more."

"Ugh!" she said, as though that was enough for Sultan. And peace was restored.

"I'm obliged to you. But — . . . I say! He didn't bite you, did he? Oh, *Sultan!*"

Sultan tried to express his disgust at the affair. Rotten business. When a fellow is fighting one can't be meticulous. And if people come interfering. Still — *sorry!* So Sultan by his code of eye and tail.

"May I see? . . . Something ought to be done to this. . . ."

She took his wrist in her hand, and her cheek and eyelashes came within a foot of his face.

Some observant element in his composition guessed, and guessed quite accurately, that she was nineteen. . . .

§ 2

She had an eyebrow like a quick stroke of a camel's-hair brush, she had a glowing face, half childish imp, half woman, she had honest hazel eyes, a voice all music, a manifest decision of character. And he must have this bite seen to at once. She lived not five minutes away. He must come with her.

She had an aunt who behaved like a mother and a mother who behaved like a genteel visitor, and they both agreed with Amanda that although Mr. Walter Long and his dreadful muzzles and everything did seem to have stamped out rabies, yet you couldn't be too careful with a dog bite. A dog bite might be injurious in all sorts of ways — particularly Sultan's bite. He was, they had to confess, a dog without refinement, a coarse-minded omnivorous dog. Both the elder ladies insisted upon regarding Benham's wound as clear evidence of some gallant rescue of Amanda from imminent danger — "she's always so *reckless* with those dogs," as though Amanda was not manifestly capable of taking care of herself; and when he had been Listerined and bandaged, they would have it that he should join them at their supper-dinner, which was already prepared and waiting. They treated him as if he were still an undergraduate, they took his arrangements in hand as though he was a favourite nephew. He must stay in Harting that night. Both the Ship and the Coach and Horses were excellent inns, and over the Downs there would be nothing for miles and miles. . . .

The house was a little long house with a verandah and a garden in front of it with flint-edged paths; the room in which they sat and ate was long and low and equipped with pieces of misfitting good furniture, an accidental-looking gilt tarnished mirror, and a sprinkling of old and middle-aged books. Some one had lit a fire, which cracked and spurted about cheerfully in a motherly fireplace, and a lamp and some candles got lit. Mrs. Wilder, Amanda's aunt, a comfortable dark broad-browed woman, directed things, and sat at the end of the table and placed Benham on her right hand between herself and Amanda. Amanda's mother remained undeveloped, a watchful little woman with at least an eyebrow like her daughter's. Her name, it seemed, was Morris. No servant appeared, but two cousins of a vague dark picturesqueness and with a stamp of thirty upon them, the first young women Benham had ever seen dressed in djibbahs, sat at the table or moved about and attended to the simple needs of the service. The reconciled dogs were in the room and shifted inquiring noses from one human being to another.

Amanda's people were so easy and intelligent and friendly, and Benham after his thirty hours of silence so freshly ready for human association, that in a very little while he could have imagined he had known and trusted this household for years. He had never met such people before, and yet there was something about them that seemed familiar — and then it occurred to him that something of their easy-going freedom was to be found in Russian novels. A photographic enlargement of somebody with a vegetarian expression of face and a special kind of slouch hat gave the atmosphere a flavour of Socialism, and a press and tools and stamps and pigments on an oak table in the corner suggested some such socialistic art as bookbinding. They were clearly 'advanced' people. And Amanda was tremendously important to them, she was their light, their pride, their most living thing. They focussed on her. When he talked to them all in general he talked to her in particular. He felt that some introduction of himself was due to these welcoming people. He tried to give it mixed with an itinerary and a sketch of his experiences. He praised the heather country and Harting Coombe and the Hartings. He told them that London had suddenly become intolerable — "In the spring sunshine."

"You live in London?" said Mrs. Wilder.

Yes. And he had wanted to think things out. In London one could do no thinking —

"Here we do nothing else," said Amanda.

"Except dog-fights," said the elder cousin.

"I thought I would just wander and think and

sleep in the open air. Have you ever tried to sleep in the open air?"

"In the summer we all do," said the younger cousin. "Amanda makes us. We go out on to the little lawn at the back."

"You see Amanda has some friends at Limpsfield. And there they all go out and camp and sleep in the woods."

"Of course," reflected Mrs. Wilder, "in April it must be different."

"It *is* different," said Benham with feeling; "the night comes five hours too soon. And it comes wet." He described his experiences and his flight to Shere and the kindly landlord and the cup of coffee. "And after that I thought with a vengeance."

"Do you write things?" asked Amanda abruptly, and it seemed to him with a note of hope.

"No. No, it was just a private puzzle. It was something I couldn't get straight."

"And you have got it straight?" asked Amanda.

"I think so."

"You were making up your mind about something?"

"Amanda *dear!*" cried her mother.

"Oh! I don't mind telling you," said Benham.

They seemed such unusual people that he was moved to unusual confidences. They had that effect one gets at times with strangers freshly met as though they were not really in the world. And there was something about Amanda that made him want to explain himself to her completely.

"What I wanted to think about was what I should do with my life."

"Haven't you any *work* —?" asked the elder cousin.

"None that I'm obliged to do."

"That's where a man has the advantage," said Amanda with the tone of profound reflection. "You can choose. And what are you going to do with your life?"

"Amanda," her mother protested, "really you mustn't!"

"I'm going round the world to think about it," Benham told her.

"I'd give my soul to travel," said Amanda.

She addressed her remark to the salad in front of her.

"But have you no ties?" asked Mrs. Wilder.

"None that hold me," said Benham. "I'm one of those unfortunates who needn't do anything at all. I'm independent. You see my riddles. East and west and north and south, it's all my way for the taking. There's not an indication."

"If I were you," said Amanda, and reflected. Then she half turned herself to him. "I should go first to India," she said, "and I should shoot, one, two, three, yes, three tigers. And then I would see Farukhabad Sikri — I was reading in a book about it yesterday — where the jungle grows in the palaces; and then I would go right up the Himalayas, and then, then I would have a walking tour in Japan, and then I would sail in a sailing ship down

to Borneo and Java and set myself up as a Ranee —
. . . And then I would think what I would do
next."

"All alone, Amanda?" asked Mrs. Wilder.

"Only when I shoot tigers. You and mother
should certainly come to Japan."

"But Mr. Benham perhaps doesn't intend to
shoot tigers, Amanda?" said Amanda's mother.

"Not at once. My way will be a little different.
I think I shall go first through Germany. And then
down to Constantinople. And then I've some idea
of getting across Asia Minor and Persia to India.
That would take some time. One must ride."

"Asia Minor ought to be fun," said Amanda.
"But I should prefer India because of the tigers. It
would be so jolly to begin with the tigers right away."

"It is the towns and governments and peoples I
want to see rather than tigers," said Benham.
"Tigers if they are in the programme. But I want
to find out about — other things."

"Don't you think there's something to be found
out at home?" said the elder cousin, blushing very
brightly and speaking with the effort of one who
speaks for conscience' sake.

"Betty's a Socialist," Amanda said to Benham with
a suspicion of apology.

"Well, we're all rather that," Mrs. Wilder protested.

"If you are free, if you are independent, then don't
you owe something to the workers?" Betty went on,
getting graver and redder with each word.

"It's just because of that," said Benham, "that I am going round the world."

§ 3

He was as free with these odd people as if he had been talking to Prothero. They were — alert. And he had been alone and silent and full of thinking for two clear days. He tried to explain why he found Socialism at once obvious and inadequate. . . .

Presently the supper things got themselves put away and the talk moved into a smaller room with several armchairs and a fire. Mrs. Wilder and the cousins and Amanda each smoked a cigarette as if it were symbolical, and they were joined by a grave grey-bearded man with a hyphenated name and slightly Socratic manner, dressed in a very blue linen shirt and collar, a very woolly mustard-coloured suit and loose tie, and manifestly devoted to one of those branches of exemplary domestic decoration that grow upon Socialist soil in England. He joined Betty in the opinion that the duty of a free and wealthy young man was to remain in England and give himself to democratic Socialism and the abolition of "profiteering." "Consider that chair," he said. But Benham had little feeling for the craftsmanship of chairs.

Under cross-examination Mr. Rathbone-Sanders became entangled and prophetic. It was evident he had never thought out his "democratic," he had rested in some vague tangle of idealism from which Benham now set himself with the zeal of a specialist

to rout him. Such an argument sprang up as one
meets with rarely beyond the happy undergraduate's
range. Everybody lived in the discussion, even
Amanda's mother listened visibly. Betty said she
herself was certainly democratic and Mrs. Wilder
had always thought herself to be so, and outside the
circle round the fire Amanda hovered impatiently,
not quite sure of her side as yet, but eager to come
down with emphasis at the first flash of intimation.

She came down vehemently on Benham's.

And being a very clear-cutting personality with
an instinct for the material rendering of things, she
also came and sat beside him on the little square-
cornered sofa.

"Of course, Mr. Rathbone-Sanders," she said, "of
course the world must belong to the people who dare.
Of course people aren't all alike, and dull people,
as Mr. Benham says, and spiteful people, and narrow people have no right to any voice at all in
things. . . ."

§ 4

In saying this she did but echo Benham's very
words, and all she said and did that evening was in
quick response to Benham's earnest expression of his
views. She found Benham a delightful novelty.
She liked to argue because there was no other talk
so lively, and she had perhaps a lurking intellectual
grudge against Mr. Rathbone-Sanders that made
her welcome an ally. Everything from her that
night that even verges upon the notable has been

told, and yet it sufficed, together with something in the clear, long line of her limbs, in her voice, in her general physical quality, to convince Benham that she was the freest, finest, bravest spirit that he had ever encountered.

In the papers he left behind him was to be found his perplexed endeavours to explain this mental leap, that after all his efforts still remained unexplained. He had been vividly impressed by the decision and courage of her treatment of the dogs; it was just the sort of thing he could not do. And there was a certain contagiousness in the petting admiration with which her family treated her. But she was young and healthy and so was he, and in a second mystery lies the key of the first. He had fallen in love with her, and that being so whatever he needed that instantly she was. He needed a companion, clean and brave and understanding. . . .

In his bed in the Ship that night he thought of nothing but her before he went to sleep, and when next morning he walked on his way over the South Downs to Chichester his mind was full of her image and of a hundred pleasant things about her. In his confessions he wrote, "I felt there was a sword in her spirit. I felt she was as clean as the wind."

Love is the most chastening of powers, and he did not even remember now that two days before he had told the wind and the twilight that he would certainly "roll and rollick in women" unless there was work for him to do. She had a peculiarly swift and

easy stride that went with him in his thoughts along
the turf by the wayside halfway and more to Chichester. He thought always of the two of them as
being side by side. His imagination became child-
ishly romantic. The open down about him with its
scrub of thorn and yew became the wilderness of the
world, and through it they went — in armour,
weightless armour — and they wore long swords.
There was a breeze blowing and larks were singing
and something, something dark and tortuous dashed
suddenly in headlong flight from before their feet.
It was an ethical problem such as those Mrs. Skelmersdale nursed in her bosom. But at the sight of
Amanda it had straightened out — and fled. . . .

And interweaving with such imaginings, he was
some day to record, there were others. She had
brought back to his memory the fancies that had
been aroused in his first reading of Plato's *Republic;*
she made him think of those women Guardians, who
were the friends and mates of men. He wanted
now to re-read that book and the *Laws.* He could
not remember if the Guardians were done in the *Laws*
as well as in the *Republic.* He wished he had both
these books in his rücksack, but as he had not, he
decided he would hunt for them in Chichester.
When would he see Amanda again? He would ask
his mother to make the acquaintance of these very
interesting people, but as they did not come to
London very much it might be some time before he
had a chance of seeing her again. And, besides, he
was going to America and India. The prospect of an

exploration of the world was still noble and attractive; but he realized it would stand very much in the way of his seeing more of Amanda. Would it be a startling and unforgivable thing if presently he began to write to her? Girls of that age and spirit living in out-of-the-way villages have been known to marry. . . .

Marriage didn't at this stage strike Benham as an agreeable aspect of Amanda's possibilities; it was an inconvenience; his mind was running in the direction of pedestrian tours in armour of no particular weight, amidst scenery of a romantic wildness. . . .

When he had gone to the house and taken his leave that morning it had seemed quite in the vein of the establishment that he should be received by Amanda alone and taken up the long garden before anybody else appeared, to see the daffodils and the early apple-trees in blossom and the pear-trees white and delicious.

Then he had taken his leave of them all and made his social tentatives. Did they ever come to London? When they did they must let his people know. He would so like them to know his mother, Lady Marayne. And so on with much gratitude.

Amanda had said that she and the dogs would come with him up the hill, she had said it exactly as a boy might have said it, she had brought him up to the corner of Up Park and had sat down there on a heap of stones and watched him until he was out of sight, waving to him when he looked back. "Come back again," she had cried.

In Chichester he found a little green-bound *Re-publedic* in a second-hand book-shop near the Cathedral, but there was no copy of the *Laws* to be found in the place. Then he was taken with the brilliant idea of sleeping the night in Chichester and going back next day viâ Harting to Petersfield station and London. He carried out this scheme and got to South Harting neatly about four o'clock in the afternoon. He found Mrs. Wilder and Mrs. Morris and Amanda and the dogs entertaining Mr. Rathbone-Sanders at tea, and they all seemed a little surprised, and, except Mr. Rathbone-Sanders, they all seemed pleased to see him again so soon. His explanation of why he hadn't gone back to London from Chichester struck him as a little unconvincing in the cold light of Mr. Rathbone-Sanders' eye. But Amanda was manifestly excited by his return, and he told them his impressions of Chichester and described the entertainment of the evening guest at a country inn and suddenly produced his copy of the *Republic*. "I found this in a book-shop," he said, "and I brought it for you, because it describes one of the best dreams of aristocracy there has ever been dreamt."

At first she praised it as a pretty book in the dearest little binding, and then realized that there were deeper implications, and became grave and said she would read it through and through, she loved such speculative reading.

She came to the door with the others and stayed at the door after they had gone in again. When he

o

looked back at the corner of the road to Petersfield she was still at the door and waved farewell to him.

He only saw a light slender figure, but when she came back into the sitting-room Mr. Rathbone-Sanders noted the faint flush in her cheek and an unwonted abstraction in her eye.

And in the evening she tucked her feet up in the armchair by the lamp and read the *Republic* very intently and very thoughtfully, occasionally turning over a page.

<h2 style="text-align:center">§ 5</h2>

When Benham got back to London he experienced an unwonted desire to perform his social obligations to the utmost.

So soon as he had had some dinner at his club he wrote his South Harting friends a most agreeable letter of thanks for their kindness to him. In a little while he hoped he should see them again. His mother, too, was most desirous to meet them. . . . That done, he went on to his flat and to various aspects of life for which he was quite unprepared.

But here we may note that Amanda answered him. Her reply came some four days later. It was written in a square schoolgirl hand, it covered three sheets of notepaper, and it was a very intelligent essay upon the *Republic* of Plato. "Of course," she wrote, "the Guardians are inhuman, but it was a glorious sort of inhumanity. They had a spirit — like sharp knives cutting through life."

It was her best bit of phrasing and it pleased

Benham very much. But, indeed, it was not her
own phrasing, she had culled it from a disquisition
into which she had led Mr. Rathbone-Sanders, and
she had sent it to Benham as she might have sent
him a flower.

§ 6

Benham re-entered the flat from which he had fled
so precipitately with three very definite plans in his
mind. The first was to set out upon his grand tour
of the world with as little delay as possible, to shut
up this Finacue Street establishment for a long time,
and get rid of the soul-destroying perfections of
Merkle. The second was to end his ill-advised
intimacy with little Mrs. Skelmersdale as generously
and cheerfully as possible. The third was to bring
Lady Marayne into social relations with the Wilder
and Morris *ménage* at South Harting. It did not
strike him that there was any incompatibility among
these projects or any insurmountable difficulty in
any of them until he was back in his flat.

The accumulation of letters, packages and telephone
memoranda upon his desk included a number of
notes and slips to remind him that both Mrs. Skelmersdale and his mother were ladies of some determination. Even as he stood turning over the pile
of documents the mechanical vehemence of the telephone filled him with a restored sense of the adverse
will in things. "Yes, mam," he heard Merkle's
voice, "yes, mam. I will tell him, mam. Will
you keep possession, mam." And then in the door-

way of the study, "Mrs. Skelmersdale, sir. Upon the telephone, sir."

Benham reflected with various notes in his hand. Then he went to the telephone.

"You Wicked Boy, where have you been hiding?"

"I've been away. I may have to go away again."

"Not before you have seen me. Come round and tell me all about it."

Benham lied about an engagement.

"Then to-morrow in the morning." . . . Impossible.

"In the afternoon. You don't *want* to see me." Benham did want to see her.

"Come round and have a jolly little evening to-morrow night. I've got some more of that harpsichord music. And I'm dying to see you. Don't you understand?"

Further lies. "Look here," said Benham, "can you come and have a talk in Kensington Gardens? You know the place, near that Chinese garden. Paddington Gate. . . ."

The lady's voice fell to flatness. She agreed. "But why not come to see me *here?*" she asked.

Benham hung up the receiver abruptly.

He walked slowly back to his study. "Phew!" he whispered to himself. It was like hitting her in the face. He didn't want to be a brute, but short of being a brute there was no way out for him from this entanglement. Why, oh! why the devil had he gone there to lunch? . . .

He resumed his examination of the waiting letters

with a ruffled mind. The most urgent thing about
them was the clear evidence of gathering anger on
the part of his mother. He had missed a lunch
party at Sir Godfrey's on Tuesday and a dinner
engagement at Philip Magnet's, quite an important
dinner in its way, with various promising young
Liberals, on Wednesday evening. And she was
furious at "this stupid mystery. Of course you're
bound to be found out, and of course there will be a
scandal." . . . He perceived that this last note
was written on his own paper. "Merkle!" he cried
sharply.

"Yessir!"

Merkle had been just outside, on call.

"Did my mother write any of these notes here?"
he asked.

"Two, sir. Her ladyship was round here three
times, sir."

"Did she see all these letters?"

"Not the telephone calls, sir. I 'ad put them on
one side. But . . . It's a little thing, sir."

He paused and came a step nearer. "You see,
sir," he explained with the faintest flavour of the
confidential softening his mechanical respect, "yesterday, when 'er ladyship was 'ere, sir, some one rang
up on the telephone —"

"But you, Merkle —"

"Exactly, sir. But 'er ladyship said '*I'll* go to
that, Merkle,' and just for a moment I couldn't
exactly think 'ow I could manage it, sir, and there
'er ladyship was, at the telephone. What passed,

sir, I couldn't 'ear. I 'eard her say, 'Any message?'
And I *fancy*, sir, I 'eard 'er say, 'I'm the 'ousemaid,'
but that, sir, I think must have been a mistake,
sir.''

"Must have been," said Benham. "Certainly —
must have been. And the call you think came
from — ?''

"There again, sir, I'm quite in the dark. But of
course, sir, it's usually Mrs. Skelmersdale, sir.
Just about her time in the afternoon. On an average, sir. . . .''

§ 7

"I went out of London to think about my life."
It was manifest that Lady Marayne did not believe him.

"Alone?" she asked.

"Of course alone."

"*Stuff!*" said Lady Marayne.

She had taken him into her own little sitting-room,
she had thrown aside gloves and fan and theatre
wrap, curled herself comfortably into the abundantly cushioned corner by the fire, and proceeded
to a mixture of cross-examination and tirade that he
found it difficult to make head against. She was
vibrating between distressed solicitude and resentful anger. She was infuriated at his going away and
deeply concerned at what could have taken him
away. "I was worried," he said. "London is too
crowded to think in. I wanted to get myself alone."

"And there I was while you were getting yourself

alone, as you call it, wearing my poor little brains out
to think of some story to tell people. I had to stuff
them up you had a sprained knee at Chexington,
and for all I knew any of them might have been
seeing you that morning. Besides what has a boy
like you to worry about? It's all nonsense, Poff."

She awaited his explanations. Benham looked
for a moment like his father.

"I'm not getting on, mother," he said. "I'm
scattering myself. I'm getting no grip. I want to
get a better hold upon life, or else I do not see what
is to keep me from going to pieces — and wasting
existence. It's rather difficult sometimes to tell
what one thinks and feels —"

She had not really listened to him.

"Who is that woman," she interrupted suddenly,
"Mrs. Fly-by-Night, or some such name, who rings
you up on the telephone?"

Benham hesitated, blushed, and regretted it.

"Mrs. Skelmersdale," he said after a little pause.

"It's all the same. Who is she?"

"She's a woman I met at a studio somewhere, and
I went with her to one of those Dolmetsch concerts."

He stopped.

Lady Marayne considered him in silence for a
little while. "All men," she said at last, "are alike.
Husbands, sons and brothers, they are all alike.
Sons! One expects them to be different. They
aren't different. Why should they be? I suppose
I ought to be shocked, Poff. But I'm not. She
seems to be very fond of you."

"She's — she's very good — in her way. She's had a difficult life. . . ."

"You can't leave a man about for a moment," Lady Marayne reflected. "Poff, I wish you'd fetch me a glass of water."

When he returned she was looking very fixedly into the fire. "Put it down," she said, "anywhere. Poff! is this Mrs. Helter-Skelter a discreet sort of woman? Do you like her?" She asked a few additional particulars and Benham made his grudging admission of facts. "What I still don't understand, Poff, is why you have been away."

"I went away," said Benham, "because I want to clear things up."

"But why? Is there some one else?"

"No."

"You went alone? All the time?"

"I've told you I went alone. Do you think I tell you lies, mother?"

"Everybody tells lies somehow," said Lady Marayne. "Easy lies or stiff ones. Don't *flourish*, Poff. Don't start saying things like a moral windmill in a whirlwind. It's all a muddle. I suppose every one in London is getting in or out of these entanglements — or something of the sort. And this seems a comparatively slight one. I wish it hadn't happened. They do happen."

An expression of perplexity came into her face. She looked at him. "Why do you want to throw her over?"

"I *want* to throw her over," said Benham.

He stood up and went to the hearthrug, and his mother reflected that this was exactly what all men did at just this phase of a discussion. Then things ceased to be sensible.

From overhead he said to her: "I want to get away from this complication, this servitude. I want to do some — some work. I want to get my mind clear and my hands clear. I want to study government and the big business of the world."

"And she's in the way?"

He assented.

"You men!" said Lady Marayne after a little pause. "What queer beasts you are! Here is a woman who is kind to you. She's fond of you. I could tell she's fond of you directly I heard her. And you amuse yourself with her. And then it's Gobble, Gobble, Gobble, Great Work, Hands Clear, Big Business of the World. Why couldn't you think of that before, Poff? Why did you begin with her?"

"It was unexpected. . . ."

"*Stuff!*" said Lady Marayne for a second time.

"Well," she said, "well. Your Mrs. Fly-by-Night, — oh it doesn't matter! — whatever she calls herself, must look after herself. I can't do anything for her. I'm not supposed even to know about her. I daresay she'll find her consolations. I suppose you want to go out of London and get away from it all. I can help you there, perhaps. I'm tired of London too. It's been a tiresome season. Oh! tiresome and disappointing! I want to go over to Ireland and travel about a little. The

Pothercareys want us to come. They've asked us twice. . . ."

Benham braced himself to face fresh difficulties. It was amazing how different the world could look from his mother's little parlour and from the crest of the North Downs.

"But I want to start round the world," he cried with a note of acute distress. "I want to go to Egypt and India and see what is happening in the East, all this wonderful waking up of the East, I know nothing of the way the world is going — . . ."

"India!" cried Lady Marayne. "The East. Poff, what is the *matter* with you? Has something happened — something else? Have you been having a love affair? — a *real* love affair?"

"Oh, *damn* love affairs!" cried Benham. "Mother! — I'm sorry, mother! But don't you see there's other things in the world for a man than having a good time and making love. I'm for something else than that. You've given me the splendidest time — . . ."

"I see," cried Lady Marayne, "I see. I've bored you. I might have known I should have bored you."

"You've *not* bored me!" cried Benham.

He threw himself on the rug at her feet. "Oh, mother!" he said, "little, dear, gallant mother, don't make life too hard for me. I've got to do my job, I've got to find my job."

"I've bored you," she wept.

Suddenly she was weeping with all the unconcealed

distressing grief of a disappointed child. She put
her pretty be-ringed little hands in front of her face
and recited the accumulation of her woes.

"I've done all I can for you, planned for you,
given all my time for you and I've *bored* you."

"Mother!"

"Don't come near me, Poff! Don't *touch* me!
All my plans. All my ambitions. Friends — every
one. You don't know all I've given up for
you. . . ."

He had never seen his mother weep before. Her
self-abandonment amazed him. Her words were
distorted by her tears. It was the most terrible
and distressing of crises. . . .

"Go away from me! How can you help me?
All I've done has been a failure! Failure! Failure!"

§ 8

That night the silences of Finacue Street heard
Benham's voice again. "I must do my job," he was
repeating, "I must do my job. Anyhow. . . ."

And then after a long pause, like a watchword and
just a little unsurely: "Aristocracy. . . ."

The next day his resolution had to bear the brunt
of a second ordeal. Mrs. Skelmersdale behaved
beautifully and this made everything tormentingly
touching and difficult. She convinced him she was
really in love with him, and indeed if he could have
seen his freshness and simplicity through her experienced eyes he would have known there was sound

reason why she should have found him exceptional. And when his clumsy hints of compensation could no longer be ignored she treated him with a soft indignation, a tender resentment, that left him soft and tender.   She looked at him with pained eyes and a quiver of the lips.   What did he think she was? And then a little less credibly, did he think she would have given herself to him if she hadn't been in love with him?   Perhaps that was not altogether true, but at any rate it was altogether true to her when she said it, and it was manifest that she did not for a moment intend him to have the cheap consolation of giving her money.   But, and that seemed odd to Benham, she would not believe, just as Lady Marayne would not believe, that there was not some other woman in the case.   He assured her and she seemed reassured, and then presently she was back at exactly the same question.   Would no woman ever understand the call of Asia, the pride of duty, the desire for the world?

One sort of woman perhaps. . . .

It was odd that for the first time now, in the sunshine of Kensington Gardens, he saw the little gossamer lines that tell that thirty years and more have passed over a face, a little wrinkling of the eyelids, a little hardening of the mouth.   How slight it is, how invisible it has been, how suddenly it appears!   And the sunshine of the warm April afternoon, heightened it may be by her determined unmercenary pose, betrayed too the faintest hint of shabbiness in her dress.   He had never noticed

these shadows upon her or her setting before and
their effect was to fill him with a strange regretful
tenderness. . . .

Perhaps men only begin to love when they cease
to be dazzled and admire. He had thought she
might reproach him, he had felt and feared she might
set herself to stir his senses, and both these expectations had been unjust to her he saw, now that he
saw her beside him, a brave, rather ill-advised and
unlucky little struggler, stung and shamed. He
forgot the particulars of that first lunch of theirs
together and he remembered his mother's second
contemptuous "*Stuff!*"

Indeed he knew now it had not been unexpected.

Why hadn't he left this little sensitive soul and
this little sensitive body alone? And since he
hadn't done so, what right had he now to back out
of their common adventure? He felt a sudden wild
impulse to marry Mrs. Skelmersdale, in a mood
between remorse and love and self-immolation,
and then a sunlit young woman with a leaping
stride in her paces, passed across his heavens, pointing to Asia and Utopia and forbidding even another
thought of the banns. . . .

"You will kiss me good-bye, dear, won't you?"
said Mrs. Skelmersdale, brimming over. "You will
do that."

He couldn't keep his arm from her little shoulders.
And as their lips touched he suddenly found himself
weeping also. . . .

His spirit went limping from that interview. She

chose to stay behind in her chair and think, she said, and each time he turned back she was sitting in the same attitude looking at him as he receded, and she had one hand on the chair back and her arm drawn up to it. The third time he waved his hat clumsily, and she started and then answered with her hand. Then the trees hid her. . . .

This sex business was a damnable business. If only because it made one hurt women. . . .

He had trampled on Mrs. Skelmersdale, he had hurt and disappointed his mother. Was he a brute? Was he a cold-blooded prig? What was this aristocracy? Was his belief anything more than a theory? Was he only dreaming of a debt to the men in the quarry, to the miners, to the men in the stokeholes, to the drudges on the fields? And while he dreamt he wounded and distressed real living creatures in the sleep-walk of his dreaming. . . .

So long as he stuck to his dream he must at any rate set his face absolutely against the establishment of any further relations with women.

Unless they were women of an entirely different type, women hardened and tempered, who would understand.

§ 9

So Benham was able to convert the unfortunate Mrs. Skelmersdale into a tender but for a long time an entirely painful memory. But mothers are not so easily disposed of, and more particularly a mother whose conduct is coloured deeply by an extraordinary

persuasion of having paid for her offspring twice
over. Nolan was inexplicable; he was, Benham
understood quite clearly, never to be mentioned
again; but somehow from the past his shadow and
his legacy cast a peculiar and perplexing shadow of
undefined obligation upon Benham's outlook. His
resolution to go round the world carried on his
preparations rapidly and steadily, but at the same
time his mother's thwarted and angry bearing produced a torture of remorse in him. It was constantly
in his mind, like the suit of the importunate widow,
that he ought to devote his life to the little lady's
happiness and pride, and his reason told him that
even if he wanted to make this sacrifice he couldn't;
the mere act of making it would produce so entirely
catastrophic a revulsion. He could as soon have
become a croquet champion or the curate of Chexington church, lines of endeavour which for him
would have led straightly and simply to sacrilegious
scandal or manslaughter with a mallet.

There is so little measure in the wild atonements
of the young that it was perhaps as well for the Research Magnificent that the remorses of this period
of Benham's life were too complicated and scattered
for a cumulative effect. In the background of his
mind and less subdued than its importance could
seem to warrant was his promise to bring the Wilder-
Morris people into relations with Lady Marayne.
They had been so delightful to him that he felt quite
acutely the slight he was putting upon them by this
delay. Lady Marayne's moods, however, had been

so uncertain that he had found no occasion to broach
this trifling matter, and when at last the occasion
came he perceived in the same instant the fullest
reasons for regretting it.

"Ah!" she said, hanging only for a moment, and
then: "you told me you were alone!" . . .

Her mind leapt at once to the personification of
these people as all that had puzzled and baffled her
in her son since his flight from London. They were
the enemy, they had got hold of him.

"When I asked you if you were alone you pretended to be angry," she remembered with a flash.
"You said, 'Do I tell lies?'"

"I *was* alone. Until — It was an accident.
On my walk I was alone."

But he flinched before her accusing, her almost
triumphant, forefinger.

From the instant she heard of them she hated
these South Harting people unrestrainedly. She
made no attempt to conceal it. Her valiant bantam
spirit caught at this quarrel as a refuge from the
rare and uncongenial ache of his secession. "And
who are they? What are they? What sort of
people can they be to drag in a passing young man?
I suppose this girl of theirs goes out every evening
— Was she painted, Poff?"

She whipped him with her questions as though
she was slashing his face. He became dead-white
and grimly civil, answering every question as though
it was the sanest, most justifiable inquiry.

"Of course I don't know who they are. How
should I know? What need is there to know?"

"There are ways of finding out," she insisted. "If I am to go down and make myself pleasant to these people because of you."

"But I implore you not to."

"And five minutes ago you were imploring me to! Of course I shall."

"Oh well! — well!"

"One has to know *something* of the people to whom one commits oneself, surely."

"They are decent people; they are well-behaved people."

"Oh! — I'll behave well. Don't think I'll disgrace your casual acquaintances. But who they are, what they are, I *will* know. . . ."

On that point Lady Marayne was to score beyond her utmost expectations.

"Come round," she said over the telephone, two mornings later. "I've something to tell you."

She was so triumphant that she was sorry for him. When it came to telling him, she failed from her fierceness.

"Poff, my little son," she said, "I'm so sorry I hardly know how to tell you. Poff, I'm sorry. I have to tell you — and it's utterly beastly."

"But what?" he asked.

"These people are dreadful people."

"But how?"

"You've heard of the great Kent and Eastern Bank smash and the Marlborough Building Society frauds eight or nine years ago?"

"Vaguely. But what has that to do with them?"

P

"That man Morris."

She stopped short, and Benham nodded for her to go on.

"Her father," said Lady Marayne.

"But who was Morris? Really, mother, I don't remember."

"He was sentenced to seven years — ten years — I forget. He had done all sorts of dreadful things. He was a swindler. And when he went out of the dock into the waiting-room — He had a signet ring with prussic acid in it — . . ."

"I remember now," he said.

A silence fell between them.

Benham stood quite motionless on the hearthrug and stared very hard at the little volume of Henley's poetry that lay upon the table.

He cleared his throat presently.

"You can't go and see them then," he said. "After all — since I am going abroad so soon — . . . It doesn't so very much matter."

§ 10

To Benham it did not seem to be of the slightest importance that Amanda's father was a convicted swindler who had committed suicide. Never was a resolved and conscious aristocrat so free from the hereditary delusion. Good parents, he was convinced, are only an advantage in so far as they have made you good stuff, and bad parents are no discredit to a son or daughter of good quality. Conceivably he had a bias against too close an examination of origins, and he held that the honour of the children should atone for the sins of the fathers and the questionable achievements of any intervening testator. Not half a dozen rich and established families in all England could stand even the most conventional inquiry into the foundations of their pride, and only a universal amnesty could prevent ridiculous distinctions. But he brought no accusation of inconsistency against his mother. She looked at things with a lighter logic and a kind of genius for the acceptance of superficial values. She was condoned and forgiven, a rescued lamb, re-established, notoriously bright and nice, and the Morrises were damned. That was their status, exclusion, damnation, as fixed as colour in Georgia or caste in Bengal. But if his mother's mind worked in that way there was no reason why his should. So far as he was concerned, he told himself, it did not matter whether Amanda was the daughter of a swindler or the daughter of a god. He had no doubt that she herself had the spirit and quality of divinity. He had seen it.

So there was nothing for it in the failure of his mother's civilities but to increase his own. He would go down to Harting and take his leave of these amiable outcasts himself. With a certain effusion. He would do this soon because he was now within sight of the beginning of his world tour. He had made his plans and prepared most of his equipment. Little remained to do but the release of Merkle, the wrappering and locking up of Finacue Street, which

could await him indefinitely, and the buying of
tickets.   He decided to take the opportunity afforded
by a visit of Sir Godfrey and Lady Marayne to the
Blights, big iron people in the North of England of
so austere a morality that even Benham was ignored
by it.   He announced his invasion in a little note
to Mrs. Wilder.   He parted from his mother on
Friday afternoon; she was already, he perceived,
a little reconciled to his project of going abroad;
and contrived his arrival at South Harting for that
sunset hour which was for his imagination the natural
halo of Amanda.

"I'm going round the world," he told them simply.
"I may be away for two years, and I thought I
would like to see you all again before I started."

That was quite the way they did things.

The supper-party included Mr. Rathbone-Sanders,
who displayed a curious tendency to drift in between
Benham and Amanda, a literary youth with a Byronic visage, very dark curly hair, and a number of
extraordinarily mature chins, a girl-friend of Betty's
who had cycled down from London, and who it appeared maintained herself at large in London by
drawing for advertisements, and a silent colourless
friend of Mr. Rathbone-Sanders.   The talk lit by
Amanda's enthusiasm circled actively round Benham's expedition.   It was clear that the idea of giving some years to thinking out one's possible work in
the world was for some reason that remained obscure
highly irritating to both Mr. Rathbone-Sanders and
the Byronic youth.   Betty too regarded it as levity

when there was "so much to be done," and the topic
whacked about and rose to something like a wrangle,
and sat down and rested and got up again reinvig-
orated, with a continuity of interest that Benham
had never yet encountered in any London gathering. He made a good case for his modern version
of the Grand Tour, and he gave them something of
his intellectual enthusiasm for the distances and
views, the cities and seas, the multitudinous wide
spectacle of the world he was to experience. He
had been reading about Benares and North China.
As he talked Amanda, who had been animated at
first, fell thoughtful and silent. And then it was
discovered that the night was wonderfully warm and
the moon shining. They drifted out into the garden,
but Mr. Rathbone-Sanders was suddenly entangled
and drawn back by Mrs. Wilder and the young
woman from London upon some technical point,
and taken to the work-table in the corner of the
dining-room to explain. He was never able to get
to the garden.

Benham found himself with Amanda upon a side
path, a little isolated by some swaggering artichokes
and a couple of apple trees and so forth from the
general conversation. They cut themselves off from
the continuation of that by a little silence, and then
she spoke abruptly and with the quickness of a
speaker who has thought out something to say and
fears interruption: "Why did you come down
here?"

"I wanted to see you before I went."

"You disturb me.   You fill me with envy."

"I didn't think of that.   I wanted to see you again."

"And then you will go off round the world, you will see the Tropics, you will see India, you will go into Chinese cities all hung with vermilion, you will climb mountains.   Oh! men can do all the splendid things.   Why do you come here to remind me of it? I have never been anywhere, anywhere at all.   I never shall go anywhere.   Never in my life have I seen a mountain.   Those Downs there — look at them! — are my highest.   And while you are travelling I shall think of you — and think of you. . . ."

"Would *you* like to travel?" he asked as though that was an extraordinary idea.

"Do you think *every* girl wants to sit at home and rock a cradle?"

"I never thought *you* did."

"Then what did you think I wanted?"

"What *do* you want?"

She held her arms out widely, and the moonlight shone in her eyes as she turned her face to him.

"Just what you want," she said; "— *the whole World!*

"Life is like a feast," she went on; "it is spread before everybody and nobody must touch it.   What am I?   Just a prisoner.   In a cottage garden. Looking for ever over a hedge.   I should be happier if I couldn't look.   I remember once, only a little time ago, there was a cheap excursion to London. Our only servant went.   She had to get up at an

unearthly hour, and I — I got up too. I helped her
to get off. And when she was gone I went up to my
bedroom again and cried. I cried with envy for any
one, any one who could go away. I've been nowhere — except to school at Chichester and three or
four times to Emsworth and Bognor — for eight
years. When you go" — the tears glittered in the
moonlight — "I shall cry. It will be worse than
the excursion to London. . . . Ever since you were
here before I've been thinking of it."

It seemed to Benham that here indeed was the
very sister of his spirit. His words sprang into his
mind as one thinks of a repartee. "But why
shouldn't you come too?" he said.

She stared at him in silence. The two white-lit
faces examined each other. Both she and Benham
were trembling.

"*Come too ?*" she repeated.

"Yes, with me."

"But — *how ?*"

Then suddenly she was weeping like a child that
is teazed; her troubled eyes looked out from under
puckered brows. "You don't mean it," she said.
"You don't mean it."

And then indeed he meant it.

"Marry me," he said very quickly, glancing
towards the dark group at the end of the garden.
"And we will go together."

He seized her arm and drew her to him. "I love
you," he said. "I love your spirit. You are not
like any one else."

There was a moment's hesitation.

Both he and she looked to see how far they were still alone.

Then they turned their dusky faces to each other. He drew her still closer.

"Oh!" she said, and yielded herself to be kissed.

Their lips touched, and for a moment he held her lithe body against his own.

"I want you," he whispered close to her. "You are my mate. From the first sight of you I knew that. . . ."

They embraced — alertly furtive.

Then they stood a little apart. Some one was coming towards them. Amanda's bearing changed swiftly. She put up her little face to his, confidently and intimately.

"Don't *tell* any one," she whispered eagerly shaking his arm to emphasize her words. "Don't tell any one — not yet. Not for a few days. . . ."

She pushed him from her quickly as the shadowy form of Betty appeared in a little path between the artichokes and raspberry canes.

"Listening to the nightingales?" cried Betty.

"Yes, aren't they?" said Amanda inconsecutively.

"That's our very own nightingale!" cried Betty advancing. "Do you hear it, Mr. Benham? No, not that one. That is a quite inferior bird that performs in the vicarage trees. . . ."

§ 11

When a man has found and won his mate then the
best traditions demand a lyrical interlude. It should
be possible to tell, in that ecstatic manner which
melts words into moonshine, makes prose almost
uncomfortably rhythmic, and brings all the freshness of every spring that ever was across the page,
of the joyous exaltation of the happy lover. This
at any rate was what White had always done in his
novels hitherto, and what he would certainly have
done at this point had he had the telling of Benham's
story uncontrolledly in his hands. But, indeed,
indeed, in real life, in very truth, the heart has not
this simplicity. Only the heroes of romance, and a
few strong simple clean-shaven Americans have that
much emotional integrity. (And even the Americans do at times seem to an observant eye to be putting in work at the job and keeping up their gladness.) Benham was excited that night, but not in
the proper bright-eyed, red-cheeked way; he did
not dance down the village street of Harting to his
harbour at the Ship, and the expression in his eyes
as he sat on the edge of his bed was not the deep
elemental wonder one could have wished there, but
amazement. Do not suppose that he did not love
Amanda, that a rich majority of his being was not
triumphantly glad to have won her, that the image
of the two armour-clad lovers was not still striding
and flourishing through the lit wilderness of his
imagination. For three weeks things had pointed

him to this. They would do everything together now, he and his mate, they would scale mountains together and ride side by side towards ruined cities across the deserts of the World. He could have wished no better thing. But at the same time, even as he felt and admitted this and rejoiced at it, the sky of his mind was black with consternation. . . .

It is remarkable, White reflected, as he turned over the abundant but confused notes upon this perplexing phase of Benham's development that lay in the third drawer devoted to the Second Limitation, how dependent human beings are upon statement. Man is the animal that states a case. He lives not in things but in expressed ideas, and what was troubling Benham inordinately that night, a night that should have been devoted to purely blissful and exalted expectations, was the sheer impossibility of stating what had happened in any terms that would be tolerable either to Mrs. Skelmersdale or Lady Marayne. The thing had happened with the suddenness of a revelation. Whatever had been going on in the less illuminated parts of his mind, his manifest resolution had been merely to bid South Harting good-bye — And in short they would never understand. They would accuse him of the meanest treachery. He could see his mother's face, he could hear her voice saying, "And so because of this sudden infatuation for a swindler's daughter, a girl who runs about the roads with a couple of retrievers hunting for a man, you must spoil all my plans, ruin my year, tell me a lot of

pretentious stuffy lies. . . ." And Mrs. Skelmersdale too would say, "Of course he just talked of
the world and duty and all that rubbish to save
my face. . . ."

It wasn't so at all.

But it looked so frightfully like it!

Couldn't they realize that he had fled out of London before ever he had seen Amanda? They might
be able to do it perhaps, but they never would. It
just happened that in the very moment when the
edifice of his noble resolutions had been ready, she
had stepped into it — out of nothingness and nowhere. She wasn't an accident; that was just the
point upon which they were bound to misjudge her;
she was an embodiment. If only he could show her
to them as she had first shown herself to him, swift,
light, a little flushed from running but not in the
least out of breath, quick as a leopard upon the
dogs. . . . But even if the improbable opportunity
arose, he perceived it might still be impossible to
produce the Amanda he loved, the Amanda of the
fluttering short skirt and the clear enthusiastic voice.
Because, already he knew she was not the only
Amanda. There was another, there might be
others, there was this perplexing person who had
flashed into being at the very moment of their
mutual confession, who had produced the entirely
disconcerting demand that nobody must be told.
Then Betty had intervened. But that sub-Amanda
and her carneying note had to be dealt with on the
first occasion, because when aristocrats love they

don't care a rap who is told and who is not told. They just step out into the light side by side. . . .

"Don't tell any one," she had said, "not for a few days. . . ."

This sub-Amanda was perceptible next morning again, flitting about in the background of a glad and loving adventuress, a pre-occupied Amanda who had put her head down while the real Amanda flung her chin up and contemplated things on the Asiatic scale, and who was apparently engaged in disentangling something obscure connected with Mr. Rathbone-Sanders that ought never to have been entangled. . . .

"A human being," White read, "the simplest human being, is a clustering mass of aspects. No man will judge another justly who judges everything about him. And of love in particular is this true. We love not persons but revelations. The woman one loves is like a goddess hidden in a shrine ; for her sake we live on hope and suffer the kindred priestesses that make up herself. The art of love is patience till the gleam returns. . . ."

Sunday and Monday did much to develop this idea of the intricate complexity of humanity in Benham's mind. On Monday morning he went up from the Ship again to get Amanda alone and deliver his ultimatum against a further secrecy, so that he could own her openly and have no more of the interventions and separations that had barred him from any intimate talk with her throughout the whole of Sunday. The front door stood open, the passage hall was empty, but as he hesitated whether he should

proclaim himself with the knocker or walk through,
the door of the little drawing-room flew open and a
black-clad cylindrical clerical person entirely unknown to Benham stumbled over the threshold,
blundered blindly against him, made a sound like
"*Moo*" and a pitiful gesture with his arm, and fled
forth. . . .

It was a curate and he was weeping bitterly. . . .

Benham stood in the doorway and watched a
clumsy broken-hearted flight down the village street.

He had been partly told and partly left to infer,
and anyhow he was beginning to understand about
Mr. Rathbone-Sanders. That he could dismiss.
But — why was the curate in tears?

§ 12

He found Amanda standing alone in the room
from which this young man had fled. She had a
handful of daffodils in her hand, and others were
scattered over the table. She had been arranging
the big bowl of flowers in the centre. He left the
door open behind him and stopped short with the
table between them. She looked up at him — intelligently and calmly. Her pose had a divine dignity.

"I want to tell them now," said Benham without
a word of greeting.

"Yes," she said, "tell them now."

They heard steps in the passage outside.
"Betty!" cried Amanda.

Her mother's voice answered, "Do you want
Betty?"

"We want you all," answered Amanda. "We have something to tell you. . . ."

"Carrie!" they heard Mrs. Morris call her sister after an interval, and her voice sounded faint and flat and unusual. There was the soft hissing of some whispered words outside and a muffled exclamation. Then Mrs. Wilder and Mrs. Morris and Betty came into the room. Mrs. Wilder came first, and Mrs. Morris with an alarmed face as if sheltering behind her. "We want to tell you something," said Amanda.

"Amanda and I are going to marry each other," said Benham, standing in front of her.

For an instant the others made no answer; they looked at each other.

"*But does he know?*" Mrs. Morris said in a low voice.

Amanda turned her eyes to her lover. She was about to speak, she seemed to gather herself for an effort, and then he knew that he did not want to hear her explanation. He checked her by a gesture.

"I *know*," he said, and then, "I do not see that it matters to us in the least."

He went to her holding out both his hands to her.

She took them and stood shyly for a moment, and then the watchful gravity of her face broke into soft emotion. "Oh!" she cried and seized his face between her hands in a passion of triumphant love and kissed him.

And then he found himself being kissed by Mrs. Morris.

She kissed him thrice, with solemnity, with thankfulness, with relief, as if in the act of kissing she transferred to him precious and entirely incalculable treasures.

CHAPTER THE FOURTH

THE SPIRITED HONEYMOON

§ 1

IT was a little after sunrise one bright morning in September that Benham came up on to the deck of the sturdy Austrian steamboat that was churning its way with a sedulous deliberation from Spalato to Cattaro, and lit himself a cigarette and seated himself upon a deck chair. Save for a yawning Greek sailor busy with a mop the first-class deck was empty.

Benham surveyed the haggard beauty of the Illyrian coast. The mountains rose gaunt and enormous and barren to a jagged fantastic silhouette against the sun; their almost vertical slopes still plunged in blue shadow, broke only into a little cold green and white edge of olive terraces and vegetation and houses before they touched the clear blue water. An occasional church or a house perched high upon some seemingly inaccessible ledge did but accentuate the vast barrenness of the land. It was a land desolated and destroyed. At Ragusa, at Salona, at Spalato and Zara and Pola Benham had seen only variations upon one persistent theme, a dwindled and uncreative human life living amidst

224

the giant ruins of preceding times, as worms live in
the sockets of a skull. Forward an unsavoury
group of passengers still slumbered amidst fruit-peel
and expectorations, a few soldiers, some squalid
brigands armed with preposterous red umbrellas,
a group of curled-up human lumps brooded over by
an aquiline individual caparisoned with brass like
a horse, his head wrapped picturesquely in a shawl.
Benham surveyed these last products of the "life
force" and resumed his pensive survey, of the coast.
The sea was deserted save for a couple of little
lateen craft with suns painted on their gaudy sails,
sea butterflies that hung motionless as if unawakened
close inshore. . . .

The travel of the last few weeks had impressed
Benham's imagination profoundly. For the first
time in his life he had come face to face with civilization in defeat. From Venice hitherward he had
marked with cumulative effect the clustering evidences of effort spent and power crumbled to nothingness. He had landed upon the marble quay of
Pola and visited its deserted amphitheatre, he had
seen a weak provincial life going about ignoble ends
under the walls of the great Venetian fortress and
the still more magnificent cathedral of Zara; he
had visited Spalato, clustered in sweltering grime
within the ample compass of the walls of Diocletian's
villa, and a few troublesome sellers of coins and iri-
descent glass and fragments of tessellated pavement
and such-like loot was all the population he had
found amidst the fallen walls and broken friezes and

Q

columns of Salona. Down this coast there ebbed
and flowed a mean residual life, a life of violence and
dishonesty, peddling trades, vendettas and war.
For a while the unstable Austrian ruled this land and
made a sort of order that the incalculable chances of
international politics might at any time shatter.
Benham was drawing near now to the utmost limit
of that extended peace. Ahead beyond the mountain capes was Montenegro and, further, Albania
and Macedonia, lands of lawlessness and confusion.
Amanda and he had been warned of the impossibility of decent travel beyond Cattaro and Cettinjé,
but this had but whetted her adventurousness and
challenged his spirit. They were going to see Albania for themselves.

The three months of honeymoon they had been
spending together had developed many remarkable
divergences of their minds that had not been in the
least apparent to Benham before their marriage.
Then their common resolve to be as spirited as possible had obliterated all minor considerations. But
that was the limit of their unanimity. Amanda
loved wild and picturesque things, and Benham
strong and clear things; the vines and brushwood
amidst the ruins of Salona that had delighted her
had filled him with a sense of tragic retrogression.
Salona had revived again in the acutest form a dispute that had been smouldering between them
throughout a fitful and lengthy exploration of north
and central Italy. She could not understand his
disgust with the mediæval colour and confusion

that had swamped the pride and state of the Roman
empire, and he could not make her feel the ambition
of the ruler, the essential discipline and responsibilities of his aristocratic idea.   While his adventurousness was conquest, hers, it was only too manifest, was brigandage.   His thoughts ran now into
the form of an imaginary discourse, that he would
never deliver to her, on the decay of states, on the
triumphs of barbarians over rulers who will not rule,
on the relaxation of patrician orders and the return
of the robber and assassin as lordship decays.   This
coast was no theatrical scenery for him; it was a
shattered empire.   And it was shattered because no
men had been found, united enough, magnificent and
steadfast enough, to hold the cities, and maintain
the roads, keep the peace and subdue the brutish
hates and suspicions and cruelties that devastated
the world.

And as these thoughts came back into his mind,
Amanda flickered up from below, light and noiseless
as a sunbeam, and stood behind his chair.

Freedom and the sight of the world had if possible brightened and invigorated her.   Her costume
and bearing were subtly touched by the romance
of the Adriatic.   There was a flavour of the pirate
in the cloak about her shoulders and the light knitted
cap of scarlet she had stuck upon her head.   She
surveyed his preoccupation for a moment, glanced
forward, and then covered his eyes with her hands.
In almost the same movement she had bent down
and nipped the tip of his ear between her teeth.

"Confound you, Amanda!"

"You'd forgotten my existence, you star-gazing Cheetah. And then, you see, these things happen to you!"

"I was thinking."

"Well — *don't*. . . . I distrust your thinking. . . . This coast is wilder and grimmer than yesterday. It's glorious. . . ."

She sat down on the chair he unfolded for her.

"Is there nothing to eat?" she asked abruptly.

"It is too early."

§ 2

"This coast is magnificent," she said presently.

"It's hideous," he answered. "It's as ugly as a heap of slag."

"It's nature at its wildest."

"That's Amanda at her wildest."

"Well, isn't it?"

"No! This land isn't nature. It's waste. Not wilderness. It's the other end. Those hills were covered with forests; this was a busy civilized coast just a little thousand years ago. The Venetians wasted it. They cut down the forests; they filled the cities with a mixed mud of population, *that* stuff. Look at it"! — he indicated the sleepers forward by a movement of his head.

"I suppose they *were* rather feeble people," said Amanda.

"Who?"

"The Venetians."

"They were traders — and nothing more. Just as we are. And when they were rich they got splendid clothes and feasted and rested. Much as we do."

Amanda surveyed him. "We don't rest."

"We idle."

"We are seeing things."

"Don't be a humbug, Amanda. We are making love. Just as they did. And it has been — ripping. In Salona they made love tremendously. They did nothing else until the barbarians came over the mountains. . . ."

"Well," said Amanda virtuously, "we will do something else."

He made no answer and her expression became profoundly thoughtful. Of course this wandering must end. He had been growing impatient for some time. But it was difficult, she perceived, to decide just what to do with him. . . .

Benham picked up the thread of his musing.

He was seeing more and more clearly that all civilization was an effort, and so far always an inadequate and very partially successful effort. Always it had been aristocratic, aristocratic in the sense that it was the work of minorities, who took power, who had a common resolution against the inertia, the indifference, the insubordination and instinctive hostility of the mass of mankind. And always the set-backs, the disasters of civilization, had been failures of the aristocratic spirit. Why had the Roman purpose faltered and shrivelled? Every order, every brotherhood, every organization carried with it the seeds of its own destruction. Must the idea of statecraft and rule perpetually reappear, reclothe itself in new forms, age, die, even as life does — making each time its almost infinitesimal addition to human achievement? Now the world is crying aloud for a renascence of the spirit that orders and controls. Human affairs sway at a dizzy height of opportunity. Will they keep their footing there, or stagger? We have got back at last to a time as big with opportunity as the early empire. Given only the will in men and it would be possible now to turn the dazzling accidents of science, the chancy attainments of the nineteenth century, into a sane and permanent possession, a new starting-point. . . . What a magnificence might be made of life!

He was aroused by Amanda's voice.

"When we go back to London, old Cheetah," she said, "we must take a house."

For some moments he stared at her, trying to get back to their point of divergence.

"Why?" he asked at length.

"We must have a house," she said.

He looked at her face. Her expression was profoundly thoughtful, her eyes were fixed on the slumbering ships poised upon the transparent water under the mountain shadows.

"You see," she thought it out, "you've got to *tell* in London. You can't just sneak back there. You've got to strike a note of your own. With all these things of yours."

"But how?"

"There's a sort of little house, I used to see them when I was a girl and my father lived in London, about Brook Street and that part. Not too far north. . . . You see going back to London for us is just another adventure. We've got to capture London. We've got to scale it. We've got advantages of all sorts. But at present we're outside. We've got to march in."

Her clear hazel eyes contemplated conflicts and triumphs.

She was roused by Benham's voice.

"What the deuce are you thinking of, Amanda?"

She turned her level eyes to his. "London," she said. "For you."

"I don't want London," he said.

"I thought you did. You ought to. I do."

"But to take a house! Make an invasion of London!"

"You dear old Cheetah, you can't be always frisking about in the wilderness, staring at the stars."

"But I'm not going back to live in London in the old way, theatres, dinner-parties, chatter —"

"Oh no! We aren't going to do that sort of thing. We aren't going to join the ruck. We'll go about in holiday times all over the world. I want to see Fusiyama. I mean to swim in the South Seas. With you. We'll dodge the sharks. But all the same we shall have to have a house in London. We have to be *felt* there."

She met his consternation fairly. She lifted her fine eyebrows. Her little face conveyed a protesting reasonableness.

"Well, *mustn't* we?"

She added, "If we want to alter the world we ought to live in the world."

Since last they had disputed the question she had thought out these new phrases.

"Amanda," he said, "I think sometimes you haven't the remotest idea of what I am after. I don't believe you begin to suspect what I am up to."

She put her elbows on her knees, dropped her chin between her hands and regarded him impudently. She had a characteristic trick of looking up with her face downcast that never failed to soften his regard.

"Look here, Cheetah, don't you give way to your early morning habit of calling your own true love a fool," she said.

"Simply I tell you I will not go back to London."

"You will go back with me, Cheetah."

"I will go back as far as my work calls me there."

"It calls you through the voice of your mate and slave and doormat to just exactly the sort of house you ought to have. . . . It is the privilege and duty of the female to choose the lair."

For a space Benham made no reply. This controversy had been gathering for some time and he wanted to state his view as vividly as possible. The Benham style of connubial conversation had long since decided for emphasis rather than delicacy.

"I think," he said slowly, "that this wanting to take London by storm is a beastly *vulgar* thing to want to do."

Amanda compressed her lips.

"I want to work out things in my mind," he went on. "I do not want to be distracted by social things, and I do not want to be distracted by picturesque things. This life — it's all very well on the surface, but it isn't real. I'm not getting hold of reality. Things slip away from me. God! but how they slip away from me!"

He got up and walked to the side of the boat.

She surveyed his back for some moments. Then she went and leant over the rail beside him.

"I want to go to London," she said.

"I don't."

"Where do you want to go?"

"Where I can see into the things that hold the world together."

"I have loved this wandering — I could wander always. But . . . Cheetah! I tell you I *want* to go to London."

He looked over his shoulder into her warm face. "*No*," he said.

"But, I ask you."

He shook his head.

She put her face closer and whispered. "Cheetah! big beast of my heart. Do you hear your mate asking for something?"

He turned his eyes back to the mountains. "I must go my own way."

"Haven't I, so far, invented things, made life amusing, Cheetah? Can't you trust the leopard's wisdom?"

He stared at the coast inexorably.

"I wonder," she whispered.

"What?"

"You *are* that, Cheetah, that lank, long, *eager* beast —."

Suddenly with a nimble hand she had unbottoned and rolled up the sleeve of her blouse. She stuck her pretty blue-veined arm before his eyes. "Look here, sir, it was you, wasn't it? It was your powerful jaw inflicted this bite upon the arm of a defenceless young leopardess —"

"Amanda!"

"Well." She wrinkled her brows.

He turned about and stood over her, he shook a finger in her face and there was a restrained intensity in his voice as he spoke.

"Look here, Amanda!" he said, "if you think that you are going to make me agree to any sort of project about London, to any sort of complication of our lives with houses in smart streets and a campaign of social assertion — by *that*, then may I be damned for an uxorious fool!"

Her eyes met his and there was mockery in her eyes.

"This, Cheetah, is the morning mood," she remarked.

"This is the essential mood. Listen, Amanda —"

He stopped short. He looked towards the gangway, they both looked. The magic word "Breakfast" came simultaneously from them.

"Eggs," she said ravenously, and led the way.

A smell of coffee as insistent as an herald's trumpet had called a truce between them.

§ 3

Their marriage had been a comparatively inconspicuous one, but since that time they had been engaged upon a honeymoon of great extent and variety. Their wedding had taken place at South Harting church in the marked absence of Lady Marayne, and it had been marred by only one untoward event. The Reverend Amos Pugh who, in spite of the earnest advice of several friends had insisted upon sharing in the ceremony, had suddenly covered his face with the sleeves of his surplice and fled with a swift rustle to the vestry, whence an uproar of inadequately smothered sorrow came as an obligato accompaniment to the more crucial passages of the service. Amanda appeared unaware of the incident at the time, but afterwards she explained things to Benham. "Curates," she said, "are such pent-up men. One ought, I suppose, to remember that. But he never had anything to go upon at all — not anything — except his own imaginations."

"I suppose when you met him you were nice to him."

"I was nice to him, of course. . . ."

They drove away from Harting, as it were, over the weeping remains of this infatuated divine. His sorrow made them thoughtful for a time, and then Amanda nestled closer to her lover and they forgot about him, and their honeymoon became so active and entertaining that only very rarely and transitorily did they ever think of him again.

The original conception of their honeymoon had been identical with the plans Benham had made for the survey and study of the world, and it was through a series of modifications, replacements and additions that it became at last a prolonged and very picturesque tour in Switzerland, the Austrian Tyrol, North Italy, and down the Adriatic coast. Amanda had never seen mountains, and longed, she said, to climb. This took them first to Switzerland. Then, in spite of their exalted aims, the devotion of their lives to noble purposes, it was evident that Amanda had no intention of scamping the detail of love, and for that what background is so richly beautiful as Italy? An important aspect of the grand tour round the world as Benham had planned it, had been interviews, inquiries and conversations with every sort of representative and understanding person he could reach. An unembarrassed young man who wants to know and does not promise to bore may reach almost any one in that way, he is as impersonal as pure reason and as mobile as a letter, but the presence of a lady in his train leaves him no longer unembarrassed. His approach has become a social event. The wife of a great or significant personage must take notice or decide not to take notice. Of course Amanda was prepared to go anywhere, just as Benham's shadow; it was the world that was unprepared. And a second leading aspect of his original scheme had been the examination of the ways of government in cities and the shifting and mixture of nations and races. It would have led to back streets, and involved and complicated details, and there was something in the fine flame of girlhood beside him that he felt was incompatible with those shadows and that dust. And also they were lovers and very deeply in love. It was amazing how swiftly that draggled shameful London sparrow-gamin, Eros, took heart from Amanda, and became wonderful, beautiful, glowing, life-giving, confident, clear-eyed; how he changed from flesh to sweet fire, and grew until he filled the sky. So that you see they went to Switzerland and Italy at last very like two ordinary young people who were not aristocrats at all, had no theory about the world or their destiny, but were simply just ardently delighted with the discovery of one another.

Nevertheless Benham was for some time under a vague impression that in a sort of way still he was going round the world and working out his destinies.

It was part of the fascination of Amanda that she was never what he had supposed her to be, and that nothing that he set out to do with her ever turned out as they had planned it. Her appreciations marched before her achievement, and when it came to climbing it seemed foolish to toil to summits over which her spirit had flitted days before. Their

Swiss expeditions which she had foreseen as glorious wanderings amidst the blue ice of crevasses and nights of exalted hardihood became a walking tour of fitful vigour and abundant fun and delight.   They spent a long day on the ice of the Aletsch glacier, but they reached the inn on its eastward side with magnificent appetites a little late for dinner.

Amanda had revealed an unexpected gift for nicknames and pretty fancies.   She named herself the Leopard, the spotless Leopard; in some obscure way she intimated that the colour was black, but that was never to be admitted openly, there was supposed to be some lurking traces of a rusty brown but the word was spotless and the implication white, a dazzling white, she would play a thousand variations on the theme; in moments of despondency she was only a black cat, a common lean black cat, and sacks and half-bricks almost too good for her. But Benham was always a Cheetah.   That had come to her as a revelation from heaven.   But so clearly he was a Cheetah.   He was a Hunting Leopard; the only beast that has an up-cast face and dreams and looks at you with absent-minded eyes like a man.   She laced their journeys with a fantastic monologue telling in the third person what the Leopard and the Cheetah were thinking and seeing and doing.   And so they walked up mountains and over passes and swam in the warm clear water of romantic lakes and loved each other mightily always, in chestnut woods and olive orchards and flower-starred alps and pine forests and awning-covered boats, and by sunset and moonlight and starshine; and out of these agreeable solitudes they came brown and dusty, striding side by side into sunlit entertaining fruit-piled market-places and envious hotels. For days and weeks together it did not seem to Benham that there was anything that mattered in life but Amanda and the elemental joys of living. And then the Research Magnificent began to stir in him again. He perceived that Italy was not India, that the clue to the questions he must answer lay in the crowded new towns that they avoided, in the packed bookshops and the talk of men, and not in the picturesque and flowery solitudes to which their lovemaking carried them.

Moods began in which he seemed to forget Amanda altogether.

This happened first in the Certosa di Pavia whither they had gone one afternoon from Milan. That was quite soon after they were married. They had a bumping journey thither in a motor-car, a little doubtful if the excursion was worth while, and they found a great amazement in the lavish beauty and decorative wealth of that vast church and its associated cloisters, set far away from any population as it seemed in a flat wilderness of reedy ditches and patchy cultivation. The distilleries and outbuildings were deserted — their white walls were covered by one monstrously great and old wisteria in flower — the soaring marvellous church was in possession of a knot of unattractive guides. One of these conducted them through the painted treasures of the gold and marble chapels; he was an elderly but animated person who evidently found Amanda more wonderful than any church. He poured out great accumulations of information and compliments before her. Benham dropped behind, went astray and was presently recovered dreaming in the great cloister. The guide showed them over two of the cells that opened thereupon, each a delightful house for a solitary, bookish and clean, and each with a little secret walled garden of its own. He was covertly tipped against all regulations and departed regretfully with a beaming dismissal from Amanda. She found Benham wondering why the Carthusians had failed to produce anything better in the world than a liqueur. "One might have imagined that men would have done something in this beautiful quiet; that there would have come thought from here or will from here."

"In these dear little nests they ought to have put lovers," said Amanda.

"Oh, of course, *you* would have made the place Thelema. . . ."

But as they went shaking and bumping back along the evil road to Milan, he fell into a deep musing. Suddenly he said, "Work has to be done. Because this order or that has failed, there is no reason why we should fail. And look at those ragged children in the road ahead of us, and those dirty women sitting in the doorways, and the foul ugliness of these gaunt nameless towns through which we go! They are what they are, because we

are what we are — idlers, excursionists.   In a world
we ought to rule. . . .

"Amanda, we've got to get to work. . . ."

That was his first display of this new mood, which
presently became a common one.   He was less and
less content to let the happy hours slip by, more and
more sensitive to the reminders in giant ruin and
deserted cell, in a chance encounter with a string of
guns and soldiers on their way to manœuvres or in
the sight of a stale newspaper, of a great world process going on in which he was now playing no part at
all.   And a curious irritability manifested itself
more and more plainly, whenever human pettiness
obtruded upon his attention, whenever some trivial
dishonesty, some manifest slovenliness, some spirit-
less failure, a cheating waiter or a wayside beggar
brought before him the shiftless, selfish, aimless
elements in humanity that war against the great
dream of life made glorious.   "Accursed things," he
would say, as he flung some importunate cripple at a
church door a ten-centime piece; "why were they
born?   Why do they consent to live?   They are
no better than some chance fungus that is because it
must."

"It takes all sorts to make a world," said Amanda.

"Nonsense," said Benham.   "Where is the mega-
therium?   That sort of creature has to go.   Our
sort of creature has to end it."

"Then why did you give it money?"

"Because — I don't want the thing to be more
wretched than it is.   But if I could prevent more

B

of them — ... What am I doing to prevent them?"

"These beggars annoy you," said Amanda after a pause. "They do me. Let us go back into the mountains."

But he fretted in the mountains.

They made a ten days' tour from Macugnaga over the Monte Moro to Sass, and thence to Zermatt and back by the Theodule to Macugnaga. The sudden apparition of douaniers upon the Monte Moro annoyed Benham, and he was also irritated by the solemn English mountain climbers at Saas Fee. They were as bad as golfers, he said, and reflected momentarily upon his father. Amanda fell in love with Monte Rosa, she wanted to kiss its snowy forehead, she danced like a young goat down the path to Mattmark, and rolled on the turf when she came to gentians and purple primulas. Benham was tremendously in love with her most of the time, but one day when they were sitting over the Findelen glacier his perceptions blundered for the first time upon the fundamental antagonism of their quality. She was sketching out jolly things that they were to do together, expeditions, entertainments, amusements, and adventures, with a voluble swiftness, and suddenly in a flash his eyes were opened, and he saw that she would never for a moment feel the quality that made life worth while for him. He saw it in a flash, and in that flash he made his urgent resolve not to see it. From that moment forth his bearing was poisoned by his secret determination not to think of this, not to admit it to his mind. And forbidden to come into his presence in its proper form, this conflict of intellectual temperaments took on strange disguises, and the gathering tension of his mind sought to relieve itself along grotesque irrelevant channels.

There was, for example, the remarkable affair of the drive from Macugnaga to Piedimulera.

They had decided to walk down in a leisurely fashion, but with the fatigues of the precipitous clamber down from Switzerland still upon them they found the white road between rock above and gorge below wearisome, and the valley hot in the late morning sunshine, and already before they reached the inn they had marked for lunch Amanda had suggested driving the rest of the way. The inn had a number of brigand-like customers consuming such sustenance as garlic and salami and wine; it received them with an indifference that bordered on disrespect, until the landlord, who seemed to be something of a beauty himself, discovered the merits of Amanda. Then he became markedly attentive. He was a large, fat, curly-headed person with beautiful eyes, a cherished moustache, and an air of great gentility, and when he had welcomed his guests and driven off the slatternly waiting-maid, and given them his best table, and consented, at Amanda's request, to open a window, he went away and put on a tie and collar. It was an attention so conspicuous that even the group of men in the far corner noticed and commented on it, and then they

commented on Amanda and Benham, assuming an
ignorance of Italian in the visitors that was only
partly justifiable. "Bellissima," "bravissima,"
"signorina," "Inglesa," one need not be born in
Italy to understand such words as these. Also
they addressed sly comments and encouragements
to the landlord as he went to and fro.

Benham was rather still and stiff during the meal,
but it ill becomes an English aristocrat to discuss
the manners of an alien population, and Amanda
was amused by the effusion of the landlord and a
little disposed to experiment upon him. She sat
radiating light amidst the shadows.

The question of the vehicle was broached. The
landlord was doubtful, then an idea, it was manifestly a questionable idea, occurred to him. He
went to consult an obscure brown-faced individual
in the corner, disappeared, and the world without
became eloquent. Presently he returned and announced that a carozza was practicable. It had
been difficult, but he had contrived it. And he
remained hovering over the conclusion of their
meal, asking questions about Amanda's mountaineering and expressing incredulous admiration.

His bill, which he presented with an uneasy flourish, was large and included the carozza.

He ushered them out to the carriage with civilities
and compliments. It had manifestly been difficult
and contrived. It was dusty and blistered, there
had been a hasty effort to conceal its recent use as
a hen-roost, the harness was mended with string.

The horse was gaunt and scandalous, a dirty white, and carried its head apprehensively. The driver had but one eye, through which there gleamed a concentrated hatred of God and man.

"No wonder he charged for it before we saw it," said Benham.

"It's better than walking," said Amanda.

The company in the inn gathered behind the landlord and scrutinized Amanda and Benham intelligently. The young couple got in. "Avanti," said Benham, and Amanda bestowed one last ineradicable memory on the bowing landlord.

Benham did not speak until just after they turned the first corner, and then something portentous happened, considering the precipitous position of the road they were upon. A small boy appeared sitting in the grass by the wayside, and at the sight of him the white horse shied extravagantly. The driver rose in his seat ready to jump. But the crisis passed without a smash. "Cheetah!" cried Amanda suddenly. "This isn't safe." "Ah!" said Benham, and began to act with the vigour of one who has long accumulated force. He rose in his place and gripped the one-eyed driver by the collar. "*Aspetto*," he said, but he meant "Stop!" The driver understood that he meant "Stop," and obeyed.

Benham wasted no time in parleying with the driver. He indicated to him and to Amanda by a comprehensive gesture that he had business with the landlord, and with a gleaming appetite upon his face went running back towards the inn.

The landlord was sitting down to a little game of dominoes with his friends when Benham reappeared in the sunlight of the doorway. There was no misunderstanding Benham's expression.

For a moment the landlord was disposed to be defiant. Then he changed his mind. Benham's earnest face was within a yard of his own, and a threatening forefinger was almost touching his nose.

"Albergo cattivissimo," said Benham. "Cattivissimo! Pranzo cattivissimo 'orrido. Cavallo cattivissimo, dangerousissimo. Gioco abominablissimo, damnissimo. Capisce. Eh?" *

The landlord made deprecatory gestures.

"*You* understand all right," said Benham. "Da me il argento per il carozzo. Subito?" †

The landlord was understood to ask whether the signor no longer wished for the carriage.

"*Subito!*" cried Benham, and giving way to a long-restrained impulse seized the padrone by the collar of his coat and shook him vigorously.

There were dissuasive noises from the company, but no attempt at rescue. Benham released his hold.

"Adesso!" ‡ said Benham.

The landlord decided to disgorge. It was at any rate a comfort that the beautiful lady was not seeing anything of this. And he could explain afterwards

* This is vile Italian. It may — with a certain charity to Benham — be rendered: "The beastliest inn! The beastliest! The beastliest, most awful lunch! The vilest horse! Most dangerous! Abominable trick! Understand?"
† "Give me back the money for the carriage. *Quickly!*"
‡ "*Now!*"

to his friends that the Englishman was clearly a luna-
tic, deserving pity rather than punishment.   He
made some sound of protest, but attempted no
delay in refunding the money Benham had prepaid.

Outside sounded the wheels of the returning carriage. They stopped. Amanda appeared in the
doorway and discovered Benham dominant.

He was a little short of breath, and as she came in
he was addressing the landlord with much earnestness in the following compact sentences.

"Attendez! Ecco! Adesso noi andiamo con
questa cattivissimo cavallo a Piedimulera. Si noi
arrivero in safety, securo that is, pagaremo. Non
altro. Si noi abbiamo accidento Dio — Dio have
mercy on your sinful soul. See! Capisce? That's
all."*

He turned to Amanda. "Get back into the
thing," he said. "We won't have these stinking
beasts think we are afraid of the job. I've just
made sure he won't have a profit by it if we smash
up. That's all. I might have known what he was
up to when he wanted the money beforehand." He
came to the doorway and with a magnificent gesture
commanded the perplexed driver to turn the carriage.

While that was being done he discoursed upon his
adjacent fellow-creatures. "A man who pays beforehand for anything in this filthy sort of life is a fool.
You see the standards of the beast. They think of

* "Now we will go with this beastly horse to Piedimulera.
If we get there safely I will pay. If we have an accident,
then ——"

nothing but their dirty little tricks to get profit, their garlic, their sour wine, their games of dominoes, their moments of lust. They crawl in this place like cockroaches in a warm corner of the fireplace until they die. Look at the scabby frontage of the house. Look at the men's faces. . . . Yes. So! Adequato. Aspettate. . . . Get back into the carriage, Amanda."

"You know it's dangerous, Cheetah. The horse is a shier. That man is blind in one eye."

"Get back into the carriage," said Benham, whitely angry. *I am going to drive!*"

"But — !"

Just for a moment Amanda looked scared. Then with a queer little laugh she jumped in again.

Amanda was never a coward when there was excitement afoot. "We'll smash!" she cried, by no means woefully.

"Get up beside me," said Benham speaking in English to the driver but with a gesture that translated him. Power over men radiated from Benham in this angry mood. He took the driver's seat. The little driver ascended and then with a grim calmness that brooked no resistance Benham reached over, took and fastened the apron over their knees to prevent any repetition of the jumping out tactics.

The recovering landlord became voluble in the doorway.

"In Piedimulera pagero," said Benham over his shoulder and brought the whip across the white outstanding ribs. "Get up!" said Benham.

Amanda gripped the sides of the seat as the carriage started into motion.

He laid the whip on again with such vigour that the horse forgot altogether to shy at the urchin that had scared it before.

"Amanda," said Benham leaning back. "If we do happen to go over on *that* side, jump out. It's all clear and wide for you. This side won't matter so —"

"*Mind!*" screamed Amanda and recalled him to his duties. He was off the road and he had narrowly missed an outstanding chestnut true.

"No, you don't," said Benham presently, and again their career became erratic for a time as after a slight struggle he replaced the apron over the knees of the deposed driver. It had been furtively released. After that Benham kept an eye on it that might have been better devoted to the road.

The road went down in a series of curves and corners. Now and then there were pacific interludes when it might have been almost any road. Then, again, it became specifically an Italian mountain road. Now and then only a row of all too infrequent granite stumps separated them from a sheer precipice. Some of the corners were miraculous, and once they had a wheel in a ditch for a time, they shaved the parapet of a bridge over a gorge and they drove a cyclist into a patch of maize, they narrowly missed a goat and jumped three gullies, thrice the horse stumbled and was jerked up in time, there were sickening moments, and withal they got down to Piedimulera unbroken and unspilt. It helped perhaps that the brake, with its handle like a barrel organ, had been screwed up before Benham took control. And when they were fairly on the level outside the town Benham suddenly pulled up, relinquished the driving into the proper hands and came into the carriage with Amanda.

"Safe now," he said compactly.

The driver appeared to be murmuring prayers very softly as he examined the brake.

Amanda was struggling with profound problems. "Why didn't you drive down in the first place?" she asked. "Without going back."

"The landlord annoyed me," he said. "I had to go back. . . . I wish I had kicked him. Hairy beast! If anything had happened, you see, he would have had his mean money. I couldn't bear to leave him."

"And why didn't you let *him* drive?" She indicated the driver by a motion of the head.

"I was angry," said Benham. "I was angry at the whole thing."

"Still —"

"You see I think I did that because he might have jumped off if I hadn't been up there to prevent him — I mean if we had had a smash. I didn't want him to get out of it."

"But you too —"

"You see I was angry. . . ."

"It's been as good as a switchback," said Amanda after reflection. "But weren't you a little careless about me, Cheetah?"

"I never thought of you," said Benham, and then as if he felt that inadequate: "You see — I was so annoyed. It's odd at times how annoyed one gets. Suddenly when that horse shied I realized what a beastly business life was — as those brutes up there live it. I want to clear out the whole hot, dirty, little aimless nest of them. . . ."

"No, I'm sure," he repeated after a pause as though he had been digesting something, "I wasn't thinking about you at all."

§ 4

The suppression of his discovery that his honeymoon was not in the least the great journey of world exploration he had intended, but merely an impulsive pleasure hunt, was by no means the only obscured and repudiated conflict that disturbed the mind and broke out upon the behaviour of Benham. Beneath that issue he was keeping down a far more intimate conflict. It was in those lower, still less recognized depths that the volcanic fire arose and the earthquakes gathered strength. The Amanda he had loved, the Amanda of the gallant stride and fluttering skirt was with him still, she marched rejoicing over the passes, and a dearer Amanda, a soft whispering creature with dusky hair, who took possession of him when she chose, a soft creature who was nevertheless a fierce creature, was also interwoven with his life. But — But there was now also a multitude of other Amandas who had this in common that they roused him to opposition, that they crossed

his moods and jarred upon his spirit. And particularly there was the Conquering Amanda not so
much proud of her beauty as eager to test it, so that
she was not unmindful of the stir she made in hotel
lounges, nor of the magic that may shine memorably
through the most commonplace incidental conversation. This Amanda was only too manifestly pleased to
think that she made peasant lovers discontented and
hotel porters unmercenary ; she let her light shine
before men. We lovers, who had deemed our own
subjugation a profound privilege, love not this
further expansiveness of our lady's empire. But
Benham knew that no aristocrat can be jealous ;
jealousy he held to be the vice of the hovel and
farmstead and suburban villa, and at an enormous
expenditure of will he ignored Amanda's waving
flags and roving glances. So, too, he denied that
Amanda who was sharp and shrewd about money
matters, that flash of an Amanda who was greedy for
presents and possessions, that restless Amanda who
fretted at any cessation of excitement, and that
darkly thoughtful Amanda whom chance observations and questions showed to be still considering an
account she had to settle with Lady Marayne. He
resisted these impressions, he shut them out of his
mind, but still they worked into his thoughts, and
presently he could find himself asking, even as he
and she went in step striding side by side through
the red-scarred pinewoods in the most perfect outward harmony, whether after all he was so happily
mated as he declared himself to be a score of times a

day, whether he wasn't catching glimpses of reality
through a veil of delusion that grew thinner and
thinner and might leave him disillusioned in the
face of a relationship —

Sometimes a man may be struck by a thought as
though he had been struck in the face, and when the
name of Mrs. Skelmersdale came into his head, he
glanced at his wife by his side as if it were something
that she might well have heard. Was this indeed the
same thing as that? Wonderful, fresh as the day
of Creation, clean as flame, yet the same! Was
Amanda indeed the sister of Mrs. Skelmersdale —
wrought of clean fire, but her sister? . . .

But also beside the inimical aspects which could
set such doubts afoot there were in her infinite variety
yet other Amandas neither very dear nor very annoy-
ing, but for the most part delightful, who entertained
him as strangers might, Amandas with an odd twist
which made them amusing to watch, jolly Amandas
who were simply irrelevant. There was for example
Amanda the Dog Mistress, with an astonishing
tact and understanding of dogs, who could explain
dogs and the cock of their ears and the droop of their
tails and their vanity and their fidelity, and why they
looked up and why they suddenly went off round the
corner, and their pride in the sound of their voices
and their dastardly thoughts and sniffing satisfac-
tions, so that for the first time dogs had souls for
Benham to see. And there was an Amanda with a
striking passion for the sleekness and soft noses of
horses. And there was an Amanda extremely

garrulous, who was a biographical dictionary and critical handbook to all the girls in the school she had attended at Chichester — they seemed a very girlish lot of girls; and an Amanda who was very knowing — knowing was the only word for it — about pictures and architecture. And these and all the other Amandas agreed together to develop and share this one quality in common, that altogether they pointed to no end, they converged on nothing. She was, it grew more and more apparent, a miscellany bound in a body. She was an animated discursiveness. That passion to get all things together into one aristocratic aim, that restraint of purpose, that imperative to focus, which was the structural essential of Benham's spirit, was altogether foreign to her composition.

There were so many Amandas, they were as innumerable as the Venuses — Cytherea, Cypria, Paphia, Popularia, Euplœa, Area, Verticordia, Etaira, Basilea, Myrtea, Libertina, Freya, Astarte, Philommedis, Telessigamma, Anadyomene, and a thousand others to whom men have bowed and built temples, a thousand and the same, and yet it seemed to Benham there was still one wanting.

The Amanda he had loved most wonderfully was that Amanda in armour who had walked with him through the wilderness of the world along the road to Chichester — and that Amanda came back to him no more.

§ 5

Amanda too was making her observations and discoveries.

These moods of his perplexed her; she was astonished to find he was becoming irritable; she felt that he needed a firm but gentle discipline in his deportment as a lover. At first he had been perfect. . . .

But Amanda was more prepared for human inconsecutiveness than Benham, because she herself was inconsecutive, and her dissatisfaction with his irritations and preoccupation broadened to no general discontent. He had seemed perfect and he wasn't. So nothing was perfect. And he had to be managed, just as one must manage a dog or a cousin or a mother or a horse. Anyhow she had got him, she had no doubt that she held him by a thousand ties, the spotless leopard had him between her teeth, he was a prisoner in the dusk of her hair, and the world was all one vast promise of entertainment.

§ 6

But the raid into the Balkans was not the tremendous success she had expected it to be. They had adventures, but they were not the richly coloured, mediaeval affairs she had anticipated. For the most part until Benham broke loose beyond Ochrida they were adventures in discomfort. In those remote parts of Europe inns die away and cease, and it had never occurred to Amanda that inns could die away anywhere. She had thought that they just became very simple and natural and quaint. And she had thought that when benighted people knocked at a door it would presently open hospitably. She had not expected shots at random from the window. And it is not usual in Albania generally for women, whether they are Christian or Moslem, to go about unveiled ; when they do so it leads to singular manifestations. The moral sense of the men is shocked and staggered, and they show it in many homely ways. Small boys at that age when feminine beauty does not yet prevail with them, pelt. Also in Mahometan districts they pelt men who do not wear fezzes, while occasionally Christians of the shawl-headed or skull-cap persuasions will pelt a fez. Sketching is always a peltable or mobable offence, as being contrary to the Koran, and sitting down tempts the pelter. Generally they pelt. The dogs of Albania are numerous, big, dirty, white dogs, large and hostile, and they attack with little hesitation. The women of Albania are secluded and remote, and indisposed to be of service to an alien sister. Roads are infrequent and most bridges have broken down. No bridge has been repaired since the later seventeenth century, and no new bridge has been made since the decline and fall of the Roman Empire. There are no shops at all. The scenery is magnificent but precipitous, and many of the high roads are difficult to trace. And there is rain. In Albania there is sometimes very heavy rain.

Yet in spite of these drawbacks they spent some

splendid hours in their exploration of that wild lost
country beyond the Adriatic headlands.   There was
the approach to Cattaro for example, through an arm
of the sea, amazingly beautiful on either shore, that
wound its way into the wild mountains and ended in
a deep blue bay under the tremendous declivity of
Montenegro. The quay, with its trees and lateen
craft, ran along under the towers and portcullised
gate of the old Venetian wall, within clustered the
town, and then the fortifications zigzagged up steeply
to a monstrous fantastic fortress perched upon a
great mountain headland that overhung the town.
Behind it the rocks, slashed to and fro with the road
to Cettinjé, continued to ascend into blue haze,
upward and upward until they became a purple
curtain that filled half the heavens.   The paved still
town was squalid by day, but in the evening it
became theatrically incredible, with an outdoor café
amidst flowers and creepers, a Hungarian military
band, a rabble of promenaders like a stage chorus in
gorgeous costumes and a great gibbous yellow moon.

And there was Kroia, which Benham and Amanda
saw first through the branches of the great trees that
bordered the broad green track they were following.
The town and its castle were poised at a tremendous
height, sunlit and brilliant against a sombre mass of
storm cloud, over vast cliffs and ravines.   Kroia continued to be beautiful through a steep laborious
approach up to the very place itself, a clustering
group of houses and bazaars crowned with a tower
and a minaret, and from a painted corridor upon

8

this crest they had a wonderful view of the great
seaward levels, and even far away the blue sea itself
stretching between Scutari and Durazzo.   The eye
fell in succession down the stages of a vast and various
descent, on the bazaars and tall minarets of the town,
on jagged rocks and precipices, on slopes of oak
forest and slopes of olive woods, on blue hills dropping away beyond blue hills to the coast.   And
behind them when they turned they saw great
mountains, sullenly magnificent, cleft into vast
irregular masses, dense with woods below and grim
and desolate above. . . .

These were unforgettable scenes, and so too was
the wild lonely valley through which they rode to
Ochrida amidst walnut and chestnut trees and
scattered rocks, and the first vision of that place
itself, with its fertile levels dotted with sheep and
cattle, its castle and clustering mosques, its spacious
blue lake and the great mountains rising up towards
Olympus under the sun.   And there was the first
view of the blue Lake of Presba seen between silvery
beech stems, and that too had Olympus in the far
background, plain now and clear and unexpectedly
snowy.   And there were midday moments when
they sat and ate under vines and heard voices singing
very pleasantly, and there were forest glades and
forest tracks in a great variety of beauty with mountains appearing through their parted branches,
there were ilex woods, chestnut woods, beech woods,
and there were strings of heavily-laden mules staggering up torrent-worn tracks, and strings of blue-

swathed mysterious-eyed women with burthens on their heads passing silently, and white remote houses and ruins and deep gorges and precipices and ancient half-ruinous bridges over unruly streams. And if there was rain there was also the ending of rain, rainbows, and the piercing of clouds by the sun's incandescence, and sunsets and the moon, first full, then new and then growing full again as the holiday wore on.

They found tolerable accommodation at Cattaro and at Cettinjé and at a place halfway between them. It was only when they had secured a guide and horses, and pushed on into the south-east of Montenegro that they began to realize the real difficulties of their journey. They aimed for a place called Podgoritza, which had a partially justifiable reputation for an inn, they missed the road and spent the night in the open beside a fire, rolled in the blankets they had very fortunately bought in Cettinjé. They supped on biscuits and Benham's brandy flask. It chanced to be a fine night, and, drawn like moths by the fire, four heavily-armed mountaineers came out of nowhere, sat down beside Benham and Amanda, rolled cigarettes, achieved conversation in bad Italian through the muleteer and awaited refreshment. They approved of the brandy highly, they finished it, and towards dawn warmed to song. They did not sing badly, singing in chorus, but it appeared to Amanda that the hour might have been better chosen. In the morning they were agreeably surprised to find one of the

Englishmen was an Englishwoman, and followed every accessible detail of her toilette with great interest. They were quite helpful about breakfast when the trouble was put to them; two vanished over a crest and reappeared with some sour milk, a slabby kind of bread, goat's cheese young but hardened, and coffee and the means of making coffee, and they joined spiritedly in the ensuing meal. It ought to have been extraordinarily good fun, this camp under the vast heavens and these wild visitors, but it was not such fun as it ought to have been because both Amanda and Benham were extremely cold, stiff, sleepy, grubby and cross, and when at last they were back in the way to Podgoritza and had parted, after some present-giving from their chance friends, they halted in a sunlit grassy place, rolled themselves up in their blankets and recovered their arrears of sleep.

Podgoritza was their first experience of a khan, those oriental substitutes for hotels, and it was a deceptively good khan, indeed it was not a khan at all, it was an inn; it provided meals, it had a kind of bar, or at any rate a row of bottles and glasses, it possessed an upper floor with rooms, separate rooms, opening on to a gallery. The room had no beds but it had a shelf about it on which Amanda and Benham rolled up in their blankets and slept. "We can do this sort of thing all right," said Amanda and Benham. "But we mustn't lose the way again."

"In Scutari," said Benham, "we will get an extra horse and a tent."

The way presently became a lake and they reached
Scutari by boat towards the dawn of the next
day. . . .

The extra horse involved the addition of its owner,
a small suspicious Latin Christian, to the company,
and of another horse for him and an ugly almost
hairless boy attendant.   Moreover the British consul
prevailed with Benham to accept the services of a
picturesque Arnaut *cavasse*, complete with a rifle,
knives, and other implements and the name of
Giorgio.   And as they got up into the highlands
beyond Scutari they began to realize the deceitful-
ness of Podgoritza and the real truth about khans.
Their next one they reached after a rainy evening,
and it was a cavernous room with a floor of indurated
mud and full of eye-stinging wood-smoke and wind
and the smell of beasts, unpartitioned, with a weakly
hostile custodian from whom no food could be got
but a little goat's flesh and bread.   The meat
Giorgio stuck upon a skewer in gobbets like cats-
meat and cooked before the fire.   For drink there
was coffee and raw spirits.   Against the wall in one
corner was a slab of wood rather like the draining
board in a scullery, and on this the guests were
expected to sleep.   The horses and the rest of the
party camped loosely about the adjacent corner
after a bitter dispute upon some unknown point
between the horse owner and the custodian.

Amanda and Benham were already rolled up on
their slanting board like a couple of chrysalids when
other company began to arrive through the open

door out of the moonlight, drawn thither by the
report of a travelling Englishwoman.

They were sturdy men in light coloured garments
adorned ostentatiously with weapons, they moved
mysteriously about in the firelit darknesses and
conversed in undertones with Giorgio. Giorgio
seemed to have considerable powers of exposition
and a gift for social organization. Presently he
came to Benham and explained that raki was available and that hospitality would do no harm; Benham and Amanda sat up and various romantic
figures with splendid moustaches came forward and
shook hands with him, modestly ignoring Amanda.
There was drinking, in which Benham shared, incomprehensible compliments, much ineffective saying
of "*Buona notte*," and at last Amanda and Benham
counterfeited sleep. This seemed to remove a check
on the conversation and a heated discussion in tense
undertones went on, it seemed interminably. . . .
Probably very few aspects of Benham and Amanda
were ignored. . . . Towards morning the twanging
of a string proclaimed the arrival of a querulous-
faced minstrel with a sort of embryonic one-stringed
horse-headed fiddle, and after a brief parley singing
began, a long high-pitched solo. The fiddle squealed
pitifully under the persuasion of a semicircular bow.
Two heads were lifted enquiringly.

The singer had taken up his position at their feet
and faced them. It was a compliment.

"*Oh!*" said Amanda, rolling over.

The soloist obliged with three songs, and then, just

as day was breaking, stopped abruptly and sprawled suddenly on the floor as if he had been struck asleep. He was vocal even in his sleep. A cock in the far corner began crowing and was answered by another outside. . . .

But this does not give a full account of the animation of the khan. *"Oh!"* said Amanda, rolling over again with the suddenness of accumulated anger.

"They're worse than in Scutari," said Benham, understanding her trouble instantly.

"It isn't days and nights we are having," said Benham a few days later, "it's days and nightmares."

But both he and Amanda had one quality in common. The deeper their discomfort the less possible it was to speak of turning back from the itinerary they had planned. . . .

They met no robbers, though an excited little English Levantine in Scutari had assured them they would do so and told a vivid story of a ride to Ipek, a delay on the road due to a sudden inexplicable lameness of his horse after a halt for refreshment, a political discussion that delayed him, his hurry through the still twilight to make up for lost time, the coming on of night and the sudden silent apparition out of the darkness of the woods about the road of a dozen armed men each protruding a gun barrel. "Sometimes they will wait for you at a ford or a broken bridge," he said. "In the mountains they rob for arms. They assassinate the Turkish soldiers even. It is better to go unarmed unless you mean to fight for it. . . . Have you got arms?"

"Just a revolver," said Benham.

But it was after that that he closed with Giorgio.

If they found no robbers in Albania, they met soon enough with bloodshed. They came to a village where a friend of a friend of Giorgio's was discovered, and they slept at his house in preference to the unclean and crowded khan. Here for the first time Amanda made the acquaintance of Albanian women and was carried off to the woman's region at the top of the house, permitted to wash, closely examined, shown a baby and confided in as generously as gesture and some fragments of Italian would permit. Benham slept on a rug on the first floor in a corner of honour beside the wood fire. There had been much confused conversation and some singing, he was dog-tired and slept heavily, and when presently he was awakened by piercing screams he sat up in a darkness that seemed to belong neither to time nor place. . . .

Near his feet was an ashen glow that gave no light.

His first perplexity gave way to dismay at finding no Amanda by his side. "Amanda!" he cried. . . .

Her voice floated down through a chink in the floor above. "What can it be, Cheetah?"

Then: "It's coming nearer."

The screaming continued, heart-rending, eviscerating shrieks. Benham, still confused, lit a match. All the men about him were stirring or sitting up and listening, their faces showing distorted and ugly in the flicker of his light. "*Che e?*" he tried. No one answered. Then one by one they stood up and went softly to the ladder that led to the stable-room below. Benham struck a second match and a third.

"Giorgio!" he called.

The cavasse made an arresting gesture and followed discreetly and noiselessly after the others, leaving Benham alone in the dark.

Benham heard their shuffling patter, one after the other, down the ladder, the sounds of a door being unbarred softly, and then no other sound but that incessant shrieking in the darkness.

Had they gone out? Were they standing at the door looking out into the night and listening?

Amanda had found the chink and her voice sounded nearer.

"It's a woman," she said.

The shrieking came nearer and nearer, long, repeated, throat-tearing shrieks. Far off there was a great clamour of dogs. And there was another sound, a whisper —?

"*Rain!*"

The shrieks seemed to turn into a side street and receded. The tension of listening relaxed. Men's voices sounded below in question and answer. Dogs close at hand barked shortly and then stopped enquiringly.

Benham seemed to himself to be sitting alone for an interminable time. He lit another match and consulted his watch. It was four o'clock and nearly dawn. . . .

Then slowly and stumbling up the ladder the men began to return to Benham's room.

"Ask them what it is," urged Amanda.

But for a time not even Giorgio would understand Benham's questions. There seemed to be a doubt whether he ought to know. The shrieking approached again and then receded. Giorgio came and stood, a vague thoughtful figure, by the embers of the fire. Explanation dropped from him reluctantly. It was nothing. Some one had been killed : that was all. It was a vendetta. A man had been missing overnight, and this morning his brother who had been prowling and searching with some dogs had found him, or rather his head. It was on this side of the ravine, thrown over from the other bank on which the body sprawled stiffly, wet through, and now growing visible in the gathering daylight. Yes — the voice was the man's wife. It was raining hard. . . . There would be shrieking for nine days. Yes, nine days. Confirmation with the fingers when Benham still fought against the facts. Her friends and relatives would come and shriek too. Two of the dead man's aunts were among the best keeners in the whole land. They could keen marvellously. It was raining too hard to go on. . . . The road would be impossible in rain. . . . Yes it was very melancholy. Her house was close at hand. Perhaps twenty or thirty women would join her. It was impossible to go on until it had stopped raining. It would be tiresome, but what could one do? . . .

§ 7

As they sat upon the parapet of a broken bridge on the road between Elbassan and Ochrida Benham was moved to a dissertation upon the condition of Albania and the politics of the Balkan peninsula.

"Here we are," he said, "not a week from London, and you see the sort of life that men live when the forces of civilization fail. We have been close to two murders —"

"Two?"

"That little crowd in the square at Scutari — That was a murder. I didn't tell you at the time."

"But I knew it was," said Amanda.

"And you see the filth of it all, the toiling discomfort of it all. There is scarcely a house here in all the land that is not filthier and viler than the worst slum in London. No man ventures far from his village without arms, everywhere there is fear. The hills are impassable because of the shepherd's dogs. Over those hills a little while ago a stranger was torn to pieces by dogs — and partially eaten. Amanda, these dogs madden me. I shall let fly at the beasts. The infernal indignity of it! But that is by the way. You see how all this magnificent country lies waste with nothing but this crawling, ugly mockery of human life."

"They sing," said Amanda.

"Yes," said Benham and reflected, "they do sing. I suppose singing is the last thing left to men. When there is nothing else you can still sit about and sing.

Miners who have been buried in mines will sing, people going down in ships."

"The Sussex labourers don't sing," said Amanda. "These people sing well."

"They would probably sing as well if they were civilized. Even if they didn't I shouldn't care. All the rest of their lives is muddle and cruelty and misery. Look at the women. There was that party of bent creatures we met yesterday, carrying great bundles, carrying even the men's cloaks and pipes, while their rascal husbands and brothers swaggered behind. Look at the cripples we have seen and the mutilated men. If we have met one man without a nose, we have met a dozen. And stunted people. All these people are like evil schoolboys; they do nothing but malicious mischief; there is nothing adult about them but their voices; they are like the heroic dreams of young ruffians in a penitentiary. You saw that man at Scutari in the corner of the bazaar, the gorgeous brute, you admired him —."

"The man with the gold inlaid pistols and the diamonds on his yataghan. He wanted to show them to us."

"Yes. You let him see you admired him."

"I liked the things on his stall."

"Well, he has killed nearly thirty people."

"In duels?"

"Good Lord! *No!* Assassinations. His shoemaker annoyed him by sending in a bill. He went to the man's stall, found him standing with his child in

his arms and blew out his brains. He blundered
against a passer-by in the road and shot him. Those
are his feats. Sometimes his pistols go off in the
bazaar just by accident."

"Does nobody kill him?"

"I wanted to," said Benham and became thoughtful for a time. "I think I ought to have made some
sort of quarrel. But then as I am an Englishman
he might have hesitated. He would have funked a
strange beast like me. And I couldn't have shot
him if he had hesitated. And if he hadn't — "

"But doesn't a blood feud come down on him?"

"It only comes down on his family. The shoemaker's son thought the matter over and squared
accounts by putting the muzzle of a gun into the small
of the back of our bully's uncle. It was easier that
way. . . . You see you're dealing with men of
thirteen years old or thereabouts, the boy who doesn't
grow up."

"But doesn't the law —?"

"There's no law. Only custom and the Turkish
tax collector.

"You see this is what men are where there is no
power, no discipline, no ruler, no responsibility.
This is a masterless world. This is pure democracy.
This is the natural state of men. This is the world
of the bully and the brigand and assassin, the world
of the mud-pelter and brawler, the world of the bent
woman, the world of the flea and the fly, the open
drain and the baying dog. This is what the British
sentimentalist thinks a noble state for men."

"They fight for freedom."

"They fight among each other. There are their private feuds and their village feuds and above all that great feud religion. In Albania there is only one religion and that is hate. But there are three churches for the better cultivation of hate and cruelty, the Latin, the Greek and the Mahometan."

"But no one has ever conquered these people."

"Any one could, the Servians, the Bulgarians, the Greeks, the Italians, the Austrians. Why, they can't even shoot! It's just the balance of power and all that foolery keeps this country a roadless wilderness. Good God, how I tire of it! These men who swagger and stink, their brawling dogs, their greasy priests and dervishes, the down-at-heel soldiers, the bribery and robbery, the cheating over the money. . . ."

He slipped off the parapet, too impatient to sit any longer, and began to pace up and down in the road.

"One marvels that no one comes to clear up this country, one itches to be at the job, and then one realizes that before one can begin here, one must get to work back there, where the fools and pedants of *Welt Politik* scheme mischief one against another. This country frets me. I can't see any fun in it, can't see the humour of it. And the people away there know no better than to play off tribe against tribe, sect against sect, one peasant prejudice against another. Over this pass the foolery grows grimmer and viler. We shall come to where the Servian plots against the Bulgarian and the Greek against both, and the Turk, with spasmodic massacres and indulgences, broods over the brew. Every division is subdivided. There are two sorts of Greek church, Exarchic, Patriarchic, both teaching by threat and massacre. And there is no one, no one, with the sense to over-ride all these squalid hostilities. All those fools away there in London and Vienna and St. Petersburg and Rome take sides as though these beastly tribes and leagues and superstitions meant anything but blank, black, damnable ignorance. One fool stands up for the Catholic Albanians, another finds heroes in the Servians, another talks of Brave Little Montenegro, or the Sturdy Bulgarian, or the Heroic Turk. There isn't a religion in the whole Balkan peninsula, there isn't a tribal or national sentiment that deserves a moment's respect from a sane man. They're things like niggers' nose-rings and Chinese secret societies; childish things, idiot things that have to go. Yet there is no one who will preach the only possible peace, which is the peace of the world-state, the open conspiracy of all the sane men in the world against the things that break us up into wars and futilities. And here am I — who have the light — *wandering!* Just wandering!"

He shrugged his shoulders and came to stare at the torrent under the bridge.

"You're getting ripe for London, Cheetah," said Amanda softly.

"I want somehow to get to work, to get my hands on definite things."

"How can we get back?"

She had to repeat her question presently.

"We can go on. Over the hills is Ochrida and then over another pass is Presba, and from there we go down into Monastir and reach a railway and get back to the world of our own times again."

§ 8

But before they reached the world of their own times Macedonia was to show them something grimmer than Albania.

They were riding through a sunlit walnut wood beyond Ochrida when they came upon the thing.

The first they saw of it looked like a man lying asleep on a grassy bank. But he lay very still indeed, he did not look up, he did not stir as they passed, the pose of his hand was stiff, and when Benham glanced back at him, he stifled a little cry of horror. For this man had no face and the flies had been busy upon him. . . .

Benham caught Amanda's bridle so that she had to give her attention to her steed.

"Ahead!" he said, "Ahead! Look, a village!"

(Why the devil didn't they bury the man? Why?

And that fool Giorgio and the others were pulling up and beginning to chatter. After all she might look back.)

Through the trees now they could see houses. He quickened his pace and jerked Amanda's horse forward. . . .

But the village was a still one. Not a dog barked.

Here was an incredible village without even a dog!

And then, then they saw some more people lying about. A woman lay in a doorway. Near her was something muddy that might have been a child, beyond were six men all spread out very neatly in a row with their faces to the sky.

"Cheetah!" cried Amanda, with her voice going up. "They've been killed. Some one has killed them."

Benham halted beside her and stared stupidly.

"It's a band," he said. "It's — propaganda. Greeks or Turks or Bulgarians."

"But their feet and hands are fastened! And — . . . *What have they been doing to them?* . . ."

"I want to kill," cried Benham. "Oh! I want to kill people. Come on, Amanda! It blisters one's eyes. Come away. Come away! Come!"

Her face was white and her eyes terror-stricken. She obeyed him mechanically. She gave one last look at those bodies. . . .

Down the deep-rutted soil of the village street they clattered. They came to houses that had been set on fire. . . .

"What is that hanging from a tree?" cried Amanda. "Oh, oh!"

"Come on. . . ."

Behind them rode the others scared and hurrying.

The sunlight had become the light of hell. There was no air but horror. Across Benham's skies these fly-blown trophies of devilry dangled mockingly in the place of God. He had no thought but to get away.

T

Presently they encountered a detachment of
Turkish soldiers, very greasy and ragged, with
worn-out boots and yellow faces, toiling up the stony
road belatedly to the village.   Amanda and Benham
riding one behind the other in a stricken silence
passed this labouring column without a gesture, but
presently they heard the commander stopping and
questioning Giorgio. . . .

Then Giorgio and the others came clattering to
overtake them.

Giorgio was too full to wait for questions.   He
talked eagerly to Benham's silence.

It must have happened yesterday, he explained.
They were Bulgarians — traitors.   They had been
converted to the Patriarchists by the Greeks — by a
Greek band, that is to say.   They had betrayed
one of their own people.   Now a Bulgarian band had
descended upon them.   Bulgarian bands it seemed
were always particularly rough on Bulgarian-speak-
ing Patriarchists. . . .

§ 9

That night they slept in a dirty little room in a
peasant's house in Resnia, and in the middle of the
night Amanda woke up with a start and heard Benham talking.   He seemed to be sitting up as he
talked.   But he was not talking to her and his voice
sounded strange.

"Flies," he said, "in the sunlight!"

He was silent for a time and then he repeated the
same words.

Then suddenly he began to declaim. "Oh! Brutes together. Apes. Apes with knives. Have they no lord, no master, to save them from such things? This is the life of men when no man rules. . . . When no man rules. . . . Not even himself. . . . It is because we are idle, because we keep our wits slack and our wills weak that these poor devils live in hell. These things happen here and everywhere when the hand that rules grows weak. Away in China now they are happening. Persia. Africa. . . . Russia staggers. And I who should serve the law, I who should keep order, wander and make love. . . . My God! may I never forget! May I never forget! Flies in the sunlight! That man's face. And those six men!

"Grip the savage by the throat.

"The weak savage in the foreign office, the weak savage at the party headquarters, feud and indolence and folly. It is all one world. This and that are all one thing. The spites of London and the mutilations of Macedonia. The maggots that eat men's faces and the maggots that rot their minds. Rot their minds. Rot their minds. Rot their minds. . . ."

To Amanda it sounded like delirium.

"*Cheetah!*" she said suddenly between remonstrance and a cry of terror.

The darkness suddenly became quite still. He did not move.

She was afraid. "Cheetah!" she said again.

"What is it, Amanda?"

"I thought —. Are you all right?"

"Quite."

"But do you feel well?"

"I've got this cold I caught in Ochrida.   I suppose I'm feverish.   But — yes, I'm well."

"You were talking."

Silence for a time.

"I was thinking," he said.

"You talked."

"I'm sorry," he said after another long pause.

§ 10

The next morning Benham had a pink spot on either cheek, his eyes were feverishly bright, he would touch no food and instead of coffee he wanted water. "In Monastir there will be a doctor," he said. "Monastir is a big place.   In Monastir I will see a doctor.   I want a doctor."

They rode out of the village in the freshness before sunrise and up long hills, and sometimes they went in the shade of woods and sometimes in a flooding sunshine.   Benham now rode in front, preoccupied, intent, regardless of Amanda, a stranger, and she rode close behind him wondering.

"When you get to Monastir, young man," she told him, inaudibly, "you will go straight to bed and we'll see what has to be done with you."

"*Ammalato*," said Giorgio confidentially, coming abreast of her.

"*Medico in Monastir*," said Amanda.

"*Si, — molti medici, Monastir*," Giorgio agreed.

Then came the inevitable dogs, big white brutes,

three in full cry charging hard at Benham and a younger less enterprising beast running along the high bank above yapping and making feints to descend.

The goatherd, reclining under the shadow of a rock, awaited Benham's embarrassment with an indolent malice.

"You *uncivilized* Beasts!" cried Benham, and before Amanda could realize what he was up to, she heard the crack of his revolver and saw a puff of blue smoke drift away above his right shoulder. The foremost beast rolled over and the goatherd had sprung to his feet. He shouted with something between anger and dismay as Benham, regardless of the fact that the other dogs had turned and were running back, let fly a second time. Then the goatherd had clutched at the gun that lay on the grass near at hand, Giorgio was bawling in noisy remonstrance and also getting ready to shoot, and the horse-owner and his boy were clattering back to a position of neutrality up the stony road. "*Bang!*" came a flight of lead within a yard of Benham, and then the goatherd was in retreat behind a rock and Giorgio was shouting "*Avanti, Avanti!*" to Amanda.

She grasped his intention and in another moment she had Benham's horse by the bridle and was leading the retreat. Giorgio followed close, driving the two baggage mules before him.

"I am tired of dogs," Benham said. "Tired to death of dogs. All savage dogs must be shot. All through the world. I am tired — "

Their road carried them down through the rocky

pass and then up a long slope in the open. Far
away on the left they saw the goatherd running and
shouting and other armed goatherds appearing
among the rocks.   Behind them the horse-owner and
his boy came riding headlong across the zone of
danger.

"Dogs must be shot," said Benham, exalted.
"Dogs must be shot."

"Unless they are *good* dogs," said Amanda, keeping beside him with an eye on his revolver.

"Unless they are good dogs to every one," said
Benham.

They rushed along the road in a turbulent dusty
huddle of horses and mules and riders.   The horse-
owner, voluble in Albanian, was trying to get past
them.   His boy pressed behind him.   Giorgio in
the rear had unslung his rifle and got it across the
front of his saddle.   Far away they heard the sound
of a shot, and a kind of shudder in the air overhead
witnessed to the flight of the bullet.   They crested a
rise and suddenly between the tree boughs Monastir
was in view, a wide stretch of white town, with many
cypress and plane trees, a winding river with many
wooden bridges, clustering minarets of pink and
white, a hilly cemetery, and scattered patches of
soldiers' tents like some queer white crop to supplement its extensive barracks.

As they hurried down towards this city of refuge a
long string of mules burthened with great bales of
green stuff appeared upon a convergent track to the
left.   Besides the customary muleteers there were,

by way of an escort, a couple of tattered Turkish soldiers. All these men watched the headlong approach of Benham's party with apprehensive inquiry. Giorgio shouted some sort of information that made the soldiers brighten up and stare up the hill, and set the muleteers whacking and shouting at their convoy. It struck Amanda that Giorgio must be telling lies about a Bulgarian band. In another moment Benham and Amanda found themselves swimming in a torrent of mules. Presently they overtook a small flock of fortunately nimble sheep, and picked up several dogs, dogs that happily disregarded Benham in the general confusion. They also comprehended a small springless cart, two old women with bundles and an elderly Greek priest, before their dusty, barking, shouting cavalcade reached the outskirts of Monastir. The two soldiers had halted behind to cover the retreat.

Benham's ghastly face was now bedewed with sweat and he swayed in his saddle as he rode. "This is *not* civilization, Amanda," he said, "this is *not* civilization."

And then suddenly with extraordinary pathos: "Oh! I want to go to *bed!* I want to go to *bed!* A bed with sheets. . . ."

To ride into Monastir is to ride into a maze. The streets go nowhere in particular. At least that was the effect on Amanda and Benham. It was as if Monastir too had a temperature and was slightly delirious. But at last they found an hotel — quite a civilized hotel. . . .

The doctor in Monastir was an Armenian with an ambition that outran his capacity to speak English. He had evidently studied the language chiefly from books. He thought *these* was pronounced "theser" and *those* was pronounced "thoser," and that every English sentence should be taken at a rush. He diagnosed Benham's complaint in various languages and failed to make his meaning clear to Amanda. One combination of words he clung to obstinately, having clearly the utmost faith in its expressiveness. To Amanda it sounded like, "May, Ah! Slays," and it seemed to her that he sought to intimate a probable fatal termination of Benham's fever. But it was clear that the doctor was not satisfied that she understood. He came again with a queer little worn book, a parallel vocabulary of half-a-dozen European languages.

He turned over the pages and pointed to a word. "May! Ah! Slays!" he repeated, reproachfully, almost bitterly.

"Oh, *measles!*" cried Amanda. . . .

So the spirited honeymoon passed its zenith.

§ 11

The Benhams went as soon as possible down to Smyrna and thence by way of Uskub tortuously back to Italy. They recuperated at the best hotel of Locarno in golden November weather, and just before Christmas they turned their faces back to England.

Benham's plans were comprehensive but entirely vague; Amanda had not so much plans as intentions. . . .

CHAPTER THE FIFTH

THE ASSIZE OF JEALOUSY

§ 1

IT was very manifest in the disorder of papers amidst which White spent so many evenings of interested perplexity before this novel began to be written that Benham had never made any systematic attempt at editing or revising his accumulation at all. There were not only overlapping documents, in which he had returned again to old ideas and restated them in the light of fresh facts and an apparent unconsciousness of his earlier effort, but there were mutually destructive papers, new views quite ousting the old had been tossed in upon the old, and the very definition of the second limitation, as it had first presented itself to the writer, had been abandoned. To begin with, this second division had been labelled "Sex," in places the heading remained, no effective substitute had been chosen for some time, but there was a closely-written memorandum, very much erased and written over and amended, which showed Benham's early dissatisfaction with that crude rendering of what he had in mind. This memorandum was tacked to an interrupted fragment of autobiography, a manuscript soliloquy in which Benham had been discussing his married life.

"It was not until I had been married for the better part of a year, and had spent more than six months in London, that I faced the plain issue between the aims I had set before myself and the claims and immediate necessities of my personal life. For all that time I struggled not so much to reconcile them as to serve them simultaneously. . . ."

At that the autobiography stopped short, and the intercalary note began.

This intercalary note ran as follows:

"I suppose a mind of my sort cannot help but tend towards simplification, towards making all life turn upon some one dominant idea, complex perhaps in its reality but reducible at last to one consistent simple statement, a dominant idea which is essential as nothing else is essential, which makes and sustains and justifies. This is perhaps the innate disposition of the human mind, at least of the European mind — for I have some doubts about the Chinese. Theology drives obstinately towards an ultimate unity in God, science towards an ultimate unity in law, towards a fundamental element and a universal material truth from which all material truths evolve, and in matters of conduct there is the same tendency to refer to a universal moral law. Now this may be a simplification due to the need of the human mind to comprehend, and its inability to do so until the load is lightened by neglecting factors. William James has suggested that on account of this, theology may be obstinately working away from the truth, that the truth may be that there are several or many incompatible and incommensurable gods; science, in the same search for unity, may follow divergent methods of inquiry into ultimately uninterchangeable generalizations; and there may be not only not one universal moral law, but no effective reconciliation of the various rights and duties of a single individual. At any rate I find myself doubtful to this day about my own personal systems of right and wrong. I can never get all my life into one focus. It is exactly like examining a rather thick section with a microscope of small penetration; sometimes one level is clear and the rest foggy and monstrous, and sometimes another.

"Now the ruling *me*, I do not doubt, is the man who has set his face to this research after aristocracy, and from the standpoint of this research it is my duty to subordinate all other considerations to this work of clearing up the conception of rule and nobility in human affairs. This is my aristocratic self. What I did not grasp for a long time, and which now grows clearer and clearer to me, is firstly that this aristocratic self is not the whole of me, it has absolutely nothing to do with a pain in my ear or in my heart, with a scar on my hand or my memory, and secondly that it is not altogether mine. Whatever knowledge I have of the quality of science, whatever will I have towards right, is of it; but if from without, from the reasoning or demonstration or reproof of some one else, there comes to me clear knowledge, clarified will, that also is as it were a part of my aristocratic self coming home to me from the outside.

How often have I not found my own mind in Prothero
after I have failed to find it in myself? It is, to be
paradoxical, my impersonal personality, this Being
that I have in common with all scientific-spirited
and aristocratic-spirited men. This it is that I am
trying to get clear from the great limitations of
humanity. When I assert a truth for the sake of
truth to my own discomfort or injury, there again
is this incompatibility of the aristocratic self and
the accepted, confused, conglomerate self of the
unanalyzed man. The two have a separate system
of obligations. One's affections, compounded as
they are in the strangest way of physical reactions
and emotional associations, one's implicit pledges
to particular people, one's involuntary reactions,
one's pride and jealousy, all that one might call
the dramatic side of one's life, may be in conflict
with the definitely seen rightnesses of one's higher
use. . . ."

The writing changed at this point.

"All this seems to me at once as old as the hills
and too new to be true. This is like the conflict
of the Superior Man of Confucius to control himself, it is like the Christian battle of the spirit with
the flesh, it savours of that eternal wrangle between
the general and the particular which is metaphysics,
it was for this aristocratic self, for righteousness'
sake, that men have hungered and thirsted, and
on this point men have left father and mother and
child and wife and followed after salvation. This
world-wide, ever-returning antagonism has filled

the world in every age with hermits and lamas, recluses and teachers, devoted and segregated lives. It is a perpetual effort to get above the simplicity of barbarism. Whenever men have emerged from the primitive barbarism of the farm and the tribe, then straightway there has emerged this conception of a specialized life a little lifted off the earth; often, for the sake of freedom, celibate, usually disciplined, sometimes directed, having a generalized aim, beyond personal successes and bodily desires. So it is that the philosopher, the scientifically concentrated man, has appeared, often, I admit, quite ridiculously at first, setting out upon the long journey that will end only when the philosopher is king. . . .

"At first I called my Second Limitation, Sex. But from the outset I meant more than mere sexual desire, lust and lustful imaginings, more than personal reactions to beauty and spirited living, more even than what is called love. On the one hand I had in mind many appetites that are not sexual yet turn to bodily pleasure, and on the other there are elements of pride arising out of sex and passing into other regions, all the elements of rivalry for example, that have strained my first definition to the utmost. And I see now that this Second Limitation as I first imagined it spreads out without any definite boundary, to include one's rivalries with old schoolfellows, for example, one's generosities to beggars and dependents, one's desire to avenge an injured friend, one's point of honour, one's regard for the

good opinion of an aunt and one's concern for the
health of a pet cat. All these things may enrich,
but they may also impede and limit the aristocratic
scheme. I thought for a time I would call this
ill-defined and miscellaneous wilderness of limitation
the Personal Life. But at last I have decided to
divide this vast territory of difficulties into two
subdivisions and make one of these Indulgence,
meaning thereby pleasurable indulgence of sense or
feeling, and the other a great mass of self-regarding
motives that will go with a little stretching under
the heading of Jealousy. I admit motives are
continually playing across the boundary of these
two divisions, I should find it difficult to argue a
case for my classification, but in practice these two
groupings have a quite definite meaning for me.
There is pride in the latter group of impulses and
not in the former; the former are always a little
apologetic. Fear, Indulgence, Jealousy, these are
the First Three Limitations of the soul of man.
And the greatest of these is Jealousy, because it
can use pride. Over them the Life Aristocratic,
as I conceive it, marches to its end. It saves itself
for the truth rather than sacrifices itself romanti-
cally for a friend. It justifies vivisection if thereby
knowledge is won for ever. It upholds that Brutus
who killed his sons. It forbids devotion to women,
courts of love and all such decay of the chivalrous
idea. And it resigns — so many things that no
common Man of Spirit will resign. Its intention
transcends these things. Over all the world it

would maintain justice, order, a noble peace, and
it would do this without indignation, without resentment, without mawkish tenderness or individualized
enthusiasm or any queen of beauty. It is of a cold
austere quality, commanding sometimes admiration
but having small hold upon the affections of men.
So that it is among its foremost distinctions that its
heart is steeled. . . ."

There this odd fragment ended and White was
left to resume the interrupted autobiography.

§ 2

What moods, what passions, what nights of despair
and gathering storms of anger, what sudden cruelties
and amazing tendernesses are buried and hidden and
implied in every love story! What a waste is there
of exquisite things! So each spring sees a million
glorious beginnings, a sunlit heaven in every opening
leaf, warm perfection in every stirring egg, hope
and fear and beauty beyond computation in every
forest tree; and in the autumn before the snows
come they have all gone, of all that incalculable
abundance of life, of all that hope and adventure,
excitement and deliciousness, there is scarcely more
to be found than a soiled twig, a dirty seed, a dead
leaf, black mould or a rotting feather. . . .

White held the ten or twelve pencilled pages
that told how Benham and Amanda drifted into
antagonism and estrangement and as he held it
he thought of the laughter and delight they must
have had together, the exquisite excitements of

her eye, the racing colour of her cheek, the gleams of light upon her skin, the flashes of wit between them, the sense of discovery, the high rare paths' they had followed, the pools in which they had swum together. And now it was all gone into nothingness, there was nothing left of it, nothing at all, but just those sheets of statement, and it may be, stored away in one single mind, like things forgotten in an attic, a few neglected faded memories. . . .

And even those few sheets of statement were more than most love leaves behind it. For a time White would not read them. They lay neglected on his knee as he sat back in Benham's most comfortable chair and enjoyed an entirely beautiful melancholy.

White too had seen and mourned the spring.

Indeed, poor dear! he had seen and mourned several springs. . . .

With a sigh he took up the manuscript and read Benham's desiccated story of intellectual estrangement, and how in the end he had decided to leave his wife and go out alone upon that journey of inquiry he had been planning when first he met her.

§ 3

Amanda had come back to England in a state of extravagantly vigorous womanhood. Benham's illness, though it lasted only two or three weeks, gave her a sense of power and leadership for which

she had been struggling instinctively ever since
they came together.   For a time at Locarno he was
lax-minded and indolent, and in that time she formed
her bright and limited plans for London.   Benham
had no plans as yet but only a sense of divergence,
as though he was being pulled in opposite directions
by two irresistible forces.   To her it was plain
that he needed occupation, some distinguished
occupation, and she could imagine nothing better
for him than a political career.   She perceived he
had personality, that he stood out among men so
that his very silences were effective.   She loved
him immensely, and she had tremendous ambitions
for him and through him.

And also London, the very thought of London,
filled her with appetite.   Her soul thirsted for
London.   It was like some enormous juicy fruit
waiting for her pretty white teeth, a place almost
large enough to give her avidity the sense of enough.
She felt it waiting for her, household, servants, a
carriage, shops and the jolly delight of buying and
possessing things, the opera, first-nights, picture
exhibitions, great dinner-parties, brilliant lunch
parties, crowds seen from a point of vantage, the
carriage in a long string of fine carriages with the
lamplit multitude peering, Amanda in a thousand
bright settings, in a thousand various dresses.
She had had love ; it had been glorious, it was still
glorious, but her love-making became now at times
almost perfunctory in the contemplation of these
approaching delights and splendours and excitements.

U

She knew, indeed, that ideas were at work in Benham's head; but she was a realist. She did not see why ideas should stand in the way of a career. Ideas are a brightness, the good looks of the mind. One talks ideas, but *the thing that is, is the thing that is.* And though she believed that Benham had a certain strength of character of his own, she had that sort of confidence in his love for her and in the power of her endearments that has in it the assurance of a faint contempt. She had mingled pride and sense in the glorious realization of the power over him that her wit and beauty gave her. She had held him faint with her divinity, intoxicated with the pride of her complete possession, and she did not dream that the moment when he should see clearly that she could deliberately use these ultimate delights to rule and influence him, would be the end of their splendour and her power. Her nature, which was just a nest of vigorous appetites, was incapable of suspecting his gathering disillusionment until it burst upon her.

Now with her attention set upon London ahead he could observe her. In the beginning he had never seemed to be observing her at all, they dazzled one another; it seemed extraordinary now to him to note how much he had been able to disregard. There were countless times still when he would have dropped his observation and resumed that mutual exaltation very gladly, but always now other things possessed her mind. . . .

There was still an immense pleasure for him in

her vigour; there was something delightful in her
pounce, even when she was pouncing on things
superficial, vulgar or destructive. She made him
understand and share the excitement of a big night
at the opera, the glitter and prettiness of a smart
restaurant, the clustering little acute adventures
of a great reception of gay people, just as she had
already made him understand and sympathize
with dogs. She picked up the art world where
he had laid it down, and she forced him to feel
dense and slow before he rebelled against her multitudinous enthusiasms and admirations. South Harting had had its little group of artistic people; it
is not one of your sleepy villages, and she slipped
back at once into the movement. Those were the
great days of John, the days before the Post Im-
pressionist outbreak. John, Orpen, Tonks, she
bought them with vigour. Artistic circles began
to revolve about her. Very rapidly she was in
possession. . . . And among other desirable things
she had, it seemed, pounced upon and captured
Lady Marayne.

At any rate it was clear that that awful hostile
silence and aloofness was to end. Benham never
quite mastered how it was done. But Amanda
had gone in one morning to Desborough Street,
very sweetly and chastely dressed, had abased herself and announced a possible (though subsequently
disproved) grandchild. And she had appreciated
the little lady so highly and openly, she had so
instantly caught and reproduced her tone, that

her success, though only temporary in its completeness, was immediate. In the afternoon Benham was amazed by the apparition of his mother amidst the scattered unsettled furnishings of the new home Amanda had chosen in Lancaster Gate. He was in the hall, the door stood open awaiting packing-cases from a van without. In the open doorway she shone, looking the smallest of dainty things. There was no effect of her coming but only of her having arrived there, as a little blue butterfly will suddenly alight on a flower.

"Well, Poff!" said Lady Marayne, ignoring abysses, "What are you up to now, Poff? Come and embrace me. . . ."

"No, not so," she said, "stiffest of sons. . . ."

She laid hold of his ears in the old fashion and kissed one eye.

"Congratulations, dear little Poff. Oh! congratulations! In heaps. I'm so *glad*."

Now what was that for?

And then Amanda came out upon the landing upstairs, saw the encounter with an involuntary cry of joy, and came downstairs with arms wide open. It was the first intimation he had of their previous meeting. He was for some minutes a stunned, entirely inadequate Benham. . . .

§ 4

At first Amanda knew nobody in London, except a few people in the Hampstead Garden suburb that she had not the slightest wish to know, and then

very quickly she seemed to know quite a lot of people. The artistic circle brought in people, Lady
Marayne brought in people; they spread. It
was manifest the Benhams were a very bright young
couple; he would certainly do something considerable presently, and she was bright and daring, jolly
to look at and excellent fun, and, when you came
to talk to her, astonishingly well informed. They
passed from one hostess's hand to another: they
reciprocated. The Clynes people and the Rush-
tones took her up; Mr. Evesham was amused
by her, Lady Beach Mandarin proclaimed her
charm like a trumpet, the Young Liberal people
made jealous advances, Lord Moggeridge found
she listened well, she lit one of the brightest week-
end parties Lady Marayne had ever gathered at
Chexington. And her descriptions of recent danger
and adventure in Albania not only entertained
her hearers but gave her just that flavour of personal
courage which completes the fascination of a young
woman. People in the gaps of a halting dinner-
table conversation would ask: "Have you met
Mrs. Benham?"

Meanwhile Benham appeared to be talking. A
smiling and successful young woman, who a year
ago had been nothing more than a leggy girl with a
good lot of miscellaneous reading in her head, and
vaguely engaged, or at least friendly to the pitch
of engagement, to Mr. Rathbone-Sanders, may be
forgiven if in the full tide of her success she does
not altogether grasp the intention of her husband's

discourse. It seemed to her that he was obsessed
by a responsibility for civilization and the idea
that he was aristocratic. (Secretly she was inclined
to doubt whether he was justified in calling himself
aristocratic; at the best his mother was county-
stuff; but still if he did there was no great harm
in it nowadays.) Clearly his line was Tory-Democ-
racy, social reform through the House of Lords
and friendly intimacy with the more spirited young
peers. And it was only very slowly and reluctantly
that she was forced to abandon this satisfactory
solution of his problem. She reproduced all the
equipment and comforts of his Finacue Street
study in their new home, she declared constantly
that she would rather forego any old social thing
than interfere with his work, she never made him
go anywhere with her without first asking if his
work permitted it. To relieve him of the burthen
of such social attentions she even made a fag or so.
The making of fags out of manifestly stricken
men, the keeping of tamed and hopeless admirers,
seemed to her to be the most natural and reasonable of feminine privileges. They did their useful little services until it pleased the Lord Cheetah
to come to his own. That was how she put it. . . .

But at last he was talking to her in tones that
could no longer be ignored. He was manifestly
losing his temper with her. There was a novel
austerity in his voice and a peculiar whiteness
about his face on certain occasions that lingered in
her memory.

He was indeed making elaborate explanations. He said that what he wanted to do was to understand "the collective life of the world," and that this was not to be done in a West-End study. He had an extraordinary contempt, it seemed, for both sides in the drama of British politics. He had extravagant ideas of beginning in some much more fundamental way. He wanted to understand this "collective life of the world," because ultimately he wanted to help control it. (Was there ever such nonsense?) The practical side of this was serious enough, however; he was back at his old idea of going round the earth. Later on that might be rather a jolly thing to do, but not until they had struck root a little more surely in London.

And then with amazement, with incredulity, with indignation, she began to realize that he was proposing to go off by himself upon this vague extravagant research, that all this work she had been doing to make a social place for him in London was as nothing to him, that he was thinking of himself as separable from her. . . .

"But, Cheetah! How can you leave your spotless leopard? You would howl in the lonely jungle!"

"Possibly I shall. But I am going."

"Then I shall come."

"No." He considered her reasons. "You see you are not interested."

"But I am."

"Not as I am. You would turn it all into a jolly holiday. You don't want to see things as I want to do. You want romance. All the world is a show for you. As a show I can't endure it. I want to lay hands on it."

"But, Cheetah!" she said, "this is separation."

"You will have your life here. And I shall come back."

"But, Cheetah! How can we be separated?"

"We are separated," he said.

Her eyes became round with astonishment. Then her face puckered.

"Cheetah!" she cried in a voice of soft distress, "I love you. What do you mean?"

And she staggered forward, tear-blinded, and felt for his neck and shoulders, so that she might weep in his arms. . . .

§ 5

"Don't say we are separated," she whispered, putting her still wet face close to his.

"No. We're mates," he answered softly, with his arm about her.

"How could we ever keep away from each uvver?" she whispered.

He was silent.

"How *could* we?"

He answered aloud. "Amanda," he said, "I mean to go round the world."

She disentangled herself from his arm and sat up beside him.

"What is to become of me," she asked suddenly in a voice of despair, "while you go round the

world? If you desert me in London," she said,
"if you shame me by deserting me in London —
If you leave me, I will never forgive you, Cheetah!
Never." Then in an almost breathless voice, and
as if she spoke to herself, "Never in all my days."

§ 6

It was after that that Amanda began to talk
about children. There was nothing involuntary
about Amanda. "Soon," she said, "we must begin
to think of children. Not just now, but a little
later. It's good to travel and have our fun, but
life is unreal until there are children in the background. No woman is really content until she is a
mother. . . ." And for nearly a fortnight nothing
more was said about that solitary journey round
the world.

But children were not the only new topic in
Amanda's talk. She set herself with an ingenious
subtlety to remind her husband that there were
other men in the world. The convenient fags,
sometimes a little embarrassed, found their inobtrusive services being brought into the light before
Benham's eyes. Most of them were much older
men than himself, elderly philanderers of whom it
seemed to him no sane man need be jealous, men
often of forty or more, but one was a contemporary,
Sir Philip Easton, a man with a touch of Spanish
blood and a suggestion of Spanish fire, who quite
manifestly was very much in love with Amanda
and of whom she spoke with a slight perceptible

difference of manner that made Benham faintly
uneasy. He was ashamed of the feeling. Easton
it seemed was a man of a peculiarly fine honour, so
that Amanda could trust herself with him to an
extent that would have been inadvisable with
men of a commoner substance, and he had a gift of
understanding and sympathy that was almost
feminine; he could cheer one up when one was
lonely and despondent. For Amanda was so method-
ical in the arrangement of her time that even in the
full rush of a London season she could find an hour
now and then for being lonely and despondent.
And he was a liberal and understanding purchaser of
the ascendant painters; he understood that side of
Amanda's interests, a side upon which Benham was
notably deficient. . . .

"Amanda seems to like that dark boy, Poff; what
is his name? — Sir Philip Easton?" said Lady
Marayne.

Benham looked at her with a slightly hostile
intelligence, and said nothing.

"When a man takes a wife, he has to keep her,"
said Lady Marayne.

"No," said Benham after consideration. "I
don't intend to be a wife-herd."

"What?"

"Wife-herd — same as goat-herd."

"Coarse, you are sometimes, Poff — nowadays."

"It's exactly what I mean. I can understand the
kind of curator's interest an Oriental finds in shepherding a large establishment, but to spend my days

looking after one person who ought to be able to look after herself —"

"She's very young."

"She's quite grown up. Anyhow I'm not a moral nursemaid."

"If you leave her about and go abroad —"

"Has she been talking to you, mother?"

"The thing shows."

"But about my going abroad?"

"She said something, my little Poff."

Lady Marayne suddenly perceived that beneath Benham's indifference was something strung very tight, as though he had been thinking inordinately. He weighed his words before he spoke again. "If Amanda chooses to threaten me with a sort of conditional infidelity, I don't see that it ought to change the plans I have made for my life. . . ."

§ 7

"No aristocrat has any right to be jealous," Benham wrote. "If he chances to be mated with a woman who does not see his vision or naturally go his way, he has no right to expect her, much less to compel her to go his way. What is the use of dragging an unwilling companion through morasses of uncongenial thought to unsought ends? What is the use of dragging even a willing pretender, who has no inherent will to seek and live the aristocratic life?

"But that does not excuse him from obedience to his own call. . . ."

He wrote that very early in his examination of the Third Limitation. Already he had thought out and judged Amanda. The very charm of her, the sweetness, the nearness and magic of her, was making him more grimly resolute to break away. All the elaborate process of thinking her over had gone on behind the mask of his silences while she had been preoccupied with her housing and establishment in London; it was with a sense of extraordinary injustice, of having had a march stolen upon her, of being unfairly trapped, that Amanda found herself faced by foregone conclusions. He was ready now even with the details of his project. She should go on with her life in London exactly as she had planned it. He would take fifteen hundred a year for himself and all the rest she might spend without check or stint as it pleased her. He was going round the world for one or two years. It was even possible he would not go alone. There was a man at Cambridge he might persuade to come with him, a don called Prothero who was peculiarly useful in helping him to hammer out his ideas. . . .

To her it became commandingly necessary that none of these things should happen.

She tried to play upon his jealousy, but her quick instinct speedily told her that this only hardened his heart. She perceived that she must make a softer appeal. Now of a set intention she began to revive and imitate the spontaneous passion of the honeymoon; she perceived for the first time clearly how wise and righteous a thing it is for a woman to bear a child. "He cannot go if I am going to have a child," she told herself. But that would mean illness, and for illness in herself or others Amanda had the intense disgust natural to her youth. Yet even illness would be better than this intolerable publication of her husband's ability to leave her side. . . .

She had a wonderful facility of enthusiasm and she set herself forthwith to cultivate a philoprogenitive ambition, to communicate it to him. Her dread of illness disappeared; her desire for offspring grew.

"Yes," he said, "I want to have children, but I must go round the world none the less."

She argued with all the concentrated subtlety of her fine keen mind. She argued with persistence and repetition. And then suddenly so that she was astonished at herself, there came a moment when she ceased to argue.

She stood in the dusk in a window that looked out upon the park, and she was now so intent upon her purpose as to be still and self-forgetful; she was dressed in a dinner-dress of white and pale green, that set off her slim erect body and the strong clear lines of her neck and shoulders very beautifully, some greenish stones caught a light from without and flashed soft whispering gleams from amidst the misty darkness of her hair. She was going to Lady Marayne and the opera, and he was bound for a dinner at the House with some young Liberals at which he was to meet two representative Indians with a grievance from Bengal. Husband and wife

had but a few moments together. She asked about
his company and he told her.

"They will tell you about India."

"Yes."

She stood for a moment looking out across the
lights and the dark green trees, and then she turned
to him.

"Why cannot I come with you?" she asked with
sudden passion. "Why cannot I see the things you
want to see?"

"I tell you you are not interested. You would
only be interested through me. That would not
help me. I should just be dealing out my premature
ideas to you. If you cared as I care, if you wanted
to know as I want to know, it would be different.
But you don't. It isn't your fault that you don't.
It happens so. And there is no good in forced
interest, in prescribed discovery."

"Cheetah," she asked, "what is it that you want
to know — that I don't care for?"

"I want to know about the world. I want to
rule the world."

"So do I."   .

"No, you want to have the world."

"Isn't it the same?"

"No. You're a greedier thing than I am, you
Black Leopard you — standing there in the dusk.
You're a stronger thing. Don't you know you're
stronger? When I am with you, you carry your
point, because you are more concentrated, more
definite, less scrupulous. When you run beside me

you push me out of my path. . . . You've made me afraid of you. . . . And so I won't go with you, Leopard. I go alone. It isn't because I don't love you. I love you too well. It isn't because you aren't beautiful and wonderful. . . ."

"But, Cheetah! nevertheless you care more for this that you want than you care for me."

Benham thought of it. "I suppose I do," he said.

"What is it that you want? Still I don't understand."

Her voice had the break of one who would keep reasonable in spite of pain.

"I ought to tell you."

"Yes, you ought to tell me."

"I wonder if I can tell you," he said very thoughtfully, and rested his hands on his hips. "I shall seem ridiculous to you."

"You ought to tell me."

"I think what I want is to be king of the world."

She stood quite still staring at him.

"I do not know how I can tell you of it. Amanda, do you remember those bodies — you saw those bodies — those mutilated men?"

"I saw them," said Amanda.

"Well. Is it nothing to you that those things happen?"

"They must happen."

"No. They happen because there are no kings but pitiful kings. They happen because the kings love their Amandas and do not care."

"But what can *you* do, Cheetah?"

"Very little. But I can give my life and all my strength. I can give all I can give."

"But how? How can you help it — help things like that massacre?"

"I can do my utmost to find out what is wrong with my world and rule it and set it right."

"*You!* Alone."

"Other men do as much. Every one who does so helps others to do so. You see — . . . In this world one may wake in the night and one may resolve to be a king, and directly one has resolved one is a king. Does that sound foolishness to you? Anyhow, it's fair that I should tell you, though you count me a fool. This — this kingship — this dream of the night — is my life. It is the very core of me. Much more than you are. More than anything else can be. I mean to be a king in this earth. *King.* I'm not mad. . . . I see the world staggering from misery to misery and there is little wisdom, less rule, folly, prejudice, limitation, the good things come by chance and the evil things recover and slay them, and it is my world and I am responsible. Every man to whom this light has come is responsible. As soon as this light comes to you, as soon as your kingship is plain to you, there is no more rest, no peace, no delight, except in work, in service, in utmost effort. As far as I can do it I will rule my world. I cannot abide in this smug city, I cannot endure its self-complacency, its routine, its gloss of success, its rottenness. . . . I shall do

little, perhaps I shall do nothing, but what I can
understand and what I can do I will do. Think of
that wild beautiful country we saw, and the mean
misery, the filth and the warring cruelty of the life
that lives there, tragedy, tragedy without dignity;
and think, too, of the limitless ugliness here, and of
Russia slipping from disorder to massacre, and
China, that sea of human beings, sliding steadily
to disaster. Do you think these are only things in
the newspapers? To me at any rate they are not
things in newspapers; they are pain and failure,
they are torment, they are blood and dust and misery.
They haunt me day and night. Even if it is utterly
absurd I will still do my utmost. It *is* absurd.
I'm a madman and you and my mother are sensible
people. . . . And I will go my way. . . . I don't
care for the absurdity. I don't care a rap."

He stopped abruptly.

"There you have it, Amanda. It's rant, perhaps. Sometimes I feel it's rant. And yet it's the
breath of life to me. . . . There you are. . . .
At last I've been able to break silence and tell
you. . . ."

He stopped with something like a sob and stood
regarding the dusky mystery of her face. She stood
quite still, she was just a beautiful outline in the
twilight, her face was an indistinctness under the
black shadow of her hair, with eyes that were two
patches of darkness.

He looked at his watch, lifting it close to his face
to see the time. His voice changed. "Well — if

x

you provoke a man enough, you see he makes speeches. Let it be a lesson to you, Amanda. Here we are talking instead of going to our dinners. The car has been waiting ten minutes."

Amanda, so still, was the most disconcerting of all Amandas. . . .

A strange exaltation seized upon her very suddenly. In an instant she had ceased to plot against him. A vast wave of emotion swept her forward to a resolution that astonished her.

"Cheetah!" she said, and the very quality of her voice had changed, "give me one thing. Stay until June with me."

"Why?" he asked.

Her answer came in a voice so low that it was almost a whisper.

"Because — now — no, I don't want to keep you any more — I am not trying to hold you any more. . . . I want. . . ."

She came forward to him and looked up closely at his face.

"Cheetah," she whispered almost inaudibly, "Cheetah — I didn't understand. But now —. I want to bear your child."

He was astonished. "Old Leopard!" he said.

"No," she answered, putting her hands upon his shoulders and drawing very close to him, "Queen — if I can be — to your King."

"You want to bear me a child!" he whispered, profoundly moved.

§ 8

The Hindu agitators at the cavernous dinner under the House of Commons came to the conclusion that Benham was a dreamer. And over against Amanda at her dinner-party sat Sir Sidney Umber, one of those men who know that their judgments are quoted.

" Who is the beautiful young woman who is seeing visions?" he asked of his neighbour in confidential undertones. . . .

He tittered. "I think, you know, she ought to seem just *slightly* aware that the man to her left is talking to her. . . ."

§ 9

A few days later Benham went down to Cambridge, where Prothero was now a fellow of Trinity and Brissenden Trust Lecturer. . . .

All through Benham's writing there was manifest a persuasion that in some way Prothero was necessary to his mind. It was as if he looked to Prothero to keep him real. He suspected even while he obeyed that upward flourish which was his own essential characteristic. He had a peculiar feeling that somehow that upward bias would betray him; that from exaltation he might presently float off, into the higher, the better, and so to complete unreality. He fled from priggishness and the terror of such sublimity alike to Prothero. Moreover, in relation to so many things Prothero in a peculiar distinctive manner *saw*. He had less self-control than Benham, less integrity of purpose, less concentration, and things that were before his eyes were by the very virtue of these defects invariably visible to him. Things were able to insist upon themselves with him. Benham, on the other hand, when facts contradicted his purpose too stoutly, had a way of becoming blind to them. He repudiated inconvenient facts. He mastered and made his world; Prothero accepted and recorded his. Benham was a will towards the universe where Prothero was a perception and Amanda a confusing responsive activity. And it was because of his realization of this profound difference between them that he was possessed by the idea of taking Prothero with him about the world, as a detachable kind of vision — rather like that eye the Graiae used to hand one another. . . .

After the busy sunlit streets of Maytime Cambridge, Prothero's rooms in Trinity, their windows full of Gothic perspectives and light-soaked blue sky, seemed cool and quiet. A flavour of scholarship pervaded them — a little blended with the flavour of innumerable breakfasts nearly but not completely forgotten. Prothero's door had been locked against the world, and he had appeared after a slight delay looking a little puffy and only apprehending who his visitor was after a resentful stare for the better part of a second. He might have been asleep, he might have been doing anything but the examination papers he appeared to be doing. The two men exchanged personal details; they had not met since

some months before Benham's marriage, and the
visitor's eye went meanwhile from his host to the
room and back to his host's face as though they were
all aspects of the thing he was after, the Prothero
humour, the earthly touch, the distinctive Prothero
flavour.   Then his eye was caught by a large red,
incongruous, meretricious-looking volume upon the
couch that had an air of having been flung aside,
Venus in Gem and Marble, its cover proclaimed. . . .

His host followed that glance and blushed. "They
send me all sorts of inappropriate stuff to review,"
he remarked.

And then he was denouncing celibacy.

The transition wasn't very clear to Benham.   His
mind had been preoccupied by the problem of how
to open his own large project.   Meanwhile Prothero
got, as it were, the conversational bit between his
teeth and bolted.   He began to say the most shock-
ing things right away, so that Benham's attention
was caught in spite of himself.

"Inflammatory classics."

"What's that?"

"Celibacy, my dear Benham, is maddening me,"
said Prothero. "I can't stand it any longer."

It seemed to Benham that somewhere, very far
away, in another world, such a statement might
have been credible.   Even in his own life, — it was
now indeed a remote, forgotten stage — there had
been something distantly akin. . . .

"You're going to marry?"

"I must."

"Who's the lady, Billy?"

"I don't know. Venus."

His little red-brown eye met his friend's defiantly.

"So far as I know, it is Venus Anadyomene."
A flash of laughter passed across his face and left it
still angrier, still more indecorously defiant. "I
like her best, anyhow. I do, indeed. But, Lord!
I feel that almost any of them —"

"Tut, tut!" said Benham.

Prothero flushed deeply but stuck to his discourse.

"Wasn't it always your principle, Benham, to
look facts in the face? I am not pronouncing an
immoral principle. Your manner suggests I am.
I am telling you exactly how I feel. That is how I
feel. I want — Venus. I don't want her to talk
to or anything of that sort. . . . I have been studying that book, yes, that large, vulgar, red book,
all the morning, instead of doing any work. Would
you like to see it? . . . *No!* . . .

"This spring, Benham, I tell you, is driving me
mad. It is a peculiarly erotic spring. I cannot
sleep, I cannot fix my mind, I cannot attend to ordinary conversation. These feelings, I understand,
are by no means peculiar to myself. . . . No,
don't interrupt me, Benham; let me talk now that
the spirit of speech is upon me. When you came in
you said, 'How are you?' I am telling you how I
am. You brought it on yourself. Well — I am
— inflamed. I have no strong moral or religious
convictions to assist me either to endure or deny
this — this urgency. And so why should I deny

it? It's one of our chief problems here. The majority of my fellow dons who look at me with secretive faces in hall and court and combination-room are in just the same case as myself. The fever in oneself detects the fever in others. I know their hidden thoughts. Their fishy eyes defy me to challenge their hidden thoughts. Each covers his miserable secret under the cloak of a wholesome manly indifference. A tattered cloak. . . . Each tries to hide his abandonment to this horrible vice of continence —"

"Billy, what's the matter with you?"

Prothero grimaced impatience. "Shall I *never* teach you not to be a humbug, Benham?" he screamed, and in screaming became calmer. "Nature taunts me, maddens me. My life is becoming a hell of shame. 'Get out from all these books,' says Nature, 'and serve the Flesh.' The Flesh, Benham. Yes — I insist — the Flesh. Do I look like a pure spirit? Is any man a pure spirit? And here am I at Cambridge like a lark in a cage, with too much port and no Aspasia. Not that I should have liked Aspasia."

"Mutual, perhaps, Billy."

"Oh! you can sneer!"

"Well, clearly — Saint Paul is my authority — it's marriage, Billy."

Prothero had walked to the window. He turned round.

"I *can't* marry," he said. "The trouble has gone too far. I've lost my nerve in the presence of women.

I don't like them any more.   They come at one —
done up in a lot of ridiculous clothes, and chattering about all sorts of things that don't matter. . . ."

He surveyed his friend's thoughtful attitude.

"I'm getting to hate women, Benham.   I'm beginning now to understand the bitterness of spinsters
against men.   I'm beginning to grasp the unkindli-
ness of priests.   The perpetual denial.   To you,
happily married, a woman is just a human being.
You can talk to her, like her, you can even admire
her calmly; you've got, you see, no grudge against
her. . . ."

He sat down abruptly.

Benham, upon the hearthrug before the empty
fireplace, considered him.

"Billy! this is delusion," he said.   "What's come
over you?"

"I'm telling you," said Prothero.

"No," said Benham.

Prothero awaited some further utterance.

"I'm looking for the cause of it.   It's feeding,
Billy.   It's port and stimulants where there is no
scope for action.   It's idleness.   I begin to see now
how much fatter you are, how much coarser."

"Idleness! Look at this pile of examination
answers.   Look at that filing system like an arsenal
of wisdom.   Useless wisdom, I admit, but anyhow
not idleness."

"There's still bodily idleness.   No.   That's your
trouble.   You're stuffy.   You've enlarged your
liver.   You sit in this room of a warm morning

after an extravagant breakfast —. And peep and covet."

"Just eggs and bacon!"

"Think of it! Coffee and toast it ought to be. Come out of it, Billy, and get aired."

"How can one?"

"Easily. Come out of it now. Come for a walk, you Pig!"

"It's an infernally warm morning."

"Walk with me to Grantchester."

"We might go by boat. You could row."

"*Walk.*"

"I ought to do these papers."

"You weren't doing them."

"No. . . ."

"Walk with me to Grantchester. All this affliction of yours is — horrid — and just nothing at all. Come out of it! I want you to come with me to Russia and about the world. I'm going to leave my wife —"

"Leave your wife!"

"Why not? And I came here hoping to find you clear-headed, and instead you are in this disgusting state. I've never met anything in my life so hot and red and shiny and shameless. Come out of it, man! How can one talk to you?"

§ 10

"You pull things down to your own level," said Benham as they went through the heat to Grantchester.

"I pull them down to truth," panted Prothero.

"Truth! As though being full of gross appetites was truth, and discipline and training some sort of falsity!"

"Artificiality. And begetting pride, Benham, begetting a prig's pride."

For a time there was more than the heat of the day between them. . . .

The things that Benham had come down to discuss were thrust into the background by the impassioned materialism of Prothero.

"I'm not talking of Love," he said, remaining persistently outrageous. "I'm talking of physical needs. That first. What is the good of arranging systems of morality and sentiment before you know what is physically possible. . . .

"But how can one disentangle physical and moral necessities?"

"Then why don't we up and find out?" said Billy.

He had no patience with the secrecy, the ignorance, the emotion that surrounded these questions. We didn't worship our ancestors when it came to building bridges or working metals or curing disease or studying our indigestion, and why should we become breathless or wordless with awe and terror when it came to this fundamental affair? Why here in particular should we give way to Holy Fear and stifled submission to traditional suppressions and the wisdom of the ages? "What is the wisdom of the ages?" said Prothero. "Think of the corners where that wisdom was born. . . . Flea-bitten sages in stone-age hovels. . . . Wandering wise man with a rolling eye, a fakir under a tree, a Jewish sheik, an Arab epileptic. . . ."

"Would you sweep away the experience of mankind?" protested Benham.

The experience of mankind in these matters had always been bitter experience. Most of it was better forgotten. It didn't convince. It had never worked things out. In this matter just as in every other matter that really signified things had still to be worked out. Nothing had been worked out hitherto. The wisdom of the ages was a Cant. People had been too busy quarrelling, fighting and running away. There wasn't any digested experience of the ages at all. Only the mis-remembered hankey-pankey of the Dead Old Man.

"Is this love-making a physical necessity for most men and women or isn't it?" Prothero demanded. "There's a simple question enough, and is there anything whatever in your confounded wisdom of the ages to tell me yes or no? Can an ordinary celibate be as healthy and vigorous as a mated man? Is a spinster of thirty-eight a healthy human being? Can she be? I don't believe so. Then why in thunder do we let her be? Here am I at a centre of learning and wisdom and I don't believe so; and there is nothing in all our colleges, libraries and roomsfull of wiseacres here, to settle that plain question for me, plainly and finally. My life is a grubby torment of cravings because it isn't settled. If sexual activity *is* a part of the balance of life, if it *is* a necessity, well let's set about making it accessible and harmless and have done with it.   Swedish exercises.   That sort of thing.   If it isn't, if it can be reduced and done without, then let us set about teaching people *how* to control themselves and reduce and get rid of this vehement passion.   But all this muffled mystery, this pompous sneak's way we take with it !''

"But, Billy!   How can one settle these things? It's a matter of idiosyncrasy.   What is true for one man isn't true for another.   There's infinite difference of temperaments !''

"Then why haven't we a classification of temperaments and a moral code for each sort?   Why am I ruled by the way of life that is convenient for Rigdon the vegetarian and fits Bowler the saint like a glove?   It isn't convenient for me.   It fits me like a hair-shirt.   Of course there are temperaments, but why can't we formulate them and exercise the elementary charity of recognizing that one man's health in these matters is another man's death? Some want love and gratification and some don't. There are people who want children and people who don't want to be bothered by children but who are full of vivid desires.   There are people whose only happiness is chastity, and women who would rather be courtesans than mothers.   Some of us would concentrate upon a single passion or a single idea; others overflow with a miscellaneous — tenderness. Yes, — and you smile !   Why spit upon and insult a miscellaneous tenderness, Benham?   Why grin

at it? Why try every one by the standards that
suit oneself? We're savages, Benham, shamefaced
savages, still. Shamefaced and persecuting.

"I was angry about sex by seventeen," he went on.
"Every year I live I grow angrier."

His voice rose to a squeal of indignation as he
talked.

"Think," he said, "of the amount of thinking and
feeling about sex that is going on in Cambridge this
morning. The hundreds out of these thousands full
of it. A vast tank of cerebration. And we put none
of it together; we work nothing out from that but
poor little couplings and casual stories, patchings
up of situations, misbehaviours, blunders, disease,
trouble, escapes; and the next generation will start,
and the next generation after that will start with
nothing but your wisdom of the ages, which isn't
wisdom at all, which is just awe and funk, taboos and
mystery and the secretive cunning of the savage. . . .

"What I really want to do is my work," said
Prothero, going off quite unexpectedly again. "That
is why all this business, this incessant craving and
the shame of it and all makes me so infernally
angry. . . ."

§ 11

"There I'm with you," cried Benham, struggling
out of the thick torrent of Prothero's prepossessions.
"What we want to do is our work."

He clung to his idea. He raised his voice to
prevent Prothero getting the word again.

"It's this, that you call Work, that I call — what do I call it? — living the aristocratic life, which takes all the coarse simplicity out of this business. If it was only submission. . . . *You* think it is only submission — giving way. . . . It isn't only submission. We'd manage sex all right, we'd be the happy swine our senses would make us, if we didn't know all the time that there was something else to live for, something far more important. And different. Absolutely different and contradictory. So different that it cuts right across all these considerations. It won't fit in. . . . I don't know what this other thing is; it's what I want to talk about with you. But I know that it *is*, in all my bones. . . . *You* know. . . . It demands control, it demands continence, it insists upon disregard."

But the ideas of continence and disregard were unpleasant ideas to Prothero that day.

"Mankind," said Benham, "is overcharged with this sex. It suffocates us. It gives life only to consume it. We struggle out of the urgent necessities of a mere animal existence. We are not so much living as being married and given in marriage. All life is swamped in the love story. . . ."

"Man is only overcharged because he is unsatisfied," said Prothero, sticking stoutly to his own view.

§ 12

It was only as they sat at a little table in the orchard at Grantchester after their lunch that Benham could make head against Prothero and recover

that largeness of outlook which had so easily touched
the imagination of Amanda.   And then he did not
so much dispose of Prothero's troubles as soar over
them.   It is the last triumph of the human understanding to sympathize with desires we do not share,
and to Benham who now believed himself to be loved
beyond the chances of life, who was satisfied and
tranquil and austerely content, it was impossible
that Prothero's demands should seem anything more
than the grotesque and squalid squealings of the
beast that has to be overridden and rejected altogether.   It is a freakish fact of our composition that
these most intense feelings in life are just those that
are most rapidly and completely forgotten; hate
one may recall for years, but the magic of love and
the flame of desire serve their purpose in our lives
and vanish, leaving no trace, like the snows of
Venice.   Benham was still not a year and a half
from the meretricious delights of Mrs. Skelmersdale, and he looked at Prothero as a marble angel
might look at a swine in its sty. . . .

What he had now in mind was an expedition to
Russia.   When at last he could sufficiently release
Prothero's attention, he unfolded the project that
had been developing steadily in him since his honeymoon experience.

He had discovered a new reason for travelling.
The last country we can see clearly, he had discovered, is our own country.   It is as hard to see one's own
country as it is to see the back of one's head.   It is
too much behind us, too much ourselves.   But

Russia is like England with everything larger, more vivid, cruder; one felt that directly one walked about St. Petersburg. St. Petersburg upon its Neva was like a savage untamed London on a larger Thames; they were seagull-haunted tidal cities, like no other capitals in Europe. The shipping and buildings mingled in their effects. Like London it looked over the heads of its own people to a limitless polyglot empire. And Russia was an aristocratic land, with a middle-class that had no pride in itself as a class; it had a British toughness and incompetence, a British disregard of logic and meticulous care. Russia, like England, was outside Catholic Christendom, it had a state church and the opposition to that church was not secularism but dissent. One could draw a score of such contrasted parallels. And now it was in a state of intolerable stress, that laid bare the elemental facts of a great social organization. It was having its South African war, its war at the other end of the earth, with a certain defeat instead of a dubious victory. . . .

"There is far more freedom for the personal life in Russia than in England," said Prothero, a little irrelevantly.

Benham went on with his discourse about Russia. . . .

"At the college of Troitzka," said Prothero, "which I understand is a kind of monster Trinity unencumbered by a University, Binns tells me that although there is a profession of celibacy within the walls, the arrangements of the town and more particularly of the various hotels are conceived in a spirit of extreme liberality."

Benham hardly attended at all to these interruptions.

He went on to point out the elemental quality of the Russian situation. He led up to the assertion that to go to Russia, to see Russia, to try to grasp the broad outline of the Russian process, was the manifest duty of every responsible intelligence that was free to do as much. And so he was going, and if Prothero cared to come too —

"Yes," said Prothero, "I should like to go to Russia."

§ 13

But throughout all their travel together that summer Benham was never able to lift Prothero away from his obsession. It was the substance of their talk as the Holland boat stood out past waiting destroyers and winking beacons and the lights of Harwich, into the smoothly undulating darkness of the North Sea; it rose upon them again as they sat over the cakes and cheese of a Dutch breakfast in the express for Berlin. Prothero filled the Sieges Allee with his complaints against nature and society, and distracted Benham in his contemplation of Polish agriculture from the windows of the train with turgid sexual liberalism. So that Benham, during this period until Prothero left him and until the tragic enormous spectacle of Russia in revolution took complete possession of him, was as it were thinking upon two floors. Upon the one he was

Y

thinking of the vast problems of a society of a hundred million people staggering on the verge of anarchy, and upon the other he was perplexed by the feverish inattention of Prothero to the tremendous things that were going on all about them. It was only presently when the serenity of his own private life began to be ruffled by disillusionment, that he began to realize the intimate connexion of these two systems of thought. Yet Prothero put it to him plainly enough.

"Inattentive," said Prothero, "of course I am inattentive. What is really the matter with all this — this social mess people are in here, is that nearly everybody is inattentive. These Big Things of yours, nobody is thinking of them really. Everybody is thinking about the Near Things that concern himself."

"The bombs they threw yesterday? The Cossacks and the whips?"

"Nudges. Gestures of inattention. If everybody was thinking of the Res Publica would there be any need for bombs?"

He pursued his advantage. "It's all nonsense to suppose people think of politics because they are in 'em. As well suppose that the passengers on a liner understand the engines, or soldiers a war. Before men can think of to-morrow, they must think of to-day. Before they can think of others, they must be sure about themselves. First of all, food; the private, the personal economic worry. Am I safe for food? Then sex, and until one is tranquil and not ashamed, not irritated and dissatisfied, how can one care for other people, or for next year or the Order of the World? How can one, Benham?"

He seized the illustration at hand. "Here we are in Warsaw — not a month after bomb-throwing and Cossack charging. Windows have still to be mended, smashed doors restored. There's blood-stains still on some of the houses. There are hundreds of people in the Citadel and in the Ochrana prison. This morning there were executions. Is it anything more than an eddy in the real life of the place? Watch the customers in the shops, the crowd in the streets, the men in the cafés who stare at the passing women. They are all swallowed up again in their own business. They just looked up as the Cossacks galloped past; they just shifted a bit when the bullets spat. . . ."

And when the streets of Moscow were agog with the grotesque amazing adventure of the Potemkin mutineers, Prothero was in the full tide of the private romance that severed him from Benham and sent him back to Cambridge — changed.

Before they reached Moscow Benham was already becoming accustomed to disregard Prothero. He was looking over him at the vast heaving trouble of Russia, which now was like a sea that tumbles under the hurrying darknesses of an approaching storm. In those days it looked as though it must be an overwhelming storm. He was drinking in the wide and massive Russian effects, the drifting crowds in the entangling streets, the houses with their strange

lettering in black and gold, the innumerable barbaric churches, the wildly driven droshkys, the sombre red fortress of the Kremlin, with its bulbous
churches clustering up into the sky, the crosses, the
innumerable gold crosses, the mad church of St.
Basil, carrying the Russian note beyond the pitch of
permissible caricature, and in this setting the obscure drama of clustering, staring, sash-wearing
peasants, long-haired students, sane-eyed women,
a thousand varieties of uniform, a running and galloping to and fro of messengers, a flutter of little
papers, whispers, shouts, shots, a drama elusive and
portentous, a gathering of forces, an accumulation
of tension going on to a perpetual clash and clamour
of bells.   Benham had brought letters of introduction to a variety of people, some had vanished, it
seemed.   They were "away," the porters said, and
they continued to be "away," — it was the formula,
he learnt, for arrest; others were evasive, a few
showed themselves extraordinarily anxious to inform
him about things, to explain themselves and things
about them exhaustively.   One young student took
him to various meetings and showed him in great
detail the scene of the recent murder of the Grand
Duke Sergius.   The buildings opposite the old
French cannons were still under repair.   "The
assassin stood just here.   The bomb fell there, look!
right down there towards the gate; that was where
they found his arm.   He was torn to fragments.
He was scraped up.   He was mixed with the
horses. . . ."

Every one who talked spoke of the outbreak of revolution as a matter of days or at the utmost weeks. And whatever question Benham chose to ask these talkers were prepared to answer. Except one. "And after the revolution," he asked, "what then? . . ." Then they waved their hands, and failed to convey meanings by reassuring gestures.

He was absorbed in his effort to understand this universal ominous drift towards a conflict. He was trying to piece together a process, if it was one and the same process, which involved riots in Lodz, fighting at Libau, wild disorder at Odessa, remote colossal battlings in Manchuria, the obscure movements of a disastrous fleet lost somewhere now in the Indian seas, steaming clumsily to its fate, he was trying to rationalize it all in his mind, to comprehend its direction. He was struggling strenuously with the obscurities of the language in which these things were being discussed about him, a most difficult language demanding new sets of visual images because of its strange alphabet. Is it any wonder that for a time he failed to observe that Prothero was involved in some entirely disconnected affair.

They were staying at the big Cosmopolis bazaar in the Theatre Square. Thither, through the doors that are opened by distraught-looking men with peacocks' feathers round their caps, came Benham's friends and guides to take him out and show him this and that. At first Prothero always accompanied Benham on these expeditions; then he began to make excuses. He would stay behind in

the hotel.   Then when Benham returned Prothero
would have disappeared.   When the porter was
questioned about Prothero his nescience was profound.

One night no Prothero was discoverable at any
hour, and Benham, who wanted to discuss a project
for going on to Kieff and Odessa, was alarmed.

"Moscow is a late place," said Benham's student
friend.   "You need not be anxious until after four
or five in the morning.   It will be quite time — *quite*
time to be anxious to-morrow.   He may be — close
at hand."

When Benham hunted up Prothero in his room
next morning he found him sleepy and irritable.

"I don't trouble if *you* are late," said Prothero,
sitting up in his bed with a red resentful face and
crumpled hair.   "I wasn't born yesterday."

"I wanted to talk about leaving Moscow."

"I don't want to leave Moscow."

"But Odessa — Odessa is the centre of interest
just now."

"I want to stay in Moscow."

Benham looked baffled.

Prothero stuck up his knees and rested his night-
shirted arms upon them.   "I don't want to leave
Moscow," he said, "and I'm not going to do so."

"But haven't we done —"

Prothero interrupted.   "You   may.   But   I
haven't.   We're not after the same things.   Things
that interest you, Benham, don't interest me.   I've
found — different things."

His expression was extraordinarily defiant.

"I want," he went on, "to put our affairs on a different footing. Now you've opened the matter we may as well go into it. You were good enough to bring me here. . . . There was a sort of understanding we were working together. . . . We aren't. . . . The long and short of it is, Benham, I want to pay you for my journey here and go on my own — independently."

His eye and voice achieved a fierceness that Benham found nearly incredible in him.

Something that had got itself overlooked in the press of other matters jerked back into Benham's memory. It popped back so suddenly that for an instant he wanted to laugh. He turned towards the window, picked his way among Prothero's carelessly dropped garments, and stood for a moment staring into the square, with its drifting, assembling and dispersing fleet of trams and its long line of blue-coated *izvoshtchiks*. Then he turned.

"Billy," he said, "didn't I see you the other evening driving towards the Hermitage?"

"Yes," said Prothero, and added, "that's it."

"You were with a lady."

"And she *is* a lady," said Prothero, so deeply moved that his face twitched as though he was going to weep.

"She's a Russian?"

"She had an English mother. Oh, you needn't stand there and look so damned ironical! She's — she's a woman. She's a thing of kindness. . . ."

He was too full to go on.

"Billy, old boy," said Benham, distressed, "I don't want to be ironical — "

Prothero had got his voice again.

"You'd better know," he said, "you'd better know.   She's one of those women who live in this hotel."

"Live in this hotel!"

"On the fourth floor.   Didn't you know?   It's the way in most of these big Russian hotels.   They come down and sit about after lunch and dinner. A woman with a yellow ticket.   Oh! I don't care.   I don't care a rap.   She's been kind to me; she's — she's dear to me.   How are you to understand?   I shall stop in Moscow.   I shall take her to England. I can't live without her, Benham.   And then — And then you come worrying me to come to your damned Odessa !"

And suddenly this extraordinary young man put his hands to his face as though he feared to lose it and would hold it on, and after an apoplectic moment burst noisily into tears.   They ran between his fingers.   "Get out of my room," he shouted, suffocatingly.   "What business have you to come prying on me?"

Benham sat down on a chair in the middle of the room and stared round-eyed at his friend.   His hands were in his pockets.   For a time he said nothing.

"Billy," he began at last, and stopped again. "Billy, in this country somehow one wants to talk like a Russian. Billy, my dear — I'm not your father, I'm not your judge. I'm — unreasonably fond of you. It's not my business to settle what is right or wrong for you. If you want to stay in Moscow, stay in Moscow. Stay here, and stay as my guest. . . ."

He stopped and remained staring at his friend for a little space.

"I didn't know," said Prothero brokenly; "I didn't know it was possible to get so fond of a person. . . ."

Benham stood up. He had never found Prothero so attractive and so abominable in his life before.

"I shall go to Odessa alone, Billy. I'll make things all right here before I go. . . ."

He closed the door behind him and went in a state of profound thought to his own room. . . .

Presently Prothero came to him with a vague inopportune desire to explain what so evidently did not need explaining. He walked about the room trying ways of putting it, while Benham packed.

In an unaccountable way Prothero's bristling little mind seemed to have shrunken to something sleek and small.

"I wish," he said, "you could stay for a later train and have lunch and meet her. She's not the ordinary thing. She's — different."

Benham plumbed depths of wisdom. "Billy," he said, "no woman *is* the ordinary thing. They are all — different. . . ."

§ 14

For a time this affair of Prothero's seemed to be a matter as disconnected from the Research Magnificent as one could imagine any matter to be. While Benham went from Moscow and returned, and travelled hither and thither, and involved himself more and more in the endless tangled threads of the revolutionary movement in Russia, Prothero was lost to all those large issues in the development of his personal situation. He contributed nothing to Benham's thought except attempts at discouragement. He reiterated his declaration that all the vast stress and change of Russian national life was going on because it was universally disregarded. "I tell you, as I told you before, that nobody is attending. You think because all Moscow, all Russia, is in the picture, that everybody is concerned. Nobody is concerned. Nobody cares what is happening. Even the men who write in newspapers and talk at meetings about it don't care. They are thinking of their dinners, of their clothes, of their money, of their wives. They hurry home. . . ."

That was his excuse.

Manifestly it was an excuse.

His situation developed into remarkable complications of jealousy and divided counsels that Benham found altogether incomprehensible. To Benham in those days everything was very simple in this business of love. The aristocrat had to love

ideally; that was all. He had to love Amanda.
He and Amanda were now very deeply in love again,
more in love, he felt, than they had ever been before.
They were now writing love-letters to each other
and enjoying a separation that was almost volup-
tuous. She found in the epistolatory treatment of
her surrender to him and to the natural fate of
women, a delightful exercise for her very considerable powers of expression. Life pointed now wonderfully to the great time ahead when there would
be a Cheetah cub in the world, and meanwhile the
Cheetah loped about the wild world upon a mighty
quest. In such terms she put it. Such foolishness
written in her invincibly square and youthful hand
went daily from London to Russia, and stacked up
against his return in the porter's office at the Cosmopolis Bazaar or pursued him down through the
jarring disorders of south-west Russia, or waited
for him at ill-chosen post-offices that deflected his
journeyings wastefully or in several instances went
altogether astray. Perhaps they supplied self-
educating young strikers in the postal service with
useful exercises in the deciphering of manuscript
English. He wrote back five hundred different ways
of saying that he loved her extravagantly. . . .

It seemed to Benham in those days that he had
found the remedy and solution of all those sexual
perplexities that distressed the world; Heroic Love
to its highest note — and then you go about your
business. It seemed impossible not to be happy and
lift one's chin high and diffuse a bracing kindliness

among the unfortunate multitudes who stewed in
affliction and hate because they had failed as yet
to find this simple, culminating elucidation.   And
Prothero — Prothero, too, was now achieving the
same grand elementariness, out of his lusts and protests and general physical squalor he had flowered
into love.   For a time it is true it made rather an
ineffective companion of him, but this was the mere
goose-stepping for the triumphal march ; this way
ultimately lay exaltation.   Benham had had as yet
but a passing glimpse of this Anglo-Russian, who was
a lady and altogether unlike her fellows ; he had
seen her for a doubtful second or so as she and
Prothero drove past him, and his impression was of a
rather little creature, white-faced with dusky hair
under a red cap, paler and smaller but with something in her, a quiet alertness, that gave her a touch
of kinship with Amanda.   And if she liked old
Prothero —   And, indeed, she must like old Prothero or could she possibly have made him so deeply
in love with her?

They must stick to each other, and then, presently, Prothero's soul would wake up and face the
world again.   What did it matter what she had
been ?

Through stray shots and red conflict, long tediums
of strained anxiety and the physical dangers of a
barbaric country staggering towards revolution,
Benham went with his own love like a lamp within
him and this affair of Prothero's reflecting its light,
and he was quite prepared for the most sympathetic

and liberal behaviour when he came back to Moscow
to make the lady's acquaintance. He intended to
help Prothero to marry and take her back to Cambridge, and to assist by every possible means in
destroying and forgetting the official yellow ticket
that defined her status in Moscow. But he reckoned without either Prothero or the young lady in
this expectation.

It only got to him slowly through his political
preoccupations that there were obscure obstacles to
this manifest course. Prothero hesitated; the lady
expressed doubts.

On closer acquaintance her resemblance to Amanda
diminished. It was chiefly a similarity of complexion. She had a more delicate face than
Amanda, and its youthful brightness was deadened;
she had none of Amanda's glow, and she spoke her
mother's language with a pretty halting limp that
was very different from Amanda's clear decisions.

She put her case compactly.

"I would not *do* in Cambridge," she said with an
infinitesimal glance at Prothero.

"Mr. Benham," she said, and her manner had the
gravity of a woman of affairs, "now do you see me in
Cambridge? Now do you see me? Kept outside
the walls? In a little *datcha?* With no occupation? Just to amuse him."

And on another occasion when Prothero was not
with her she achieved still completer lucidity.

"I would come if I thought he wanted me to
come," she said. "But you see if I came he would

not want me to come. Because then he would have
me and so he wouldn't want me. He would just
have the trouble. And I am not sure if I should
be happy in Cambridge. I am not sure I should
be happy enough to make him happy. It is a very
learned and intelligent and charming society, of
course; but here, *things happen*. At Cambridge
nothing happens — there is only education. There
is no revolution in Cambridge; there are not even
sinful people to be sorry for. . . . And he says
himself that Cambridge people are particular. He
says they are liberal but very, very particular, and
perhaps I could not always act my part well. Sometimes I am not always well behaved. When there
is music I behave badly sometimes, or when I am
bored. He says the Cambridge people are so
liberal that they do not mind what you are, but he
says they are so particular that they mind dreadfully
how you are what you are. . . . So that it comes
to exactly the same thing. . . ."

"Anna Alexievna," said Benham suddenly, "are
you in love with Prothero?"

Her manner became conscientiously scientific.

"He is very kind and very generous — too generous. He keeps sending for more money — hundreds of roubles, I try to prevent him."

"Were you *ever* in love?"

"Of course. But it's all gone long ago. It was
like being hungry. Only very fine hungry. Exquisite hungry. . . . And then being disgusted. . . ."

"He is in love with you."

"What is love?" said Anna. "He is grateful.
He is by nature grateful." She smiled a smile, like
the smile of a pale Madonna who looks down on her
bambino.

"And you love nothing?"

"I love Russia — and being alone, being completely alone. When I am dead perhaps I shall be
alone. Not even my own body will touch me then."

Then she added, "But I shall be sorry when he
goes."

Afterwards Benham talked to Prothero alone.
"Your Anna," he said, "is rather wonderful. At
first, I tell you now frankly I did not like her very
much, I thought she looked 'used,' she drank vodka
at lunch, she was gay, uneasily ; she seemed a sham
thing. All that was prejudice. She thinks ; she's
generous, she's fine."

"She's tragic," said Prothero as though it was
the same thing.

He spoke as though he noted an objection. His
next remark confirmed this impression. "That's
why I can't take her back to Cambridge," he said.

"You see, Benham," he went on, "she's human.
She's not really feminine. I mean, she's — unsexed.
She isn't fitted to be a wife or a mother any more.
We've talked about the possible life in England, very
plainly. I've explained what a household in Cambridge would mean. . . . It doesn't attract her.
. . . In a way she's been let out from womanhood,
forced out of womanhood, and I see now that when
women are let out from womanhood there's no put-

ting them back. I could give a lecture on Anna.
I see now that if women are going to be wives and
mothers and homekeepers and ladies, they must be
got ready for it from the beginning, sheltered, never
really let out into the wild chances of life. She has
been. Bitterly. She's *really* emancipated. And
it's let her out into a sort of nothingness. She's no
longer a woman, and she isn't a man. She ought to
be able to go on her own — like a man. But I
can't take her back to Cambridge. Even for her
sake."

His perplexed eyes regarded Benham.

"You won't be happy in Cambridge — alone,"
said Benham.

"Oh, damnably not! But what can I do? I
had at first some idea of coming to Moscow for good
— teaching."

He paused. "Impossible. I'm worth nothing
here. I couldn't have kept her."

"Then what are you going to do, Billy?"

"I don't *know* what I'm going to do, I tell you.
I live for the moment. To-morrow we are going
out into the country."

"I don't understand," said Benham with a gesture of resignation. "It seems to me that if a man
and woman love each other — well, they insist upon
each other. What is to happen to her if you leave
her in Moscow?"

"Damnation! Is there any need to ask that?"

"Take her to Cambridge, man. And if Cambridge objects, teach Cambridge better manners."

Prothero's face was suddenly transfigured with rage.

"I tell you she won't come!" he said.

"Billy!" said Benham, "you should make her!"

"I can't."

"If a man loves a woman he can make her do anything — "

"But I don't love her like that," said Prothero, shrill with anger. "I tell you I don't love her like that."

Then he lunged into further deeps. "It's the other men," he said, "it's the things that have been. Don't you understand? Can't you understand? The memories — she must have memories — they come between us. It's something deeper than reason. It's in one's spine and under one's nails. One could do anything, I perceive, for one's very own woman. . . ."

"*Make* her your very own woman," said the exponent of heroic love.

"I shirk deeds, Benham, but you shirk facts. How could any man make her his very own woman now? You — you don't seem to understand — *anything*. She's nobody's woman — for ever. That — that might-have-been has gone for ever. . . . It's nerves — a passion of the nerves. There's a cruelty in life and — She's *kind* to me. She's so kind to me. . . ."

And then again Prothero was weeping like a vexed child.

z

§ 15

The end of Prothero's first love affair came to Benham in broken fragments in letters. When he looked for Anna Alexievna in December — he never learnt her surname — he found she had left the Cosmopolis Bazaar soon after Prothero's departure and he could not find whither she had gone. He never found her again. Moscow and Russia had swallowed her up.

Of course she and Prothero parted; that was a foregone conclusion. But Prothero's manner of parting succeeded in being at every phase a shock to Benham's ideas. It was clear he went off almost callously; it would seem there was very little crying. Towards the end it was evident that the two had quarrelled. The tears only came at the very end of all. It was almost as if he had got through the passion and was glad to go. Then came regret, a regret that increased in geometrical proportion with every mile of distance.

In Warsaw it was that grief really came to Prothero. He had some hours there and he prowled the crowded streets, seeing girls and women happy with their lovers, abroad upon bright expeditions and full of delicious secrets, girls and women who ever and again flashed out some instant resemblance to Anna. . . .

In Berlin he stopped a night and almost decided that he would go back. "But now I had the damned frontier," he wrote, "between us."

It was so entirely in the spirit of Prothero, Benham thought, to let the "damned frontier" tip the balance against him.

Then came a scrawl of passionate confession, so passionate that it seemed as if Prothero had been transfigured. "I can't stand this business," he wrote. "It has things in it, possibilities of emotional disturbance — you can have no idea! In the train — luckily I was alone in the compartment — I sat and thought, and suddenly, I could not help it, I was weeping — noisy weeping, an uproar! A beastly German came and stood in the corridor to stare. I had to get out of the train. It is disgraceful, it is monstrous we should be made like this. . . .

"Here I am stranded in Hanover with nothing to do but to write to you about my dismal feelings. . . ."

After that surely there was nothing before a broken-hearted Prothero but to go on with his trailing wing to Trinity and a life of inappeasable regrets; but again Benham reckoned without the invincible earthliness of his friend. Prothero stayed three nights in Paris.

"There is an extraordinary excitement about Paris," he wrote. "A levity. I suspect the gypsum in the subsoil — some as yet undescribed radiations. Suddenly the world looks brightly cynical. . . . None of those tear-compelling German emanations. . . .

"And, Benham, I have found a friend.

"A woman. Of course you will laugh, you will

sneer. You do not understand these things. . . .
Yet they are so simple. It was the strangest accident brought us together. There was something
that drew us together. A sort of instinct. Near
the Boulevard Poissonière. . . ."

"Good heavens!" said Benham. "A sort of
instinct!"

"I told her all about Anna!"

"Good Lord!" cried Benham.

"She understood. Perfectly. None of your so-
called 'respectable' women could have understood.
. . . At first I intended merely to talk to her. . . ."

Benham crumpled the letter in his hand.

"Little Anna Alexievna!" he said, "you were
too clean for him."

§ 16

Benham had a vision of Prothero returning from
all this foreign travel meekly, pensively, a little sadly,
and yet not without a kind of relief, to the grey
mildness of Trinity. He saw him, capped and
gowned, and restored to academic dignity again,
nodding greetings, resuming friendships.

The little man merged again into his rare company
of discreet Benedicts and restrained celibates at the
high tables. They ate on in their mature wisdom
long after the undergraduates had fled. Presently
they would withdraw processionally to the combination room. . . .

There would be much to talk about over the
wine.

Benham speculated what account Prothero would give of Moscow. . . .

He laughed abruptly.

And with that laugh Prothero dropped out of Benham's world for a space of years. There may have been other letters, but if so they were lost in the heaving troubles of a revolution-strained post-office. Perhaps to this day they linger sere and yellow in some forgotten pigeon-hole in Kishinev or Ekaterinoslav. . . .

§ 17

In November, after an adventure in the trader's quarter of Kieff which had brought him within an inch of death, and because an emotional wave had swept across him and across his correspondence with Amanda, Benham went back suddenly to England and her. He wanted very greatly to see her and also he wanted to make certain arrangements about his property. He returned by way of Hungary, and sent telegrams like shouts of excitement whenever the train stopped for a sufficient time. "Old Leopard, I am coming, I am coming," he telegraphed, announcing his coming for the fourth time. It was to be the briefest of visits, very passionate, the mutual refreshment of two noble lovers, and then he was returning to Russia again.

Amanda was at Chexington, and there he found her installed in the utmost dignity of expectant maternity. Like many other people he had been a little disposed to regard the bearing of children as a

common human experience ; at Chexington he came
to think of it as a rare and sacramental function.
Amanda had become very beautiful in quiet, grey,
dove-like tones ; her sun-touched, boy's complexion
had given way to a soft glow of the utmost loveliness,
her brisk little neck that had always reminded him
of the stalk of a flower was now softened and
rounded ; her eyes were tender, and she moved about
the place in the manner of one who is vowed to
a great sacrifice. She dominated the scene, and
Lady Marayne, with a certain astonishment in her
eyes and a smouldering disposition to irony, was
the half-sympathetic, half-resentful priestess of
her daughter-in-law's unparalleled immolation. The
motif of motherhood was everywhere, and at his
bedside he found — it had been put there for him
by Amanda — among much other exaltation of
woman's mission, that most wonderful of all philoprogenitive stories, Hudson's *Crystal Age*.

Everybody at Chexington had an air of being
grouped about the impending fact. An epidemic of
internal troubles, it is true, kept Sir Godfrey in the
depths of London society, but to make up for his
absence Mrs. Morris had taken a little cottage down
by the river and the Wilder girls were with her, both
afire with fine and subtle feelings and both, it
seemed, and more particularly Betty, prepared to
be keenly critical of Benham's attitude.

He did a little miss his cue in these exaltations,
because he had returned in a rather different vein of
exaltation.

In missing it he was assisted by Amanda herself, who had at moments an effect upon him of a priestess confidentially disrobed. It was as if she put aside for him something official, something sincerely maintained, necessary, but at times a little irksome. It was as if she was glad to take him into her confidence and unbend. Within the pre-natal Amanda an impish Amanda still lingered.

There were aspects of Amanda that it was manifest dear Betty must never know. . . .

But the real Amanda of that November visit even in her most unpontifical moods did not quite come up to the imagined Amanda who had drawn him home across Europe. At times she was extraordinarily jolly. They had two or three happy walks about the Chexington woods; that year the golden weather of October had flowed over into November, and except for a carpet of green and gold under the horse-chestnuts most of the leaves were still on the trees. Gleams of her old wanton humour shone on him. And then would come something else, something like a shadow across the world, something he had quite forgotten since his idea of heroic love had flooded him, something that reminded him of those long explanations with Mr. Rathbone-Sanders that had never been explained, and of the curate in the doorway of the cottage and his unaccountable tears.

On the afternoon of his arrival at Chexington he was a little surprised to find Sir Philip Easton coming through the house into the garden, with an

accustomed familiarity. Sir Philip perceived him
with a start that was instantly controlled, and
greeted him with unnatural ease.

Sir Philip, it seemed, was fishing and reading and
playing cricket in the neighbourhood, which struck
Benham as a poor way of spending the summer, the
sort of soft holiday a man learns to take from
scholars and literary men. A man like Sir Philip, he
thought, ought to have been aviating or travelling.

Moreover, when Sir Philip greeted Amanda it
seemed to Benham that there was a flavour of established association in their manner. But then Sir
Philip was also very assiduous with Lady Marayne.
She called him "Pip," and afterwards Amanda called
across the tennis-court to him, "Pip!" And then he
called her "Amanda." When the Wilder girls came
up to join the tennis he was just as brotherly. . . .

The next day he came to lunch.

During that meal Benham became more aware
than he had ever been before of the peculiar deep
expressiveness of this young man's eyes. They
watched him and they watched Amanda with a
solicitude that seemed at once pained and tender.
And there was something about Amanda, a kind of
hard brightness, an impartiality and an air of something undefinably suspended, that gave Benham an
intuitive certitude that that afternoon Sir Philip
would be spoken to privately, and that then he would
pack up and go away in a state of illumination from
Chexington. But before he could be spoken to he
contrived to speak to Benham.

They were left to smoke after lunch, and then it was he took advantage of a pause to commit his little indiscretion.

"Mrs. Benham," he said, "looks amazingly well — extraordinarily well, don't you think?"

"Yes," said Benham, startled. "Yes. She certainly keeps very well."

"She misses you terribly," said Sir Philip; "it is a time when a woman misses her husband. But, of course, she does not want to hamper your work. . . ."

Benham felt it was very kind of him to take so intimate an interest in these matters, but on the spur of the moment he could find no better expression for this than a grunt.

"You don't mind," said the young man with a slight catch in the breath that might have been apprehensive, "that I sometimes bring her books and flowers and things? Do what little I can to keep life interesting down here? It's not very congenial. . . . She's so wonderful — I think she is the most wonderful woman in the world."

Benham perceived that so far from being a modern aristocrat he was really a primitive barbarian in these matters.

"I've no doubt," he said, "that my wife has every reason to be grateful for your attentions."

In the little pause that followed Benham had a feeling that Sir Philip was engendering something still more personal. If so, he might be constrained to invert very gently but very firmly the bowl of chrysanthemums over Sir Philip's head, or kick him

in an improving manner. He had a ridiculous belief
that Sir Philip would probably take anything of the
sort very touchingly. He scrambled in his mind
for some remark that would avert this possibility.

"Have you ever been in Russia?" he asked hastily.
"It is the most wonderful country in Europe. I
had an odd adventure near Kiev. During a pogrom."

And he drowned the developing situation in a
flood of description. . . .

But it was not so easy to drown the little things
that were presently thrown out by Lady Marayne.
They were so much more in the air. . . .

§ 18

Sir Philip suddenly got out of the picture even as
Benham had foreseen.

"Easton has gone away," he remarked three days
later to Amanda.

"I told him to go. He is a bore with you about.
. . . But otherwise he is rather a comfort, Cheetah." She meditated upon Sir Philip. "And he's
an *honourable* man," she said. "He's safe. . . ."

§ 19

After that visit it was that the notes upon love and
sex began in earnest. The scattered memoranda
upon the perfectness of heroic love for the modern
aristocrat ended abruptly. Instead there came the
first draft for a study of jealousy. The note was
written in pencil on Chexington notepaper and mani-

festly that had been supported on the ribbed cover
of a book. There was a little computation in the
corner, converting forty-five degrees Réaumur into
degrees Fahrenheit, which made White guess it
had been written in the Red Sea. But, indeed, it
had been written in a rather amateurishly stoked
corridor-train on Benham's journey to the gathering
revolt in Moscow. . . .

"I think I have been disposed to underrate the
force of sexual jealousy. . . . I thought it was
something essentially contemptible, something that
one dismissed and put behind oneself in the mere
effort to be aristocratic, but I begin to realize that
it is not quite so easily settled with. . . .

"One likes to know. . . . Possibly one wants
to know too much. . . . In phases of fatigue, and
particularly in phases of sleeplessness, when one is
leaving all that one cares for behind, it becomes an
irrational torment. . . .

"And it is not only in oneself that I am astonished
by the power of this base motive. I see, too, in the
queer business of Prothero how strongly jealousy,
how strongly the sense of proprietorship, weighs with
a man. . . .

"There is no clear reason why one should insist
upon another human being being one's ownest own
— utterly one's own. . . .

"There is, of course, no clear reason for most
human motives. . . .

"One does. . . .

"There is something dishonouring in distrust

— to both the distrusted and the one who distrusts. . . ."

After that, apparently, it had been too hot and
stuffy to continue.

§ 20

Benham did not see Amanda again until after the
birth of their child. He spent his Christmas in
Moscow, watching the outbreak, the fitful fighting
and the subsequent break-up, of the revolution, and
taking care of a lost and helpless English family
whose father had gone astray temporarily on the
way home from Baku. Then he went southward to
Rostov and thence to Astrakhan. Here he really
began his travels. He determined to get to India by
way of Herat and for the first time in his life rode
out into an altogether lawless wilderness. He went
on obstinately because he found himself disposed to
funk the journey, and because discouragements were
put in his way. He was soon quite cut off from all
the ways of living he had known. He learnt what it
is to be flea-bitten, saddle-sore, hungry and, above
all, thirsty. He was haunted by a dread of fever,
and so contrived strange torments for himself with
overdoses of quinine. He ceased to be traceable
from Chexington in March, and he reappeared in
the form of a telegram from Karachi demanding
news in May. He learnt he was the father of a
man-child and that all was well with Amanda.

He had not expected to be so long away from any
communication with the outer world, and something

in the nature of a stricken conscience took him back
to England.   He found a second William Porphyry
in the world, dominating Chexington, and Amanda
tenderly triumphant and passionate, the Madonna
enthroned.   For William Porphyry he could feel no
emotion.   William Porphyry was very red and ugly
and protesting, feeble and aggressive, a matter for
a skilled nurse.   To see him was to ignore him and
dispel a dream.   It was to Amanda Benham turned
again.

For some days he was content to adore his
Madonna and listen to the familiar flatteries of her
love.   He was a leaner, riper man, Amanda said,
and wiser, so that she was afraid of him. . . .

And then he became aware that she was requiring
him to stay at her side.   "We have both had our
adventures," she said, which struck him as an odd
phrase.

It forced itself upon his obstinate incredulity that
all those conceptions of heroic love and faithfulness
he had supposed to be so clearly understood between
them had vanished from her mind.   She had absolutely forgotten that twilight moment at the window
which had seemed to him the crowning instant, the
real marriage of their lives.   It had gone, it had left
no recoverable trace in her.   And upon his interpre-
tations of that he had loved her passionately for a
year.   She was back at exactly the ideas and intentions that ruled her during their first settlement
in London.   She wanted a joint life in the social
world of London, she demanded his presence, his

attention, the daily practical evidences of love. It was all very well for him to be away when the child was coming, but now everything was different. Now he must stay by her.

This time he argued no case. These issues he had settled for ever. Even an indignant dissertation from Lady Marayne, a dissertation that began with appeals and ended in taunts, did not move him. Behind these things now was India. The huge problems of India had laid an unshakeable hold upon his imagination. He had seen Russia, and he wanted to balance that picture by a vision of the east. . . .

He saw Easton only once during a week-end at Chexington. The young man displayed no further disposition to be confidentially sentimental. But he seemed to have something on his mind. And Amanda said not a word about him. He was a young man above suspicion, Benham felt. . . .

And from his departure the quality of the correspondence of these two larger carnivores began to change. Except for the repetition of accustomed endearments, they ceased to be love letters in any sense of the word. They dealt chiefly with the "Cub," and even there Benham felt presently that the enthusiasm diminished. A new amazing quality for Amanda appeared — triteness. The very writing of her letters changed as though it had suddenly lost backbone. Her habitual liveliness of phrasing lost its point. Had she lost her animation? Was she ill unknowingly? Where had the light

gone? It was as if her attention was distracted.
. . . As if every day when she wrote her mind was
busy about something else.

Abruptly at last he understood. A fact that had
never been stated, never formulated, never in any
way admitted, was suddenly pointed to convergently
by a thousand indicating fingers, and beyond question perceived to be *there*. . . .

He left a record of that moment of realization.

"Suddenly one night I woke up and lay still, and
it was as if I had never seen Amanda before. Now
I saw her plainly, I saw her with that same dreadful
clearness that sometimes comes at dawn, a pitiless,
a scientific distinctness that has neither light nor
shadow. . . .

"Of course," I said, and then presently I got up
very softly. . . .

"I wanted to get out of my intolerable, close,
personal cabin. I wanted to feel the largeness of
the sky. I went out upon the deck. We were off
the coast of Madras, and when I think of that
moment, there comes back to me also the faint flavour
of spice in the air, the low line of the coast, the cool
flooding abundance of the Indian moonlight, the
swish of the black water against the side of the
ship. And a perception of infinite loss, as if the limitless heavens above this earth and below to the very
uttermost star were just one boundless cavity from
which delight had fled. . . .

"Of course I had lost her. I knew it with absolute certainty. I knew it from her insecure temper-

ament, her adventurousness, her needs. I knew it from every line she had written me in the last three months. I knew it intuitively. She had been unfaithful. She must have been unfaithful.

"What had I been dreaming about to think that it would not be so?"

§ 21

"Now let me write down plainly what I think of these matters. Let me be at least honest with myself, whatever self-contradictions I may have been led into by force of my passions. Always I have despised jealousy. . . .

"Only by the conquest of four natural limitations is the aristocratic life to be achieved. They come in a certain order, and in that order the spirit of man is armed against them less and less efficiently. Of fear and my struggle against fear I have told already. I am fearful. I am a physical coward until I can bring shame and anger to my assistance, but in overcoming fear I have been helped by the whole body of human tradition. Every one, the basest creatures, every Hottentot, every stunted creature that ever breathed poison in a slum, knows that the instinctive constitution of man is at fault here and that fear is shameful and must be subdued. The race is on one's side. And so there is a vast traditional support for a man against the Second Limitation, the limitation of physical indulgence. It is not so universal as the first, there is a grinning bawling humour on the side of grossness, but common pride is against it. And in this matter my temperament has been my help: I am fastidious, I eat little, drink little, and feel a shivering recoil from excess. It is no great virtue; it happens so; it is something in the nerves of my skin. I cannot endure myself unshaven or in any way unclean; I am tormented by dirty hands or dirty blood or dirty memories, and after I had once loved Amanda I could not — unless some irrational impulse to get equal with her had caught me — have broken my faith to her, whatever breach there was in her faith to me. . . .

"I see that in these matters I am cleaner than most men and more easily clean; and it may be that it is in the vein of just that distinctive virtue that I fell so readily into a passion of resentment and anger.

"I despised a jealous man. There is a traditional discredit of jealousy, not so strong as that against cowardice, but still very strong. But the general contempt of jealousy is curiously wrapped up with the supposition that there is no cause for jealousy, that it is unreasonable suspicion. Given a cause then tradition speaks with an uncertain voice. . . .

"I see now that I despised jealousy because I assumed that it was impossible for Amanda to love any one but me; it was intolerable to imagine anything else, I insisted upon believing that she was as fastidious as myself and as faithful as myself, made indeed after my image, and I went on disregarding the most obvious intimations that she was not, until that still moment in the Indian Ocean, when silently,

2 A

gently as a drowned body might rise out of the depths
of a pool, that knowledge of love dead and honour
gone for ever floated up into my consciousness.

"And then I felt that Amanda had cheated me!
Outrageously.   Abominably.

"Now, so far as my intelligence goes, there is not
a cloud upon this question. My demand upon
Amanda was outrageous and I had no right whatever to her love or loyalty.   I must have that very
clear. . . .

"This aristocratic life, as I conceive it, must be,
except accidentally here and there, incompatible
with the domestic life. It means going hither and
thither in the universe of thought as much as in the
universe of matter, it means adventure, it means
movement and adventure that must needs be hopelessly encumbered by an inseparable associate, it
means self-imposed responsibilities that will not fit
into the welfare of a family. In all ages, directly
society had risen above the level of a barbaric tribal
village, this need of a release from the family for
certain necessary types of people has been recognized. It was met sometimes informally, sometimes
formally, by the growth and establishment of special
classes and orders, of priests, monks, nuns, of pledged
knights, of a great variety of non-family people,
whose concern was the larger collective life that
opens out beyond the simple necessities and duties
and loyalties of the steading and of the craftsman's
house. Sometimes, but not always, that release
took the form of celibacy; but besides that there

have been a hundred institutional variations of the common life to meet the need of the special man, the man who must go deep and the man who must go far. A vowed celibacy ceased to be a tolerable rule for an aristocracy directly the eugenic idea entered the mind of man, because a celibate aristocracy means the abandonment of the racial future to a proletariat of base unleaderly men. That was plain to Plato. It was plain to Campanelea. It was plain to the Protestant reformers. But the world has never yet gone on to the next step beyond that recognition, to the recognition of feminine aristocrats, rulers and the mates of rulers, as untrammelled by domestic servitudes and family relationships as the men of their kind. That I see has always been my idea since in my undergraduate days I came under the spell of Plato. It was a matter of course that my first gift to Amanda should be his *Republic*. I loved Amanda transfigured in that dream. . . .

"There are no such women. . . .

"It is no excuse for me that I thought she was like-minded with myself. I had no sound reason for supposing that. I did suppose that. I did not perceive that not only was she younger than myself, but that while I had been going through a mill of steely education, kept close, severely exercised, polished by discussion, she had but the weak training of a not very good school, some scrappy reading, the vague discussions of village artists, and the draped and decorated novelties of the 'advanced.' It all went to nothing on the impact of the world. . . .

She showed herself the woman the world has always known, no miracle, and the alternative was for me to give myself to her in the ancient way, to serve her happiness, to control her and delight and companion her, or to let her go. . . .

"The normal woman centres upon herself; her mission is her own charm and her own beauty and her own setting; her place is her home. She demands the concentration of a man. Not to be able to command that is her failure. Not to give her that is to shame her. As I had shamed Amanda. . . ."

§ 22

"There are no such women." He had written this in and struck it out, and then at some later time written it in again. There it stayed now as his last persuasion, but it set White thinking and doubting. And, indeed, there was another sheet of pencilled broken stuff that seemed to glance at quite another type of womanhood.

§ 23

"It is clear that the women aristocrats who must come to the remaking of the world will do so in spite of limitations at least as great as those from which the aristocratic spirit of man escapes. These women must become aristocratic through their own innate impulse, they must be self-called to their lives, exactly as men must be; there is no making an aristocrat without a predisposition for rule and nobility. And they have to discover and struggle against just exactly the limitations that we have to struggle against. They have to conquer not only fear but indulgence, indulgence of a softer, more insidious quality, and jealousy — proprietorship. . . .

"It is as natural to want a mate as to want bread, and a thousand times in my work and in my wanderings I have thought of a mate and desired a mate. A mate — not a possession. It is a need almost naïvely simple. If only one could have a woman who thought of one and with one! Though she were on the other side of the world and busied about a thousand things. . . .

"'*With* one,' I see it must be rather than '*of* one.' That 'of one' is just the unexpurgated egotistical demand coming back again. . . .

"Man is a mating creature. It is not good to be alone. But mating means a mate. . . .

"We should be lovers, of course; that goes without saying. . . .

"And yet not specialized lovers, not devoted, *attending* lovers. 'Dancing attendance' — as they used to say. We should meet upon our ways as the great carnivores do. . . .

"That at any rate was a sound idea. Though we only played with it.

"But that mate desire is just a longing that can have no possible satisfaction now for me. What is the good of dreaming? Life and chance have played a trick upon my body and soul. I am mated, though I am mated to a phantom. I loved and I love Amanda, not Easton's Amanda, but Amanda in armour, the Amanda of my dreams. Sense, and particularly the sense of beauty, lies deeper than reason in us. There can be no mate for me now unless she comes with Amanda's voice and Amanda's face and Amanda's quick movements and her clever hands. . . .

§ 24

"Why am I so ungrateful to her still for all the happiness she gave me?

"There were things between us two as lovers, — love, things more beautiful than anything else in the world, things that set the mind hunting among ineffectual images in a search for impossible expression, images of sunlight shining through blood-red petals, images of moonlight in a scented garden, of marble gleaming in the shade, of far-off wonderful music heard at dusk in a great stillness, of fairies dancing softly, of floating happiness and stirring delights, of joys as keen and sudden as the knife of an assassin, assassin's knives made out of tears, tears that are happiness, wordless things; and surprises, expectations, gratitudes, sudden moments of contemplation, the sight of a soft eyelid closed in sleep, shadowy tones in the sound of a voice heard unexpectedly; sweet, dear magical things that I can find no words for. . . .

"If she was a goddess to me, should it be any affair of mine that she was not a goddess to herself; that she could hold all this that has been between us more cheaply than I did? It does not change one jot of

it for me.   At the time she did not hold it cheaply.
She forgets where I do not forget. . . ."

§ 25

Such were the things that Benham could think
and set down.

Yet for whole days he was possessed by the
thought of killing Amanda and himself.

He did not at once turn homeward.   It was in
Ceylon that he dropped his work and came home.
At Colombo he found a heap of letters awaiting him,
and there were two of these that had started at the
same time.   They had been posted in London on one
eventful afternoon.   Lady Marayne and Amanda
had quarrelled violently.   Two earnest, flushed,
quick-breathing women, full of neat but belated
repartee, separated to write their simultaneous
letters.   Each letter trailed the atmosphere of that
truncated encounter.   Lady Marayne told her story
ruthlessly.   Amanda, on the other hand, generalized, and explained.   Sir Philip's adoration of her
was a love-friendship, it was beautiful, it was pure.
Was there no trust nor courage in the world?   She
would defy all jealous scandal.   She would not
even banish him from her side.   Surely the Cheetah
could trust her.   But the pitiless facts of Lady
Marayne went beyond Amanda's explaining.   The
little lady's dignity had been stricken.   "I have
been used as a cloak," she wrote.

Her phrases were vivid.   She quoted the very
words of Amanda, words she had overheard at Chex-

ington in the twilight. They were no invention. They were the very essence of Amanda, the lover. It was as sure as if Benham had heard the sound of her voice, as if he had peeped and seen, as if she had crept by him, stooping and rustling softly. It brought back the living sense of her, excited, flushed, reckless; his wild-haired Amanda of infinite delight. . . . All day those words of hers pursued him. All night they flared across the black universe. He buried his face in the pillows and they whispered softly in his ear.

He walked his room in the darkness longing to smash and tear.

He went out from the house and shook his ineffectual fists at the stirring quiet of the stars.

He sent no notice of his coming back. Nor did he come back with a definite plan. But he wanted to get at Amanda.

§ 26

It was with Amanda he had to reckon. Towards Easton he felt scarcely any anger at all. Easton he felt only existed for him because Amanda willed to have it so.

Such anger as Easton did arouse in him was a contemptuous anger. His devotion filled Benham with scorn. His determination to serve Amanda at any price, to bear the grossest humiliations and slights for her, his humility, his service and tenderness, his care for her moods and happiness, seemed to Benham a treachery to human nobility.

That rage against Easton was like the rage of a trade-unionist against a blackleg. Are all the women to fall to the men who will be their master-slaves and keepers? But it was not simply that Benham felt men must be freed from this incessant attendance; women too must free themselves from their almost instinctive demand for an attendant. . . .

His innate disposition was to treat women as responsible beings. Never in his life had he thought of a woman as a pretty thing to be fooled and won and competed for and fought over. So that it was Amanda he wanted to reach and reckon with now, Amanda who had mated and ruled his senses only to fling him into this intolerable pit of shame and jealous fury. But the forces that were driving him home now were the forces below the level of reason and ideas, organic forces compounded of hate and desire, profound aboriginal urgencies. He thought, indeed, very little as he lay in his berth or sulked on deck; his mind lay waste under a pitiless invasion of exasperating images that ever and again would so wring him that his muscles would tighten and his hands clench or he would find himself restraining a snarl, the threat of the beast, in his throat.

Amanda grew upon his imagination until she overshadowed the whole world. She filled the skies. She bent over him and mocked him. She became a mystery of passion and dark beauty. She was the sin of the world. One breathed her in the winds of the sea. She had taken to herself the greatness of elemental things. . . .

So that when at last he saw her he was amazed to see her, and see that she was just a creature of common size and quality, a rather tired and very frightened-looking white-faced young woman, in an evening-dress of unfamiliar fashion, with little common trinkets of gold and colour about her wrists and neck.

In that instant's confrontation he forgot all that had brought him homeward. He stared at her as one stares at a stranger whom one has greeted in mistake for an intimate friend.

For he saw that she was no more the Amanda he hated and desired to kill than she had ever been the Amanda he had loved.

§ 27

He took them by surprise. It had been his intention to take them by surprise. Such is the inelegance of the jealous state.

He reached London in the afternoon and put up at a hotel near Charing Cross. In the evening about ten he appeared at the house in Lancaster Gate. The butler was deferentially amazed. Mrs. Benham was, he said, at a theatre with Sir Philip Easton, and he thought some other people also. He did not know when she would be back. She might go on to supper. It was not the custom for the servants to wait up for her.

Benham went into the study that reduplicated his former rooms in Finacue Street and sat down before the fire the butler lit for him. He sent the man to bed, and fell into profound meditation.

It was nearly two o'clock when he heard the sound of her latchkey and went out at once upon the landing.

The half-door stood open and Easton's car was outside. She stood in the middle of the hall and relieved Easton of the gloves and fan he was carrying.

"Good-night," she said, "I am so tired."

"My wonderful goddess," he said.

She yielded herself to his accustomed embrace, then started, stared, and wrenched herself out of his arms.

Benham stood at the top of the stairs looking down upon them, white-faced and inexpressive. Easton dropped back a pace. For a moment no one moved nor spoke, and then very quietly Easton shut the half-door and shut out the noises of the road.

For some seconds Benham regarded them, and as he did so his spirit changed. . . .

Everything he had thought of saying and doing vanished out of his mind.

He stuck his hands into his pockets and descended the staircase. When he was five or six steps above them, he spoke. "Just sit down here," he said, with a gesture of one hand, and sat down himself upon the stairs. "*Do* sit down," he said with a sudden testiness as they continued standing. "I know all about this affair. Do please sit down and let us talk. . . . Everybody's gone to bed long ago."

"Cheetah!" she said. "Why have you come back like this?"

Then at his mute gesture she sat down at his feet.

"I wish you would sit down, Easton," he said in a voice of subdued savagery.

"Why have you come back?" Sir Philip Easton found his voice to ask.

"*Sit* down," Benham spat, and Easton obeyed unwillingly.

"I came back," Benham went on, "to see to all this. Why else? I don't — now I see you — feel very fierce about it. But it has distressed me. You look changed, Amanda, and fagged. And your hair is untidy. It's as if something had happened to you and made you a stranger. . . . You two people are lovers. Very natural and simple, but I want to get out of it. Yes, I want to get out of it. That wasn't quite my idea, but now I see it is. It's queer, but on the whole I feel sorry for you. All of us, poor humans —. There's reason to be sorry for all of us. We're full of lusts and uneasiness and resentments that we haven't the will to control. What do you two people want me to do to you? Would you like a divorce, Amanda? It's the clean, straight thing, isn't it? Or would the scandal hurt you?"

Amanda sat crouched together, with her eyes on Benham.

"Give us a divorce," said Easton, looking to her to confirm him.

Amanda shook her head.

"I don't want a divorce," she said.

"Then what do you want?" asked Benham with sudden asperity.

"I don't want a divorce," she repeated. "Why

do you, after a long silence, come home like this, abruptly, with no notice?"

"It was the way it took me," said Benham, after a little interval.

"You have left me for long months."

"Yes. I was angry. And it was ridiculous to be angry. I thought I wanted to kill you, and now I see you I see that all I want to do is to help you out of this miserable mess — and then get away from you. You two would like to marry. You ought to be married."

"I would die to make Amanda happy," said Easton.

"Your business, it seems to me, is to live to make her happy. That you may find more of a strain. Less tragic and more tiresome. I, on the other hand, want neither to die nor live for her." Amanda moved sharply. "It's extraordinary what amazing vapours a lonely man may get into his head. If you don't want a divorce then I suppose things might go on as they are now."

"I hate things as they are now," said Easton. "I hate this falsehood and deception."

"You would hate the scandal just as much," said Amanda.

"I would not care what the scandal was unless it hurt you."

"It would be only a temporary inconvenience," said Benham. "Every one would sympathize with you. . . . The whole thing is so natural. . . . People would be glad to forget very soon. They did with my mother."

"No," said Amanda, "it isn't so easy as that."

She seemed to come to a decision.

"Pip," she said. "I want to talk to — *him* — alone."

Easton's brown eyes were filled with distress and perplexity. "But why?" he asked.

"I do," she said.

"But this is a thing for *us*."

"Pip, I want to talk to him alone. There is something — something I can't say before you. . . ."

Sir Philip rose slowly to his feet.

"Shall I wait outside?"

"No, Pip. Go home. Yes, — there are some things you must leave to me."

She stood up too and turned so that she and Benham both faced the younger man. The strangest uneasiness mingled with his resolve to be at any cost splendid. He felt — and it was a most unexpected and disconcerting feeling — that he was no longer confederated with Amanda; that prior, more fundamental and greater associations prevailed over his little new grip upon her mind and senses. He stared at husband and wife aghast in this realization. Then his resolute romanticism came to his help. "I would trust you —" he began. "If you tell me to go —"

Amanda seemed to measure her hold upon him.

She laid her hand upon his arm. "Go, my dear Pip," she said. "Go."

He had a moment of hesitation, of anguish, and it seemed to Benham as though he eked himself out

with unreality, as though somewhen, somewhere, he
had seen something of the sort in a play and filled
in a gap that otherwise he could not have supplied.

Then the door had closed upon him, and Amanda,
pale and darkly dishevelled, faced her husband,
silently and intensely.

"*Well?*" said Benham.

She held out her arms to him.

"Why did you leave me, Cheetah?   Why did you
leave me?"

§ 28

Benham affected to ignore those proffered arms.
But they recalled in a swift rush the animal anger
that had brought him back to England.   To remind
him of desire now was to revive an anger stronger
than any desire.   He spoke seeking to hurt her.

"I am wondering now," he said, "why the devil I
came back."

"You had to come back to me."

"I could have written just as well about these
things."

"*Cheetah*," she said softly, and came towards him
slowly, stooping forward and looking into his eyes,
"you had to come back to see your old Leopard.
Your wretched Leopard. Who has rolled in the
dirt.   And is still yours."

"Do you want a divorce?   How are we to fix
things, Amanda?"

"Cheetah, I will tell you how we will fix things."

She dropped upon the step below him. She laid her hands with a deliberate softness upon him, she gave a toss so that her disordered hair was a little more disordered, and brought her soft chin down to touch his knees. Her eyes implored him.

"Cheetah," she said. "You are going to forgive."

He sat rigid, meeting her eyes.

"Amanda," he said at last, "you would be astonished if I kicked you away from me and trampled over you to the door. That is what I want to do."

"Do it," she said, and the grip of her hands tightened. "Cheetah, dear! I would love you to kill me."

"I don't want to kill you."

Her eyes dilated. "Beat me."

"And I haven't the remotest intention of making love to you," he said, and pushed her soft face and hands away from him as if he would stand up.

She caught hold of him again. "Stay with me," she said.

He made no effort to shake off her grip. He looked at the dark cloud of her hair that had ruled him so magically, and the memory of old delights made him grip a great handful almost inadvertently as he spoke. "Dear Leopard," he said, "we humans are the most streaky of conceivable things. I thought I hated you. I do. I hate you like poison. And also I do not hate you at all."

Then abruptly he was standing over her.

She rose to her knees.

"Stay here, old Cheetah!" she said. "This is your house. I am your wife."

He went towards the unfastened front door.

"Cheetah!" she cried with a note of despair.

He halted at the door.

"Amanda, I will come to-morrow. I will come in the morning, in the sober London daylight, and then we will settle things."

He stared at her, and to her amazement he smiled. He spoke as one who remarks upon a quite unexpected fact. . . .

"Never in my life, Amanda, have I seen a human being that I wanted so little to kill."

§ 29

White found a fragment that might have been written within a week of those last encounters of Benham and Amanda.

"The thing that astonished me most in Amanda was the change in her mental quality.

"With me in the old days she had always been a sincere person; she had deceived me about facts, but she had never deceived me about herself. Her personal, stark frankness had been her essential strength. And it was gone. I came back to find Amanda an accomplished actress, a thing of poses and calculated effects. She was a surface, a sham, a Lorelei. Beneath that surface I could not discover anything individual at all. Fear and a grasping quality, such as God gave us all when he gave us hands; but the individual I knew, the humorous

2 B

wilful Spotless Leopard was gone. Whither, I cannot imagine. An amazing disappearance. Clean
out of space and time like a soul lost for ever.

"When I went to see her in the morning, she was
made up for a scene, she acted an intricate part,
never for a moment was she there in reality. . . .

"I have got a remarkable persuasion that she lost
herself in this way, by cheapening love, by making
base love to a lover she despised. . . . There can
be no inequality in love. Give and take must
balance. One must be one's natural self or the whole
business is an indecent trick, a vile use of life! To
use inferiors in love one must needs talk down to
them, interpret oneself in their insufficient phrases,
pretend, sentimentalize. And it is clear that unless
oneself is to be lost, one must be content to leave
alone all those people that one can reach only by
sentimentalizing. But Amanda — and yet somehow I love her for it still — could not leave any one
alone. So she was always feverishly weaving nets
of false relationship. Until her very self was forgotten. So she will go on until the end. With
Easton it had been necessary for her to key herself
to a simple exalted romanticism that was entirely
insincere. She had so accustomed herself to these
poses that her innate gestures were forgotten. She
could not recover them; she could not even reinvent
them. Between us there were momentary gleams
as though presently we should be our frank former
selves again. They were never more than momentary. . . ."

And that was all that this astonishing man had seen fit to tell of his last parting from his wife.

Perhaps he did Amanda injustice. Perhaps there was a stronger thread of reality in her desire to recover him than he supposed. Clearly he believed that under the circumstances Amanda would have tried to recover anybody.

She had dressed for that morning's encounter in a very becoming and intimate wrap of soft mauve and white silk, and she had washed and dried her dark hair so that it was a vapour about her face. She set herself with a single mind to persuade herself and Benham that they were inseparable lovers, and she would not be deflected by his grim determination to discuss the conditions of their separation. When he asked her whether she wanted a divorce, she offered to throw over Sir Philip and banish him for ever as lightly as a great lady might sacrifice an objectionable poodle to her connubial peace.

Benham passed through perplexing phases, so that she herself began to feel that her practice with Easton had spoilt her hands. His initial grimness she could understand, and partially its breakdown into irritability. But she was puzzled by his laughter. For he laughed abruptly.

"You know, Amanda, I came home in a mood of tremendous tragedy. And really, — you are a Lark."

And then overriding her altogether, he told her what he meant to do about their future and the future of their little son.

"You don't want a divorce and a fuss. Then I'll

leave things.   I perceive I've no intention of marry-
ing any more.   But you'd better do the straight
thing.   People forget and forgive.   Especially when
there is no one about making a fuss against you.

"Perhaps, after all, there is something to be said
for shirking it.   We'll both be able to get at the boy
then.   You'll not hurt him, and I shall want to see
him.   It's better for the boy anyhow not to have a
divorce.

"I'll not stand in your way.   I'll get a little flat
and I shan't come too much to London, and when I
do, you can get out of town.   You must be discreet
about Easton, and if people say anything about
him, send them to me.   After all, this is our private
affair.

"We'll go on about money matters as we have been
going.   I trust to you not to run me into overwhelming debts.   And, of course, if at any time,
you do want to marry — on account of children or
anything — if nobody knows of this conversation
we can be divorced then. . . ."

Benham threw out these decisions in little dry
sentences while Amanda gathered her forces for her
last appeal.

It was an unsuccessful appeal, and at the end she
flung herself down before him and clung to his knees.
He struggled ridiculously to get himself clear, and
when at last he succeeded she dropped prostrate
on the floor with her dishevelled hair about her.

She heard the door close behind him, and still she
lay there, a dark Guinevere, until with a start she

heard a step upon the thick carpet without. He had come back. The door reopened. There was a slight pause, and then she raised her face and met the blank stare of the second housemaid. There are moments, suspended fragments of time rather than links in its succession, when the human eye is more intelligible than any words.

The housemaid made a rapid apologetic noise and vanished with a click of the door.

"*Damn!*" said Amanda.

Then slowly she rose to her knees.

She meditated through vast moments.

"It's a cursed thing to be a woman," said Amanda.

She stood up. She put her hand on the telephone in the corner and then she forgot about it. After another long interval of thought she spoke.

"Cheetah!" she said, "Old Cheetah! . . .

"I didn't *think* it of you. . . ."

Then presently with the even joyless movements of one who does a reasonable business, with something indeed of the manner of one who packs a trunk, she rang up Sir Philip Easton.

§ 30

The head chambermaid on the first floor of the Westwood Hotel in Danebury Street had a curious and perplexing glimpse of Benham's private processes the morning after this affair.

Benham had taken Room 27 on the afternoon of his return to London. She had seen him twice or three times, and he had struck her as a coldly dec-

orous person, tall, white-faced, slow speaking; the
last man to behave violently or surprise a head
chambermaid in any way. On the morning of his
departure she was told by the first-floor waiter that
the occupant of Room 26 had complained of an
uproar in the night, and almost immediately she
was summoned to see Benham.

He was standing facing the door and in a position
which did a little obscure the condition of the room
behind him. He was carefully dressed, and his
manner was more cold and decorous than ever.
But one of his hands was tied up in a white bandage.

"I am going this morning," he said, "I am going
down now to breakfast. I have had a few little
accidents with some of the things in the room and I
have cut my hand. I want you to tell the manager
and see that they are properly charged for on the
bill. . . . Thank you."

The head chambermaid was left to consider the
accidents.

Benham's things were all packed up and the room
had an air of having been straightened up neatly and
methodically after a destructive cataclysm. One or
two items that the chambermaid might possibly have
overlooked in the normal course of things were carefully exhibited. For example, the sheet had been
torn into half a dozen strips and they were lying side
by side on the bed. The clock on the mantelpiece
had been knocked into the fireplace and then pounded
to pieces. All the looking-glasses in the room were
smashed, apparently the electric lamp that stood on

the night table by the bedside had been wrenched off
and flung or hammered about amidst the other
breakables. And there was a considerable amount
of blood splashed about the room. The head
chambermaid felt unequal to the perplexities of the
spectacle and summoned her most convenient friend,
the head chambermaid on the third floor, to her aid.
The first-floor waiter joined their deliberations and
several housemaids displayed a respectful interest
in the matter. Finally they invoked the manager.
He was still contemplating the scene of the disorder
when the precipitate retreat of his subordinates
warned him of Benham's return.

Benham was smoking a cigarette and his bearing
was reassuringly tranquil.

"I had a kind of nightmare," he said. "I am
fearfully sorry to have disarranged your room. You
must charge me for the inconvenience as well as
for the damage."

§ 31

"An aristocrat cannot be a lover."

"One cannot serve at once the intricacies of the
wider issues of life and the intricacies of another
human being. I do not mean that one may not
love. One loves the more because one does not
concentrate one's love. One loves nations, the
people passing in the street, beasts hurt by the
wayside, troubled scoundrels and university dons
in tears. . . .

"But if one does not give one's whole love and life

into a woman's hands I do not think one can expect
to be loved.

"An aristocrat must do without close personal
love. . . ."

This much was written at the top of a sheet of
paper. The writing ended halfway down the page.
Manifestly it was an abandoned beginning. And it
was, it seemed to White, the last page of all this
confusion of matter that dealt with the Second and
Third Limitations. Its incompleteness made its
expression perfect. . . .

There Benham's love experience ended. He
turned to the great business of the world. Desire and
Jealousy should deflect his life no more; like Fear
they were to be dismissed as far as possible and
subdued when they could not be altogether dismissed.
Whatever stirrings of blood or imagination there
were in him after that parting, whatever failures
from this resolution, they left no trace on the rest
of his research, which was concerned with the hates
of peoples and classes and war and peace and the
possibilities science unveils and starry speculations
of what mankind may do.

§ 32

But Benham did not leave England again until he
had had an encounter with Lady Marayne.

The little lady came to her son in a state of extraordinary anger and distress. Never had she
seemed quite so resolute nor quite so hopelessly dispersed and mixed. And when for a moment it

seemed to him that she was not as a matter of fact dispersed and mixed at all, then with an instant eagerness he dismissed that one elucidatory gleam. "What are you doing in England, Poff?" she demanded. "And what are you going to do?

"Nothing! And you are going to leave her in your house, with your property and a lover. If that's it, Poff, why did you ever come back? And why did you ever marry her? You might have known; her father was a swindler. She's begotten of deceit. She'll tell her own story while you are away, and a pretty story she'll make of it."

"Do you want me to divorce her and make a scandal?"

"I never wanted you to go away from her. If you'd stayed and watched her as a man should, as I begged you and implored you to do. Didn't I tell you, Poff? Didn't I warn you?"

"But now what am I to do?"

"There you are! That's just a man's way. You get yourself into this trouble, you follow your passions and your fancies and fads and then you turn to me! How can I help you now, Poff? If you'd listened to me before!"

Her blue eyes were demonstratively round.

"Yes, but —"

"I warned you," she interrupted. "I warned you. I've done all I could for you. It isn't that I haven't seen through her. When she came to me at first with that made-up story of a baby! And all about loving me like her own mother. But I did

what I could. I thought we might still make the
best of a bad job. And then —. I might have
known she couldn't leave Pip alone. . . . But for
weeks I didn't dream. I wouldn't dream. Right
under my nose. The impudence of it!"

Her voice broke. "Such a horrid mess! Such a
hopeless, horrid mess!"

She wiped away a bright little tear. . . .

"It's all alike. It's your way with us. All of
you. There isn't a man in the world deserves to
have a woman in the world. We do all we can for
you. We do all we can to amuse you, we dress for
you and we talk for you. All the sweet, warm little
women there are! And then you go away from
us! There never was a woman yet who pleased
and satisfied a man, who did not lose him. Give
you everything and off you must go! Lovers,
mothers. . . ."

It dawned upon Benham dimly that his mother's
troubles did not deal exclusively with himself.

"But Amanda," he began.

"If you'd looked after her properly, it would have
been right enough. Pip was as good as gold until
she undermined him. . . . A woman can't wait
about like an umbrella in a stand. . . . He was
just a boy. . . . Only of course there she was — a
novelty. It is perfectly easy to understand. She
flattered him. . . . Men are such fools."

"Still — it's no good saying that now."

"But she'll spend all your money, Poff! She'll
break your back with debts. What's to prevent

her? With him living on her! For that's what it comes to practically."

"Well, what am I to do?"

"You aren't going back without tying her up, Poff? You ought to stop every farthing of her money — every farthing. It's your duty."

"I can't do things like that."

"But have you no Shame? To let that sort of thing go on!"

"If I don't feel the Shame of it —   And I don't."

"And that money —.   I got you that money, Poff! It was my money."

Benham stared at her perplexed. "What am I to do?" he asked.

"Cut her off, you silly boy! Tie her up! Pay her through a solicitor. Say that if she sees him *once* again —"

He reflected. "No," he said at last.

"Poff!" she cried, "every time I see you, you are more and more like your father. You're going off — just as he did. That baffled, *mulish* look — priggish — solemn! Oh! it's strange the stuff a poor woman has to bring into the world. But you'll do nothing. I know you'll do nothing. You'll stand everything. You — you Cuckold! And she'll drive by me, she'll pass me in theatres with the money that ought to have been mine! Oh! Oh!"

She dabbed her handkerchief from one swimming eye to the other. But she went on talking. Faster and faster, less and less coherently; more and more wildly abusive. Presently in a brief pause of the storm Benham sighed profoundly. . . .

It brought the scene to a painful end. . . .

For weeks her distress pursued and perplexed him.

He had an extraordinary persuasion that in some obscure way he was in default, that he was to blame for her distress, that he owed her — he could never define what he owed her.

And yet, what on earth was one to do?

And something his mother had said gave him the odd idea that he had misjudged his father, that he had missed depths of perplexed and kindred goodwill. He went down to see him before he returned to India. But if there was a hidden well of feeling in Mr. Benham senior, it had been very carefully boarded over. The parental mind and attention were entirely engaged in a dispute in the *School World* about the heuristic method. Somebody had been disrespectful to Martindale House and the thing was rankling almost unendurably. It seemed to be a relief to him to show his son very fully the essentially illogical position of his assailant. He was entirely inattentive to Benham's carefully made conversational opportunities. He would be silent at times while Benham talked and then he would break out suddenly with: "What seems to me so unreasonable, so ridiculous, in the whole of that fellow's second argument — if one can call it an argument — . . . A man who reasons as he does is bound to get laughed at. If people will only see it. . . ."

CHAPTER THE SIXTH

The New Haroun al Raschid

§ 1

BENHAM corresponded with Amanda until the summer of 1913. Sometimes the two wrote coldly to one another, sometimes with warm affection, sometimes with great bitterness. When he met White in Johannesburg during the strike period of 1913, he was on his way to see her in London and to settle their relationship upon a new and more definite footing. It was her suggestion that they should meet.

About her he felt an enormous, inexorable, dissatisfaction. He could not persuade himself that his treatment of her and that his relations to her squared with any of his preconceptions of nobility, and yet at no precise point could he detect where he had definitely taken an ignoble step. Through Amanda he was coming to the full experience of life. Like all of us he had been prepared, he had prepared himself, to take life in a certain way, and life had taken him, as it takes all of us, in an entirely different and unexpected way. . . . He had been ready for noble deeds and villainies, for achievements and failures, and here as the dominant fact of his personal life was a perplexing riddle. He could not hate and condemn her for ten minutes at a time without a flow of exoneration; he could not think of her tolerantly or lovingly without immediate shame and resentment, and with the utmost will in the world he could not banish her from his mind.

During the intervening years he had never ceased to have her in his mind; he would not think of her it is true if he could help it, but often he could not help it, and as a negative presence, as a thing denied, she was almost more potent than she had been as a thing accepted. Meanwhile he worked. His nervous irritability increased, but it did not hinder the steady development of his Research.

Long before his final parting from Amanda he had worked out his idea and method for all the more personal problems in life; the problems he put together under his headings of the first three "Limitations." He had resolved to emancipate himself from fear, indulgence, and that instinctive preoccupation with the interests and dignity of self which he chose to term Jealousy, and with the one tremendous exception of Amanda he had to a large extent succeeded. Amanda. Amanda. Amanda. He stuck the more grimly to his Research to drown that beating in his brain.

Emancipation from all these personal things he held now to be a mere prelude to the real work of a man's life, which was to serve this dream of a larger human purpose. The bulk of his work was to discover and define that purpose, that purpose which must be the

directing and comprehending form of all the activities
of the noble life.   One cannot be noble, he had come
to perceive, at large; one must be noble to an end.
To make human life, collectively and in detail, a thing
more comprehensive, more beautiful, more generous
and coherent than it is to-day seemed to him the
fundamental intention of all nobility.   He believed
more and more firmly that the impulses to make and
help and subserve great purposes are abundantly present in the world, that they are inhibited by hasty
thinking, limited thinking and bad thinking, and that
the real ennoblement of human life was not so much a
creation as a release.   He lumped the preventive and
destructive forces that keep men dispersed, unhappy,
and ignoble under the heading of Prejudice, and he
made this Prejudice his fourth and greatest and most
difficult limitation.   In one place he had written it,
"Prejudice or Divisions."   That being subdued in
oneself and in the world, then in the measure of
its subjugation, the new life of our race, the great
age, the noble age, would begin.

So he set himself to examine his own mind and the
mind of the world about him for prejudice, for ham-
pering follies, disguised disloyalties and mischievous
distrusts, and the great bulk of the papers that White
struggled with at Westhaven Street were devoted to
various aspects of this search for "Prejudice."   It
seemed to White to be at once the most magnificent
and the most preposterous of enterprises.   It was
indeed no less than an enquiry into all the preventable
sources of human failure and disorder. . . .   And it

was all too manifest to White also that the last
place in which Benham was capable of detecting a
prejudice was at the back of his own head. . . .

Under this Fourth Limitation he put the most
remarkable array of influences, race-hatred, national
suspicion, the evil side of patriotism, religious and
social intolerance, every social consequence of muddle
headedness, every dividing force indeed except the
purely personal dissensions between man and man.
And he developed a metaphysical interpretation of
these troubles. "No doubt," he wrote in one place,
"much of the evil between different kinds of men is
due to uncultivated feeling, to natural bad feeling,
but far more is it due to bad thinking." At times he
seemed on the verge of the persuasion that most
human trouble is really due to bad metaphysics.
It was, one must remark, an extraordinary journey
he had made; he had started from chivalry and
arrived at metaphysics; every knight he held must
be a logician, and ultimate bravery is courage of the
mind. One thinks of his coming to this conclusion
with knit brows and balancing intentness above
whole gulfs of bathos — very much as he had once
walked the Leysin Bisse. . . .

"Men do not know how to think," he insisted —
getting along the planks; "and they will not realize
that they do not know how to think. Nine-tenths
of the wars in the world have arisen out of miscon-
ceptions. . . . Misconception is the sin and dishonour of the mind, and muddled thinking as ignoble
as dirty conduct. . . . Infinitely more disastrous."

And again he wrote: "Man, I see, is an over-
practical creature, too eager to get into action.
There is our deepest trouble.   He takes conclusions
ready-made, or he makes them in a hurry.   Life is so
short that he thinks it better to err than wait.   He
has no patience, no faith in anything but himself.
He thinks he is a being when in reality he is only a
link in a being, and so he is more anxious to be complete than right.   The last devotion of which he is
capable is that devotion of the mind which suffers
partial performance, but insists upon exhaustive
thought.   He scamps his thought and finishes his
performance, and before he is dead it is already being
abandoned and begun all over again by some one
else in the same egotistical haste. . . ."

It is, I suppose, a part of the general humour of life
that these words should have been written by a man
who walked the plank to fresh ideas with the dizziest
difficulty unless he had Prothero to drag him forward,
and who acted time after time with an altogether
disastrous hastiness.

§ 2

Yet there was a kind of necessity in this journey
of Benham's from the cocked hat and wooden sword
of Seagate and his early shame at cowardice and
baseness to the spiritual megalomania of his complete
Research Magnificent.   You can no more resolve
to live a life of honour nowadays and abstain from
social and political scheming on a world-wide scale,
than you can profess religion and refuse to think

2 c

about God. In the past it was possible to take all
sorts of things for granted and be loyal to unexamined
things. One could be loyal to unexamined things
because they were unchallenged things. But now
everything is challenged. By the time of his second
visit to Russia, Benham's ideas of conscious and
deliberate aristocracy reaching out to an idea of
universal responsibility had already grown into the
extraordinary fantasy that he was, as it were, an
uncrowned king in the world. To be noble is to be
aristocratic, that is to say, a ruler. Thence it follows
that aristocracy is multiple kingship, and to be an
aristocrat is to partake both of the nature of philosopher and king. . . .

Yet it is manifest that the powerful people of this
world are by no means necessarily noble, and that
most modern kings, poor in quality, petty in spirit,
conventional in outlook, controlled and limited, fall
far short of kingship. Nevertheless, there *is* nobility,
there *is* kingship, or this earth is a dustbin and mankind but a kind of skin-disease upon a planet. From
that it is an easy step to this idea, the idea whose first
expression had already so touched the imagination of
Amanda, of a sort of diffused and voluntary kingship
scattered throughout mankind. The aristocrats are
not at the high table, the kings are not enthroned,
those who are enthroned are but pretenders and
simulacra, kings of the vulgar; the real king and
ruler is every man who sets aside the naïve passions
and self-interest of the common life for the rule and
service of the world.

This is an idea that is now to be found in much contemporary writing. It is one of those ideas that seem to appear simultaneously at many points in the world, and it is impossible to say now how far Benham was an originator of this idea, and how far he simply resonated to its expression by others. It was far more likely that Prothero, getting it heaven knows where, had spluttered it out and forgotten it, leaving it to germinate in the mind of his friend. . . .

This lordly, this kingly dream became more and more essential to Benham as his life went on. When Benham walked the Bisse he was just a youngster resolved to be individually brave; when he prowled in the jungle by night he was there for all mankind. With every year he became more and more definitely to himself a consecrated man as kings are consecrated. Only that he was self-consecrated, and anointed only in his heart. At last he was, so to speak, Haroun al Raschid again, going unsuspected about the world, because the palace of his security would not tell him the secrets of men's disorders. He was no longer a creature of circumstances, he was kingly, unknown, Alfred in the Camp of the Danes. In the great later accumulations of his Research the personal matter, the introspection, the intimate discussion of motive, becomes less and less. He forgets himself in the exaltation of kingliness. He worries less and less over the particular rightness of his definite acts. In these later papers White found Benham abstracted, self-forgetful, trying to find out with an ever increased self-detachment, with

an ever deepening regal solicitude, why there are
massacres, wars, tyrannies and persecutions, why
we let famine, disease and beasts assail us, and want
dwarf and cripple vast multitudes in the midst of
possible plenty.   And when he found out and as far
as he found out, he meant quite simply and earnestly
to apply his knowledge. . . .

§ 3

The intellectualism of Benham intensified to the
end.   His definition of Prejudice impressed White as
being the most bloodless and philosophical formula
that ever dominated the mind of a man.

"Prejudice," Benham had written, "is that common incapacity of the human mind to understand
that a difference in any respect is not a difference in
all respects, reinforced and rendered malignant by
an instinctive hostility to what is unlike ourselves.
We exaggerate classification and then charge it with
mischievous emotion by referring it to ourselves." .
And under this comprehensive formula he proceeded
to study and attack Family Prejudice, National
Prejudice, Race Prejudice, War, Class Prejudice,
Professional Prejudice, Sex Prejudice, in the most
industrious and elaborate manner.   Whether one
regards one's self or others he held that these prejudices are evil things.   "From the point of view
of human welfare they break men up into wars and
conflicts, make them an easy prey to those who trade
upon suspicion and hostility, prevent sane collective
co-operations, cripple and embitter life.   From the

point of view of personal aristocracy they make men vulgar, violent, unjust and futile. All the conscious life of the aristocrat must be a constant struggle against false generalizations; it is as much his duty to free himself from that as from fear, indulgence, and jealousy; it is a larger and more elaborate task, but it is none the less cardinal and essential. Indeed it is more cardinal and essential. The true knight has to be not only no coward, no self-pamperer, no egotist. He has to be a philosopher. He has to be no hasty or foolish thinker. His judgment no more than his courage is to be taken by surprise.

"To subdue fear, desire and jealousy, is the aristocrat's personal affair, it is his ritual and discipline, like a knight watching his arms; but the destruction of division and prejudice and all their forms and establishments, is his real task, that is the common work of knighthood. It is a task to be done in a thousand ways; one man working by persuasion, another by example, this one overthrowing some crippling restraint upon the freedom of speech and the spread of knowledge, and that preparing himself for a war that will shatter a tyrannous presumption. Most imaginative literature, all scientific investigation, all sound criticism, all good building, all good manufacture, all sound politics, every honesty and every reasoned kindliness contribute to this release of men from the heat and confusions of our present world."

It was clear to White that as Benham progressed with this major part of his research, he was more and more possessed by the idea that he was not making his own personal research alone, but, side by side with a vast, masked, hidden and once unsuspected multitude of others ; that this great idea of his was under kindred forms the great idea of thousands, that it was breaking as the dawn breaks, simultaneously to great numbers of people, and that the time was not far off when the new aristocracy, the disguised rulers of the world, would begin to realize their common bent and effort.   Into these latter papers there creeps more and more frequently a new phraseology, such expressions as the "Invisible King" and the "Spirit of Kingship," so that as Benham became personally more and more solitary, his thoughts became more and more public and social.

Benham was not content to define and denounce the prejudices of mankind.   He set himself to study just exactly how these prejudices worked, to get at the nature and habits and strengths of each kind of prejudice, and to devise means for its treatment, destruction or neutralization.   He had no great faith in the power of pure reasonableness ; his psychological ideas were modern, and he had grasped the fact that the power of most of the great prejudices that strain humanity lies deeper than the intellectual level.   Consequently he sought to bring himself into the closest contact with prejudices in action and prejudices in conflict in order to discover their sub-rational springs.

A large proportion of that larger moiety of the material at Westhaven Street which White from his

extensive experience of the public patience decided
could not possibly "make a book," consisted of
notes and discussions upon the first-hand observations Benham had made in this or that part of the
world.   He began in Russia during the revolutionary
trouble of 1906, he went thence to Odessa, and from
place to place in Bessarabia and Kieff, where during
a pogrom he had his first really illuminating encounter with race and culture prejudice. His
examination of the social and political condition of
Russia seems to have left him much more hopeful
than was the common feeling of liberal-minded
people during the years of depression that followed
the revolution of 1906, and it was upon the race
question that his attention concentrated.

The Swadeshi outbreak drew him from Russia to
India.   Here in an entirely different environment
was another discord of race and culture, and he found
in his study of it much that illuminated and corrected
his impressions of the Russian issue.   A whole drawer
was devoted to a comparatively finished and very
thorough enquiry into human dissensions in lower
Bengal.   Here there were not only race but culture
conflicts, and he could work particularly upon the
differences between men of the same race who were
Hindus, Christians and Mahometans respectively.
He could compare the Bengali Mahometan not only
with the Bengali Brahminist, but also with the
Mahometan from the north-west.   "If one could
scrape off all the creed and training, would one find
much the same thing at the bottom, or something

fundamentally so different that no close homogeneous social life and not even perhaps a life of just compromise is possible between the different races of mankind?"

His answer to that was a confident one. "There are no such natural and unalterable differences in character and quality between any two sorts of men whatever, as would make their peaceful and kindly co-operation in the world impossible," he wrote.

But he was not satisfied with his observations in India. He found the prevalence of caste ideas antipathetic and complicating. He went on after his last parting from Amanda into China, it was the first of several visits to China, and thence he crossed to America. White found a number of American press-cuttings of a vehemently anti-Japanese quality still awaiting digestion in a drawer, and it was clear to him that Benham had given a considerable amount of attention to the development of the "white" and "yellow" race hostility on the Pacific slope; but his chief interest at that time had been the negro. He went to Washington and thence south; he visited Tuskegee and Atlanta, and then went off at a tangent to Hayti. He was drawn to Hayti by Hesketh Pritchard's vivid book, *Where Black Rules White*, and like Hesketh Pritchard he was able to visit that wonderful monument to kingship, the hidden fastness of La Ferrière, the citadel built a century ago by the "Black Napoleon," the Emperor Christophe. He went with a young American demonstrator from Harvard.

§ 4

It was a memorable excursion. They rode from
Cap Haytien for a day's journey along dusty uneven
tracks through a steaming plain of luxurious vegetation, that presented the strangest mixture of un-
bridled jungle with populous country. They passed
countless villages of thatched huts alive with curiosity
and swarming with naked black children, and yet all
the time they seemed to be in a wilderness. They
forded rivers, they had at times to force themselves
through thickets, once or twice they lost their way,
and always ahead of them, purple and sullen, the
great mountain peak with La Ferrière upon its crest
rose slowly out of the background until it dominated
the landscape. Long after dark they blundered
upon rather than came to the village at its foot where
they were to pass the night. They were interrogated
under a flaring torch by peering ragged black soldiers,
and passed through a firelit crowd into the presence
of the local commandant to dispute volubly about
their right to go further. They might have been
in some remote corner of Nigeria. Their papers,
laboriously got in order, were vitiated by the fact,
which only became apparent by degrees, that the
commandant could not read. They carried their
point with difficulty.

But they carried their point, and, watched and
guarded by a hungry half-naked negro in a kepi and
the remains of a sky-blue pair of trousers, they
explored one of the most exemplary memorials of

imperialism that humanity has ever made. The
roads and parks and prospects constructed by this
vanished Emperor of Hayti, had long since disappeared, and the three men clambered for hours up ravines and precipitous jungle tracks, occasionally crossing the winding traces of a choked and ruined road
that had once been the lordly approach to his fastness.
Below they passed an abandoned palace of vast extent, a palace with great terraces and the still traceable outline of gardens, though there were green
things pushing between the terrace steps, and trees
thrust out of the empty windows.   Here from a bel-
vedere of which the skull-like vestige still remained,
the negro Emperor Christophe, after fourteen years
of absolute rule, had watched for a time the smoke of
the burning of his cane-fields in the plain below, and
then, learning that his bodyguard had deserted him,
had gone in and blown out his brains.

He had christened the place after the best of
examples, "Sans Souci."

But the citadel above, which was to have been his
last defence, he never used. The defection of his
guards made him abandon that. To build it, they
say, cost Hayti thirty thousand lives. He had the
true Imperial lavishness. So high it was, so lost in a
wilderness of trees and bush, looking out over a land
relapsed now altogether to a barbarism of patch
and hovel, so solitary and chill under the tropical
sky — for even the guards who still watched over its
suspected treasures feared to live in its ghostly
galleries and had made hovels outside its walls —

and at the same time so huge and grandiose — there were walls thirty feet thick, galleries with scores of rust-eaten cannon, circular dining-halls, king's apartments and queen's apartments, towering battlements and great arched doorways —'that it seemed to Benham to embody the power and passing of that miracle of human history, tyranny, the helpless bowing of multitudes before one man and the transitoriness of such glories, more completely than anything he had ever seen or imagined in the world before.   Beneath the battlements — they are choked above with jungle grass and tamarinds and many flowery weeds — the precipice fell away a sheer two thousand feet, and below spread a vast rich green plain populous and diversified, bounded at last by the blue sea, like an amethystine wall.   Over this precipice Christophe was wont to fling his victims, and below this terrace were bottle-shaped dungeons where men, broken and torn, thrust in at the neck-like hole above, starved and died : it was his headquarters here, here he had his torture chambers and the means for nameless cruelties. . . .

"Not a hundred years ago," said Benham's companion, and told the story of the disgraced favourite, the youth who had offended.

"Leap," said his master, and the poor hypnotized wretch, after one questioning glance at the conceivable alternatives, made his last gesture of servility, and then stood out against the sky, swayed, and with a convulsion of resolve, leapt and shot headlong down through the shimmering air.

Came presently the little faint sound of his fall.

The Emperor satisfied turned away, unmindful of the fact that this projectile he had launched had caught among the bushes below, and presently struggled and found itself still a living man. It could scramble down to the road and, what is more wonderful, hope for mercy. An hour and it stood before Christophe again, with an arm broken and bloody and a face torn, a battered thing now but with a faint flavour of pride in its bearing. "Your bidding has been done, Sire," it said.

"So," said the Emperor, unappeased. "And you live? Well — Leap again. . . ."

And then came other stories. The young man told them as he had heard them, stories of ferocious wholesale butcheries, of men standing along the walls of the banqueting chamber to be shot one by one as the feast went on, of exquisite and terrifying cruelties, and his one note of wonder, his refrain was, "*Here!* Not a hundred years ago. . . . It makes one almost believe that somewhere things of this sort are being done now."

They ate their lunch together amidst the weedy flowery ruins. The lizards which had fled their coming crept out again to bask in the sunshine. The soldier-guide and guard scrabbled about with his black fingers in the ruinous and rifled tomb of Christophe in a search for some saleable memento. . . .

Benham sat musing in silence. The thought of deliberate cruelty was always an actual physical

distress to him.   He sat bathed in the dreamy afternoon sunlight and struggled against the pictures that
crowded into his mind, pictures of men aghast at
death, and of fear-driven men toiling in agony, and of
the shame of extorted obedience and of cringing and
crawling black figures, and the defiance of righteous
hate beaten down under blow and anguish.   He saw
eyes alight with terror and lips rolled back in agony,
he saw weary hopeless flight before striding proud
destruction, he saw the poor trampled mangled dead,
and he shivered in his soul. . . .

He hated Christophe and all that made Christophe ;
he hated pride, and then the idea came to him that it
is not pride that makes Christophes but humility.

There is in the medley of man's composition, deeper
far than his superficial working delusion that he is a
separated self-seeking individual, an instinct for co-
operation and obedience.   Every natural sane man
wants, though he may want it unwittingly, kingly
guidance, a definite direction for his own partial life.
At the bottom of his heart he feels, even if he does not
know it definitely, that his life is partial.   He is
driven to join himself on.   He obeys decision and the
appearance of strength as a horse obeys its rider's
voice.   One thinks of the pride, the uncontrolled
frantic will of this black ape of all Emperors, and one
forgets the universal docility that made him possible.
Usurpation is a crime to which men are tempted
by human dirigibility.   It is the orderly peoples who
create tyrants, and it is not so much restraint above
as stiff insubordination below that has to be taught

to men. There are kings and tyrannies and im-
perialisms, simply because of the unkingliness of men.

And as he sat upon the battlements of La Ferrière,
Benham cast off from his mind his last tolerance for
earthly kings and existing States, and expounded to
another human being for the first time this long-
cherished doctrine of his of the Invisible King who is
the lord of human destiny, the spirit of nobility, who
will one day take the sceptre and rule the earth. . . .
To the young American's naïve American response
to any simply felt emotion, he seemed with his
white earnestness and his glowing eyes a veritable
prophet. . . .

"This is the root idea of aristocracy," said Benham.

"I have never heard the underlying spirit of
democracy, the real true Thing in democracy, so
thoroughly expressed," said the young American.

§ 5

Benham's notes on race and racial cultures gave
White tantalizing glimpses of a number of picturesque
experiences.   The adventure in Kieff had first roused
Benham to the reality of racial quality.   He was
caught in the wheels of a pogrom.

"Before that time I had been disposed to minimize
and deny race.   I still think it need not prevent men
from the completest social co-operation, but I see
now better than I did how difficult it is for any man to
purge from his mind the idea that he is not primarily
a Jew, a Teuton, or a Kelt, but a man. You can
persuade any one in five minutes that he or she

belongs to some special and blessed and privileged sort of human being; it takes a lifetime to destroy that persuasion. There are these confounded differences of colour, of eye and brow, of nose or hair, small differences in themselves except that they give a foothold and foundation for tremendous fortifications of prejudice and tradition, in which hostilities and hatreds may gather. When I think of a Jew's nose, a Chinaman's eyes or a negro's colour I am reminded of that fatal little pit which nature has left in the vermiform appendix, a thing no use in itself and of no significance, but a gathering-place for mischief. The extremest case of race-feeling is the Jewish case, and even here, I am convinced, it is the Bible and the Talmud and the exertions of those inevitable professional champions who live upon racial feeling, far more than their common distinction of blood, which holds this people together banded against mankind."

Between the lines of such general propositions as this White read little scraps of intimation that linked with the things Benham let fall in Johannesburg to reconstruct the Kieff adventure.

Benham had been visiting a friend in the country on the further side of the Dnieper. As they drove back along dusty stretches of road amidst fields of corn and sunflower and through bright little villages, they saw against the evening blue under the full moon a smoky red glare rising from amidst the white houses and dark trees of the town. "The pogrom's begun," said Benham's friend, and was surprised

when Benham wanted to end a pleasant day by
going to see what happens after the beginning of a
pogrom.

He was to have several surprises before at last
he left Benham in disgust and went home by himself. ·

For Benham, with that hastiness that so flouted his
exalted theories, passed rapidly from an attitude of
impartial enquiry to active intervention. The two
men left their carriage and plunged into the network
of unlovely dark streets in which the Jews and traders
harboured. . . . Benham's first intervention was on
behalf of a crouching and yelping bundle of humanity
that was being dragged about and kicked at a street
corner. The bundle resolved itself into a filthy little
old man, and made off with extraordinary rapidity,
while Benham remonstrated with the kickers.
Benham's tallness, his very Gentile face, his good
clothes, and an air of tense authority about him
had its effect, and the kickers shuffled off with
remarks that were partly apologies. But Benham's friend revolted. This was no business of
theirs.

· Benham went on unaccompanied towards the
glare of the burning houses.

For a time he watched. Black figures moved between him and the glare, and he tried to find out the
exact nature of the conflict by enquiries in clumsy
Russian. He was told that the Jews had insulted a
religious procession, that a Jew had spat at an ikon,
that the shop of a cheating Jew trader had been set

on fire, and that the blaze had spread to the adjacent group of houses. He gathered that the Jews were running out of the burning block on the other side "like rats." The crowd was mostly composed of town roughs with a sprinkling of peasants. They were mischievous but undecided. Among them were a number of soldiers, and he was surprised to see a policemen, brightly lit from head to foot, watching the looting of a shop that was still untouched by the flames.

He held back some men who had discovered a couple of women's figures slinking along in the shadow beneath a wall. Behind his remonstrances the Jewesses escaped. His anger against disorder was growing upon him. . . .

Late that night Benham found himself the leading figure amidst a party of Jews who had made a counter attack upon a gang of roughs in a court that had become the refuge of a crowd of fugitives. Some of the young Jewish men had already been making a fight, rather a poor and hopeless fight, from the windows of the house near the entrance of the court, but it is doubtful if they would have made an effective resistance if it had not been for this tall excited stranger who was suddenly shouting directions to them in sympathetically murdered Russian. It was not that he brought powerful blows or subtle strategy to their assistance, but that he put heart into them and perplexity into his adversaries because he was so manifestly non-partizan. Nobody could ever have mistaken Benham for a Jew. When at last

2 D

towards dawn a not too zealous governor called out the troops and began to clear the streets of rioters, Benham and a band of Jews were still keeping the gateway of that court behind a hasty but adequate barricade of furniture and handbarrows.

The ghetto could not understand him, nobody could understand him, but it was clear a rare and precious visitor had come to their rescue, and he was implored by a number of elderly, dirty, but very intelligent-looking old men to stay with them and preserve them until their safety was assured.

They could not understand him, but they did their utmost to entertain him and assure him of their gratitude.   They seemed to consider him as a representative of the British Government, and foreign intervention on their behalf is one of those unfortunate fixed ideas that no persecuted Jews seem able to abandon.

Benham found himself, refreshed and tended, sitting beside a wood fire in an inner chamber richly flavoured by humanity and listening to a discourse in evil but understandable German.   It was a discourse upon the wrongs and the greatness of the Jewish people — and it was delivered by a compact middle-aged man with a big black beard and long-lashed but animated eyes.   Beside him a very old man dozed and nodded approval.   A number of other men crowded the apartment, including several who had helped to hold off the rioters from the court.   Some could follow the talk and ever again endorsed the speaker in Yiddish or Russian ; others listened with tantalized expressions, their brows knit, their lips moving.

It was a discourse Benham had provoked. For now he was at the very heart of the Jewish question, and he could get some light upon the mystery of this great hatred at first hand. He did not want to hear tales of outrages, of such things he knew, but he wanted to understand what was the irritation that caused these things.

So he listened. The Jew dilated at first on the harmlessness and usefulness of the Jews.

"But do you never take a certain advantage?" Benham threw out.

"The Jews are cleverer than the Russians. Must we suffer for that?"

The spokesman went on to the more positive virtues of his race. Benham suddenly had that uncomfortable feeling of the Gentile who finds a bill being made against him. Did the world owe Israel nothing for Philo, Aron ben Asher, Solomon Gabriol, Halévy, Mendelssohn, Heine, Meyerbeer, Rubinstein, Joachim, Zangwill? Does Britain owe nothing to Lord Beaconsfield, Montefiore or the Rothschilds? Can France repudiate her debt to Fould, Gaudahaux, Oppert, or Germany to Fürst, Steinschneider, Herxheimer, Lasker, Auerbach, Traube and Lazarus and Benfey? . . .

Benham admitted under the pressure of urgent tones and gestures that these names did undoubtedly include the cream of humanity, but was it not true that the Jews did press a little financially upon the inferior peoples whose lands they honoured in their exile?

The man with the black beard took up the challenge bravely.

"They are merciful creditors," he said. "And it is their genius to possess and control. What better stewards could you find for the wealth of nations than the Jews? And for the honours? That always had been the rôle of the Jews — stewardship. Since the days of Joseph in Egypt. . . ."

Then in a lower voice he went on to speak of the deficiencies of the Gentile population. He wished to be just and generous but the truth was the truth. The Christian Russians loved drink and laziness; they had no sense of property; were it not for unjust laws even now the Jews would possess all the land of South Russia. . . .

Benham listened with a kind of fascination. "But," he said.

It was so. And with a confidence that aroused a protest or so from the onlookers, the Jewish apologist suddenly rose up, opened a safe close beside the fire and produced an armful of documents.

"Look!" he said, "all over South Russia there are these!"

Benham was a little slow to understand, until half a dozen of these papers had been thrust into his hand. Eager fingers pointed, and several voices spoke. These things were illegalities that might some day be legal; there were the records of loans and hidden transactions that might at any time put all the sur-

rounding soil into the hands of the Jew.   All South
Russia was mortgaged. . . .

"But is it so?" asked Benham, and for a time
ceased to listen and stared into the fire.

Then he held up the papers in his hand to secure
silence and, feeling his way in unaccustomed German,
began to speak and continued to speak in spite of a
constant insurgent undertone of interruption from
the Jewish spokesman.

All men, Benham said, were brothers.   Did they
not remember Nathan the Wise?

"I did not claim him," said the spokesman, misunderstanding.   "He is a character in fiction."

But all men are brothers, Benham maintained.
They had to be merciful to one another and give their
gifts freely to one another.   Also they had to consider
each other's weaknesses.   The Jews were probably
justified in securing and administering the property
of every community into which they came, they
were no doubt right in claiming to be best fitted for
that task, but also they had to consider, perhaps
more than they did, the feelings and vanities of the
host population into which they brought these
beneficent activities.   What was said of the ignorance, incapacity and vice of the Roumanians and
Russians was very generally believed and accepted,
but it did not alter the fact that the peasant, for all
his incapacity, did like to imagine he owned his own
patch and hovel and did have a curious irrational
hatred of debt. . . .

The faces about Benham looked perplexed.

"*This*," said Benham, tapping the papers in his hand. "They will not understand the ultimate benefit of it. It will be a source of anger and fresh hostility. It does not follow because your race has supreme financial genius that you must always follow its dictates to the exclusion of other considerations. . . ."

The perplexity increased.

Benham felt he must be more general. He went on to emphasize the brotherhood of man, the right to equal opportunity, equal privilege, freedom to develop their idiosyncrasies as far as possible, unhindered by the idiosyncrasies of others. He could feel the sympathy and understanding of his hearers returning. "You see," said Benham, "you must have generosity. You must forget ancient scores. Do you not see the world must make a fresh beginning?"

He was entirely convinced he had them with him. The heads nodded assent, the bright eyes and lips followed the slow disentanglement of his bad German.

"Free yourselves and the world," he said.

Applause.

"And so," he said breaking unconsciously into English, "let us begin by burning these *beastly* mortgages!"

And with a noble and dramatic gesture Benham cast his handful on the fire. The assenting faces became masks of horror. A score of hands clutched at those precious papers, and a yell of dismay and anger filled the room. Some one caught at his throat from behind. "Don't kill him!" cried some one. "He fought for us!"

§ 6

An hour later Benham returned in an extraordinarily dishevelled and battered condition to his hotel. He found his friend in anxious consultation with the hotel proprietor.

"We were afraid that something had happened to you," said his friend.

"I got a little involved," said Benham.

"Hasn't some one clawed your cheek?"

"Very probably," said Benham.

"And torn your coat? And hit you rather heavily upon the neck?"

"It was a complicated misunderstanding," said Benham. "Oh! pardon! I'm rather badly bruised upon that arm you're holding."

§ 7

Benham told the story to White as a jest against himself.

"I see now of course that they could not possibly understand my point of view," he said. . . .

"I'm not sure if they quite followed my German. . . .

"It's odd, too, that I remember saying, 'Let's burn these mortgages,' and at the time I'm almost sure I didn't know the German for mortgage. . . ."

It was not the only occasion on which other people had failed to grasp the full intention behind Benham's

proceedings. His aristocratic impulses were apt to
run away with his conceptions of brotherhood, and
time after time it was only too manifest to White
that Benham's pallid flash of anger had astonished
the subjects of his disinterested observations extremely. His explorations in Hayti had been ter-
minated abruptly by an affair with a native policeman that had necessitated the intervention of the
British Consul. It was begun with that suddenness
that was too often characteristic of Benham, by his
hitting the policeman. It was in the main street of
Cap Haytien, and the policeman had just clubbed an
unfortunate youth over the head with the heavily
loaded wooden club which is the normal instrument
of Haytien discipline. His blow was a repartee, part
of a triangular altercation in which a large, voluble,
mahogany-coloured lady whose head was tied up
in a blue handkerchief played a conspicuous part,
but it seemed to Benham an entirely unjustifiable
blow.

He allowed an indignation with negro policemen
in general that had been gathering from the very
moment of his arrival at Port-au-Prince to carry him
away. He advanced with the kind of shout one
would hurl at a dog, and smote the policeman to the
earth with the stout stick that the peculiar social
atmosphere of Hayti had disposed him to carry.
By the local standard his blow was probably a
trivial one, but the moral effect of his indignant
pallor and a sort of rearing tallness about him on
these occasions was always very considerable. Un-

happily these characteristics could have no effect
on a second negro policeman who was approaching
the affray from behind, and he felled Benham by a
blow on the shoulder that was meant for the head,
and with the assistance of his colleague overpowered
him, while the youth and the woman vanished.

The two officials dragged Benham in a state of
vehement protest to the lock-up, and only there,
in the light of a superior officer's superior knowledge, did they begin to realize the grave fact of
his British citizenship.

The memory of the destruction of the Haytien
fleet by a German gunboat was still vivid in Port-
au-Prince, and to that Benham owed it that in spite
of his blank refusal to compensate the man he had
knocked over, he was after two days of anger, two
days of extreme insanitary experience, and much
meditation upon his unphilosophical hastiness, released.

Quite a number of trivial incidents of a kindred
sort diversified his enquiries into Indian conditions.
They too turned for the most part on his facile
exasperation at any defiance of his deep-felt desire
for human brotherhood. At last indeed came
an affair that refused ultimately to remain trivial,
and tangled him up in a coil that invoked newspaper articles and heated controversies.

The effect of India upon Benham's mind was a
peculiar mixture of attraction and irritation. He
was attracted by the Hindu spirit of intellectualism
and the Hindu repudiation of brutality, and he was

infuriated by the spirit of caste that cuts the great
world of India into a thousand futile little worlds,
all aloof and hostile one to the other. "I came to
see India," he wrote, "and there is no India. There
is a great number of Indias, and each goes about
with its chin in the air, quietly scorning everybody
else."

His Indian adventures and his great public controversy on caste began with a tremendous row with
an Indian civil servant who had turned an Indian
gentleman out of his first-class compartment, and
culminated in a disgraceful fracas with a squatting
brown holiness at Benares, who had thrown aside
his little brass bowlful of dinner because Benham's
shadow had fallen upon it.

"You unendurable snob!" said Benham, and then
lapsing into the forceful and inadvisable: "By
Heaven, you *shall* eat it! . . ."

§ 8

Benham's detestation of human divisions and
hostilities was so deep in his character as to seem
almost instinctive. But he had too a very clear
reason for his hostility to all these amazing breaks
in human continuity in his sense of the gathering
dangers they now involve. They had always, he
was convinced, meant conflict, hatred, misery and
the destruction of human dignity, but the new conditions of life that have been brought about by
modern science were making them far more dangerous than they had ever been before. He believed

that the evil and horror of war was becoming more and more tremendous with every decade, and that the free play of national prejudice and that stupid filching ambitiousness that seems to be inseparable from monarchy, were bound to precipitate catastrophe, unless a real international aristocracy could be brought into being to prevent it.

In the drawer full of papers labelled "Politics," White found a paper called "The Metal Beast." It showed that for a time Benham had been greatly obsessed by the thought of the armaments that were in those days piling up in every country in Europe. He had gone to Essen, and at Essen he had met a German who had boasted of Zeppelins and the great guns that were presently to smash the effete British fleet and open the Imperial way to London.

"I could not sleep," he wrote, "on account of this man and his talk and the streak of hatred in his talk. He distressed me not because he seemed exceptional, but because he seemed ordinary. I realized that he was more human than I was, and that only killing and killing could come out of such humanity. I thought of the great ugly guns I had seen, and of the still greater guns he had talked about, and how gloatingly he thought of the destruction they could do. I felt as I used to feel about that infernal stallion that had killed a man with its teeth and feet, a despairing fear, a sense of monstrosity in life. And this creature who had so disturbed me was only a beastly snuffy little man in an ill-fitting frock-coat, who laid his knife and fork by their tips on the edge of his plate, and picked his teeth with gusto and breathed into my face as he talked to me. The commonest of representative men. I went about that Westphalian country after that, with the conviction that headless, soulless, blood-drinking metal monsters were breeding all about me. I felt that science was producing a poisonous swarm, a nest of black dragons. They were crouching here and away there in France and England, they were crouching like beasts that bide their time, mewed up in forts, kennelled in arsenals, hooded in tarpaulins as hawks are hooded. . . . And I had never thought very much about them before, and there they were, waiting until some human fool like that frock-coated thing of spite, and fools like him multiplied by a million, saw fit to call them out to action. Just out of hatred and nationalism and faction. . . .''

Then came a queer fancy.

"Great guns, mines, battleships, all that cruelty-apparatus; I see it more and more as the gathering revenge of dead joyless matter for the happiness of life. It is a conspiracy of the lifeless, an enormous plot of the rebel metals against sensation. That is why in particular half-living people seem to love these things. La Ferrière was a fastness of the kind of tyranny that passes out of human experience, the tyranny of the strong man over men. Essen comes, the new thing, the tyranny of the strong machine. . . .

"Science is either slave or master. These people — I mean the German people and militarist people generally — have no real mastery over the scientific and economic forces on which they seem to ride. The monster of steel and iron carries Kaiser and Germany and all Europe captive. It has persuaded them to mount upon its back and now they must follow the logic of its path. Whither? . . . Only kingship will ever master that beast of steel which has got loose into the world. Nothing but the sense of unconquerable kingship in us all will ever dare withstand it. . . . Men must be kingly aristocrats — it isn't *may* be now, it is *must* be — or, these confederated metals, these things of chemistry and metallurgy, these explosives and mechanisms, will trample the blood and life out of our race into mere red-streaked froth and filth. . . ."

Then he turned to the question of this metallic beast's release. Would it ever be given blood?

"Men of my generation have been brought up in this threat of a great war that never comes; for forty years we have had it, so that it is with a note of incredulity that one tells oneself, "After all this war may happen. But can it happen?"

He proceeded to speculate upon the probability whether a great war would ever devastate western Europe again, and it was very evident to White that he wanted very much to persuade himself against that idea. It was too disagreeable for him to think it probable. The paper was dated 1910. It was in October, 1914, that White, who was still working upon the laborious uncertain account of Benham's life and thought he has recently published, read what Benham had written. Benham concluded that the common-sense of the world would hold up this danger until reason could get "to the head of things."

"There are already mighty forces in Germany," Benham wrote, "that will struggle very powerfully to avoid a war. And these forces increase. Behind the coarseness and the threatenings, the melodrama and the display of the vulgarer sort there arises a great and noble people. . . . I have talked with Germans of the better kind. . . . You cannot have a whole nation of Christophes. . . . There also the true knighthood discovers itself. . . . I do not believe this war will overtake us."

"*Well!*" said White.

"I must go back to Germany and understand Germany better," the notes went on.

But other things were to hold Benham back from that resolve. Other things were to hold many men back from similar resolves until it was too late for them. . . .

"It is preposterous that these monstrous dangers should lower over Europe, because a certain threatening vanity has crept into the blood of a people, because a few crude ideas go inadequately controlled. . . . Does no one see what that metallic beast will do if they once let it loose? It will trample cities; it will devour nations. . . ."

White read this on the 9th of October, 1914. One crumpled evening paper at his feet proclaimed in startled headlines: "Rain of Incendiary Shells. Antwerp Ablaze." Another declared untruthfully but impressively: "Six Zeppelins drop Bombs over the Doomed City."

He had bought all the evening papers, and had read and re-read them and turned up maps and worried over strategic problems for which he had no data at all — as every one did at that time — before he was able to go on with Benham's manuscripts.

These pacific reassurances seemed to White's war-troubled mind like finding a flattened and faded flower, a girl's love token, between the pages of some torn and scorched and blood-stained book picked out from a heap of loot after rapine and murder had had their fill. . . .

"How can we ever begin over again?" said White, and sat for a long time staring gloomily into the fire, forgetting forgetting, forgetting too that men who are tired and weary die, and that new men are born to succeed them. . . .

"We have to begin over again," said White at last, and took up Benham's papers where he had laid them down. . . .

§ 9

One considerable section of Benham's treatment of the Fourth Limitation was devoted to what he called the Prejudices of Social Position. This section alone was manifestly expanding into a large treatise upon the psychology of economic organization. . . .

It was only very slowly that he had come to realize the important part played by economic and class hostilities in the disordering of human affairs. This was a very natural result of his peculiar social circumstances. Most people born to wealth and ease take the established industrial system as the natural method in human affairs; it is only very reluctantly and by real feats of sympathy and disinterestedness that they can be brought to realize that it is natural only in the sense that it has grown up and come about, and necessary only because nobody is strong and clever enough to rearrange it. Their experience of it is a satisfactory experience. On the other hand, the better off one is, the wider is one's outlook and the more alert one is to see the risks and dangers of international dissensions. Travel and talk to foreigners open one's eyes to aggressive possibilities; history and its warnings become conceivable. It is in the nature of things that socialists and labour parties should minimize international obligations and necessities, and equally so that autocracies and aristocracies and plutocracies should be negligent of and impatient about social reform.

But Benham did come to realize this broader conflict between worker and director, between poor man and possessor, between resentful humanity and enterprise, between unwilling toil and unearned opportunity. It is a far profounder and subtler conflict than any other in human affairs. "I can foresee a time," he wrote, "when the greater national

and racial hatreds may all be so weakened as to be
no longer a considerable source of human limitation
and misery, when the suspicions of complexion and
language and social habit are allayed, and when the
element of hatred and aggression may be clean
washed out of most religious cults, but I do not
begin to imagine a time, because I cannot imagine
a method, when there will not be great friction
between those who employ, those who direct collective action, and those whose part it is to be the
rank and file in industrialism. This, I know, is a
limitation upon my confidence due very largely to
the restricted nature of my knowledge of this sort
of organization. Very probably resentment and
suspicion in the mass and self-seeking and dishonesty
in the fortunate few are not so deeply seated, so
necessary as they seem to be, and if men can be
cheerfully obedient and modestly directive in war
time, there is no reason why ultimately they should
not be so in the business of peace. But I do not
understand the elements of the methods by which
this state of affairs can be brought about.

"If I were to confess this much to an intelligent
working man I know that at once he would answer
'Socialism,' but Socialism is no more a solution of
this problem than eating is a solution when one is
lost in the wilderness and hungry. Of course
everybody with any intelligence wants Socialism,
everybody, that is to say, wants to see all human
efforts directed to the common good and a common
end, but brought face to face with practical prob-

2 ᴃ

lems Socialism betrays a vast insufficiency of
practical suggestions. I do not say that Socialism
would not work, but I do say that so far Socialists
have failed to convince me that they could work it.
The substitution of a stupid official for a greedy
proprietor may mean a vanished dividend, a limited
output and no other human advantage whatever.
Socialism is in itself a mere eloquent gesture, in-
spiring, encouraging, perhaps, but beyond that not
very helpful, towards the vast problem of moral
and material adjustment before the race. That
problem is incurably miscellaneous and intricate,
and only by great multitudes of generous workers,
one working at this point and one at that, secretly
devoted knights of humanity, hidden and dispersed
kings, unaware of one another, doubting each his
right to count himself among those who do these
kingly services, is this elaborate rightening of work
and guidance to be done."

So from these most fundamental social difficulties
he came back to his panacea. All paths and all
enquiries led him back to his conception of aristocracy, conscious, self-disciplined, devoted, self-ex-
amining yet secret, making no personal nor class
pretences, as the supreme need not only of the
individual but the world.

§ 10

It was the Labour trouble in the Transvaal
which had brought the two schoolfellows together
again. White had been on his way to Zimbabwe.

An emotional disturbance of unusual intensity had
driven him to seek consolations in strange scenery
and mysterious desolations. It was as if Zimbabwe
called to him. Benham had come to South Africa
to see into the question of Indian immigration, and
he was now on his way to meet Amanda in London.
Neither man had given much heed to the gathering
social conflict on the Rand until the storm burst
about them. There had been a few paragraphs in
the papers about a dispute upon a point of labour
etiquette, a question of the recognition of Trade
Union officials, a thing that impressed them both as
technical, and then suddenly a long incubated
quarrel flared out in rioting and violence, the burning of houses and furniture, attacks on mines,
attempts to dynamite trains. White stayed in
Johannesburg because he did not want to be stranded
up country by the railway strike that was among the
possibilities of the situation. Benham stayed because he was going to London very reluctantly, and
he was glad of this justification for a few days' delay.
The two men found themselves occupying adjacent
tables in the Sherborough Hotel, and White was
the first to recognize the other. They came together
with a warmth and readiness of intimacy that neither
would have displayed in London.

White had not seen Benham since the social days
of Amanda at Lancaster Gate, and he was astonished
at the change a few years had made in him. The
peculiar contrast of his pallor and his dark hair had
become more marked, his skin was deader, his

features seemed more prominent and his expression intenser. His eyes were very bright and more sunken under his brows. He had suffered from yellow fever in the West Indies, and these it seemed were the marks left by that illness. And he was much more detached from the people about him; less attentive to the small incidents of life, more occupied with inner things. He greeted White with a confidence that White was one day to remember as pathetic.

"It is good to meet an old friend," Benham said. "I have lost friends. And I do not make fresh ones. I go about too much by myself, and I do not follow the same tracks that other people are following. . . ."

What track was he following? It was now that White first heard of the Research Magnificent. He wanted to know what Benham was doing, and Benham after some partial and unsatisfactory explanation of his interest in insurgent Hindoos, embarked upon larger expositions. "It is, of course, a part of something else," he amplified. He was writing a book, "an enormous sort of book." He laughed with a touch of shyness. It was about "everything," about how to live and how not to live. And "aristocracy, and all sorts of things." White was always curious about other people's books. Benham became earnest and more explicit under encouragement, and to talk about his book was soon to talk about himself. In various ways, intentionally and inadvertently, he told White much.

These chance encounters, these intimacies of the
train and hotel, will lead men at times to a stark
frankness of statement they would never permit
themselves with habitual friends.

About the Johannesburg labour trouble they
talked very little, considering how insistent it was
becoming. But the wide propositions of the Research Magnificent, with its large indifference to
immediate occurrences, its vast patience, its tremendous expectations, contrasted very sharply in
White's memory with the bitterness, narrowness
and resentment of the events about them. For him
the thought of that first discussion of this vast in-
choate book into which Benham's life was flowering,
and which he was ultimately to summarize, trailed
with it a fringe of vivid little pictures; pictures of
crowds of men hurrying on bicycles and afoot under a
lowering twilight sky towards murmuring centres of
disorder, of startling flares seen suddenly afar off,
of the muffled galloping of troops through the
broad dusty street in the night, of groups of men
standing and watching down straight broad roads,
roads that ended in groups of chimneys and squat
buildings of corrugated iron. And once there was
a marching body of white men in the foreground
and a complicated wire fence, and a clustering mass
of Kaffirs watching them over this fence and talking
eagerly amongst themselves.

"All this affair here is little more than a hitch in
the machinery," said Benham, and went back to
his large preoccupation. . . .

But White, who had not seen so much human disorder as Benham, felt that it was more than that. Always he kept the tail of his eye upon that eventful background while Benham talked to him.

When the firearms went off he may for the moment have even given the background the greater share of his attention. . . .

§ 11

It was only as White burrowed through his legacy of documents that the full values came to very many things that Benham said during these last conversations. The papers fitted in with his memories of their long talks like text with commentary; so much of Benham's talk had repeated the private writings in which he had first digested his ideas that it was presently almost impossible to disentangle what had been said and understood at Johannesburg from the fuller statement of those patched and corrected manuscripts. The two things merged in White's mind as he read. The written text took upon itself a resonance of Benham's voice; it eked out the hints and broken sentences of his remembered conversation.

But some things that Benham did not talk about at all, left by their mere marked absence an impression on White's mind. And occasionally after Benham had been talking for a long time there would be an occasional aphasia, such as is often apparent in the speech of men who restrain themselves from betraying a preoccupation. He would

say nothing about Amanda or about women in
general, he was reluctant to speak of Prothero,
and another peculiarity was that he referred
perhaps half a dozen times or more to the
idea that he was a "prig." He seemed to be de-
fending himself against some inner accusation, some
unconquerable doubt of the entire adventure of his
life. These half hints and hints by omission exercised the quick intuitions of White's mind very keenly, and he drew far closer to an understanding of Benham's reserves than Benham ever suspected. . . .

At first after his parting from Amanda in London
Benham had felt completely justified in his treatment of her. She had betrayed him and he had
behaved, he felt, with dignity and self-control. He
had no doubt that he had punished her very effectively, and it was only after he had been travelling in China with Prothero for some time and
in the light of one or two chance phrases in her
letters that he began to have doubts whether he
ought to have punished her at all. And one night
at Shanghai he had a dream in which she stood
before him, dishevelled and tearful, his Amanda,
very intensely his Amanda, and said that she was
dirty and shameful and spoilt for ever, because he
had gone away from her. Afterwards the dream
became absurd: she showed him the black leopard's
fur as though it was a rug, and it was now moth-
eaten and mangey, the leopard skin that had been
so bright and wonderful such a little time ago, and
he awoke before he could answer her, and for a long

time he was full of unspoken answers explaining
that in view of her deliberate unfaithfulness the
position she took up was absurd. She had spoilt
her own fur. But what was more penetrating and
distressing in this dream was not so much the case
Amanda stated as the atmosphere of unconquerable
intimacy between them, as though they still belonged
to each other, soul to soul, as though nothing that
had happened afterwards could have destroyed their
common responsibility and the common interest of
their first unstinted union. She was hurt, and of
course he was hurt. He began to see that his marriage to Amanda was still infinitely more than a
technical bond.

And having perceived that much he presently
began to doubt whether she realized anything of the
sort. Her letters fluctuated very much in tone, but
at times they were as detached and guarded as a
schoolgirl writing to a cousin. Then it seemed to
Benham an extraordinary fraud on her part that she
should presume to come into his dream with an entirely deceptive closeness and confidence. She began
to sound him in these latter letters upon the possibility of divorce. This, which he had been quite disposed to concede in London, now struck him as an
outrageous suggestion. He wrote to ask her why,
and she responded exasperatingly that she thought it
was "better." But, again, why better? It is remarkable that although his mind had habituated
itself to the idea that Easton was her lover in London, her thought of being divorced, no doubt to

marry again, filled him with jealous rage. She asked him to take the blame in the divorce proceedings. There, again, he found himself ungenerous. He did not want to do that. Why should he do that? As a matter of fact he was by no means reconciled to the price he had paid for his Research Magnificent; he regretted his Amanda acutely. He was regretting her with a regret that grew when by all the rules of life it ought to be diminishing.

It was in consequence of that regret and his controversies with Prothero while they travelled together in China that his concern about what he called priggishness arose. It is a concern that one may suppose has a little afflicted every reasonably self-conscious man who has turned from the natural passionate personal life to religion or to public service or any abstract devotion. These things that are at least more extensive than the interests of flesh and blood have a trick of becoming unsubstantial, they shine gloriously and inspiringly upon the imagination, they capture one and isolate one and then they vanish out of sight. It is far easier to be entirely faithful to friend or lover than it is to be faithful to a cause or to one's country or to a religion. In the glow of one's first service that larger idea may be as closely spontaneous as a handclasp, but in the darkness that comes as the glow dies away there is a fearful sense of unreality. It was in such dark moments that Benham was most persecuted by his memories of Amanda and most distressed by this suspicion that the Research Magnificent was a priggishness, a pretentious logomachy. Prothero could indeed hint as much so skilfully that at times the dream of nobility seemed an insult to the sunshine, to the careless laughter of children, to the good light in wine and all the warm happiness of existence. And then Amanda would peep out of the dusk and whisper, "Of course if you could leave me —! Was I not *life?* Even now if you cared to come back to me — For I loved you best and loved you still, old Cheetah, long after you had left me to follow your dreams. . . . Even now I am drifting further into lies and the last shreds of dignity drop from me; a dirty, lost, and shameful leopard I am now, who was once clean and bright. . . . You could come back, Cheetah, and you could save me yet. If you would love me. . . ."

In certain moods she could wring his heart by such imagined speeches, the very quality of her voice was in them, a softness that his ear had loved, and not only could she distress him, but when Benham was in this heartache mood, when once she had set him going, then his little mother also would rise against him, touchingly indignant, with her blue eyes bright with tears; and his frowsty father would back towards him and sit down complaining that he was neglected, and even little Mrs. Skelmersdale would reappear, bravely tearful on her chair looking after him as he slunk away from her through Kensington Gardens; indeed every personal link he

had ever had to life could in certain moods pull him
back through the door of self-reproach Amanda
opened and set him aching and accusing himself of
harshness and self-concentration.   The very kit-
tens of his childhood revived forgotten moments of
long-repented hardness.   For a year before Prothero was killed there were these heartaches.   That
tragedy gave them their crowning justification.
All these people said in this form or that, "You
owed a debt to us, you evaded it, you betrayed us,
you owed us life out of yourself, love and services,
and you have gone off from us all with this life that
was ours, to live by yourself in dreams about the
rule of the world, and with empty phantoms of power
and destiny.   All this was intellectualization.   You
sacrificed us to the thin things of the mind.   There
is no rule of the world at all, or none that a man like
you may lay hold upon.   The rule of the world is a
fortuitous result of incalculably multitudinous forces.
But all of us you could have made happier.   You
could have spared us distresses.   Prothero died
because of you.   Presently it will be the turn of your
father, your mother — Amanda perhaps. . . ."

He made no written note of his heartaches, but he
made several memoranda about priggishness that
White read and came near to understanding.   In
spite of the tugging at his heart-strings, Benham was
making up his mind to be a prig.   He weighed the
cold uningratiating virtues of priggishness against
his smouldering passion for Amanda, and against his
obstinate sympathy for Prothero's grossness and

his mother's personal pride, and he made his choice.
But it was a reluctant choice.

One fragment began in the air. "Of course I had
made myself responsible for her life. But it was,
you see, such a confoundedly energetic life, as vigorous and as slippery as an eel. . . . Only by giving
all my strength to her could I have held Amanda.
. . . So what was the good of trying to hold
Amanda? . . .

"All one's people have this sort of claim upon one.
Claims made by their pride and their self-respect, and
their weaknesses and dependences. You've no right
to hurt them, to kick about and demand freedom
when it means snapping and tearing the silly suffering tendrils they have wrapped about you. The
true aristocrat I think will have enough grasp,
enough steadiness, to be kind and right to every
human being and still do the work that ought to be
his essential life. I see that now. It's one of the
things this last year or so of loneliness has made me
realize ; that in so far as I have set out to live the
aristocratic life I have failed. Instead I've discovered it — and found myself out. I'm an over-
strung man. I go harshly and continuously for
one idea. I live as I ride. I blunder through my
fences, I take off too soon. I've no natural ease of
mind or conduct or body. I am straining to keep
hold of a thing too big for me and do a thing beyond
my ability. Only after Prothero's death was it
possible for me to realize the prig I have always
been, first as regards him and then as regards

Amanda and my mother and every one.   A necessary unavoidable priggishness. . . .

"I do not see how certain things can be done without prigs, people, that is to say, so concentrated and
specialized in interest as to be a trifle inhuman, so
resolved as to be rather rhetorical and forced. . . .
All things must begin with clumsiness, there is no
assurance about pioneers. . . .

"Some one has to talk about aristocracy, some
one has to explain aristocracy. . . .   But the very
essence of aristocracy, as I conceive it, is that it does
not explain nor talk about itself. . . .

"After all it doesn't matter what I am. . . .   It's
just a private vexation that I haven't got where I
meant to get.   That does not affect the truth I
have to tell. . . .

"If one has to speak the truth with the voice of a
prig, still one must speak the truth.   I have worked
out some very considerable things in my research,
and the time has come when I must set them out
clearly and plainly.   That is my job anyhow.   My
journey to London to release Amanda will be just
the end of my adolescence and the beginning of my
real life.   It will release me from my last entanglement with the fellow creatures I have always failed
to make happy. . . .   It's a detail in the work.
. . .   And I shall go on.

"But I shall feel very like a man who goes back
for a surgical operation.

"It's very like that.   A surgical operation, and
when it is over perhaps I shall think no more about it.

"And beyond these things there are great masses of work to be done. So far I have but cleared up for myself a project and outline of living. I must begin upon these masses now, I must do what I can upon the details, and, presently, I shall see more clearly where other men are working to the same ends. . . ."

§ 12

Benham's expedition to China with Prothero was essentially a wrestle between his high resolve to work out his conception of the noble life to the utmost limit and his curiously invincible affection and sympathy for the earthliness of that inglorious little don. Although Benham insisted upon the dominance of life by noble imaginations and relentless reasonableness, he would never altogether abandon the materialism of life. Prothero had once said to him, "You are the advocate of the brain and I of the belly. Only, only we respect each other." And at another time, "You fear emotions and distrust sensations. I invite them. You do not drink gin because you think it would make you weep. But if I could not weep in any other way I would drink gin." And it was under the influence of Prothero that Benham turned from the haughty intellectualism, the systematized superiorities and refinements, the caste marks and defensive dignities of India to China, that great teeming stinking tank of humorous yellow humanity.

Benham had gone to Prothero again after a bout of elevated idealism. It was only very slowly that he reconciled his mind to the idea of an entirely solitary pursuit of his aristocratic dream. For some time as he went about the world he was trying to bring himself into relationship with the advanced thinkers, the liberal-minded people who seemed to promise at least a mental and moral co-operation. Yet it is difficult to see what co-operation was possible unless it was some sort of agreement that presently they should all shout together. And it was after a certain pursuit of Rabindranath Tagore, whom he met in Hampstead, that a horror of perfect manners and perfect finish came upon him, and he fled from that starry calm to the rich uncleanness of the most undignified fellow of Trinity. And as an advocate and exponent of the richness of the lower levels of life, as the declared antagonist of caste and of the uttermost refinements of pride, Prothero went with Benham by way of Siberia to the Chinese scene.

Their controversy was perceptible at every dinner-table in their choice of food and drink. Benham was always wary and Prothero always appreciative. It peeped out in the distribution of their time, in the direction of their glances. Whenever women walked about, Prothero gave way to a sort of ethnological excitement. "That girl — a wonderful racial type." But in Moscow he was sentimental. He insisted on going again to the Cosmopolis Bazaar, and when he had ascertained that Anna Alexievna had vanished and left no trace he prowled the streets until the small hours.

In the eastward train he talked intermittently of her. "I should have defied Cambridge," he said.

But at every stopping station he got out upon the platform ethnologically alert. . . . .

Theoretically Benham was disgusted with Prothero. Really he was not disgusted at all. There was something about Prothero like a sparrow, like a starling, like a Scotch terrier. . . . These, too, are morally objectionable creatures that do not disgust. . . .

Prothero discoursed much upon the essential goodness of Russians. He said they were a people of genius, that they showed it in their faults and failures just as much as in their virtues and achievements. He extolled the "germinating disorder" of Moscow far above the "implacable discipline" of Berlin. Only a people of inferior imagination, a base materialist people, could so maintain its attention upon precision and cleanliness. Benham was roused to defence against this paradox. "But all exaltation neglects," said Prothero. "No religion has ever boasted that its saints were spick and span." This controversy raged between them in the streets of Irkutsk. It was still burning while they picked their way through the indescribable filth of Pekin.

"You say that all this is a fine disdain for material things," said Benham. "But look out there!"

Apt to their argument a couple of sturdy young women came shuffling along, cleaving the crowd in the narrow street by virtue of a single word and two brace of pails of human ordure.

"That is not a fine disdain for material things,"
said Benham. "That is merely individualism and
unsystematic living."

"A mere phase of frankness. Only frankness is
left to them now. The Manchus crippled them,
spoilt their roads and broke their waterways.
European intervention paralyses every attempt they
make to establish order on their own lines. In the
Ming days China did not reek. . . . And, anyhow,
Benham, it's better than the silly waste of London. . . ."

And in a little while Prothero discovered that
China had tried Benham and found him wanting,
centuries and dynasties ago.

What was this new-fangled aristocratic man, he
asked, but the ideal of Confucius, the superior
person, "the son of the King"? There you had the
very essence of Benham, the idea of self-examination, self-preparation under a vague Theocracy.
("Vaguer," said Benham, "for the Confucian
Heaven could punish and reward.") Even the
elaborate sham modesty of the two dreams was the
same. Benham interrupted and protested with
heat. And this Confucian idea of the son of the
King, Prothero insisted, had been the cause of
China's paralysis. "My idea of nobility is not
traditional but expectant," said Benham. "After
all, Confucianism has held together a great pacific
state far longer than any other polity has ever
lasted. I'll accept your Confucianism. I've not
the slightest objection to finding China nearer

2 F

salvation than any other land. Do but turn it round so that it looks to the future and not to the past, and it will be the best social and political culture in the world. That, indeed, is what is happening. Mix Chinese culture with American enterprise and you will have made a new lead for mankind."

From that Benham drove on to discoveries. "When a man thinks of the past he concentrates on self; when he thinks of the future he radiates from self. Call me a neo-Confucian; with the cone opening forward away from me, instead of focussing on me. . . ."

"You make me think of an extinguisher," said Prothero.

"You know I am thinking of a focus," said Benham. "But all your thought now has become caricature. . . . You have stopped thinking. You are fighting after making up your mind. . . ."

Prothero was a little disconcerted by Benham's prompt endorsement of his Chinese identification. He had hoped it would be exasperating. He tried to barb his offence. He amplified the indictment. All cultures must be judged by their reaction and fatigue products, and Confucianism had produced formalism, priggishness, humbug. . . . No doubt its ideals had had their successes; they had unified China, stamped the idea of universal peace and good manners upon the greatest mass of population in the world, paved the way for much beautiful art and literature and living. "But in the end, all your stern orderliness, Benham," said Prothero, "only leads to me.   The human spirit rebels against this everlasting armour on the soul. After Han came T'ang. Have you never read Ling Po? There's scraps of him in English in that little book you have — what is it? — the *Lute of Jade?*   He was the inevitable Epicurean; the Omar Khayyam after the Prophet. Life must relax at last. . . ."

"No!" cried Benham. "If it is traditional, I admit, yes; but if it is creative, no. . . ."

Under the stimulation of their undying controversy Benham was driven to closer enquiries into Chinese thought. He tried particularly to get to mental grips with English-speaking Chinese. "We still know nothing of China," said Prothero. "Most of the stuff we have been told about this country is mere middle-class tourists' twaddle. We send merchants from Brixton and missionaries from Glasgow, and what doesn't remind them of these delectable standards seems either funny to them or wicked. I admit the thing is slightly pot-bound, so to speak, in the ancient characters and the ancient traditions, but for all that, they *know*, they *have*, what all the rest of the world has still to find and get. When they begin to speak and write in a modern way and handle modern things and break into the soil they have scarcely touched, the rest of the world will find just how much it is behind. . . . Oh! not soldiering; the Chinese are not such fools as that, but *life*. . . ."

Benham was won to a half belief in these assertions.

He came to realize more and more clearly that

while India dreams or wrestles weakly in its sleep, while Europe is still hopelessly and foolishly given over to militant monarchies, racial vanities, delirious religious feuds and an altogether imbecile fumbling with loaded guns, China, even more than America, develops steadily into a massive possibility of ordered and aristocratic liberalism. . . .

The two men followed their associated and disconnected paths. Through Benham's chance speeches and notes, White caught glimpses, as one might catch glimpses through a moving trellis, of that bilateral adventure. He saw Benham in conversation with liberal-minded mandarins, grave-faced, bald-browed persons with disciplined movements, who sat with their hands thrust into their sleeves talking excellent English; while Prothero pursued enquiries of an intenser, more recondite sort with gentlemen of a more confidential type. And, presently, Prothero began to discover and discuss the merits of opium.

For if one is to disavow all pride and priggishness, if one is to find the solution of life's problem in the rational enjoyment of one's sensations, why should one not use opium? It is art materialized. It gives tremendous experiences with a minimum of exertion, and if presently its gifts diminish one need but increase the quantity. Moreover, it quickens the garrulous mind, and steadies the happiness of love. Across the varied adventures of Benham's journey in China fell the shadow first of a suspicion and then of a certainty. . . .

The perfected and ancient vices of China wrapped about Prothero like some tainted but scented robe, and all too late Benham sought to drag him away. And then in a passion of disgust turned from him.

"To this," cried Benham, "one comes! Save for pride and fierceness!"

"Better this than cruelty," said Prothero talking quickly and clearly because of the evil thing in his veins. "You think that you are the only explorer of life, Benham, but while you toil up the mountains I board the house-boat and float down the stream. For you the stars, for me the music and the lanterns. You are the son of a mountaineering don, and I am a Chinese philosopher of the riper school. You force yourself beyond fear of pain, and I force myself beyond fear of consequences. What are we either of us but children groping under the black cloak of our Maker? — who will not blind us with his light. Did he not give us also these lusts, the keen knife and the sweetness, these sensations that are like pineapple smeared with saltpetre, like salted olives from heaven, like being flayed with delight. . . . And did he not give us dreams fantastic beyond any lust whatever? What is the good of talking? Speak to your own kind. I have gone, Benham. I am lost already. There is no resisting any more, since I have drugged away resistance. Why then should I come back? I know now the symphonies of the exalted nerves; I can judge; and I say better lie and hear them to the end than come back again to my old life, to my little tin-whistle solo,

my — effort! My *effort!* . . . I ruin my body.
I know. But what of that? . . . I shall soon be
thin and filthy. What of the grape-skin when one
has had the pulp?''

"But," said Benham, "the cleanness of life!"

"While I perish," said Prothero still more
wickedly, "I say good things. . . .''

§ 13

White had a vision of a great city with narrow
crowded streets, hung with lank banners and gay
with vertical vermilion labels, and of a pleasant
large low house that stood in a garden on a hillside,
a garden set with artificial stones and with beasts
and men and lanterns of white porcelain, a garden
which overlooked this city. Here it was that
Benham stayed and talked with his host, a man
robed in marvellous silks and subtle of speech even
in the European languages he used, and meanwhile
Prothero, it seemed, had gone down into the wicked-
ness of the town below. It was a very great town
indeed, spreading for miles along the banks of a
huge river, a river that divided itself indolently
into three shining branches so as to make islands of
the central portion of the place. And on this river
swarmed for ever a vast flotilla of ships and boats,
boats in which people lived, boats in which they
sought pleasure, moored places of assembly, high-
pooped junks, steamboats, passenger sampans, cargo
craft, such a water town in streets and lanes, endless
miles of it, as no other part of the world save China

can display.   In the daylight it was gay with countless sunlit colours embroidered upon a fabric of
yellow and brown, at night it glittered with a hundred
thousand lights that swayed and quivered and were
reflected quiveringly upon the black flowing waters.

And while Benham sat and talked in the garden
above came a messenger who was for some reason
very vividly realized by White's imagination.   He
was a tall man with lack-lustre eyes and sunken
cheeks that made his cheek bones very prominent,
and gave his thin-lipped mouth something of the
geniality of a skull, and the arm he thrust out of
his yellow robe to hand Prothero's message to Benham was lean as a pole.   So he stood out in White's
imagination, against the warm afternoon sky and
the brown roofs and blue haze of the great town
below, and was with one exception the distinctest
thing in the story.   The message he bore was
scribbled by Prothero himself in a nerveless scrawl:
"Send a hundred dollars by this man.   I am in a
frightful fix."

Now Benham's host had been twitting him with
the European patronage of opium, and something in
this message stirred his facile indignation.   Twice
before he had had similar demands.   And on the
whole they had seemed to him to be unreasonable
demands.   He was astonished that while he was
sitting and talking of the great world-republic of
the future and the secret self-directed aristocracy
that would make it possible, his own friend, his
chosen companion, should thus, by this inglorious

request and this ungainly messenger, disavow him.
He felt a wave of intense irritation.

"No," he said, "I will not."

And he was too angry to express himself in any
language understandable by his messenger.

His host intervened and explained after a few
questions that the occasion was serious. Prothero,
it seemed, had been gambling.

"No," said Benham. "He is shameless. Let
him do what he can."

The messenger was still reluctant to go.

And scarcely had he gone before misgivings seized
Benham.

"Where *is* your friend?" asked the mandarin.

"I don't know," said Benham.

"But they will keep him! They may do all
sorts of things when they find he is lying to them."

"Lying to them?"

"About your help."

"Stop that man," cried Benham suddenly realizing
his mistake. But when the servants went to stop
the messenger their intentions were misunderstood,
and the man dashed through the open gate of the
garden and made off down the winding road.

"Stop him!" cried Benham, and started in pursuit, suddenly afraid for Prothero.

The Chinese are a people of great curiosity, and a
small pebble sometimes starts an avalanche. . . .

White pieced together his conception of the circles
of disturbance that spread out from Benham's pursuit of Prothero's flying messenger.

For weeks and months the great town had been uneasy in all its ways because of the insurgent spirits from the south and the disorder from the north, because of endless rumours and incessant intrigue.   The stupid manœuvres of one European "power" against another, the tactlessness of missionaries, the growing Chinese disposition to meet violence and force with violence and force, had fermented and brewed the possibility of an outbreak.   The sudden resolve of Benham to get at once to Prothero was like the firing of a mine.   This tall, pale-faced, incomprehensible stranger charging through the narrow streets that led to the pleasure-boats in the south river seemed to many a blue-clad citizen like the White Peril embodied.   Behind him came the attendants of the rich man up the hill; but they surely were traitors to help this stranger.

Before Benham could at all realize what was happening he found his way to the river-boat on which he supposed Prothero to be detained, barred by a vigorous street fight.   Explanations were impossible; he joined in the fight.

For three days that fight developed round the mystery of Prothero's disappearance.

It was a complicated struggle into which the local foreign traders on the river-front and a detachment of modern drilled troops from the up-river barracks were presently drawn.   It was a struggle that was never clearly explained, and at the end of it they found Prothero's body flung out upon a waste place near a little temple on the river bank, stabbed while he was asleep. . . .

And from the broken fragments of description that Benham let fall, White had an impression of him hunting for all those three days through the strange places of a Chinese city, along narrow passages, over queer Venetian-like bridges, through the vast spaces of empty warehouses, in the incense-scented darkness of temple yards, along planks that passed to the dark hulls of secret barges, in quick-flying boats that slipped noiselessly among the larger craft, and sometimes he hunted alone, sometimes in company, sometimes black figures struggled in the darkness against dim-lit backgrounds and sometimes a swarm of shining yellow faces screamed and shouted through the torn paper windows. . . . And then at the end of this confused effect of struggle, this Chinese kinematograph film, one last picture jerked into place and stopped and stood still, a white wall in the sunshine come upon suddenly round a corner, a dirty flagged passage and a stiff crumpled body that had for the first time an inexpressive face. . . .

§ 14

Benham sat at a table in the smoking-room of the Sherborough Hotel at Johannesburg and told of these things. White watched him from an arm-chair. And as he listened he noted again the intensification of Benham's face, the darkness under his brows, the pallor of his skin, the touch of red in his eyes. For there was still that red gleam in Benham's eyes; it shone when he looked out of a darkness into a light. And he sat forward with his arms folded under him, or moved his long lean hand about over the things on the table.

"You see," he said, "this is a sort of horror in my mind. Things like this stick in my mind. I am always seeing Prothero now, and it will take years to get this scar off my memory again. Once before — about a horse, I had the same kind of distress. And it makes me tender, sore-minded about everything. It will go, of course, in the long run, and it's just like any other ache that lays hold of one. One can't cure it. One has to get along with it. . . .

"I know, White, I ought to have sent that money, but how was I to know then that it was so imperative to send that money? . . .

"At the time it seemed just pandering to his vices. . . .

"I was angry. I shall never subdue that kind of hastiness altogether. It takes me by surprise. Before the messenger was out of sight I had repented. . . .

"I failed him. I have gone about in the world dreaming of tremendous things and failing most people. My wife too. . . ."

He stopped talking for a little time and folded his arms tight and stared hard in front of himself, his lips compressed.

"You see, White," he said, with a kind of setting of the teeth, "this is the sort of thing one has to stand. Life is imperfect. Nothing can be done perfectly. And on the whole —" He spoke still more slowly, "I would go through again with the very same things that have hurt my people. If I had to live over again. I would try to do the things without hurting the people, but I would do the things anyhow. Because I'm raw with remorse, it does not follow that on the whole I am not doing right. Right doing isn't balm. If I could have contrived not to hurt these people as I have done, it would have been better, just as it would be better to win a battle without any killed or wounded. I was clumsy with them and they suffered, I suffer for their suffering, but still I have to stick to the way I have taken. One's blunders are accidents. If one thing is clearer than another it is that the world isn't accident-proof. . . .

But I wish I had sent those dollars to Prothero. . . . God! White, but I lie awake at night thinking of that messenger as he turned away. . . . Trying to stop him. . . .

"I didn't send those dollars. So fifty or sixty people were killed and many wounded. . . . There for all practical purposes the thing ends. Perhaps it will serve to give me a little charity for some other fool's haste and blundering. . . .

"I couldn't help it, White. I couldn't help it. . . .

"The main thing, the impersonal thing, goes on. One thinks, one learns, one adds one's contribution of experience and understanding. The spirit of the race goes on to light and comprehension. In spite of accidents. In spite of individual blundering.

"It would be absurd anyhow to suppose that nobility is so easy as to come slick and true on every occasion. . . .

"If one gives oneself to any long aim one must reckon with minor disasters. This Research I undertook grows and grows. I believe in it more and more. The more it asks from me the more I give to it. When I was a youngster I thought the thing I wanted was just round the corner. I fancied I would find out the noble life in a year or two, just what it was, just where it took one, and for the rest of my life I would live it. Finely. But I am just one of a multitude of men, each one going a little wrong, each one achieving a little right. And the noble life is a long, long way ahead. . . . We are working out a new way of living for mankind, a new rule, a new conscience. It's no small job for all of us. There must be lifetimes of building up and lifetimes of pulling down and trying again. Hope and disappointments and much need for philosophy. . . . I see myself now for the little workman I am upon this tremendous undertaking. And all my life hereafter goes to serve it. . . ."

He turned his sombre eyes upon his friend. He spoke with a grim enthusiasm. "I'm a prig. I'm a fanatic, White. But I have something clear, something better worth going on with than any adventure of personal relationship could possibly be. . . ."

And suddenly he began to tell White as plainly as he could of the faith that had grown up in his mind. He spoke with a touch of defiance, with the tense force of a man who shrinks but overcomes his shame. "I will tell you what I believe."

He told of his early dread of fear and baseness, and of the slow development, expansion and complication of his idea of self-respect until he saw that there is no honour nor pride for a man until he refers his life to ends and purposes beyond himself. An aristocrat must be loyal. So it has ever been, but a modern aristocrat must also be lucid; there it is that one has at once the demand for kingship and the repudiation of all existing states and kings. In this manner he had come to his idea of a great world republic that must replace the little warring kingdoms of the present, to the conception of an unseen kingship ruling the whole globe, to his King Invisible, who is the Lord of Truth and all sane loyalty. "There," he said, "is the link of our order, the new knighthood, the new aristocracy, that must at last rule the earth. There is our Prince. He is in me, he is in you; he is latent in all mankind. I have worked this out and tried it and lived it, and I know that outwardly and inwardly this is the way a man must live, or else be a poor thing and a base one. On great occasions and small occasions I have failed myself a thousand times, but no failure lasts if your faith lasts. What I have learnt, what I have thought out and made sure, I want now to tell the world. Somehow I will tell it, as a book I suppose, though I do not know if I

shall ever be able to make a book. But I have away
there in London or with me here all the masses of
notes I have made in my search for the life that is
worth while living. . . . We who are self-appointed
aristocrats, who are not ashamed of kingship, must
speak to one another. . . .

"We can have no organization because organiza-
tions corrupt. . . .

"No recognition. . . .

"But we can speak plainly. . . ."

(As he talked his voice was for a space drowned by
the jingle and voices of mounted police riding past
the hotel.)

"But on one side your aristocracy means revolution," said White. "It becomes a political conspiracy."

"Manifestly. An open conspiracy. It denies the
king upon the stamps and the flag upon the wall. It
is the continual proclamation of the Republic of
Mankind."

§ 15

The earlier phases of violence in the Rand outbreak in 1913 were manifest rather in the outskirts of
Johannesburg than at the centre. "Pulling out"
was going on first at this mine and then that, there
were riots in Benoni, attacks on strike breakers and
the smashing up of a number of houses. It was not
until July the 4th that, with the suppression of a
public meeting in the market-place, Johannesburg
itself became the storm centre.

Benham and White were present at this market-place affair, a confused crowded occasion, in which a little leaven of active men stirred through a large uncertain multitude of decently dressed onlookers. The whole big square was astir, a swaying crowd of men. A ramshackle platform improvised upon a trolley struggled through the swarming straw hats to a street corner, and there was some speaking. At first it seemed as though military men were using this platform, and then it was manifestly in possession of an excited knot of labour leaders with red rosettes. The military men had said their say and got down. They came close by Benham, pushing their way across the square. "We've warned them," said one. A red flag, like some misunderstood remark at a tea-party, was fitfully visible and incomprehensible behind the platform. Somebody was either pitched or fell off the platform. One could hear nothing from the speakers except a minute bleating. . . .

Then there were shouts that the police were charging. A number of mounted men trotted into the square. The crowd began a series of short rushes that opened lanes for the passage of the mounted police as they rode to and fro. These men trotted through the crowd, scattering knots of people. They carried pick-handles, but they did not seem to be hitting with them. It became clear that they aimed at the capture of the trolley. There was only a feeble struggle for the trolley; it was captured and hauled through the scattered spectators in the square to the

protection of a small impassive body of regular
cavalry at the opposite corner.   Then quite a number
of people seemed to be getting excited and fighting.
They appeared to be vaguely fighting the foot-police,
and the police seemed to be vaguely pushing through
them and dispersing them.   The roof of a little one-
story shop became prominent as a centre of vigorous
stone-throwing.

It was no sort of battle.   Merely the normal inconsecutiveness of human affairs had become exaggerated and pugnacious.   A meeting was being pre-
vented, and the police engaged in the operation
were being pelted or obstructed. Mostly people
were just looking on.

"It amounts to nothing," said Benham.   "Even if
they held a meeting, what could happen?   Why does
the Government try to stop it?"

The drifting and charging and a little booing went
on for some time.   Every now and then some one
clambered to a point of vantage, began a speech and
was pulled down by policemen.   And at last across
the confusion came an idea, like a wind across a
pond.

The strikers were to go to the Power Station.

That had the effect of a distinct move in the game.
The Power Station was the centre of Johannesburg's
light and energy.   There if anywhere it would be
possible to express one's disapproval of the administration, one's desire to embarrass and confute it.
One could stop all sorts of things from the Power
Station.   At any rate it was a repartee to the sup-

2 G

pression of the meeting. Everybody seemed glad-
dened by a definite project.

Benham and White went with the crowd.

At the intersection of two streets they were held up
for a time; the scattered drift of people became congested. Gliding slowly across the mass came an
electric tram, an entirely unbattered tram with even
its glass undamaged, and then another and another.
Strikers, with the happy expression of men who have
found something expressive to do, were escorting
the trams off the street. They were being meticulously careful with them. Never was there less mob
violence in a riot. They walked by the captured
cars almost deferentially, like rough men honoured
by a real lady's company. And when White and
Benham reached the Power House the marvel grew.
The rioters were already in possession and going
freely over the whole place, and they had injured
nothing. They had stopped the engines, but they
had not even disabled them. Here too manifestly
a majority of the people were, like White and Benham, merely lookers-on.

"But this is the most civilized rioting," said Benham. "It isn't rioting; it's drifting. Just as
things drifted in Moscow. Because nobody has the
rudder. . . .

"What maddens me," he said, "is the democracy
of the whole thing. White! I *hate* this modern democracy. Democracy and inequality! Was
there ever an absurder combination? What is the
good of a social order in which the men at the top are

commoner, meaner stuff than the men underneath, the same stuff, just spoilt, spoilt by prosperity and opportunity and the conceit that comes with advantage? This trouble wants so little, just a touch of aristocracy, just a little cultivated magnanimity, just an inkling of responsibility, and the place might rise instantly out of all this squalor and evil temper. . . . What does all this struggle here amount to? On one side unintelligent greed, unintelligent resentment on the other; suspicion everywhere. . . .

"And you know, White, at bottom *they all want to be decent!*

"If only they had light enough in their brains to show them how.

"It's such a plain job they have here too, a new city, the simplest industries, freedom from war, everything to make a good life for men, prosperity, glorious sunshine, a kind of happiness in the air. And mismanagement, fear, indulgence, jealousy, prejudice, stupidity, poison it all. A squabble about working on a Saturday afternoon, a squabble embittered by this universal shadow of miner's phthisis that the masters were too incapable and too mean to prevent.

"Oh, God!" cried Benham, "when will men be princes and take hold of life? When will the kingship in us wake up and come to its own? . . . Look at this place! Look at this place! . . . The easy, accessible happiness! The manifest prosperity. The newness and the sunshine. And the silly bitterness, the rage, the mischief and miseries! . . ."

And then: "It's not our quarrel. . . ."

"It's amazing how every human quarrel draws one in to take sides. Life is one long struggle against the incidental. I can feel my anger gathering against the Government here in spite of my reason. I want to go and expostulate. I have a ridiculous idea that I ought to go off to Lord Gladstone or Botha and expostulate. . . . What good would it do? They move in the magic circles of their own limitations, an official, a politician — how would they put it? — 'with many things to consider. . . .'

"It's my weakness to be drawn into quarrels. It's a thing I have to guard against. . . .

"What does it all amount to? It is like a fight between navvies in a tunnel to settle the position of the Pole star. It doesn't concern us. . . . Oh! it doesn't indeed concern us. It's a scuffle in the darkness, and our business, the business of all brains, the only permanent good work is to light up the world. . . . There will be mischief and hatred here and suppression and then forgetfulness, and then things will go on again, a little better or a little worse. . . ."

"I'm tired of this place, White, and of all such places. I'm tired of the shouting and running, the beating and shooting. I'm sick of all the confusions of life's experience, which tells only of one need amidst an endless multitude of distresses. I've seen my fill of wars and disputes and struggles. I see now how a man may grow weary at last of life and its disorders, its unreal exacting disorders, its blunders and its remorse. No! I want to begin upon the realities I have made for myself. For they

are the realities. I want to go now to some quiet
corner where I can polish what I have learnt, sort
out my accumulations, be undisturbed by these
transitory symptomatic things. . . .

"What was that boy saying? They are burning
the *Star* office. . . . Well, let them. . . ."

And as if to emphasize his detachment, his aver-
sion, from the things that hurried through the night
about them, from the red flare in the sky and the
distant shouts and revolver shots and scuffling flights
down side streets, he began to talk again of aristocracy and the making of greatness and a new great
spirit in men. All the rest of his life, he said, must
be given to that. He would say his thing plainly
and honestly and afterwards other men would say
it clearly and beautifully ; here it would touch a man
and there it would touch a man ; the Invisible King
in us all would find himself and know himself a little
in this and a little in that, and at last a day would
come, when fair things and fine things would rule
the world and such squalor as this about them would
be as impossible any more for men as a Stone Age
Corroboree. . . .

Late or soon?

Benham sought for some loose large measure of
time.

"Before those constellations above us have changed
their shapes. . . .

"Does it matter if we work at something that will
take a hundred years or ten thousand years? It will
never come in our lives, White. Not soon enough for

that. But after that everything will be soon — when one comes to death then everything is at one's finger-tips — I can feel that greater world I shall never see as one feels the dawn coming through the last darkness. . . ."

§ 16

The attack on the Rand Club began while Benham and White were at lunch in the dining-room at the Sherborough on the day following the burning of the *Star* office. The Sherborough dining-room was on the first floor, and the Venetian window beside their table opened on to a verandah above a piazza. As they talked they became aware of an excitement in the street below, shouting and running and then a sound of wheels and the tramp of a body of soldiers marching quickly. White stood up and looked. "They're seizing the stuff in the gunshops," he said, sitting down again. "It's amazing they haven't done it before."

They went on eating and discussing the work of a medical mission at Mukden that had won Benham's admiration. . . .

A revolver cracked in the street and there was a sound of glass smashing. Then more revolver shots. "That's at the big club at the corner, I think," said Benham and went out upon the verandah.

Up and down the street mischief was afoot. Outside the Rand Club in the cross street a considerable mass of people had accumulated, and was being hustled by a handful of khaki-clad soldiers. Down

the street people were looking in the direction of the
market-place and then suddenly a rush of figures
flooded round the corner, first a froth of scattered
individuals and then a mass, a column, marching
with an appearance of order and waving a flag.   It
was a poorly disciplined body, it fringed out into a
swarm of sympathizers and spectators upon the side
walk, and at the head of it two men disputed.   They
seemed to be differing about the direction of the
whole crowd.   Suddenly one smote the other with
his fist, a blow that hurled him sideways, and then
turned with a triumphant gesture to the following
ranks, waving his arms in the air.   He was a tall
lean man, hatless and collarless, greyhaired and wild-
eyed.   On he came, gesticulating gauntly, past the
hotel.

And then up the street something happened.
Benham's attention was turned round to it by a
checking, by a kind of catch in the breath, on the
part of the advancing procession under the verandah.

The roadway beyond the club had suddenly become clear.   Across it a dozen soldiers had appeared
and dismounted methodically and lined out, with
their carbines in readiness.   The mounted men at
the club corner had vanished, and the people there
had swayed about towards this new threat.   Quite
abruptly the miscellaneous noises of the crowd ceased.
Understanding seized upon every one.

These soldiers were going to fire. . . .

The brown uniformed figures moved like autom-
ata ; the rifle shots rang out almost in one report. . . .

There was a rush in the crowd towards doorways and side streets, an enquiring pause, the darting back of a number of individuals into the roadway and then a derisive shouting. Nobody had been hit. The soldiers had fired in the air.

"But this is a stupid game," said Benham. "Why did they fire at all?"

The tall man who had led the mob had run out into the middle of the road. His commando was a little disposed to assume a marginal position, and it had to be reassured. He was near enough for Benham to see his face. For a time it looked anxious and thoughtful. Then he seemed to jump to his decision. He unbuttoned and opened his coat wide as if defying the soldiers. "Shoot," he bawled, "Shoot, if you dare!"

A little uniform movement of the soldiers answered him. The small figure of the officer away there was inaudible. The coat of the man below flapped like the wings of a crowing cock before a breast of dirty shirt, the hoarse voice cracked with excitement, "Shoot, if you dare. Shoot, if you dare! See!"

Came the metallic bang of the carbines again, and in the instant the leader collapsed in the road, a sprawl of clothes, hit by half a dozen bullets. It was an extraordinary effect. As though the figure had been deflated. It was incredible that a moment before this thing had been a man, an individual, a hesitating complicated purpose.

"Good God!" cried Benham, "but — this is horrible!"

The heap of garments lay still. The red hand that stretched out towards the soldiers never twitched.

The spectacular silence broke into a confusion of sounds, women shrieked, men cursed, some fled, some sought a corner from which they might still see, others pressed forward. "Go for the swine!" bawled a voice, a third volley rattled over the heads of the people, and in the road below a man with a rifle halted, took aim, and answered the soldiers' fire. "Look out!" cried White who was watching the soldiers, and ducked. "This isn't in the air!"

Came a straggling volley again, like a man running a metal hammer very rapidly along iron corrugations, and this time people were dropping all over the road. One white-faced man not a score of yards away fell with a curse and a sob, struggled up, staggered for some yards with blood running abundantly from his neck, and fell and never stirred again. Another went down upon his back clumsily in the roadway and lay wringing his hands faster and faster until suddenly with a movement like a sigh they dropped inert by his side. A straw-hatted youth in a flannel suit ran and stopped and ran again. He seemed to be holding something red and strange to his face with both hands; above them his eyes were round and anxious. Blood came out between his fingers. He went right past the hotel and stumbled and suddenly sprawled headlong at the opposite corner. The majority of the crowd had already vanished into doorways and side streets. But there was still shouting and there was still a remnant of amazed

and angry men in the roadway — and one or two
angry women. They were not fighting. Indeed
they were unarmed, but if they had had weapons
now they would certainly have used them.

"But this is preposterous!" cried Benham.
"Preposterous. Those soldiers are never going to
shoot again! This must stop."

He stood hesitating for a moment and then turned
about and dashed for the staircase. "Good
Heaven!" cried White. "What are you going to
do?"

Benham was going to stop that conflict very much
as a man might go to stop a clock that is striking
unwarrantably and amazingly. He was going to
stop it because it annoyed his sense of human dignity.

White hesitated for a moment and then followed,
crying "Benham!"

But there was no arresting this last outbreak of
Benham's all too impatient kingship. He pushed
aside a ducking German waiter who was peeping
through the glass doors, and rushed out of the hotel.
With a gesture of authority he ran forward into the
middle of the street, holding up his hand, in which he
still held his dinner napkin clenched like a bomb.
White believes firmly that Benham thought he would
be able to dominate everything. He shouted out
something about "Foolery!"

Haroun al Raschid was flinging aside all this sublime indifference to current things. . . .

But the carbines spoke again.

Benham seemed to run unexpectedly against some-

thing invisible. He spun right round and fell down
into a sitting position. He sat looking surprised.

After one moment of blank funk White drew out
his pocket handkerchief, held it arm high by way
of a white flag, and ran out from the piazza of the
hotel.

§ 17

"Are you hit?" cried White dropping to his
knees and making himself as compact as possible.
"Benham!"

Benham, after a moment of perplexed thought
answered in a strange voice, a whisper into which a
whistling note had been mixed.

"It was stupid of me to come out here. Not my
quarrel. Faults on both sides. And now I can't
get up. I will sit here a moment and pull myself together. Perhaps I'm — I must be shot. But it
seemed to come — inside me. . . . If I should be
hurt. Am I hurt? . . . Will you see to that book
of mine, White? It's odd. A kind of faintness.
. . . What?"

"I will see after your book," said White and glanced
at his hand because it felt wet, and was astonished to
discover it bright red. He forgot about himself then,
and the fresh flight of bullets down the street.

The immediate effect of this blood was that he said
something more about the book, a promise, a definite
promise. He could never recall his exact words, but
their intention was binding. He conveyed his
absolute acquiescence with Benham's wishes what-

ever they were. His life for that moment was unreservedly at his friend's disposal. . . .

White never knew if his promise was heard. Benham had stopped speaking quite abruptly with that "What?"

He stared in front of him with a doubtful expression, like a man who is going to be sick, and then, in an instant, every muscle seemed to give way, he shuddered, his head flopped, and White held a dead man in his arms.

THE END

Printed in the United States of America.

THE following pages contain advertisements of a few of the Macmillan novels

The Wife of Sir Isaac Harman

By H. G. WELLS

Cloth, 12mo, $1.50

"Easily the best piece of fiction of the book season." — *Graphic*.

"The book has all the attractive Wells whimsies, piquancies, and fertilities of thought, and the story is absolutely good to read."— *N. Y. World*.

"This time Mr. Wells is very little of a socialist, considerable of a philosopher, prevailingly humorous, and always clever." — *The Bellman*.

"A new novel by H. G. Wells is always a treat, and *The Wife of Sir Isaac Harman* will prove no disappointment. . . . The book in many ways is one of the most successful this versatile sociologist has turned out." — *La Follette's Magazine*.

"Mr. Wells is perhaps the most significant novelist of the day."
— *Bookseller, Newsdealer, and Stationer*.

"Mr. Wells has never done better work in social analysis and character sketching than this novel." — *Independent*.

———

THE MACMILLAN COMPANY
Publishers   **64-66 Fifth Avenue**   **New York**

Old Delabole

By EDEN PHILLPOTTS

Author of " Brunel's Tower," etc.

Cloth, 12mo

A critic in reviewing *Brunel's Tower* remarked that it would seem that Eden Phillpotts was now doing the best work of his career. There was sufficient argument for this contention in the novel then under consideration and further demonstration of its truth is found in *Old Delabole*, which, because of its cheerful and wise philosophy and its splendid feeling for nature and man's relation to it, will perhaps ultimately take its place as its author's best. The scene is laid in Cornwall. Delabole is a slate mining town and the tale which Mr. Phillpotts tells against it as a background, one in which a matter of honor or of conscience is the pivot, is dramatic in situation and doubly interesting because of the moral problem which it presents. Mr. Phillpotts's artistry and keen perception of those motives which actuate conduct have never been better exhibited.

God's Puppets

By WILLIAM ALLEN WHITE

Author of " A Certain Rich Man."

Cloth, 12mo

Here are brought together a number of the more notable short stories by one whose reputation in this field is as great as in the novel form — for has Mr. White not delighted thousands of readers with *The Court of Boyville* and *In Our Town*, short intimate studies of life at first hand which, while quite different from the material in the new volume, nevertheless show mastery of the art? Mr. White is a slow and careful writer, a fact to which the long intervals between his books bear witness, but each work has proved itself worth waiting for, and *God's Puppets* will be found no exception. It gives us of the best of his creative genius.

———

THE MACMILLAN COMPANY

Publishers   64–66 Fifth Avenue   New York

The Star Rover

By JACK LONDON

Author of "The Call of the Wild," "The Sea Wolf," "The Mutiny of the Elsinore," etc. With frontispiece in colors by Jay Hambidge.

Cloth, 12mo

Daring in its theme and vivid in execution, this is one of the most original and gripping stories Mr. London has ever written. The fundamental idea upon which the plot rests — the supremacy of mind over body — has served to inspire writers before, but rarely, if indeed ever, has it been employed as strikingly or with as much success as in this book. With a wealth of coloring and detail the author tells of what came of an attempt on the part of the hero to free his spirit from his body, of the wonderful adventures this "star rover" had, adventures covering long lapses of years and introducing strange people in stranger lands. It is a work that will make as lasting an impression upon the reader as did *The Sea Wolf* and *The Call of the Wild*.

Heart's Kindred

By ZONA GALE

Author of "Christmas," "The Loves of Pelleas and Etarre," etc.

Cloth, 12mo

There is much of timely significance in Miss Gale's new book. For example, one of the most interesting and powerful of its scenes takes place at a meeting of the Women's Peace Congress and in the course of the action there are introduced bits of the actual speeches delivered at the most recent session of this congress. But *Heart's Kindred* is not merely a plea for peace; it is rather the story of the making of a man — and of the rounding out of a woman's character, too. In the rough, unpolished, but thoroughly sincere Westerner and the attractive young woman who brings out the good in the man's nature, Miss Gale has two as absorbing people as she has ever created. In *Heart's Kindred* is reflected that humanness and breadth of vision which was first found in *Friendship Village* and *The Loves of Pelleas and Etarre* and made Miss Gale loved far and wide.

THE MACMILLAN COMPANY

Publishers   64-66 Fifth Avenue   New York

A New Novel (Title Undetermined)

By JAMES STEPHENS
Author of "The Crock of Gold," "Here Are Ladies," etc.

Cloth, 12mo

The announcement of a new novel by the author of "The Crock of Gold" is a promise of a rare treat to all lovers of literature. Mr. Stephens has taken his place among the really important writers of the day, one whose books evidence a wise and kindly philosophy, a droll Irish wit and a keen understanding of human nature. The present work, as have all that have come before it, sounds a new and vibrant note.

Short Stories

By RABINDRANATH TAGORE

Illustrated, decorated cloth, 12mo

Some of the more notable of Mr. Tagore's short stories are here presented in translations by the author and with illustrations by native Indian artists. Ernest Rhys in his biography of Tagore devotes much space to a consideration of him as a short story writer, advancing the opinion that this particular form of literature is one of the most important expressions of Tagore's genius. Now for the first time English readers are given the opportunity of acquainting themselves with this new Tagore and of forming their own estimate of him. None of the material in this volume has ever appeared before in English.

The Stranger

By ARTHUR BULLARD (Albert Edwards)
Author of "Comrade Yetta," etc.

Cloth, 12mo

That Mr. Bullard, who made his reputation under the *nom de plume* of Edwards, is a writer of exceeding power the reception which has been accorded his previous novels testifies. In his new book, as in the case of its predecessors, he has chosen as his theme one of the big problems of modern life, and he has dealt with it in that same vigorous, frank, and keen fashion. The story is one which grips the reader not only for the interest inherent in its plot, but for the tremendous significance of its analysis of certain vital issues with which society is to-day confronted.

THE MACMILLAN COMPANY

Publishers   64-66 Fifth Avenue   New York

A Far Country

By WINSTON CHURCHILL

Author of " The Inside of the Cup," etc.

Illustrated, $1.50

" No one can afford to miss reading 'A Far Country,' or reading it can fail to be interested. The themes Mr. Churchill handles are the big themes confronting all America and in the fortunes and misfortunes of his characters he indicates energies and developments that are nation-wide. It touches on what is vital . . . and it will help in no small degree to broaden our thought and clarify our vision. Many people read ' The Inside of the Cup,' but 'A Far Country' should reach a wider audience." — *New York Times.*

" A powerfully written story, displaying wonderful scope and clarity of vision. Presents a wonderful study of American emotions."
— *Boston Globe.*

" A story worthily complete . . . vastly encouraging. The kind of a book that points to a hope and a right road."
— *New York World.*

" Mr. Churchill has done a difficult thing well. . . . We congratulate him on an achievement well worth while." — *Chicago Post.*

" A great piece of art, comprising admirable humanization, plot and sympathy, diverse as intrinsic . . . and many interesting side issues. Any author might well be proud of such an achievement."
— *Chicago Herald.*

" 'A Far Country'" is a strong story that is vital and compelling.
. . . Adds one more leaf to Mr. Churchill's literary laurels."
— *Philadelphia Ledger.*

THE MACMILLAN COMPANY

Publishers   64-66 Fifth Avenue   New York

THE HARBOR

By ERNEST POOLE

$1.40

Mr. Poole has written a novel of remarkable power and vision in which are depicted the great changes taking place in American life, business, and ideals in the present generation. Under the tremendous influence of the great New York harbor with its docks, warehouses, its huge liners and its workers, a young writer passes, in the development of his life and work, from a blind worship of enterprise and efficiency to a deeper knowledge and understanding of humanity.

"By all odds the best American novel that has appeared in many a long day. It is earnest, sincere, broad in scope and purpose, well balanced, combining intellect and emotion."— *N. Y. Times*.

"'The Harbor' is well worth reading, both for what it gives and the manner in which that is given."— *N. Y. Post*.

"An extremely vivid story, . . . a great deal of the living New York is in it."— *Brooklyn Eagle*.

"A fine new American story, in the spirit of the hour, . . . A work which must be placed at once among the rare books that count."
— *N. Y. World*.

"'The Harbor' is the first really notable novel produced by the New Democracy."— *N. Y. Tribune*.

THE MACMILLAN COMPANY

Publishers   64-66 Fifth Avenue   New York

Alice and A Family

By ST. JOHN G. ERVINE

Cloth, $1.25

St. John G. Ervine's new novel, "Alice and A Family," is primarily a story of humor, its message a cheery one. No book of the season was more favorably received than "Mrs. Martin's Man," which at once placed Mr. Ervine in that class of writers which may be looked to for really distinctive contributions to contemporary fiction. Splendid as was that first work, however, "Alice and A Family" needs no reflected glory. On its merit alone it will be found well worth the reading.

"It is a pleasant surprise to greet Mr. Ervine in another mood — a mood that is no less important because it is less serious than the mood of "Mrs. Martin's Man." — *Boston Transcript*.

"There is not a single character in the book that is not well portrayed. The author apparently writes of what he knows, of a social environment with which he is thoroughly familiar. Alice and her adopted family are interesting, flesh-and-blood persons. St. John Ervine has firmly established his claim to a place in the ranks of those younger writers to whom we look for the worth-while novels of the future." — *New York Times*.

"There is fun in the story, its local color is evidently true, and it is as clever as it is entertaining." — *Outlook*.

"Here is a book of sweetly sane humor depicting in broad strokes, yet shrewd, the lives of the very poor." — *Reedy's Mirror*.

THE MACMILLAN COMPANY

Publishers   64-66 Fifth Avenue   New York

www.ingramcontent.com/pod-product-compliance
Lightning Source LLC
Chambersburg PA
CBHW020920020726
47495CB00002B/269